Sign up for our newsletter to hear
about new and upcoming releases.

www.ylva-publishing.com

OTHER BOOKS BY JAE

JUST
Physical

JAE

ACKNOWLEDGMENTS

Thank you to all of my readers who wrote me an e-mail, demanding that Jill, who was a supporting character in my novel *Damage Control*, get her own novel. As you can see, I take instructions well!

A big thank-you also goes to my critique partners, Alison Grey and RJ Nolan, and to my beta readers, who encouraged and helped me along the way: Andrea, Anne-France, Amy, Christiane, Danielle, Erin, and Michele.

I'm also grateful to my editor, Lauren Sweet, whose amazing insight into plot and structure helped shape this book.

PROLOGUE

THE LAST TIME JILL HAD been seriously sick was when she came down with pneumonia at the age of seven, but in the last two months, she'd spent more time in doctors' offices than on set or in her own house. She grinned halfheartedly. *I doubt I'll get a lollipop for good behavior this time.*

She sat in the waiting area, leafing through a five-month-old magazine without really reading it. The clock on the wall above her was ticking noisily, each tick sounding as loud as a drum. Or maybe it was the thumping of her heart that was filling her ears.

Calm down. It's just your damn leg, not something life-threatening. Normally, Jill was an incorrigible optimist, but she had a bad feeling about this.

None of the many health-care professionals she'd seen in the last eight weeks had been able to help her or at least find out what was wrong with her leg. The pins-and-needles sensation in her left big toe, which she had blamed on the pointy-toed shoes she had to wear on set, had spread to the entire foot and then up her calf. Now her left leg was numb from her toes to her hip.

Her blood tests looked normal, though, and so did an X-ray. They had ruled out diabetes, Lyme disease, vitamin B12 deficiency, orthopedic problems, and a trapped nerve. Rest hadn't helped, and neither had physical therapy. She was beginning to think they suspected her of being a hypochondriac—one more wannabe Hollywood diva who thought the world was a stage and delivered a rendition of *The Dying Swan* every time she had a simple cold.

Finally, Dr. Stevens had scheduled an MRI. After weeks of waiting...waiting for appointments, then waiting for the results, she might finally find out today what was wrong with her.

"Ms. Corrigan?" a nurse called. "Dr. Stevens will see you now."

A lump formed in Jill's throat. She followed the nurse down what felt like the longest hallway she had ever encountered. She white-knuckled her cane as she took a seat across the desk from Dr. Stevens. His puke-green walls hadn't gotten any more attractive since her last visit.

"So," Dr. Stevens said. "How are you doing?"

She wished he'd cut out the small talk and get right to the point. "Fine," she said. Describing her symptoms again wouldn't do her any good; he already knew them.

"That's good." He nodded repeatedly, shuffled his feet beneath the desk, and peeked at the report in front of him.

Even when she craned her neck, she couldn't make out any of the words.

He fingered the report. "I have good news and bad news."

Jill gritted her teeth. Oh no, she would not allow him to play this game with her. She had never been one to draw out things unnecessarily, and she wasn't about to start now. Firmly, she put both hands on his desk. "Just tell me, please."

"It's not a brain tumor."

Jill blew out a breath. After he had sent her to get an MRI scan of her brain and spinal cord, she had halfway suspected that he was thinking she might have cancer. Okay, this had to be the good news. What was the bad news, then? Nothing could be worse than a brain tumor, right? She leaned forward. "What is it, then?"

"Well, diagnosing it is a real challenge because there's no one specific test that can confirm it all by itself, but…" The doctor stared at the radiology report instead of looking her in the eyes.

Clearly, he had failed Bedside Manner 101. She rapped her knuckles on the desk to make him look back at her. Her cane, which she had leaned against the desk, thudded to the floor, but she didn't care. "But what?"

Dr. Stevens scratched his nose. "From the symptoms you're describing and that episode of blurred vision you experienced a couple of years ago—"

"That just lasted for a day or two, nothing like this." She waved at her leg. "And I was under a lot of pressure to find roles back then, so it was probably just stress."

The doctor slowly shook his head. "I don't think so. The bright spots on the MRI indicate areas of inflammation in the CNS, and with your history of neurological symptoms, I'm pretty sure it's MS—multiple sclerosis. It's an autoimmune disorder, which means that your immune system attacks the protective sheath around your nerve fibers…"

Jill didn't hear the rest of what he was saying. The two letters echoed through her mind. *MS.* She tried to remember what she had heard about it—which wasn't much. *Isn't that what Mr. Rosner has?* Her parents' neighbor was in a wheelchair, unable to even lift a hand.

"No," she said loudly, interrupting the doctor midsentence. "That's not possible, is it? I'm only twenty-five."

Dr. Stevens's gaze softened. "I'm sorry to say so, but that's a typical age for the onset of MS."

A numbness of a different kind spread through her, shackling her to the chair, while her thoughts raced at a frantic pace, bombarding her with questions and grim images of what the future might hold for her. Finally, she managed to get out one of them. "Will I end up in a wheelchair?"

The doctor lifted his hands and then dropped them to his lap. "There's no way to tell. The course of MS is different for everyone. You seem to have the relapsing-remitting type, which means that you'll experience flare-ups followed by periods without symptoms. They might change and get worse over time, but it's impossible to predict the course of your disease."

"Periods," Jill repeated, trying to understand how her life had changed so drastically in such a short time. "How long?"

"Like I just said, it's different for everyone. If you're lucky, maybe one or two relapses a year."

Jill suppressed a snort. At the moment, she didn't feel very lucky. "If I really have MS..." Saying it out loud made her head spin. "Is there nothing I can do to treat it?"

"Of course there is. I'll refer you to a neurologist, who'll discuss treatment options with you. He might want to put you on a round of corticosteroids to treat your recent attack. And there are medications that can delay flare-ups."

"But there's no cure?"

The doctor sighed. "No. At least not yet."

Silence spread through the room until Dr. Stevens asked, "Do you have any other questions?"

Jill had hundreds of them, but she couldn't grasp any of them long enough to voice it, so she just shook her head.

He stood, handed her a stack of brochures, and a card. "That's the address of a local support group. You might want to go to a meeting."

Jill took the brochures and the card without glancing at them or saying anything. She left the doctor's office on legs that felt even shakier than before. For what felt like an eternity but might have been just minutes, she sat in her car without starting the engine and stared through the windshield, not seeing a thing. Something pricked behind her eyes, but no tears would fall.

"Okay. Get a grip." She clutched the steering wheel with both hands, trying to ground herself in reality. "This isn't the end of the world."

Then why did it feel as if it were?

After two days of pacing around her house, sleeping just for an hour or two at a time, sheer exhaustion finally forced Jill to sink down onto the couch. She eyed the brochures lying there. After a moment's hesitation, she reached out and took the one on top.

She'd started to read it yesterday, but after encountering words such as *bladder issues*, *choosing a mobility device*, and *daily injections*, she had quickly put the brochure away. Now she forced herself to read on, even though her stomach clenched with every word. Was this really what her future would hold?

"Come on. You can do this. You're not going to let this disease defeat you," she said out loud, as if that would make it true. Without allowing herself to stop, she reached for the next brochure. This one was titled "Getting Help" and listed counseling and self-help group options.

Jill imagined herself sitting in a circle of chairs and wheelchairs, telling perfect strangers about any bladder issues she might develop. She shook her head and smiled despite herself. No, a support group wasn't for her.

The last page of the brochure listed other places to get support—including family members.

Jill groaned. *Oh shit.* She hadn't even thought about her parents and James. Did she really have to tell them? It wasn't as if they were a big part of her life. They saw each other maybe once a year, and all her mother ever talked about on the phone was Jill's brother, perfect James, who—unlike Jill—had the right kind of job and the right kind of relationship. But since Jill had strayed from that path of perfection when she'd come out and moved to Hollywood, they hadn't supported her when she'd struggled to find roles, nor had they been there for her when her first girlfriend had broken up with her.

It made no sense to get them involved, she decided. If she ended up needing help, she'd be better off paying someone for it. Maybe she'd hire a housekeeper. That way, she could save her energy for important things, not for ironing and cleaning, which she hated anyway.

Now ready to find out more about how to manage this damn disease, she opened her laptop and clicked through a few websites, reading bits and pieces until she finally ended up on the YouTube channel of a young woman. It was a video diary that described life with MS. She watched the entry on diet tips and then one about exercise, glad to hear there was something, however small, she could do.

The next video started automatically. The subject—MS and relationships—made Jill reach for the touchpad to click over to the next video. She was single, and starting a new relationship was the last thing on her mind right now. In fact, she didn't think she'd ever get involved with anyone again. She didn't want to live with MS, so how could she do it to a person she loved?

But the young woman's voice, now choked-up instead of upbeat as it had been in the previous videos, made her stop and listen.

"It's not that I don't get it," the woman in the video said, sniffling. "I mean, living with the prospect that he might one day have to feed me and dress me and push me around in a wheelchair... That's a lot to take in. No one wants to take on that kind of responsibility at twenty. Everyone warned me, telling me how much of a burden the situation is for the partner of a person with MS and how MS puts a lot of strain on a relationship. But I wanted to believe that we were different. That we would make it. Through the good times and the bad, right?"

The young woman pulled a tissue from a box, then another one and finally a third. "He didn't even wait until I was out of the hospital. He just moved out without much of an explanation, other than saying he felt trapped and couldn't do it anymore." The rest of her words were unintelligible because she was sobbing into her bunch of tissues.

Jesus. That asshole just abandoned her.

After a minute of crying and venting, the woman calmed enough so Jill could understand her again. "Why can't he be more like Michael? He takes such good care of Sara, drives her to doctor's appointments, and even helps her with bathing and dressing."

Jill wasn't sure that was any better. Just because a couple stayed together didn't mean they were happy. How could they be under such circumstances?

She tapped the touchpad and closed the browser. Her determination grew to never, ever put herself—or someone she loved—in that position. It was better if she stayed alone. Someone in her situation had no right to tie a partner to her and expect the poor woman to take care of her. That burden was hers and hers alone.

She had always been the take-it-or-leave-it type when it came to relationships anyway. While she'd been in love a time or two, she'd never been the clingy type who had to be in a relationship or feel lonely.

With a decisive nod, she closed the laptop. Staying single would be for the best.

CHAPTER 1

Eighteen months later

"S̶u̶s̶a̶n̶a̶?̶" J̶i̶l̶l̶ ̶c̶a̶l̶l̶e̶d̶ ̶t̶o̶w̶a̶r̶d̶ ̶t̶h̶e̶ kitchen. "I'm heading over to Grace's. Can you set the alarm when you go? And don't feed you-know-who too many treats while I'm gone."

"Me?" her housekeeper called back in her most innocent tone. "I don't do that. He just likes to keep me company in the kitchen because he's a real love sponge."

Jill snorted. "Yeah. That and an anything-edible-that-dropped-to-the-kitchen-floor sponge." When she reached for her car keys and walked to the door, Tramp came running from the kitchen.

"Oh no." She shook her head and pushed him back a little. "You stay here with your grandmother."

"I heard that." Susana Rosales stepped into the hall, combing back her salt-and-pepper hair with one hand. "I'm not old enough to be a grandmother."

"Not yet," Jill answered with a grin. "I hear Tomás finally has a girlfriend."

Susana beamed at her. "Sí. It seems seeing you naked didn't traumatize him for life after all."

They looked at each other and started laughing.

A year ago, it hadn't been a laughing matter at all. Jill sobered as she thought back to the day she had discovered that taking hot baths was no longer a good idea. The heat had made her MS symptoms flare, and she had nearly passed out before managing to make it out of the tub. She'd stumbled out of the bathroom—and into the arms of Susana's sixteen-year-old son, who had just stepped down from a ladder after changing a lightbulb in her room. It had been a toss-up as to who had been more mortified: Jill or Tomás.

"Traumatized?" Jill repeated and shook her head. "Nah. If anything, seeing me naked would have spoiled him for other women."

Susana flicked the dish towel she'd tucked into her apron in her direction and tsked. "Go, or I'll tell Tomás not to mow your lawn after all."

Laughing, Jill escaped out the door and to her car. A push of a button on her remote control opened the wrought-iron double-swing gate in front of her home in Glendale. She felt like a character in a spy thriller as she guided the car onto the street, peeking left and right to make sure no paparazzi were lurking.

After she had come out as a lesbian and a woman with MS last June, they had followed her around as if they were a starving pack of wolves and she a tasty rabbit, even though they hadn't given her the time of day before. *That's Hollywood for you. You have to die, go into rehab, or at least get diagnosed with a chronic illness to get any attention.*

When she was sure the coast was clear, she drove to Grace's cottage in Topanga Canyon. The hidden home had been a safe haven for Grace and her girlfriend, Lauren, when they first got together. Jill had spent some time up in the cottage too, especially last year, during the media frenzy after she had been forced to reveal her MS to the public. Back then, Lauren had still been her publicist, but in the past months, she had become a friend.

Grace's SUV and Lauren's Honda Civic were in the driveway when Jill reached the end of the steep dirt path.

Ooh, great! Jill parked her bright red Beetle convertible and rubbed her hands. She couldn't wait to find out what the casting director of *Shaken to the Core* had said. Would he give her the lead role in the historical drama Lauren had written—or at least let her audition for it? She had been captivated by Lauren's script from the moment Lauren had shown it to her. It wasn't just the historical setting and the suspenseful action scenes of two young women trying to survive the earthquake and fires of 1906. This was finally a script with not just one but two strong female characters. Truth be told, Jill was sick of always playing the witty sidekick or the dorky best friend. Now, with Lauren putting in a good word for her, she might finally have a chance to prove herself in a more challenging role.

Grace opened the door wearing a turquoise bikini that was almost the same color as her eyes.

Not that Jill was looking into her eyes. Her gaze was drawn down to her friend's generous cleavage. She stared for a second, startled by the unexpected sight and the reminder that her libido was still alive and kicking.

"Come on in," Grace said, giving her a hug. Her skin was warm, and drops of water clung to it. "We're outside in the hot tub." She led the way to the stone patio at the back of the cottage.

Jeez. Jill shook her head at herself. *You're not so desperate that you'd ogle your best friend, are you?* Okay, maybe she should cut herself some slack after more than eighteen months of not looking at, much less touching, another woman. Besides, even priests and gay men ogled Grace. She hadn't been voted one of the sexiest women alive for nothing.

When they stepped through the sliding glass door, Lauren lifted a hand out of the bubbling water and gave a short wave. "Hey, Jill. Want to join us?" She pointed at the redwood hot tub that was big enough for three.

Jill playfully clutched her chest. "Skinny dipping with the two of you? Thanks for the very tempting offer, but I'm not sure my heart could take it." Her heart was just fine, but immersing herself in hot water still wasn't a good idea. Any rise in body temperature could make her symptoms flare and force her to use a cane for the rest of the day. But she didn't mention that. There was no reason to constantly remind the people in her life about her damn MS, now that it was in remission.

Grace gave her a look that said she knew exactly why Jill had rejected the offer. Thankfully, she said nothing.

Lauren smiled, leaned back, and watched Grace climb back in. "Suit yourself. Grace and I get it all to ourselves, then."

Jill's friends looked at each other and seemed to forget that they weren't alone.

Jill smiled wistfully. She was happy for Grace, really. After her failed marriage and all the bullshit she'd been through last year, she deserved whatever happiness she could get. But sometimes, a part of Jill rebelled at the unfairness of her own situation. Her friends had it all—they were successful, healthy, and in love, while she...

Oh, come on. Stop the pity party! You're doing just fine. She sat on a deck chair in the shade and cleared her throat. "So, did you get a chance to talk to the casting director?"

"Um, yes, I did," Lauren answered.

"You did?" Grace asked. "Why didn't you say anything?"

"Well, I just met with him earlier today, and when I got back..."

Grinning, Jill shook her head at her friends. "Let me guess... You got a little distracted."

Lauren's gaze strayed to Grace's bare shoulders, which were peeking out of the water. A wide grin formed on her face. "A lot distracted, actually."

"So," Jill said, "what did the casting director say?"

The smile disappeared from Lauren's face. She might have once been one of Hollywood's top PR experts, but she couldn't act to save her life.

Jill suppressed a sigh. "He said no."

Biting her lip, Lauren nodded. "I'm sorry. I know you really wanted that role."

"It's okay," Jill said, trying not to let her disappointment show. "Maybe I wouldn't have been a good fit anyway."

"You would have been perfect," Grace said, her cheeks reddened either by the hot water or her passionate defense. "You're strong and tough with just a hint of vulnerability. That would have worked great for the role. Not to mention that you're gay, so you would have had no problem kissing another woman. I really can't understand why they wouldn't let you audition."

"It's a pretty challenging role," Lauren said quietly.

Grace frowned at her girlfriend of six months. "You think Jill isn't up to it? You saw her in *Ava's Heart*. She acted circles around the rest of the supporting cast! She—"

"I'm not talking about that kind of challenge. The script calls for a lot of physical action. The two lead actresses will have to do some of their own stunts."

Jill bit down on the inside of her cheek. So that was the true reason. It wasn't her looks or her acting skills. It was the MS. She hadn't had an attack for seven months and two weeks. At times, she could almost forget that she even had MS. The people in the industry never forgot, though. Disaster movies were expensive. The powers that be didn't want to risk production being held up by an actress who couldn't keep up.

"I understand," she said as calmly as possible, even though she was raging inside. What good would it do to make her friends feel bad about it too?

"I don't," Grace said, her famous sky-blue eyes darkened to a thundercloud gray. "Why couldn't they at least offer her a supporting role? One that didn't involve so much running and jumping and climbing over mountains of debris?"

Years of acting experience enabled Jill to look calm while her friends talked about her as if weren't even present. She knew they meant well.

"Actually, I was able to convince the casting director to take a look at her head shot." Lauren swiveled around on the hot tub's bench seat to face Jill. "With your green eyes, red hair, and fair complexion, you look exactly the way I imagine Lucy Sharpe to look like. You're even the right age."

Lucy Sharpe... Jill tried to remember who that was. Maybe it was just her imagination, but since the MS had started, her memory didn't seem to be the same. Sometimes it took her forever to learn her lines.

"The lady doctor, remember?" Lauren prompted when Jill directed a questioning look her way.

Ah. Jill nodded. She was also a strong female character, and she starred in nearly as many scenes as the two leading ladies, but she wasn't a main character. Jill forced a grin. "Ooh, so I'd get to play doctor?"

"If you want the role..." Lauren searched her face.

"Sure, what's not to want?" Jill swallowed her pride. It wasn't as if casting directors had been knocking down her door in the past nine months since her double outing.

Lauren brightened. "Okay. I'll let them know, then."

"Do you think they'll go for it?" Jill asked.

"They'd better." Lauren flashed a grim smile. "The casting director is my godfather, and after he shot me down about you playing Kathryn Winthrop, he owes me."

Even though it might be stupid, Jill shook her head. "I don't want to get the role just because the casting director is doing you a personal favor."

11

"Are you kidding? They'd be lucky to get you. I think you bring just the right kind of spunk to the role. Besides…" Lauren gave her a playful leer. "I'm sure you'll look great in a corset."

Jill groaned. "I hate period costumes. You can't breathe in those things. Next time, write a script about a female version of Casanova who does nothing but lie by the pool and seduce women all day. I'd be perfect for that role."

Both of her friends snorted and splashed water at her.

"Hey!"

The walkie-talkie crackled to life. "Crash?" came the stunt coordinator's voice through the device. "You still there?"

Crash grinned. She was standing on the rooftop of a six-story building. Where was she supposed to go? "Still here and ready to rumble."

"We need a few more minutes to set up the cameras," he said.

"Okay. I'll stand by."

The walkie-talkie fell silent.

Normally, Crash didn't mind the waiting involved in making a movie. In her five years in the stunt business, she had gotten used to it. But up here on the rooftop, the dry March wind was so much stronger than on the ground that it made her eyes tear. She had to repeatedly reach up, wipe her eyes, and brush strands of her blonde wig out of her face.

While she waited, she went through her reminders: keep an eye on the wind currents, to make it less likely she would jump into a sudden gust that would blow her off course and make her overshoot the air bag. Hit the inflated bag straight in the middle, so she wouldn't get a bad bounce and smash against the building or the ground.

She took a deep, steadying breath. While a certain risk always remained, the stunt was safe. She'd checked out the equipment and had done a practice jump earlier today.

Finally, the stunt coordinator's voice came through the walkie-talkie again. "Ready?"

Crash peered down the building to the blue heavy-duty air bag below and made sure the safety spotters were in the correct places. "Ready to roll."

"Remember to do a face-off and—"

"I know the drill," she told him.

The second-unit director's commands came through the walkie-talkie as he instructed his crew. "Roll camera."

"Rolling."

Crash eyed the spot on the rooftop ledge where she had to go over in order to hit the air bag just right.

"In three, two, one…"

At the countdown, Crash's body started to buzz with excitement. The thrill of doing a high fall never got old, no matter how often she'd done it. She planted her feet more firmly and waited for the final cue.

"Go!"

She jumped over the ledge face-first, kicking her legs and flailing her arms just the way the director wanted it. The ground rushed up fast. *Wait, wait, wait…* She gave the cameramen as much time as she could so they'd have plenty of material to shoot before rotating her body.

She landed flat on her back, her chin tucked into her chest, with the impact as evenly distributed as she could. A bit of air whooshed out of the bag.

Everything went quiet for a moment. Then the crew broke into applause.

Crash lifted up on one elbow, looked behind her, and grinned. *Perfect landing.* She had hit the white X in the center of the air bag.

Their stunt coordinator, who was also the second-unit director, walked over. "You okay?"

She smoothly rolled off the air bag and dropped to the ground. "Yeah. Need me to do that again?"

"No. You nailed it on the first take. Nice job."

"Too bad," Crash grumbled. With the adrenaline still pumping through her body, she was ready to climb back up and do it all over again.

He looked her up and down as if taking her measurements. "Do you have more stunt work lined up for the next few months?"

"Not yet." Crash wasn't at a point in her career yet where she would constantly work. Just when she had started getting bigger jobs, she hurt her leg in a motorcycle stunt. Then, on her first job after that had healed, a fire stunt had gone wrong. Memories of heat searing her skin flashed through Crash's mind, and she stifled the impulse to rub the burn scar on the back of her neck. The screw-up hadn't been her fault, but that didn't matter. If people thought she was still skittish about it, word would get around, and stunt coordinators would stop hiring her. Nothing was more dangerous than a stunt person who couldn't keep a lid on their fear.

"You might want to hit up a buddy of mine, Ben Brower." The second-unit director handed her a business card. "They start shooting a historical drama with lots of action scenes in mid-May, and they're still looking for a girl to double one of the actresses and maybe play a few extras in the more dangerous scenes."

"Woman," Crash said.

He frowned. "What?"

"They're looking for a *woman* to double one of the actresses," Crash said softly, but without flinching away from his gaze.

His frown deepened. "That's what I just said, isn't it?"

Crash decided to let it go. The second-unit director looked as if he were old enough to have gotten his start doubling for John Wayne, so compared to his age, she really was little more than a girl. He was offering work, so he hadn't meant it in a belittling way. "So, who would I be doubling?" she asked. "The lead actress?"

"No, one of the supporting actresses. Jill Something-or-another."

Great. So she'd be doubling for some unknown wannabe starlet who probably had one scene in the movie. Crash sighed. Well, it was better than nothing, and he had said she could play an extra in some of the more dangerous scenes. If she did well, it might get her on the list of candidates for bigger, more exciting work. "Okay," she said. "I'll give Mr. Brower a call."

"It's a movie about the great earthquake and fires of 1906, so you'll probably have to do some fire stunts. You're up for that, aren't you?"

Crash gritted her teeth. News in the stunt business traveled fast. "I'm up for it," she said as evenly as possible and pocketed the card. "Thanks."

CHAPTER 2

"And cut," Floyd Manning called. He gave Jill a nod. "Thank you, that was great."

Jill stuck her index finger into the high neck of her starched blouse and tugged, while trying to adjust her corset with the other hand. She didn't know how women in 1906 had lived like this every day. She'd been saddled with the corset and the two petticoats for less than a day, yet she was already sick of them.

"Why don't you take a short break?" Floyd eyed her with a wrinkle of concern between his eyebrows. "We won't need you for the next hour."

Truth be told, Jill could use a break, but she didn't want any special consideration. "Um, wasn't I supposed to head over to the second-unit set?"

The director shook his head. "That's not necessary. We'll get someone from the stunt department to do it. Just join them after your break so they can shoot the lead-in."

Jill gave up on her attempts to get the corset to fit more comfortably and narrowed her eyes at Floyd. "Nikki and Shawn are running through walls of fire, climbing tons of debris, and dodging panicked horses, and you think I can't even trip over a bedpan?"

Floyd got up from the director's chair and walked over to her, probably so none of the crew and cast would overhear what he had to say. "It's not that I think you can't do it. But if you get hurt, we'll have to stop production while you heal. That means a lot of lost money. If the stunt person gets hurt, we just call in another one."

After seven years in the business, Jill knew that was how things worked, but she still felt there was more to it than the routine procedure. "Yeah, but it's not like I'm supposed to do a backflip and land on a galloping horse. I'm tripping over a bedpan, for Christ's sake!"

Folding his arms across his skinny chest, Floyd faced her squarely. "It's not as easy as it looks. You could still get hurt."

"Would you let me try if I didn't have MS?" Jill asked.

A slight flinch. "It's not like that," he said but couldn't look her in the eyes anymore.

Bingo. She'd been right. Not that it gave her any satisfaction. She opened her mouth, about to tell him where he could shove his unwanted consideration, but then she bit her tongue. He probably meant well, or he had the producers and their insurance company breathing down his neck. Besides, it wouldn't do her any good to get a reputation as a diva who flew off the handle when things didn't go her way.

She inflated her cheeks and then blew out a breath. "All right. If you're sure you want to bother a stunt person for an easy thing like that…"

"I'm sure," he said.

When he didn't add anything else, she turned and walked to her trailer. At times like this, she really regretted coming out to the press and the public—not as a lesbian, but as a person with MS.

Well, it wasn't as if you had much choice. The paparazzi had snapped pictures of Grace helping her to her trailer when her symptoms had flared. The press and the public had promptly concluded that they were having an affair. If she hadn't revealed the truth, the rumors would have gotten out of control, hurting her friend's career, because back then, her fans had still assumed Grace to be happily married to action star Nick Sinclair.

Jill entered the trailer and flopped down on the couch. Exhaustion settled over her without warning, so she closed her eyes, not even bothering to get out of her costume. She'd rest here for a moment and then head over to the second-unit set. Maybe Ben, the second-unit director and stunt coordinator, would let her try no matter what Floyd said.

Crash grunted as the pink-haired wardrobe assistant laced up her corset. Man, this thing was worse than a stunt harness.

The young woman stepped back and eyed her from head to toe. Usually, women didn't frown like that when they regarded her half-dressed body.

"What?" Crash asked and peered down her body too.

"Um, you're about the same age, height, and weight as Ms. Corrigan, but…uh, you need a little something…" She gestured at Crash's chest and then stuffed some padding into the corset.

Chuckling, Crash held still. She had yet to meet the actress she would double, so she had no idea about her bra size. Of course she had planned to pay her a visit and study the way she moved so she could copy her as closely as possible, but the stunt coordinator had called her in two weeks early, saying there'd been a change of plans and they needed her right away.

She didn't yet have the call sheet or the stunt script, but when she had arrived, the second-unit set had been buzzing with activity. The rigging coordinator had set up a ratchet and debris cannons, so apparently, one of the stunt performers would be thrown through a wall or a window by some kind of explosion. She hoped she'd get to do that gag or another, equally exciting stunt.

Once she was in costume and had her makeup done, she headed back to the set. Her petticoats rustled, and she looked down at the long skirt she was wearing. It always felt a bit strange. While her job sometimes made it necessary to wear a dress or a skirt, the last time she'd worn one off-set had been her sixth birthday. *Good thing they pay me well for this.* At least the high-neck blouse and the ankle-length skirt would cover the pads she'd wear for some of the stunts. Usually, stuntwomen had it harder than their male colleagues since they didn't get to wear baggy pants and long-sleeved tops that could hide their pads.

When she stopped a PA and asked him where Ben was, he directed her toward one of the buildings. They were shooting in an old, abandoned hospital that reminded her of the one in *One Flew Over the Cuckoo's Nest.* She followed other cast and crew members up the stairs and found herself in a long room, with two rows of metal-framed beds lined up along the walls. Gas light fixtures hung from the ceiling.

All the cables, lighting equipment, and the technology of a modern movie set contrasted sharply with the cast moving around in period costumes—the women wearing skirts or dresses and the men trousers, vests, and bowler hats.

An actress in a white nurse's uniform sat at a desk in the center of the room, listening to something Ben was explaining.

Crash's steps echoed across the shiny hardwood floor.

Ben looked up and waved her over. "There you are. Thanks for coming in on such short notice."

"Sure. So, what do you need me to do?" Crash looked around, but there was no equipment set up that would give her any indication of what kind of stunt they wanted her to do.

"Well..." Ben stepped away from the actress behind the desk and scratched his neck.

Was he hesitating to tell her because it was a dangerous gag, maybe one involving fire? Crash swallowed. She wanted to shove her hands into her pants pockets while she waited for his reply but then realized she was wearing a skirt.

"Nothing big," Ben finally said. He handed her a stack of stapled pages—the list of scenes they would shoot that day.

Her name was on one of the scenes. There was just one line of description for the stunt she was supposed to do.

> Dr. Lucy Hamilton Sharpe walks over to one of the patients, stumbles across a bedpan, and crashes into a metal cart.

She turned the page over, thinking there had to be more. Nothing. This was a joke, right? No one booked a SAG-eligible stunt performer for something like that. She squinted over at Ben. "Uh, you want me to do...what?"

"Stumble over a bedpan."

"Seriously?"

He nodded and scratched the stubble on his chin, looking a bit embarrassed. "I know, I know."

She stepped closer to him so no one could overhear her. "Let me guess. The actress I'm doubling for is a bit..." She waved her hand while searching for the right word. "Difficult."

Someone cleared her throat behind Crash.

When she turned, she came face-to-face with a woman who wore a costume that was identical to hers.

Oh shit. That's the actress I'm doubling. Just her luck.

She didn't look like the spoiled Hollywood diva Crash had expected. In fact, Jill Corrigan was exactly the type of woman who usually caught Crash's eye. Compared to some of the actresses Crash had met, she wasn't stunning, but there was a vibrancy, a spark to her that made Crash take notice anyway. The actress's flaming-red hair contrasted with her fair skin, and for a moment, Crash thought it was a wig, just like the one she was wearing, but then a second look revealed that it was real. She stood eye to eye with Crash's five foot eight, and yep, the wardrobe lady had been right—she was indeed a bit better endowed than Crash.

What are you doing? Crash forced her gaze up and took in the charming smattering of freckles across the actress's nose, which were visible even through her stage makeup. *Cute. Definitely cute.*

But now the actress's green eyes sparked with annoyance, destroying any hope that maybe she hadn't heard what Crash had said about her being difficult. Jill folded her arms across her chest, which looked a bit out of place in her historical costume. "I happen to think that I'm fairly easy to work with. That is, unless someone assumes things about me without even meeting me first."

"Uh..." Well, if Jill refused to shoot the stumbling-over-a-bed-pan scene herself, she probably was a bit of a diva. But Crash knew better than to voice her thoughts. She'd have to work with this woman for the next two or three months, after all. "Hi," she said with her most disarming smile. "Crash Patterson. Nice to meet you." She held out her hand.

After a few moments, the actress reached out and accepted her handshake. Her grip was firm. "Jill Corrigan." She eyed Crash with a small wrinkle on her forehead that was just too adorable. "What kind of name is Crash?"

"The name of someone who doesn't mind stumbling over bedpans," she said and then mentally slapped herself. The quip wouldn't help establish an amiable working relationship.

"Just to make one thing perfectly clear. I would rather do the scene myself, but Floyd wants to have a stunt person take over. It wasn't my decision."

Crash hadn't worked with the director before, but he didn't seem the type who would coddle his actors. Was there something going on between him and the pretty actress, and that was why he didn't want her to do this very simple stunt? It wouldn't be the first time a set romance had impacted the production schedule, but Crash didn't like it. She had never let her private life interfere with her work. In fact, she hadn't even had a private life her first two years in the business. She'd been too busy introducing herself to any stunt coordinator who would talk to her and doing any gag, no matter how small. Kind of like the one she was supposed to do now.

"No big deal," she said. "I really don't mind."

Jill mumbled something that sounded like "Well, I do," before turning toward Ben and dragging him toward the edge of the set.

Crash watched them, observed Jill's gestures as she talked to Ben and waved her arm to indicate the set. She told herself she wasn't ogling her; she was just trying to familiarize herself with the actress's body language so she could adjust her own on camera.

Finally, Ben shook his head to whatever Jill had requested.

"Excuse me," someone said behind Crash.

The camera crew and the sound people were setting up their equipment all around her.

Crash quickly got out of their way.

Normally, Jill knew exactly how to use her Irish charm to get whatever she wanted. Not this time, apparently.

Ben kept shaking his head, no matter what she said. "No, Jill. I can't just ignore Floyd's decision. You don't want me to get in trouble with the boss, do you?"

Jill sighed. "No. Of course not."

Nikki, one of the movie's leading ladies, joined them. She wrapped one arm around Jill and gently nudged her. "Why are you so eager to get fake urine all over your costume anyway?"

A grin slowly made its way onto Jill's face. "Well, when you put it that way... Maybe I should be glad that the stuntwoman is doing it." Despite her words, she couldn't bring herself to be relieved. Shame and anger made her cheeks burn. She hated that the stuntwoman now assumed her to be a prissy diva who had requested a stunt double because she was afraid to chip a nail. Crash Patterson seemed to be the only person in the room who had no idea that Jill had MS. Hard to believe that anyone in Hollywood had missed the tabloid frenzy last June, but it seemed Crash had managed somehow. Normally, Jill would be glad about it, but now it meant the stuntwoman thought she was a slacker.

Jill glanced over at Crash. Wearing the wig and the same costume, she could be mistaken for Jill from behind, but a closer look revealed that she didn't look like Jill at all. While people often referred to Jill as cute, Crash was gorgeous, in that nonclassical, almost androgynous way that would have immediately captured Jill's interest in the past. The woman's jawline was a bit too square and her nose a bit too strong for her to ever make it as an actress, but Jill liked her dimpled chin and her striking blue eyes.

She watched as Ben and Crash—or whatever her real name was—did a quick walk-through of the scene. Lighting was adjusted and the boom mikes moved back a bit, and then the cameras were rolling.

"And...action!" Ben called.

It was weird to see someone who looked so much like her, at least from behind and with a wig, walk down the row of beds. Was it just her imagination, or had Crash even adjusted her long, loose-limbed stride to the way Jill moved? Either she was really that good, or it was the skirt that changed the way she moved.

Halfway toward her patient, Crash tripped over the bedpan. It looked real, as if she hadn't known it was there. Crash almost fell and then careened into a metal cart that held medical supplies, which went flying in all directions.

"Cut!" Ben called. He reviewed the take on his monitors, then immediately nodded. "Great. I don't think we need to do it again."

Crash took off her wig, revealing short, disheveled black hair, and grinned. "Well, that was easy money."

Jill gritted her teeth. When the stuntwoman glanced over at her, she scowled and looked away. While it was Floyd who'd made that decision, it was hard not to resent Crash for being allowed to do what she no longer could.

"Jill?" Ben called. "Ready to film the lead-in?"

"Ready," she answered, resolved to bag it in one take too. She'd show that stuntwoman that she wasn't a difficult diva who held up production whenever she felt like it.

They didn't have time to break for a hot, sit-down meal from catering, so once Jill was done with her scenes for the day, she changed out of her costume and headed over to the craft services tent to see if there was any leftover food.

She ran her hands down the seams of her pants while she walked. God, after thirteen hours in petticoats, skirt, and corset, jeans had never felt so good. She grinned inwardly. *I might just set up a shrine to Levi Strauss!*

Someone cleared her throat behind her and said, "Hi."

Quickly, Jill snatched her hands away, embarrassed to have been caught practically caressing her own legs. Her cheeks heated, so she refused to turn around. She had a pretty good idea of who was behind her anyway. That low voice with the faint Texas accent was unmistakable.

"Long day, huh?" Crash commented.

Jill nodded but otherwise didn't react to Crash's obvious attempt to start a conversation. She wasn't in the mood to make small talk with someone who had called her difficult in front of half the crew. She was working hard not to cause any trouble on the set, and she wasn't about to let this stuntwoman—who didn't even know how lucky she was to have her body do anything she asked it to do—make her look bad.

When she stepped up to the twelve-foot-long craft services table that had been set up on one end of the tent, Crash joined her.

Out of the corner of her eye, Jill saw that Crash had changed out of her costume too, apparently just as eager to get rid of the corset as Jill had been. Her low-rise jeans fit her like a second skin, making Jill's dormant libido take notice. They had filmed some of the same scenes today, so the director would have the best material to choose from, but while Jill felt ready to drop, Crash looked fresh as a daisy.

Figures. At least temperatures were still relatively cool for the middle of May in LA, so except for the fatigue, her symptoms didn't flare up.

Other actors and crew had wrapped their scenes too and were now descending on the food like a locust swarm.

Jill threw a longing glance at the rapidly disappearing brownies, grilled cheese sandwiches, and muffins. In the past, she would have grabbed some of that food too, but she tried to stick to a healthier diet these days.

Suppressing a sigh, she put a mango-lettuce-cucumber wrap onto her paper plate and reached for an apple—only to have her hand collide with another set of fingers reaching for the same piece of fruit.

A shiver ran through her body. Quickly, she snatched her hand away. Not turning toward Crash, she felt more than saw Crash watch her. "What?"

"Listen," Crash said and gestured for Jill to go ahead and take the coveted apple. "I wanted to apologize for calling you difficult. I shouldn't have said that."

Jill weighed the apple in her hand. "Then why did you?"

"Well, I'm not usually hired for a simple scene like that, so I assumed—"

"You know what they say about people who make assumptions, don't you?"

Crash folded her arms over her chest and regarded her with a dismayed expression. "Are you always this...?"

"Difficult?" Jill finished for her.

One corner of Crash's mouth twitched. "I didn't say that."

"But you thought it," Jill countered.

"Oh, now you're a mind reader too?"

"I don't have to be a mind reader to know what you're thinking." Jill knew she was a bit touchy, but she couldn't help being hurt that this stranger had formed an opinion about her so quickly.

At a stand-off, they stared at each other. Crash's blue eyes were almost eerie, and it irritated Jill even more how fascinating she found them.

"Ms. Patterson?" One of the PAs peered into the tent. "Mr. Brower is looking for you."

"Tell him I'm on my way," Crash said but made no move to follow him out of the tent. When the PA walked away, she turned back to Jill. "I really want us to be able to work together."

"That's one thing you don't have to worry about. If you knew me at all, you'd know that I never allow my personal feelings to interfere with my work." No matter what Crash thought of her, she was a professional.

Crash didn't look happy with the way they left things, but she finally gave her a nod. "I'd better go see what Ben wants. See you tomorrow."

Jill watched the tent flap fall closed behind Crash. God, it was going to be a long three months of shooting.

CHAPTER 3

Two sound technicians who'd sneaked off for a smoke stared at Jill as she passed them on the way to her car.

What is it, boys? Never seen a woman in her underwear before? Chuckling, she glanced down at the pair of knee-length drawers and the chemise she was wearing. She unlocked her Beetle and let herself sink behind the wheel with a relieved sigh. Sitting down felt good, and so did being inside the car, where it was warmer. This was only the third day of filming, yet she was already exhausted. Today's night shoot was kicking her ass, but Jill was determined to prove herself in the upcoming fight scene—even if she was only allowed to film the lead-in and the close-ups.

Just when she reached for the jacket on the passenger seat, her cell phone rang. She fumbled it out of the jacket pocket and glanced at the display.

Great. Her mother was calling. If she didn't answer, she'd later have to listen to her ranting and raving about how worried she'd been. Sighing, she swiped her finger across the screen to accept the call. "Hi, Mom."

"Finally! I've been trying to reach you for hours!"

"I'm still on set, so I couldn't have my cell phone with me. I just went to the car for a minute. Did something happen?"

"Oh, yes!"

Jill gripped the steering wheel with her free hand. "Is Dad okay?"

"What? Oh, yes, nothing like that. Your brother got a promotion! Isn't that great?"

"Yes," Jill said dutifully. "It's wonderful." *And it would be wonderful too if you didn't scare me half to death!*

Her mother started to go on and on about the promotion.

"Mom, I really can't talk right now. We're doing a night shoot, and I have to get back to the set."

"I just wanted to give you the good news and ask if you got my e-mail," her mother said.

The e-mail sat unread in her in-box, but there was a good chance it had to do either with her brother's great accomplishments or with MS. Since her mother had chosen to tell her about James's promotion on the phone, that left option number two. "The one about the MS health advice?"

"Yes."

Bingo. Jill halfheartedly listened to her mother's monologue about acupuncture, bee sting venom, and pH balance, all of which she was supposed to try out. Shaking her head, she thumped the steering wheel with her free hand. Since she'd finally told her parents about the MS last year, she'd stopped being their daughter and started being the family patient. Her mother hadn't even asked how the shooting of *Shaken to the Core* was going.

"Mom, I need to go," she said when her mother started talking about some aloe vera drink. She hung up, threw the phone onto the passenger seat, and closed her eyes for a moment.

When Crash started to shiver in the cool night air, she slipped her leather jacket over her costume, not caring how ridiculous it might look.

It seemed to take forever until the cameras and the rest of the equipment had been set up. Why was it that everything always seemed to take twice as long on night shoots?

Spotlights cut through the darkness, illuminating a sea of tents that, in the movie, housed the injured and sick after the hospital had burned down.

When her colleague who would play the looter breaking into the makeshift hospital arrived, she went over the fight choreography with him.

After two run-throughs, both she and Ben were satisfied that all would go smoothly.

"Okay, let's get this over with so we can finally go home and get some sleep," Ben said. He looked around. "Where's Jill?"

Crash peered around too but couldn't locate her anywhere. Come to think of it, she hadn't seen her for the last half hour.

"I think she headed to her car to get a jacket," one of the PAs said.

Crash looked over to the parking lot, but everything was pitch-dark over there. A hint of worry skittered down her spine. Why was it taking Jill so long to get her jacket?

Ben let out a sigh. "Can someone go and get her? We're losing time here, people!"

"I'll go," Crash said before anyone else could volunteer. Maybe this would give her the opportunity to apologize again.

In the last two days, she'd had a lot of time to watch Jill while she waited for her next stunt. It hadn't taken her long to figure out that Jill was not the difficult diva she'd first thought her to be. Even after half a dozen takes, Jill was always ready to repeat a shot as often as it took to get it right. She never complained, and she never treated any member of the crew with disrespect.

Crash jogged toward the parking lot. Once she'd left the circle of light on the set, she couldn't see much.

Voices drifted over from the edge of the parking lot. When her eyes adjusted to the near darkness, she could make out two members of the sound crew who'd wandered off for a smoke.

Crash continued on her way. She'd seen Jill arrive in a cute Beetle convertible this morning, and she tried to remember where Jill had parked it.

Finally, she made out the Beetle across the parking lot. Gravel crunched under her ankle-high costume boots as she strode over.

Someone was sitting in the car.

Crash bent and peered through the window.

Jill sat behind the wheel, her head leaned back and her eyes closed. She was wearing the same historic underwear that Crash had on, but she looked much better in it. A jacket was lying across her knees, as if she hadn't quite managed to put it on.

Just when Crash was about to get worried, Jill's lips parted and she started snoring so loudly that it could be heard even through the closed car door.

Relieved laughter burst from Crash's lips. She watched her for a while. Jill looked so cute—not to mention exhausted—that Crash hated to wake her. But she had no choice. Ben and the rest of the crew were waiting.

Softly, she knocked on the side window.

The snoring instantly stopped. Jill's head jerked up, and she smashed her knee into the steering wheel. She rubbed her leg and looked around as if needing a few seconds to remember where she was.

When their gazes met, Crash grinned and gave a sheepish wave.

Jill opened the door and climbed out of the car, still looking half asleep.

"Not used to staying up all night?" Crash asked and then shook her head at herself. *You'd better cut out the teasing—and the flirting—before she gets mad again.*

"Something like that," Jill mumbled.

"Sorry to wake you, but everyone's waiting." They headed toward the set.

"I'm fine," Jill said. "You can let go."

Puzzled, Crash peered over at her and only then realized that she'd taken hold of Jill's elbow to safely guide her through the darkness. She quickly let go.

Jill crossed the parking lot as fast as she could. The knee-length drawers didn't allow her to wear her foot brace today, so she couldn't outrun Crash.

It was bad enough that the damn fatigue had made her fall asleep while at work, but why did it have to be Crash of all people who found her? The stuntwoman already thought she was a spoiled diva who didn't pull her own weight on the set.

"Jill?" Crash said as they were about to step into the circle of light surrounding the tents.

Jill just wanted to get back to work. Annoyed—more with herself and her fatigue than with Crash—she turned around. "What?"

"I...I really am sorry."

"No big deal," Jill said with a wave of her hand. "I wasn't really asleep, just resting my eyes for a second."

"Not for waking you. For saying...what I did about you. It was a stupid assumption to make, and I'd like to leave it behind us."

The faint light and the distance between them made it hard to make out her expression, but her words sounded honest. Either she was a better actress than Jill had given her credit for, or she could be taken at face value.

"So?" Crash held out her hand. "Do you accept my apology?"

Jill took two steps toward her so she could see her better. She glanced down at Crash's hand and then back up at her face.

Traditionally, blue eyes were thought of as cold, but Crash's looked warm and sincere.

"Apology accepted," Jill said and laid her hand into Crash's.

Crash's strong fingers cradled hers carefully. The simple touch felt unexpectedly good, reminding Jill how long it had been since a woman had held her hand.

Quickly, she pulled her hand away, not allowing herself to linger. "We need to get back to the set," she said and marched off without waiting for Crash's reply.

Once they reached the set, Ben called Jill over to show her the sequence of motions that she would need to execute so the camera could capture her face during the fight with the looter. "He enters and finds you in the tent, asleep in the middle of the medical supplies. When you don't move out of the way, he shoves you back to get to the supplies. You stumble backward and fall." He pointed to the mat they'd set up in one of the tents. "Crash will do that part. One of your hands finds a broken-off branch on the ground, and you grab it as you get back up. You take a swing at him, but he blocks it and the two of you tussle for the weapon." He turned and looked at Crash. "Can you show her?"

"Sure." Crash shrugged out of her leather jacket so she could move more freely. "I can even teach her how to fall safely if she wants to do the stunt herself." She looked back and forth between Ben and Jill, careful not to make the same mistake as before and assume that Jill wouldn't want to do any of her own stunts.

Jill opened her mouth, but before she could answer, Ben shook his head and said, "No, I'd rather you do it. Just show her what she needs to do so we can shoot the close-ups with her."

What the hell was going on? Crash was used to producers and directors hesitating to allow their actors to do their own stunts, but this seemed a bit over the top. By now, Crash doubted that the director was so overprotective of Jill because they were lovers. Maybe it was just wishful thinking, but her gaydar kept insisting that Jill was a lesbian. Even if she wasn't, she didn't seem to be the type who would allow herself to be coddled while at work.

But now wasn't the time to solve this puzzle. Crash grabbed the branch with both hands. "You swing it like you would a baseball bat. Like this." She demonstrated and then handed over the branch for Jill to try.

Jill swung the branch, looking as if she'd done it a thousand times before.

Maybe she really is a lesbian. After all, we're supposed to be good at softball. Crash grinned to herself.

"What?" Jill asked.

"Nothing." She led Jill over to the tent so they could practice right where they would shoot the scene. "Now take a swing at me."

Jill hesitated.

"Don't worry. You won't hurt me. I'll block it."

Halfheartedly, Jill tried to hit her with the branch.

Crash blocked it, grabbed the branch, and pulled.

Their bodies collided, with both of them holding on to the branch. "He tries to take the makeshift weapon from you, but you refuse to let go." She tugged on the branch, pulling Jill even closer. The ruffles of Jill's chemise brushed Crash's chest, and she caught a whiff of Jill's perfume, nearly making her lose her grip on the branch.

"Like this?"

"Yes, exactly," Crash said, annoyed with herself for sounding so breathless. "He slowly pushes you toward the tent post until you can't back up anymore." She did it.

Jill's back hit the tent post, but she hardly even noticed; she was too busy staring into Crash's ice-blue eyes, which looked fierce and wild in the spotlights filtering in through the tent walls.

"And then?" she asked. Why was her voice so hoarse? *Get yourself together, or Ben will think you either have the hots for Crash or aren't fit enough to do this simple scene.*

"And then," Crash said, "he grabs the branch with both hands and presses it to your throat." With Jill still holding on to the middle of the branch, Crash grabbed it at both ends, brought it up horizontally, and laid it against Jill's throat, exerting only the slightest pressure.

They stared at each other, their hands touching on the branch, their faces only inches apart.

Crash licked her lips as if her mouth had suddenly gone dry, and Jill mirrored the gesture.

Are you crazy? She tried to shake herself out of it. She had no business lusting after anyone, least of all a woman who was so physically active and full of energy. A woman who most likely had no idea that Jill had MS and that she would end up a burden, not an equal partner.

For Christ's sake, she'd just fallen asleep in her car when all she'd wanted to do was get her jacket. Until someone found a cure for MS or at least the goddamn fatigue, she would never be able to keep up with someone like Crash.

She let go of the branch and slid out from between Crash and the tent pole. Distance. She needed some distance so she could think clearly.

"You okay?" Crash asked but didn't try to follow her. Her voice sounded a bit husky too.

"Fine," Jill croaked. "So, that's when one of the nurses comes in and hits the guy over the head, right?"

"Uh, yes, exactly. All you need to do is stand there and look surprised as he goes down."

Jill gave a decisive nod. She glanced at Ben, who stood at the tent's entrance. "Okay. I'm ready."

Four days later, Jill had just settled on the couch with the script when a knock sounded on her trailer door.

Jill groaned. "Not yet," she muttered, aware that she sounded like a whining teenager who had been ordered to go to bed. She was supposed to have one more hour before they needed her back on set—and she needed that hour to go over her lines for tomorrow's scenes.

By the time she got home that night, she knew she'd be exhausted and any attempt to memorize lines would feel like wading through molasses, so she'd rather do it now.

When she opened the door and peeked out, it wasn't a PA sent to summon her back to the set. Instead, Crash stood on the top step, still in the Lucy Sharpe costume, but without the wig. Her short, black hair looked strangely out of place in the turn-of-the-century garb. With a broad grin, she presented a shiny apple. "I didn't see you at the craft services table, so I thought I'd bring you a snack."

Jill took the apple, careful not to touch Crash's fingers in the process. "Thanks."

They stood facing each other in silence for several moments.

"Um, do you want to come in?" Jill asked and opened the trailer door wider.

"Sure." Crash followed her in. Her vibrancy filled the trailer, immediately making it seem much smaller. She looked around and let out a whistle. "Nice digs."

After a week of shooting, Jill was already so used to her home away from home that she didn't notice the details anymore. She took in the tiny kitchenette at one end of the trailer, the comfortable couch along one wall, and the small table with two chairs in the other corner, trying to see them through Crash's eyes. "You think so?"

"Yeah. I think it's even nicer than Nikki's and Shawn's trailers."

Crash had been in their co-stars' trailers? She shoved away the thought, firmly telling herself it didn't matter to her one way or the other. Instead, she focused on the apple and took a big bite out of it.

"I'm not even sure theirs have air-conditioning," Crash said.

Jill nearly choked on her bite of apple. *Dammit.* Lauren must have found out from Grace what effect heat had on Jill, so she had pulled some strings to get her the nicest trailer with the best air-conditioning on set. She didn't know whether to be grateful or angry with her friend and former publicist.

"Careful." Crash stepped closer and softly patted her on the back. "Women and apples don't have the best of history."

Finally, Jill managed to stop coughing and took a deep breath. Crash's scent filled her nose—an irresistible mix of shampoo, fresh sweat, and horses from one of the stunts earlier that day. She took a step back and focused on the conversation. "That's what people think, but actually, the Bible doesn't say that the fruit was an apple."

Another grin flashed across Crash's face. "I wouldn't know one way or another. I was talking about Snow White."

Jill flopped down on one end of the couch, inviting Crash with a nod of her head to take the other. She grinned at her. "I didn't take you for a fan of fairy tales."

"What can I say? I'm a sucker for happy endings." Crash sat and stretched out her legs, getting comfortable despite the corset she was wearing. "So, how do you know so much about the Bible?"

"Are you saying I don't look like the typical devout Irish Catholic girl to you?"

"Um..."

Jill laughed and took pity on her. "I'm not religious. I've always preferred to rely on myself rather than some higher power. But my brother is big on religion. He quoted from the scripture whenever he had me over for dinner."

"Had?" Crash repeated.

Damn. She was too perceptive for her own good. Jill resolved to be more careful about what she said around Crash in the future. While she didn't mind sharing funny anecdotes about past movies and TV shows she had filmed, she preferred not to share too much about her private life with her colleagues. "Well, I'm here in LA, and the rest of my family lives in Ohio, so we don't get the chance to have dinner together anymore," she said. It was the truth—but not the real reason why she no longer had dinner with her brother. She hadn't talked to him since the day she'd told him about the MS. Instead of telling her he was sorry or offering help, he had suggested it was her punishment for defying God by doing unnatural things with other women.

Crash looked at her. Something in her blue eyes told Jill that she sensed there was more to it, but Crash finally nodded and accepted that no further explanation would be forthcoming. She reached for the script that lay on the middle cushion between them. "I hope I didn't interrupt you memorizing your lines."

"That's okay. It wasn't going too well anyway."

"Yeah? Why not?"

Jill shrugged. "I'm not sure." It could be the MS messing with her focus or her memory, or maybe it was the fact that some aspects of her character's behavior didn't ring true to her and that was why the lines were giving her such trouble.

"Would it help if I ran lines with you for a while?" Crash asked.

"Are you sure you've got the time?"

"Oh yeah. I'm bored to death out there, waiting for them to need me for another gag."

"Gag?"

"Stunt," Crash said. She looked at Jill, her head tilted to the side like an overeager puppy begging for a treat.

Jill had to smile. "Sure, why not." Running lines with Crash might be fun, and maybe it would help her memorize her lines. "I'm granting you asylum in my air-conditioned domicile, as long as you don't mind being threatened by a scalpel."

"Uh, excuse me?"

Jill chuckled. "You'll see."

Crash reached across the middle cushion and picked up the stapled script pages.

"The highlighted lines are mine, so just read the rest," Jill said.

Crash took a minute to skim the first page before giving Jill a nod to show that she was ready. Instead of staying on the couch, she stood and moved around the room, as Jill had done in the past when learning her lines, before she'd learned to conserve her energy. She looked so powerful and energetic that Jill couldn't help envying her.

"You need to get out of here, ma'am," Crash said. She wasn't just reading the text, but acting it out, lowering her voice to sound like the soldier who'd just rushed into the makeshift hospital.

Jill stood as well and bent over the coffee table, pretending to be busy with a patient. "Doctor," she said without looking up. "And we *are* getting out—but not without our patients. I need to stabilize her first."

"There's no time! If the fire reaches the park, the tents will go up in flames within seconds!"

Jill didn't answer. She remained bent over her imaginary patient.

Crash crossed the trailer in two long steps, marching like a soldier on a mission. She cursed under her breath, grabbed Jill by the shoulders, and dragged her toward the door.

"What are you doing? If you—"

Shaking her head, Crash let go of her. "The script says, 'What do you think you are doing, Corporal?'"

Jill stepped closer and half turned so she could look at the script pages Crash was holding. *Damn.* She was right. Jill closed her eyes for a moment and repeated the line three times to herself, hoping it would finally stick in her memory. "Okay, let's try this again," she said when she opened her eyes.

They ran through the lines again from the beginning. Jill attempted to get into the scene, trying out different gestures and inflections. But something was still off, making her stumble over her lines at times.

Finally, she plopped down on the couch and shook her head. "See what I mean? This isn't working, and I'm still not sure why."

Crash sat next to her. "Well, I'm not an acting coach, and far be it from me to tell a seasoned actress like you how to do her job..."

"But?" Jill prompted.

"I think the scene needs more...fire."

"More fire? That's what they're running from."

Crash threw the script down on the coffee table. "No, I mean more fire from you. More anger."

"Um, excuse me. I'm butting heads with an armed soldier, refusing to leave. I'd think that's enough anger, isn't it?"

"Yeah, but...I just don't feel it."

Groaning, Jill let her head fall back against the couch. "Damn. I think you're right. I just don't get why Lauren wrote the scene this way."

"Lauren?"

"Oh. She's the screenwriter who wrote *Shaken to the Core*. And she's a friend of mine," Jill added after a moment's hesitation. "I mean, Lucy is a trained doctor. Shouldn't she be calm and level-headed in the face of this crisis? Shouldn't she trust the soldier to do his job, just the way she's doing hers? Why get so angry with him?"

Crash seemed to consider it for a moment before shaking her head. "I think she's angry at much more than him."

"What do you mean?" When Jill turned on the couch to face her more fully, their skirts brushed and she sensed the warmth of Crash's knee against hers. Quickly, she moved back a bit.

"You have to view this scene in context and consider Lucy's background. I only read bits and pieces of the script while I was waiting for a stunt yesterday, but didn't she grow up on a ranch?"

Jill nodded. "She did. Her mother was the first female veterinarian in the US."

"And Lucy is one of only eight thousand lady doctors in 1906," Crash added.

"Right." To prepare for her role, Jill had read the memoir of one of the first women to graduate from a medical college, so she knew what that meant. "She's a woman living and working in a man's world." A thought occurred to her. "Just like you."

"Things are much easier for stuntwomen nowadays, but I've heard some stories from women who used to be in the business twenty or thirty years ago…" Crash shook her head. "Let's just say I understand why Lucy wouldn't react too well to being ordered around when she's trying to do her job."

Jill looked at her with new respect. She hadn't expected Crash to be able to provide such insights into her character.

Crash laughed. "What? You thought I was all brawn, no brains?"

Jill's cheeks warmed, and she cursed the fair complexion she had inherited from the Irish side of her family. "Well, far be it from me to underestimate your intellect, but I think Ben hired you for your athletic skills."

Crash let out an exaggerated sigh. "Story of my life. People just want me for my body."

A witty—and slightly flirty—reply was already on the tip of her tongue, but Jill bit it back. *Back to work.* "Could we try the scene again?"

"Sure. I'm all yours."

So she wasn't the only flirt around. Too bad it couldn't go anywhere. "Let's take it from 'There's no time.'"

Crash nodded and moved back to the door, as if she had just entered. "There's no time! If the fire reaches the park, the tents will go up in flames within seconds!"

Jill stiffened her shoulders but kept working on her patient.

Urgently, Crash strode toward her and grabbed her by the shoulders.

Jill allowed herself to connect with all the anger she'd bottled up inside in the last two years. Anger at this damn disease that made her future unpredictable at best. Anger at the doctors who were just as helpless as she was. Anger at the acquaintances who told her how good she looked every time they saw her, as if that somehow meant she couldn't possibly be sick.

Rage bubbled up from the deepest core of her being until the next line almost burst from her lips. "What do you think you are doing, Corporal?" She grabbed hold of the coffee table with one hand and swung up the nearest object with the other, waving it threateningly. "If you don't let go of me this instant, I'm going to stab you with—"

"The remote control?" Crash burst out laughing.

Jill's gaze went to the object in her hand, which was indeed the remote control. "My scalpel," she said, trying to hold on to her anger, but then she couldn't help it. She joined Crash's laughter.

They fell onto the couch next to each other, holding their sides.

A knock on the door interrupted their hilarity.

Jill wiped her eyes. God, she couldn't remember the last time she'd laughed like this. It felt good. She took a calming breath and called, "Yes?"

The door swung open, revealing a PA with a walkie-talkie hanging around his neck. He looked from Jill to Crash with a curious expression, obviously having heard their laughter through the door. Then his gaze zeroed in on the remote control Jill hadn't realized she was still clutching.

Jill looked over at Crash, who gazed back with one corner of her mouth twitching.

They burst out laughing again.

"Uh, they need you in five minutes, Ms. Corrigan," the PA said and left with a puzzled shake of his head.

When she could talk again, Jill shook the remote control at Crash. "If I burst out laughing while we're shooting the scene, you're in trouble."

"Me?" Crash clutched her chest with a faux innocent expression.

Jill dropped the remote control onto the couch and walked to the door. "Better stick to stunt work. Your acting skills are seriously lacking."

Grinning, Crash followed her back to the set.

CHAPTER 4

WHEN JILL GOT HER FIRST good look at the large concrete deck they had built in the studio's back lot, she stopped midstep to gape up at it.

An entire building had been erected on the platform—or rather what was left of it after an earthquake had hit it. Only one wall and a portion of another remained standing, and most of the roof had caved in. The chimney had crashed down, and the crew was installing a wire cage so one of the stuntwomen could safely be buried under the debris.

"Impressive, isn't it?" Crash said as she walked up to Jill. "They built it on hydraulic actuators, so the floor will really be shaking once we start shooting. Should be a lot of fun."

Two years ago, Jill would have readily agreed. The whole setup reminded her of a simulator in an amusement park—and she was about to get a free ride. But now that her balance was less than stellar, she was a bit worried about how she would hold up on that swaying platform. She nodded in reply to Crash's words, but secretly feared that this scene would be even more of a challenge than the scene with the soldier the day before—which had needed four takes before she'd managed to make it through the scene without bursting into laughter.

Ben and Floyd walked over. Normally, Floyd stayed at the first-unit location to shoot with the leading actresses, but it seemed not even the director had wanted to miss the big spectacle.

"Ready?" Ben asked.

Still looking at the platform, Jill nodded.

He seemed to sense her hesitation. "Are you sure you're up for it? We could have Crash—"

"No," Jill said, finally wrenching her gaze away from this newest challenge and looking him in the eyes. She had already argued with Floyd for an hour before he had agreed to let her do this scene, and she wasn't about to repeat the same with Ben. "I'm good. Crash can take over when the wall comes tumbling down, but the rest has a lot of close-ups. This scene is important and much more emotionally challenging than the bedpan scene. I want...I need to do it myself."

Ben traded gazes with Floyd, then nodded.

The rigger and his assistant attached a safety wire to the harness Jill wore beneath her costume. "Okay, one final check and we're good to go," the rigger said. "Um, Crash, could you...?"

"Uh, sure." Crash shouldered past them, bent, and gave Jill an impish grin. "May I?" She grasped the hem of Jill's dress and nodded down at it.

Jill grinned back. "Don't you think you should buy me dinner first?"

Crash barked out a startled laugh. Then she sobered, tilted her head, and looked up at Jill from her half-bent position. "Actually, I'd like that," she said so quietly that only Jill could hear it. "If you want, we could—"

"I was joking." Jill wanted to step back, get some distance between them, but Crash still held on to her dress, so she was forced to remain where she was.

"Right. There I go again, making assumptions about you. I thought you might be," Crash lowered her voice even more, "gay."

"I am, but..."

"It's okay," Crash said with a hint of a smile. "I know it's hard to believe, but you're not the first woman to turn me down."

Jill bit the inside of her cheek until it started to hurt. She felt bad letting Crash believe she wasn't interested in her specifically, but what could she say without explaining why she'd decided to forgo dating and relationships? Other than with Grace, she hadn't talked about it with anyone, and she wasn't about to start, especially not here.

Now all business, Crash lifted up the dress and the two petticoats beneath it.

The old-fashioned drawers covered most of Jill's body, but instead of the corset, she was wearing the body harness today.

Crash checked the two straps around Jill's upper thighs, tugging on the buckles to make sure they were securely fastened. Her fingertips traced the straps upward.

Oh God. Arousal hit her hard, making her clit twitch.

"They're not too tight, are they?" Crash asked from halfway under her skirt.

"No," Jill got out. Definitely not too tight. The blood flow to her crotch was just fine, thank you very much.

Crash tugged on the straps once, then, thankfully, retreated. She got up from her kneeling position and trailed her fingers over the straps hidden beneath the costume bodice—directly beneath Jill's breasts.

Jill's nipples instantly hardened. *Down, girls!* She prayed that Crash didn't notice.

Finally, Crash was satisfied with the fit of the torso straps. "Good to go," she announced and stepped back. Even her tan couldn't hide the flush on her cheeks.

Jill bit back a grim smile. Even though she'd had to reject Crash's dinner invitation, she couldn't help being glad she wasn't the only one affected. She tugged down the petticoats and the dress and made sure they fell just right over her lace-up boots.

Ben and Crash grabbed her hands and helped her climb up onto the concrete deck.

She ignored the way Crash's strong hand felt holding hers and focused on the rest of her body. It was still tingling, but she hoped it was just the after-effects of Crash's touch, not her MS symptoms threatening to flare up. Her left side felt a bit stiff, and the restricting dress and body harness weren't helping. The safety wire, which would be edited out in post-production, pulled taut as she climbed over the rubble.

"Okay, that's far enough," Ben called.

All around the large concrete deck, smaller platforms with cameras were moved into position.

"Cameras ready?"

"Ready."

"Sound ready?"

"Ready."

"And...action!" Ben shouted.

Jill forgot her concerns and immersed herself into her role. She became Dr. Lucy Sharpe—healthy Lucy, who could climb over debris to get to someone trapped beneath. She barely felt the debris dig into her skin as she went down on all fours and started removing stones and bits of plaster with her bare hands.

The ground beneath her started shaking as the city was hit by aftershocks. Large fans blew dust, ash, and tiny pieces of plaster into her face, so she had to squint to see anything. She grabbed bricks and threw them left and right in her frantic attempt to free the trapped person.

Heat rose around her while she worked as the flames came closer and closer to the crumbled house.

Every brick seemed to weigh a ton, but a moan from under the rubble spurred her on.

Finally, after lifting away the dented remainders of a washbasin, she caught sight of the woman. Blood ran down her face and matted her hair.

Jill knew it was only some very convincing film makeup, but for a moment, the sight still made her queasy.

The woman's eyes fluttered open.

Jill tried to pull her out, but the woman grabbed hold of the debris with both hands. "We need to get out of here!" Jill shouted. "The fire is nearly upon us!"

"My boy!" The woman looked around, her eyes wide with panic. "Please! We have to find him!"

"Cut!" Ben shouted.

Jill got to her feet and turned toward him, stumbling as a bit of debris slid out from under her feet. She caught herself, arms spread wide to help keep her balance.

"Sorry." Ben pointed upward, to where the sun had disappeared behind a cloud. "We lost the light. Let's go again once we get it back."

Jill lost track of time as they shot take after take of the scene. Circumstances seemed to conspire against her: the stage makeup of the trapped woman had started to dissolve, so they had to send someone up to fix it. Then the dust made the cameraman sneeze in the middle of shooting. Each time, they had to cover the poor woman with fake bricks again, and Jill had to make her way back across the debris, only to do it all over again.

The heat from the fire burning next to the platform made her sweat. The dress stuck to her chest. Even the large green screen they had erected on one side of the concrete deck, where CGI would later create the ruins of other buildings, seemed to reflect the heat back at her.

With each take, fatigue settled on her like another layer of dust, and it took more effort to move the damn bricks. An electric current crept up her left leg. Her entire left side felt as if she had been burned by the fire, but each time she checked, her skin looked completely normal.

Jill knew what it was: a warning sign. She needed to cool down. If she kept working in this heat, her symptoms would get worse until she couldn't move a muscle and would have to be carried down this mountain of debris.

But whenever she glanced down in between takes and looked into the skeptical faces of Ben and Floyd, she wanted to try harder to prove them wrong. *You can do it! Just once more.*

"Guys," the stuntwoman who was playing the trapped victim finally called down to the crew. "I don't know about you, but I think the two of us need a break."

Jill had to restrain herself from hugging the woman for saying it first. She hadn't wanted to be the one who called for a break. It would have felt as if she were admitting defeat, letting her MS beat her. She just hoped she would be able to make it back up on this moving pile of debris once she had climbed down. The deck felt as if it were still shaking as she made her way toward the edge, but she knew the hydraulic actuators had been shut off; it was her muscles that were shaking.

Crash helped down her colleague, who had reached the edge of the platform first, then unhooked the safety wire from the harness Jill wore and helped her down too.

No longer having the energy to climb down gracefully, Jill nearly fell into Crash's arms.

Crash caught her. Her closeness made Jill's body temperature climb even more until she almost expected steam to come out of her ears. Her legs felt like overcooked spaghetti.

"You okay?" Crash asked, her breath tickling Jill's ear.

A new current of electricity went through Jill, but this one had nothing to do with the MS. She nodded with as much energy as she could muster. "I'm fine. I just need a drink...I mean, something to drink."

"Do you want me to get you—?"

Jill cut her off with a wave of her hand. "No, thanks." Just a cold beverage wouldn't do. She needed a bowl of the ice the craft services people always kept around for her. If she ran it along her arms and neck for a few minutes, her body temperature would go down and the MS symptoms would disappear or at least lessen.

"Okay," Ben said. "Why don't you two take five while we set up everything to go again."

Jill didn't have to be told twice. As fast as her shaky legs would carry her, she fled to the craft services tent.

Crash watched Jill's retreating back. The actress looked as if she was about to collapse from a heatstroke or something. Crash wanted to hurry after her, but she sensed that Jill didn't want her to make a fuss.

Just the opposite of Crash's ex, who had been vying for her attention twenty-four/seven, and when Crash—busy with her career—had failed to give her constant admiration, she had found someone else. Not just anyone else but Crash's mentor, the woman who had taken her under her wing when she had first gotten into the stunt business.

After that, Crash had sworn off women for a while, at least for anything more than a fling. Now, nearly two years after Kyleigh had broken her heart, her emotional wounds had healed and she felt ready to get involved with another woman on a more serious basis.

She certainly wouldn't mind getting involved with Jill Corrigan—for a fling or maybe even something more. Too bad Jill wasn't interested in her. At least that was what she said. Her body language seemed to say something else, though.

Ben and Floyd looked toward the craft services tent, where Jill had disappeared.

"I told you they shouldn't have cast her," Ben said.

Anger gripped Crash. It surprised her how protective of Jill she felt, but she didn't stop to question it. She faced him squarely. "What's that supposed to mean? Jill did a fantastic job with that scene!"

Ben held up both hands in a defensive gesture. "Nothing. She's a good actress and a real trooper, but with the MS and everything..."

Crash felt as if the wire attached to a stunt harness had just jerked her to a sudden halt, knocking the air from her lungs. She stared at the second-unit director. "She...? Jill has MS?"

"I assumed everyone knew," Ben said. "I guess you didn't."

Her vocal cords refused to work, so she just shook her head.

"Didn't you pay any attention to the tabloids last year? It was all over town. Hell, all over the country!"

Crash never paid much attention to the gossip rags or the Hollywood rumor mill, especially not last year, when she'd recovered from her accidents and the breakup with Kyleigh. "No," she said around the large lump in her throat. "I had no idea."

She wanted to go after Jill, but Ben's voice held her back. "Why don't we shoot your scenes while we wait for Jill to get back?"

Crash glanced toward the craft services tent and then back at him before nodding. This way, she would at least give Jill a break. She tried to forget about Jill and focus just on the upcoming stunt while the rigger attached her to the wire, but that was easier said than done. Visions of Jill, helplessly bound to a wheelchair, flashed through her mind. *MS... God.* Could people die from that?

"Crash?" Ben said. "You okay?"

"Oh, yeah. Sorry." She quickly climbed up onto the concrete deck and got into position.

The cameras started rolling, and the platform began to shake beneath her.

How fitting, Crash thought. That was exactly how she felt: shaken to the core, just like the title of the movie.

"Cut," Ben shouted. "That's a wrap for today, folks. See you tomorrow."

"Hallelujah," the stuntwoman who'd played the trapped earthquake victim mumbled.

Jill gave her a commiserating glance. "Amen, sister." She had thought the redeeming words would never come and they would have to do take after take of this scene until sunset.

When she got up from her kneeling position, relief weakened her knees. Or maybe it was sheer exhaustion. She didn't care. All she cared about was finally making it off this damn pile of rubble. She felt as if she had just fought a three-day battle against an enemy that outnumbered her. Unfortunately, the MS was an opponent that couldn't be beaten.

With her arms spread to both sides to help keep her balance, she made her way over bricks and other debris until she reached the edge of the platform.

It wasn't much more than a yard off the ground, but even that distance felt like having to jump off a plane without a parachute. Normally, her foot brace helped stabilize her ankle, but she couldn't wear it for this scene because the plastic was too rigid and made crouching and crawling over the debris nearly impossible.

She sat on the edge of the concrete deck and let her feet dangle down so she was closer to the ground, praying that her left leg would hold up when she jumped.

"Wait!"

Jill had been so focused on safely getting down that Crash's calling out startled her. She looked up.

Crash left her conversation with Ben and the stuntwoman doubling for Shawn and rushed over. She unhooked Jill's safety wire and held out her hands to catch her.

"Thanks," Jill said. "I'm fine." Crash had already helped her down once, and Jill didn't want to start behaving like a damsel who needed help every single time.

Crash let her arms drop and then folded them across her chest. A frown marred her face. "Has anyone ever told you that you're as stubborn as a mule?"

"A person or two might have mentioned it," Jill said with a tired grin. She waved at Crash to clear the space in front of her.

For a moment, Crash looked as if she wanted to ignore her wishes, grab her around the waist, and lift her down. Then she shook her head and stepped back.

Jill slid forward on her ass. When she pushed off the platform, her dress caught on a piece of concrete that was sticking up. The ripping of fabric sounded overly loud to Jill.

She landed unevenly, trying to keep her weight mostly on her stronger right foot, and clutched the platform to keep herself upright. When she trusted her legs to hold her, she let go and reached behind herself with one hand. A large rip ran diagonally across her backside.

Despite her exhaustion—or maybe because of it—laughter bubbled up.

"You okay?" Crash eyed her as if she doubted Jill's mental soundness, but then a grin spread over her face too. She still stood with her hands held out, ready to catch Jill if needed.

"Yeah. I'm fine, but I think my days as wardrobe's favorite are numbered. The dress is toast." She had never thought she'd ever be grateful she had to wear two petticoats, but now those articles of clothing kept her from revealing her drawers to the entire cast and crew of *Shaken to the Core*. "See you tomorrow."

With as much dignity as she could muster, she pushed past Crash and walked toward her trailer, glad that the long hem of her dress hid that she was favoring her left leg.

She felt Crash's gaze on her all the way to the trailer and up the three metal stairs that were akin to climbing Mount Everest.

With a sigh of relief, she pulled the door closed behind her and turned up the air conditioner as high as it could go. The cold blasts of air felt heavenly. As her body cooled down, the burning sensation on the left side of her body and the numbness in her leg receded. Still, she kept close to the wall as she made her way over to the couch, just in case she had to catch herself.

She dropped onto the couch, sank back, and closed her eyes. Elation at having finished the shoot warred with frustration, but mainly, she was just tired. So tired. She knew she should get up and drive home or at least get into the trailer's tiny shower and clean herself up, but she just couldn't summon the energy to move.

A knock sounded on the door.

Bone-weary, Jill stayed where she was, hoping her visitor would take the hint and go away.

But the knock came again.

Groaning, she opened her eyes and pushed herself into an upright position. "Yes?"

She wasn't overly surprised when Crash peeked into her trailer. "Sorry to disturb you."

"No problem. Come on in. I was just going over my lines for tomorrow." Too late she realized that tomorrow's script pages were nowhere to be seen. She hoped Crash wouldn't notice.

Crash looked as if she didn't believe her, but she said nothing.

"So, what can I do for you?" Jill asked.

"The question is, what can I do for you," Crash said. She entered, closed the door behind her, and pointed at Jill's costume. "I remembered that you're still wearing the stunt harness, and I thought you might need some help getting out of that thing."

"Oh." Jill glanced down at herself. She'd forgotten about the harness. "Thanks, but I can manage." Truth be told, she had no idea how to take off the contraption, but accepting help didn't come easily for her.

Crash stepped closer and looked down at her. "Really?"

There was something in her blue eyes...something that hadn't been there before. Not pity, exactly, more like compassion mixed with sorrow.

Jill's overheated body went cold. She squeezed her eyes shut for a moment and then opened them again. The expression in Crash's eyes was still the same. "You know," Jill whispered.

Crash nodded. Her jaw muscles bunched.

Dammit. Jill's eyes stung. She told herself it was just the dust and ash the large fans had blown on her all day. She didn't care if Crash knew, right? Jill never cared what people thought.

But that feeling of regret, anger, and vulnerability right behind her sternum just wouldn't go away. She had liked the fact that Crash hadn't known and had treated her like an attractive woman, not like an MS patient.

"Does it hurt?" Crash asked.

For a moment, Jill thought she was talking about the MS, but then she realized she'd been rubbing her chest through the harness. "No, it's fine. Just not the most comfortable."

"Come on, let's take it off."

"I bet you say that to all the women," Jill said, hiding behind a grin.

"Nah." Crash returned the grin, but her eyes remained serious. "Usually, they take off their clothes without me having to tell them."

Jill shrugged. She still didn't move to take off her dress. "Guess I'm special, then."

"You're especially stubborn; that's what you are."

"Yeah, we established that already."

Crash perched on the coffee table and looked at her, now eye to eye. "Well, I'm a Leo, and you know what they say about my sun sign. We're pretty stubborn too."

Jill snorted and shook her head. "Isn't Taurus supposed to be the stubborn one?"

"You got me there. I don't know a thing about astrology, but I do know how to take off a stunt harness, so…" Crash gestured toward Jill's dress.

Jesus. Leo or not, Crash was pretty stubborn. If Jill wanted to get some rest anytime soon, she had to give in and get this over with. "Okay, okay." She lifted her hands to the bodice of her dress, but the tiny buttons wouldn't cooperate. They simply refused to slide through the buttonholes. That was exactly why she had banned articles of clothing with buttons from her wardrobe for the most part, but on the set, she had to wear them.

She was tempted to tear off the buttons, but she was probably already in the doghouse with the wardrobe people for ripping the back of the dress, so she kept fumbling with the buttons, trying to get her still-numb left hand to cooperate.

"Did I mention I know how to take off a dress too?" Crash said.

"I'll just bet you do," Jill mumbled without looking up from her battle with the buttons.

Finally, one slid through the buttonhole.

Suppressing a triumphant cry, she started to work on the next. Several minutes later, she had them all open and slipped out of the dress. The two petticoats followed. Now she stood in front of Crash in a pair of knee-length drawers, a lacy chemise, and the stunt harness. The old-fashioned underwear covered nearly all of her body, but she still felt strangely exposed. Ignoring the feeling, she looked over at Crash with a challenging stare. "There."

"Okay, so let's see…" Crash stood from where she had perched on the coffee table and rubbed her fingers together as if to warm them, even though she wouldn't actually have to touch Jill's skin to remove the harness.

Just the thought of Crash touching her bare skin sent a shiver through Jill's body. *Traitor.* Her entire left side had been either numb or burning for most of the day; her balance was off, and she was walking with a limp, but her body still reacted to Crash's closeness. *Figures.*

Crash reached for the first strap that held the stunt harness closed around Jill's torso and tore the Velcro open, then slid the strap through the titanium buckle. Her fingers brushed Jill's side on their way up to the next strap, sending another shiver through Jill. With her hands on the Velcro, Crash paused. "You okay? I'm not hurting you, am I?"

Jill bit her lip and shook her head. "No. I'm fine." She tried to distract herself by mentally repeating lines of tomorrow's scenes. As Crash's fingers moved higher, to the strap right below her breasts, she switched to nursery rhymes.

Crash opened the last buckle and then knelt to remove the straps around Jill's upper thighs. A chuckle drifted up. Again, Crash paused and peered up at Jill. "Mary had a little lamb?"

"What?"

"You were humming 'Mary had a little lamb,'" Crash said with a broad grin.

"Oh." Heat shot up Jill's neck. Her tired mind searched for an explanation she could offer—one other than *I was trying to distract myself from the way your fingers feel on my body.* "Uh, I guess I, um, must be hungry."

Crash slid the padded leg straps free, stood, and helped Jill out of the safety vest. "Want me to get you something? There's a Greek restaurant nearby if you have a hankering for lamb."

Jill dropped onto the couch and gestured for Crash to sit too. "Okay, let's get one thing straight once and for all. I might have MS, but I'm not helpless."

"I never said—"

One wave of Jill's hand stopped her. "I'm not helpless," Jill repeated. "This is a set, not a hospital, and you are the stuntwoman doubling for me, not my nurse. If I have a hankering for lamb, I'm perfectly capable of calling the restaurant and ordering takeout."

It wasn't the first time Jill had delivered a speech like that. Most other people had retreated, hurt by those frank words. Crash's normally clear blue eyes clouded over for a moment before she nodded. "Fair enough." She took Jill's cell phone, which was lying on the coffee table, and pressed it into her hand. "Can you order the chicken gyros for me? No tzatziki, please."

Clutching the phone, Jill stared at her. She opened her mouth, about to reprimand her and tell her she wasn't invited to dinner, but instead, she heard herself chuckle and say, "You're unbelievable, you know that? And I don't mean it in a good way."

Crash just grinned. "Share a baklava with me?"

"Share? Are you crazy? If we're ordering baklava, you can get your own."

"You say the sweetest things." Crash pressed her hand to her chest with a dreamy expression on her face.

After sending her a halfhearted glare, Jill turned away from Crash to hide her smile and called the Greek restaurant and then Susana to let her know she'd be late picking up Tramp.

While Crash unpacked the paper takeout bags, Jill walked over to the mini fridge, pleased to feel her left leg cooperate. "Diet Coke?"

"Do you have any water?" Crash asked. "I try to avoid soda if I can."

Was she a health nut? Her body certainly looked as if she took good care of it. *Focus. Her body is none of your business.* Jill grabbed a can of Coke and a bottle of water and carried them over to the couch.

They sat side by side, sipping their beverages and digging into their food.

Jill moaned at the taste of her lamb souvlaki, deliciously marinated in rosemary, oregano, and lemon.

They ate in silence for several minutes.

"Can I ask you something?" *What the heck...?* Jill hadn't meant to say that. But admittedly, she was curious about Crash.

Crash looked up from her box of gyros. "Sure." She took a sip of water. "If I get to ask you something in return."

Jill instantly regretted her question. She knew what Crash would ask now that she had found out about the MS. Since revealing her disease to the public, she got the same type of questions over and over. But Jill had started it, so she wasn't about to back down now. Reluctantly, she nodded.

"So, what's your question?" Crash leaned back and sprawled out her legs, the picture of relaxation, so totally comfortable in her own skin that Jill couldn't help envying her.

Dozens of questions shot through Jill's mind. She'd always been a curious person, but it amazed her how much she wanted to know about Crash. Finally, she settled on "What's your real name?"

"Ooh, you're going right for the jugular." Crash grinned at her and popped a piece of chicken into her mouth.

"Let me guess. You could tell me, but then you'd have to kill me."

"Kill you? Nah. I could think of much more pleasant things to do with you."

Her words and her low voice, smooth as honey, with just a hint of a Texas drawl, made Jill tingle all over—a tingling very unlike that in her left leg. *Snap out of it.* She cleared her throat. "Don't try to distract me. Your real name." She waved her fingers at Crash. "Tell me."

"Okay." Crash put down her plastic fork and sat up straight. "Ready?"

Jill nodded.

"My real name is Edna Myrtle Patterson."

"Uh…" Jill eyed her warily, not wanting to say anything wrong in case Crash wasn't joking. "Really?"

"What? It's a perfectly good name for a nice girl from Texas," Crash drawled. Then she couldn't keep up her serious facade any longer and burst out laughing.

Jill socked her in the shoulder. "Liar. Your name isn't really Edna Myrtle…is it?"

"No. My parents are not that cruel."

"So, what is it? Come on!" Jill wriggled her fingers in a gimme motion.

"Kristine No-Middle-Name Patterson."

"Kristine," Jill repeated, testing out the sound of the name. She decided she liked it. With a glance at Crash's athletic frame and her strong jawline, she asked, "Do you go by Kris?"

Crash energetically shook her head. "Nope. I've got enough of the lesbian stereotype going on, thank you very much." She ruffled her short, wind-blown hair. "It's Kristine."

"No middle name?"

"No middle name," Crash confirmed. "After having four boys, my parents had given up hope of ever getting a daughter, so they hadn't picked out a first name, much less a middle name for a girl. I was lucky they didn't name me Christopher, which was the name they had picked out for child number five."

Jill laughed. "So you have four brothers?"

"Five," Crash said with an affectionate smile. "My little brother, Cody, is a year younger than me."

"Wow. Five brothers." Jill shook her head. She couldn't imagine growing up like that. "I suddenly feel like saying 'I'm sorry.' Having one brother is more than enough for me."

"Nah. It wasn't that bad," Crash said. "Raising five boys prepared my mother for having a daughter like me… Although she would probably say that there is no way to prepare for that, other than having good insurance."

"So maybe Crash is a fitting name for you after all," Jill said with a smile. "Even if it doesn't seem to be the best nickname for a stuntwoman. I mean, who wants to be known for crashing?"

Crash shook her head. "That's not how I got my nickname. When I first started out in the stunt business, I did a lot of driving gags. I kind of specialized in crashing cars—on purpose, mind you."

Jill tried to imagine having a job like that, but she couldn't wrap her head around it. Why would a reasonably sane person voluntarily risk life and limb every single day? Jill would have given anything to be healthy again, while Crash readily accepted being hurt, maybe even ending up in a wheelchair or possibly dying, every time she went to work. "How did you get into stunts?"

"You realize that's a second question, don't you? Does that mean I'll get to ask you a second one too?"

Shit. Jill's mother had always told her that her curiosity would be her downfall one day. It seemed she'd been right after all. Or maybe not, because Jill's biggest flaw wasn't her curiosity—it was her inability to back down. She sighed. "All right."

"I've always been very athletic," Crash said. "In my family, everything revolved around sports. My father is a football coach, and my mother used to be a gymnast. I started taking Taekwondo classes when I was seven; I was into horses, and I took pretty much every sport you can think of in high school. Everyone always thought I'd either break my neck at a young age or win fame and fortune as a sports star."

"But you haven't done either," Jill said with a glance at Crash's strong yet slender neck.

"Not yet." Crash grinned. She chewed a forkful of her gyros, which by now was probably just as cold as Jill's lamb souvlaki, and swallowed before continuing. "When I was sixteen, there was a movie being shot not far from where I lived, and they were looking for a teenager who could ride a horse out of a burning barn."

Jill's eyebrows crept up her forehead. "Your parents let you do that?"

"Well, I broke it to them little by little," Crash said with a mischievous smile. "By the time they found out that detail about the burning barn, they had already agreed to let me do it."

"I'm beginning to see why even raising five boys couldn't prepare your mother for having a child like you," Jill said. "So, after that burning barn stunt, you tasted blood and started working as a stuntwoman?"

Crash let out a snort. "I wish. I had to wait until I was eighteen. Even then, it wasn't easy to break into the business, especially for a woman. There aren't that many stunt jobs, so I spent my first two or three years in LA introducing myself to a lot of stunt coordinators and teaching Taekwondo to a lot of kids before I had done enough gags to qualify for SAG membership."

Jill nodded slowly. "I know what you mean. I had to kiss a lot of frogs too before I started getting better roles."

"Literally?" Crash asked.

"Thank God no. Although I once did a commercial where I had to kiss a guy who did look a bit like a toad."

"Ugh," they both said at the same time and then laughed.

They grinned at each other, and Jill thought again how warm Crash's blue eyes seemed. Then she reminded herself that she had no business getting lost in Crash's baby blues and moved a few inches away on the couch.

"My turn," Crash said.

Jill stiffened but nodded for Crash to go ahead and ask. A deal was a deal, after all.

Crash had just opened her mouth to ask her first question when a knock sounded at the door and one of the PAs poked his head into the trailer.

"Sorry to interrupt, Ms. Corrigan. Mr. Manning sent me over to see if you're still here. He's going over the dailies and thought you might want to see them too."

Jill looked from him to Crash. "Um…"

"Saved by the PA," Crash said with a slight smile. "Go ahead. I'll save my questions for another time."

With everyone else, Jill would have breathed a sigh of relief, hoping that the other person would have forgotten about it by the time they talked again, but she already knew Crash wouldn't forget. Suppressing a sigh, she glanced back at the PA. "Tell him I'll be right there."

CHAPTER 5

FRIDAY EVENING, CRASH GROANED AS she got out of the shower and dried off. Since she'd started working as a stuntwoman, hardly a day had gone by without some minor pains and bruises from a dangerous gag or extensive training, and she wondered how it compared to having MS.

She wasn't normally one to brood or obsess over things she had no control over, but since finding out Jill had a chronic illness two days ago, it was all she could think of.

Come on. She's just some actress you're doubling. One of many. But she knew she was lying to herself—and not very successfully. Jill was as special as she was stubborn. There was a spark of life in Jill's green eyes that made it hard to believe she was sick. Under different circumstances, Crash could see herself asking Jill out. Well, she *had* asked her out when Jill had joked about buying her dinner first. But that had been before she had found out Jill had MS. Things were different now.

Really? She towel-dried her hair and glanced at herself in the mirror. Did she no longer consider Jill dating material, just because she had MS?

The thought made her cringe. On the one hand, Crash didn't want to believe she was that superficial. She had encountered that attitude too often in the stunt industry. As soon as you were no longer perfectly healthy, Hollywood dropped you like a hot potato.

But on the other hand, MS was a serious disease and she would be stupid to jump into anything with both feet. Even though Crash might be ready for a relationship again, she had promised herself to be more careful with her heart. Getting involved with someone who came with so much baggage wasn't the way to do that.

It was all a moot point anyway. Jill had made it clear that she didn't want to go out with her, so why was she even thinking about this?

Barefoot, she padded over to the kitchen to make herself a smoothie and then opened her laptop to check the weather report for the next week.

She was scheduled to do a ratchet stunt on Thursday, faking an explosion of a gas pipe that had been shattered by the earthquake. Things could heat up on set, so some June Gloom would make it more bearable. The thought of a giant ball of fire coming toward her, the flames licking at her face, made her shiver. She clutched the laptop with both hands and consciously slowed her breathing.

Calm down. Ben takes safety seriously.

This wasn't the set of *Point of Impact*. But no amount of reasoning could sooth the hasty thrumming of her heart. She'd just have to tough it out. Once she'd made it through this stunt with a tiny bit of fire involved, she hoped she'd be able to handle the big fire gag coming up at the end of the movie.

Sighing, she scrolled down to Thursday's weather. Just her luck. Apparently, LA would get an early heat wave next week. Rehearsing that ratchet stunt over and over while the sun beat down on them wouldn't be fun. Well, at least the ice-cold fire gel would feel refreshing on her overheated skin.

She clicked over to her e-mail. Her oldest brother had sent baby pictures, claiming his youngest took after his aunt since he was always getting into some mischief. Snorting, she shot off a quick reply and then closed her e-mail. With her hand already on the lid of the laptop, about to close it, she paused.

Before she could talk herself out of it, she entered "multiple sclerosis" into the search box and hit enter.

Twenty-three million results.

She clicked on the first link and started to read. She breathed a little more easily after finding out that MS wasn't considered a fatal disease, but the rest of the information made her head buzz and her heart feel heavy. *Damage to the CNS. No cure. Blurred vision. Unstable walking. Heat sensitivity. Muscle weakness. Fatigue. Slurred speech. Bladder problems.* The list of possible symptoms went on and on, and apparently, there was no way of telling how the illness would affect each individual.

Now a lot of things about Jill made sense—why she wasn't allowed to do most of her own stunts and why she retreated to her air-conditioned trailer instead of hanging around on set during breaks.

After a while, she stopped reading and reached for her smoothie. God, she could use something stronger than the blueberry-banana mix. Was Jill experiencing all of those symptoms? And why on earth had a woman with these kinds of problems chosen to star in a disaster movie and not in a nice little comedy or something?

Crash snorted. After working with Jill for two weeks, she knew the answer to that question already. The more someone else insisted Jill couldn't do something, the more Jill wanted to do it.

Oh, yeah, and you aren't like that at all, right? She remembered repeating a difficult wire stunt eighteen times, refusing to give up until she got the timing just right. The difference was that she got to strip off the stunt harness and the safety wire at the end of the day, while Jill would have to live with her symptoms for the rest of her life.

Her chest felt tight. She was tempted to just close the laptop and try to forget about this damn MS, but as a stuntwoman, she had learned not to back off when things got scary. She squared her shoulders, carried the laptop over to the couch, and settled down for an evening of research.

Monday was just as hot as the weather report had promised. Crash and the rest of the stunt department had been measuring, calculating, and preparing for hours and then rehearsing the gag for several more hours. She really doubted that their audience could appreciate how much work went into a scene that lasted three seconds on the screen.

Finally, even Ben couldn't stand working in the heat any longer, so he allowed them to break for lunch.

Most of her colleagues headed over to where the catering service was handing out hot meals. After a moment's hesitation, Crash walked toward the craft services tent instead, where smaller snacks were available for the cast and the crew all day. She told herself it was because the tent held healthier food choices and because it would be less busy, but deep down, she knew it was because the tent was Jill's refuge when she wasn't in her trailer. Crash had observed her disappearing into the tent any chance she got in between scenes.

She pushed back the flap and smiled.

The craft services tent was empty except for one person. Jill stood at the long table, her left side toward Crash. She had the sleeves of her costume pushed up, and several buttons on the high-necked blouse were open.

Crash was just about to call out a greeting when Jill reached into a bowl and took out an ice cube. She ran it over her palms and trailed it along the inside of her wrists, where her skin was even paler, then to the bend of her elbow until just a sliver of ice remained. Immediately, she took another cube. She lifted up her flaming-red hair and rubbed the ice along the back of her neck. Her eyes closed, and her head tilted back as she let out a sigh of relief.

Crash's mouth went dry, and she wished she had a handful of ice too so she could cool herself down.

The next ice cube traced a path along the elegant slope of Jill's neck and then across her collarbones.

Crash imagined following its path with her lips, flicking drops of water from Jill's skin with her tongue.

The heat of Jill's skin melted the ice. Droplets of water slid down her throat and into the cleavage of her costume. Jill reached into the bowl once more, put an ice cube into her mouth, and sucked on it.

A low groan escaped Crash. *God, that's hot.*

Then she immediately felt guilty for thinking so. Jill wasn't doing sexy things with ice cubes to turn her on. She didn't even know Crash was there, watching like some voyeur, and the ice cubes weren't devices of seduction; they served a strictly medical purpose. According to Crash's research, most MS patients suffered from heat sensitivity. Any rise in their body temperature could make their symptoms flare, and ice was a good way to counteract that.

Unfortunately, Jill's cooling-off techniques had the opposite effect on Crash's body temperature. She glanced back and forth between the ground and the path of the ice over Jill's skin. Was she allowed to find it hot, even though it had to do with Jill's MS?

Jill was still an attractive woman. Was Crash being respectful by trying not to think of her *that way*, or was she reducing her to an MS patient, even though Jill was so much more than that?

Crash wasn't sure what the right thing to do was. *Well, ogling Jill without her knowledge isn't.*

Loud voices headed toward the tent—probably someone from the grip department in search of some candy for dessert.

Jill turned toward the approaching voices.

Quickly, Crash slipped from the tent before she could be discovered. She'd go eat with her colleagues, giving Jill—and herself—a chance to cool down.

CHAPTER 6

As a redhead who got sunburned easily, Jill had never really been a sun worshipper, but right now, moving to the Arctic felt like a nice option.

June had only just begun, but the air already hung thick and muggy over Los Angeles, and smoke from a forest fire curled up over the San Gabriel Mountains. Temperatures had hovered just below the eighty-five-degree mark since Monday. Too bad she couldn't wear her cooling vest beneath the costume. She couldn't wait for next week, when they would fly up to San Francisco and shoot in cooler weather for a few days.

The clouds blocking out the sun every now and then didn't bring much relief. She was grateful for the parasol that was part of her costume, lending at least some shade while she had to wait around for the grips to set up the green screen and camera cranes for the next scene. When she stepped out of the way to give them room to work, her foot made a scuffing sound on the cobblestones.

She looked around, making sure no one was watching, before experimentally taking another step. Her toes immediately dropped down, dragging across the ground.

Great. Foot drop. She eyed the distance to her trailer, where she always kept an ankle-foot brace that fit into her costume shoes, just in case she needed it. But she'd have to ask for a break to put it on, and she hated to hold up shooting.

Just as she was weighing her options, the cloud cover got thicker, obscuring the sun. Distant rumbling warned them that one of the area's rare thunderstorms was approaching fast.

While her colleagues threw worried glances up at the sky, Jill nearly let out a relieved laugh. For once, the weather seemed to be on her side.

Chaos broke out as the first lightning bolt flashed across the sky.

"Get the cameras and the equipment inside," Floyd shouted over a clap of thunder.

Most members of the cast and crew were from the West Coast, so they weren't used to thunderstorms. Jill, however, had spent several summers with her grandparents in Florida—the lightning capital of the country—as a teenager. In the ensuing commotion, she grabbed a lighting stand and pretended to carry it to safety while using it as a cane. She grinned triumphantly when she reached her trailer without anyone seeming to notice her limping.

But she had cheered too soon. Someone stood on the top step of her trailer. Was it a grip who had noticed her little excursion with the lighting stand? Cautiously, Jill moved closer.

The person turned and directed her trademark crooked grin at her.

Phew. It was just Crash, not a member of the crew come to investigate the theft of the lighting stand. Although judging by the way Jill's heart beat faster, her body didn't think of her as *just Crash.* "What are you doing here? I thought you were shooting with the second unit?"

"I was, but we're done for the day. Am I interrupting something between you and your friend?" Crash asked, pointing at the piece of equipment Jill was holding on to. "You two look awfully cozy."

Jill rolled her eyes. "And here I thought you were a stuntwoman, not a comedian."

"Well, I have many skills."

Another bolt of lightning flashed above them.

"Unless one of those many skills is acting as a lightning rod, you might want to move away from those metal stairs," Jill said.

"Said the woman carrying a piece of metal," Crash answered.

Oops. Dragging the stand with her, Jill limped up the three steps.

When her toes caught on the second step, making her stumble, Crash jumped to her aid and wrapped one arm around her. "I've got you." She reached for the lighting stand with her free hand. "Both of you."

Crash's warmth against her side made Jill feel even more overheated. If she kept standing here for much longer, she'd collapse into a puddle at Crash's feet. She reached into the beaded purse that was part of her costume, got out the key, and unlocked the door.

"Thanks," she said. "You can let go. I'm fine now." She pushed away from Crash and dragged herself into the trailer. As soon as she entered, she turned on the air-conditioning and then gestured at Crash. "Come on in."

Angling the lighting stand, Crash carried it in. She looked almost comical clutching the thing, and Jill had to laugh despite the circumstances.

"So," Jill said as Crash closed the door behind them, "what brings you to my humble abode?"

Crash lifted one shoulder into a half-shrug. "Well, it's got the best air-conditioning on the set, so..."

Jill fixed her with a narrow-eyed stare. "You want me to believe that you keep hanging around my trailer because of the air-conditioning?" Unlike Jill, Crash didn't seem to suffer much in the heat. The T-shirt she wore didn't even have sweat stains. Besides, she had already wrapped up work for the day and could just drive home.

"It also has the nicest view," Crash said.

With a disbelieving snort, Jill looked through one of the small windows to the dusty back lot and the rows of white trailers outside. "You call that a nice view?"

"I wasn't talking about what you see when you look outside," Crash said. A grin curled up the corners of her mouth, but the expression in her eyes was completely serious.

Folding her arms across her chest, Jill gave her a strict look. "You can stay…as long as you turn off the blarney."

A sigh came from Crash. "Whatever happened to women who could accept a compliment graciously?"

"They have lived in Hollywood, the city of meaningless flattery, for too long," Jill answered. She limped toward the trailer's tiny bathroom. "I'll go get changed. I don't think we'll shoot another scene anytime soon."

"Need any help getting out of that dress?"

Was there a suggestive undertone in Crash's voice? Jill wasn't sure, but she wanted to nip this in the bud once and for all. She turned back around to face Crash. "I'm amending the conditions of your asylum in my trailer. No flattery. No suggestive remarks. I'm not on the market, so just keep it professional, okay?"

"That wasn't a suggestive remark." One corner of Crash's mouth twitched into a hint of a smile. "Well, okay, maybe a little." She held her thumb and forefinger an inch apart. "But mostly, I just wanted to help. I can tell that the heat is getting to you, and I remember how much trouble you had with those pesky buttons."

Jill hated having her inadequacies pointed out to her. "That's very kind of you," she said stiffly. "But if I need help, I'll let you know."

"Yeah, right after you cure cancer and bring about world peace," Crash muttered just loudly enough for Jill to hear.

Jill bit back a smile. Why was it that Crash made her smile even when her symptoms were flaring up and they were butting heads? She turned her back and tried to open the first of the tiny buttons on the front of her dress.

The damn thing seemed to escape her fingers, which felt as awkward as if she were wearing three pairs of mittens.

"Jill, come on. Let me help," Crash said behind her. "It's no big deal."

"Maybe not for you," Jill mumbled. For a moment, she considered other options—taking her nail clippers to the buttons. *Okay, now you're being ridiculous.* Wardrobe would kill her if she ruined another dress. Plus using the clippers took coordination too, which she didn't have at the moment.

She turned toward Crash, took a deep breath, and let it escape. "All right."

"All right?" Crash repeated, looking surprised. "You mean you'll actually let me undress you?"

Images of Crash unhooking her bra and then bending to kiss her breasts flashed through Jill's mind. *No.* Firmly, Jill pushed those fantasies away, because that was all they'd ever be—fantasies. Acting on them wouldn't be fair to either of them.

She licked her dry lips. "You can help me with the buttons. I'll take care of the rest."

Crash nodded and took a step toward her.

They stood facing each other. Outside, lightning flashed, bathing the trailer in a pattern of light and shadows.

"Okay, let's see…" Crash lifted her hands to the row of buttons on Jill's costume bodice.

Jill's gaze was drawn down. She watched as Crash's fingers—slender yet strong—struggled a bit with the top button. Were her hands, usually so competent whenever Jill had watched her shoot a stunt, trembling a little? It was probably just because she wasn't used to undressing someone—at least not in this context.

Finally, the top button slid through its hole and Crash moved on to the next. Her hands an inch from Jill's chest, she paused and looked up at her face. "Are you okay?"

Jill bit her lip and nodded. This was just so confusing. Exciting and embarrassing at the same time and, most of all, terribly intimate—not just in a sexual way. Only once, on the morning of the most important press conference of her life, had she allowed Grace to help her dress. Somehow, having Grace hook her bra for her hadn't evoked so many complex emotions.

She wanted to pull away or push Crash's hands aside, but that would only make Crash aware of what a big deal this was for her.

To distract herself, she focused on the rolling thunder and the flashes of lightning outside. The weather seemed to echo the storm brewing inside of her.

Finally, the last button fell open, and Jill shrugged the dress from her shoulders. It fell to the floor, revealing the corset and the old-fashioned drawers she wore.

Normally, Jill wasn't shy about people seeing her in a state of undress, but now she felt strangely exposed. "Thanks," she said, her voice a bit rough. "I can take it from here." No need to torture herself by allowing Crash to put her hands on her any more than necessary. The memory of how it had felt when Crash had helped her take off the stunt harness was still ingrained in every cell of her body.

"Nonsense," Crash answered. "The corset is damn near impossible to take off on your own. Let me help you with that."

Jill let out a sigh, but knowing Crash wouldn't give in, she finally turned. She felt Crash's heat behind her and her breath on her neck as Crash bent her head and unknotted the laces of the corset. Goose bumps formed all over her body.

"Who the hell invented a thing like this?" Crash grunted.

"No idea. Some sadist, probably." When the ties loosened and Crash lifted the corset away from her chest, she sucked in a breath. "Thanks." Very aware of the fact that she wasn't wearing a bra beneath the thin chemise, she hastened toward the bathroom as fast as her still slightly dragging foot allowed. "Let me get a T-shirt."

She firmly closed the door behind her, turned on the faucet in the tiny sink, and splashed cold water onto her face. After drying off and slipping a T-shirt over her head, she was starting to feel more in control.

When she stepped out of the claustrophobically small bathroom, Crash stood by the trailer's window, looking outside.

Maybe she did enjoy the view from the trailer after all. Jill smiled. She stepped next to Crash and peered outside too.

Lightning bolts zigzagged across the darkened sky, but the thunderstorm brought little rain.

"That's one thing I miss here in LA," Crash said, almost as if talking to herself. "I can count the number of thunderstorms I have seen since moving here on one or two hands."

"Hmm, I don't know. With all the wildfires they cause, I'm kind of glad we don't get them more often." Talking about the weather was a relief. It helped get some much-needed distance after the intimacy of letting Crash help her undress.

"You've got a point." Crash turned away from the window and faced Jill. She slowly ran her gaze over Jill's body, from her bare feet to her disheveled hair.

Ripples of awareness followed her gaze. Jill crossed her arms over her still braless chest.

Crash looked away. Another lightning flashed, then Crash asked, "Remember the two answers you owe me?"

Jill swallowed. "Yeah," she said cautiously.

"Can I ask one question now?"

Every muscle in her body tense, Jill nodded.

"Are you uncomfortable around me?" Crash asked.

It took Jill several seconds to grasp that Crash hadn't asked an MS-related question. Now she almost wished for one. A denial was already on the tip of her tongue, but she held it back. Crash had answered both of her questions honestly and had revealed personal information, so she owed her the same.

"Because if you are," Crash said when Jill kept silent, "I want you to know there's no reason for it. I know I come across like a bit of a female Casanova, especially around you, but—"

Jill turned toward her and held up one hand, stopping her. "At the risk of sounding like a lame cliché... It's not you. It's me."

Crash groaned. "That does sound like a lame cliché."

"Yeah, but in this case, it's true. You're a flirt, but not in an obnoxious way. I bet most women, even the straight ones, don't mind a bit."

"But you do," Crash said.

Jill sighed. "I'm not a stick-in-the-mud. I appreciate some flirting as much as the next woman, but most often flirting leads to dating and dating leads to having a committed relationship. Before you know it, you're U-Hauling and talking about getting a Golden Retriever."

"What's wrong with a Golden Retriever? They're really sweet dogs. Not the most clever, but…" A warning glance from Jill made her trail off. "Okay, all joking aside. I get it. You're not into relationships."

"They're just not a good idea for someone like me," Jill said, trying to sound matter-of-fact.

"Someone like you?" Crash cocked her head.

Was she purposefully being obtuse?

A clap of thunder interrupted, giving Jill a moment to consider whether she really wanted to get into this with Crash. She hated talking about it, but Crash deserved to know, so Jill took a deep breath and forced herself to look Crash in the eyes. "Someone with MS."

Crash's forehead furrowed. "You think people with MS shouldn't be in relationships?"

"I can't speak for anyone else, but that's the decision I made for myself. It's not one I made lightly, but I think it's for the best."

"Why would you think that?"

"A relationship should be an equal give and take, but in five or ten or twenty years, my partner might have to become a caregiver. I don't want to do that to anyone, so I have no business being in a relationship." A wave of anger at the unfairness of it swept over her and then turned into grief. She pushed back both feelings. It was the right thing to do; she knew that.

Crash studied her with a serious expression. "What if you'd been in a relationship when you were diagnosed? I take it you weren't?"

"No. My last girlfriend and I broke up a few weeks before the first symptoms started, and I've lived like a nun ever since." She forced a grin onto her face. "Well, one in more attractive garb, but anyway…"

For once, Crash didn't return the smile or respond to the joke.

Jill sighed. "I don't know, okay? I wasn't in a relationship and won't ever be again, so it's pointless to even think about it."

"Ever," Crash repeated. "Wow. That's a long time to be alone."

A lump the size of a fist formed in Jill's throat, preventing her from speaking, so she just shrugged.

For several seconds, only the sound of their breathing filled the trailer.

"Do you really think it'll get so bad that you couldn't be a good partner anymore?" Crash asked quietly.

Thinking about it made the lump spread to her chest. She forced herself to get the words out. Crash needed to hear them, just in case she still harbored ideas of asking her out—and maybe Jill needed to hear them too, as a reminder of why she had to ignore the attraction between them. "I've got a fifty-fifty chance of my MS turning secondary progressive within the next ten years. That means there'll be no more remissions, just a slow, steady worsening of my symptoms. I could end up in a wheelchair, unable to even feed myself."

Crash's jaw muscles bunched, and she gulped audibly. "But...but you could be one of the fifty percent who don't get worse."

"I hope so," Jill said, holding on to that thought with all her strength until she felt the lump dissolve a little. "But I can't tie another person to me just based on hope. Can you understand that?"

Slowly, Crash nodded. "Kind of. I just—"

A knock on the door interrupted whatever Crash had been about to say. One of the PAs stuck his head inside of the trailer. His gaze roved over Jill's T-shirt and her historical underwear. "Uh, you'd better get back into your costume. They need you on the set in five."

Jill looked to the piece of sky visible behind him. The cloud cover had lifted, and no more lightning bolts flashed from the sky. Jill hadn't even noticed that the thunderstorm had stopped while she and Crash had talked. "I'll be there in a minute," she told the PA.

"I'll send over someone from wardrobe to help you with that...corset thingy," he said, pointing at the corset that lay abandoned on the couch.

"Okay." Better the wardrobe lady than Crash offering to help her again. She felt raw and needed some distance.

When the PA left, she turned to Crash. "Do you want to ask your second question now too?" If they got this over with now, at least Crash would be forced to keep it short.

Crash shook her head. She looked shell-shocked, as if she were still digesting what Jill had told her. "You know what? I'll take a rain check on that second question. See you tomorrow."

Before Jill could reply, the trailer door fell shut behind Crash.

Crash slowly climbed down the three steps from Jill's trailer.

Outside, grips and set technicians were running around, trying to make up for the time they'd lost during the thunderstorm. PAs with walkie-talkies shooed extras into the right positions.

The chaos on set felt strangely distant, though. Crash's mind was back in the trailer, and Jill's words still rang in her ears.

Fifty-fifty chance. Jill's whole life, reduced to a coin toss.

No wonder she didn't want to get involved with anyone. If she were in Jill's shoes, Crash wasn't sure she would want to drag a potential partner into it either. It was a courageous decision, and Crash couldn't help admiring Jill for it.

At the same time, the thought of Jill staying alone, facing whatever life and her MS threw at her completely on her own... Crash shook her head. It just felt so wrong. Jill deserved someone in her life.

Someone? You mean you? Part of her wanted to shout yes, but another, bigger part was scared. No amount of stunt training could help her fight that fear.

Why was she even thinking about this? It was crazy, really. She barely knew Jill, and what she knew of her should make her want to stay away.

Besides, Jill had made it clear that she didn't want to get involved. Even if Crash could get her to change her mind, was she ready to date someone who could take a turn for the worse at any time? Did she really want to gamble on that fifty-fifty chance?

When no answers came, Crash trudged to her car and drove home, away from it all. For now, she had other things to worry about.

Tomorrow, she would have to do a stunt involving fire for the first time since nearly getting burned to a crisp on the set of *Point of Impact*. She couldn't afford to be distracted by thoughts of Jill.

Despite that mental admonishment, she thought of nothing else all the way home.

CHAPTER 7

CRASH COVERED A WIDE YAWN with one hand while she went over the safety checks, testing the wire pulleys, the cable, and her harness. Staying up until three in the morning the night before a stunt wasn't a good idea. She'd gone to bed at a reasonable hour, but thoughts of the stunt kept her tossing and turning, so she had gotten back up to research secondary progressive MS.

They had rehearsed the ratchet stunt without the wall earlier. Since it had taken the set designers forever to create a wall that looked like a solid brick structure but was actually just drywall, they could do this stunt only once.

Don't mess it up.

She glanced over at Jill, who stood out of camera range along with some of the other actors, watching the stunt crew. Apparently, it was only a half day for Jill, so she had changed out of her costume. When their gazes met, she gave Crash a nod.

Crash scanned her face for any sign of fatigue and her posture for any symptoms of numbness or pain, but she didn't find any. Jill looked healthy and attractive in a pair of tight jeans and a form-fitting T-shirt.

It was hard to wrap her head around the fact that Jill's apparent health was just an illusion that could change any day.

What the heck are you doing? Focus on the stunt, or you'll end up a pile of ashes! Crash forced her attention back to the job at hand. The ratchet gag she could do in her sleep, but the added element of the fire made her muscles knot with tension.

She watched warily as the technical crew set up four propane tanks just out of view of the cameras. The scar on the back of her neck started to burn as if the flames from those tanks had set it on fire. *Calm down. If all goes according to plan, the fire won't even touch you.*

"You okay?" Ben asked as he set a bucket of fire gel down next to her.

She tore her gaze away from the propane tanks and nodded while rubbing the back of her neck.

The rigger hooked the ratchet cable to the harness under Crash's costume, and Ben slathered fire gel onto her hands and face.

Now they had to move fast, because the gel would dry quickly and no longer protect her from the heat of the flames.

Adrenaline replaced her earlier tiredness, and she felt wide-awake. God, she hated fire stunts. Why the hell had she said yes when Ben had asked her if she wanted to do the stunt, even though she wasn't doubling Jill in this scene?

She knew the answer, of course. Once you started running from your fears, you were done in the stunt business. She also didn't want to appear weak or scared in front of her colleagues. She'd worked too hard to establish herself as a stunt performer who could pretty much do it all—high falls, wire work, fight scenes, stunt driving, and fire jobs.

"Ready?" Ben asked.

Crash gave him a thumbs-up sign. She was breathing much too fast, nearly hyperventilating. Her gaze went to Jill, who looked back with a worried expression and mouthed something.

"Are you sure?" Ben asked. "You look—"

"I'm fine. Get on with it."

Not looking happy, Ben repeated the thumbs-up sign to the crew.

The cameras began rolling, and the countdown started. "Three, two, one…go!"

Crash held her breath, even though her instincts told her to suck as much air into her lungs as she could. If she did, she would singe her lungs. She tucked her chin into her chest and leaned forward at the waist so that the wire rigged to her harness remained taut.

A crew member opened the gas feed. The fireball from the propane tanks raced toward Crash. The scorching heat hit her in the face. For a moment, she thought they had miscalculated and the flames would reach her.

She barely held back a scream.

Just before the fire could engulf her, the ratchet kicked in, yanking her back and off her feet.

She smashed through the wall behind her, landed on a pile of pads, rolled, and used her momentum to come to her feet. Dizziness gripped her for a second, and again it made her think of Jill. Was this what she experienced during the MS flare-ups? She shook off both the distracting thought and the dizziness, brushed pieces of drywall off her costume, and gratefully took the wet towel someone handed her.

The fire gel was starting to burn in her eyes, so she quickly wiped it off before walking over to Ben. Adrenaline still pumped through her veins, making her a bit shaky. "How did it look?"

He waved her over so she could look at the monitor he was watching.

Once he pressed replay, the monitor showed an explosion that created a giant fireball and threw an unsuspecting woman through the air.

Nausea swept over her. She swallowed hard. It didn't look as if she had a snowball's chance in hell of surviving.

"Good job," Ben said and patted her on the back. "Go get changed."

Crash didn't need to be told twice. She rushed toward the wardrobe trailer as fast as she could without running.

Jill watched as Crash turned away from the monitor and quickly crossed the cobblestones of the set. Her face was pale beneath the traces of transparent goop that was clinging to her skin despite her attempts to wipe it off.

Crash looked as if she was about to pass her without comment, but then she stopped and said, "Hi, Jill. You okay?"

"Me?" Jill pointed at her own chest. "You are the one who was just thrown through a wall by an explosion." The mere mention of the stunt made her shiver.

"Yeah, you. You were frowning."

"Because—" Jill bit her lip. She admitted to herself that she had been worried about Crash, but if she told her that, she'd make her think she was interested in her. *Oh, and you aren't? Lie to her all you want, but be honest with yourself.* Deep down, she knew that she'd never been half as worried about any other stunt person, no matter what daredevil thing they did. "I'm fine, really. But you don't look so good. You didn't get hurt, did you?"

"Nah. Just tired. Late night."

"I see." Images of things that might have kept Crash up flashed before Jill's mind's eye, most of them involving hot, sweaty sex. She quickly shook them off. Since she no longer had the energy for marathon sex, she had no right to want to be the woman Crash spent her nights with.

"I need to get over to wardrobe," Crash said. "See you later."

Jill watched her walk away. Was it just her imagination, or was there something going on with Crash—something more than just being tired? She wasn't normally so abrupt and uncommunicative.

None of your business. You're not her girlfriend. Jill wanted to shrug it off, but her gut feeling wouldn't let her. Crash had looked really pale. What if she had hurt herself and was just too proud to admit it?

She'd pick up tomorrow's call sheet from the production office and check up on Crash in wardrobe on her way back. If Crash was fine, she'd drive home and try to put her out of her mind once and for all.

When she climbed the three steps to the wardrobe trailer ten minutes later, a weird sound made her pause.

There it was again—a gagging sound. It came from somewhere behind the trailer.

As fast as she could, Jill hurried down the steps and around.

Crash stood bent over, both palms planted on the trailer, bracing herself as she retched and vomited.

Without thinking twice, Jill rushed over. "Crash! Are you okay?" She groaned as soon as she'd said it. *The prize for the stupidest question in history goes to Jill Corrigan. Does that sound like she's okay?*

Still heaving, Crash held up a hand to indicate she couldn't speak.

Gently, Jill touched a hand to Crash's back. God, she was trembling, and the T-shirt she now wore felt damp. "What happened? Are you hurt?"

Crash shook her head. She dry-heaved once more and then finally straightened and turned.

Jill pulled an unused tissue from her pocket and held herself back before she could wipe Crash's face. "Here." She pressed it into her hands.

"Thanks," Crash mumbled, her voice rough, either from vomiting or because she was embarrassed.

"What happened?" Jill asked again when Crash was done.

"Nothing. That stunt was just…pretty taxing."

Most of the stunts Jill had seen her perform so far had seemed taxing to her. But in the three weeks since shooting had begun, she had seen Crash do dangerous things that she would have never attempted even for a million bucks. Crash had never batted an eye, and she had certainly never lost her lunch over a stunt. "There's more to it than that, isn't there?"

Crash inhaled through her nose and let the breath escape through her mouth. "Yeah. But I don't want to talk about it." After a second, she added more softly, "Especially not here."

Jill looked around and nodded. They had that in common—they both didn't want to show any weakness at work. "Okay. Come on. I'll drive you home."

"I can drive myself."

"Now who's stubborn?" Jill nudged her. "I let you help with my buttons. Now it's your turn to be the damsel in distress."

Crash made a face but then had to laugh. "All right. Show me to your carriage, gallant knight."

Jill hooked her arm through Crash's and set them off in the direction of the parking lot. It felt wonderful to be the one to take care of Crash, instead of being the one receiving help. For a moment, she felt guilty for enjoying Crash's plight, but then she mentally shrugged and focused on getting Crash home.

The more distance they brought between them and the set, the more Crash's stomach settled—and the sillier she started to feel. *I can't believe I did that. Barfing my guts out after a gag, like a damn newbie.*

She mentally shook her head at herself and peeked over at Jill, who was focused on the dense LA traffic. Crash hadn't wanted anyone—especially not Jill—to see her like that. *Hiding behind the wardrobe trailer to throw up... Not the kind of impression I wanted to make.*

Then she immediately rebuked herself. They weren't dating, so there was no need to impress her. But she couldn't help it. She wanted Jill to think of her as strong and capable, not as someone who buckled under pressure.

Suppressing a sigh, she glanced over at her again. Was this how Jill felt when she had to accept help?

"...right?" Jill said.

"Huh?"

"Do I make a right here?" Jill asked.

Crash looked up and realized they were approaching Franklin Avenue. "Yes. Sorry." She gave Jill directions to the quiet, tree-lined street where she lived. "You can stop here." She pointed to her two-story apartment complex. "That's me."

Jill shut off the engine and craned her neck. "Nice."

"Yeah. It's just a ten-minute walk from Griffith Park, so I can go hiking without having to worry about parking."

They sat in silence for a moment.

"Do you want to come up for a coffee or something?" Crash asked after a while.

Jill turned her head toward her and gave her a chiding look. "Really? That's the best line you've got? No wonder you're single."

Crash laughed. "Not *that* kind of something. I really meant just a cup of coffee between friends. Or don't you do friendships either?" If circumstances were different, friendship wouldn't be what she wanted—at least not all she wanted—but with the way things were, it might be for the best.

After a moment's hesitation, Jill nodded. "I do—as long as it's not the lesbian kind."

"The lesbian kind?" Crash chuckled. "What do you mean?"

"Lesbians often seem to think that friendship is some kind of foreplay. If they agree to be friends, it's always with the unspoken addition of 'until we'll be more.'"

"I know what you mean." But hoping for that kind of friendship with Jill was madness. Her last girlfriend had cheated on her because Crash hadn't been there for her twenty-four/seven. If she hadn't been ready for that sort of commitment with Kyleigh, she certainly wasn't ready for any kind of relationship with Jill. "So let's agree to be the non-lesbian type of friends."

Jill started the car and followed Crash's directions to her spot in the underground garage of her apartment building. "Lots of milk, no sugar," she said when she shut off the engine.

"Um, excuse me?"

"That's the way I like my coffee." With an impish grin, Jill released her seat belt and got out of the car.

Chuckling, Crash climbed out too. She already felt much better than she had half an hour before. Amazing what the right kind of company could do.

While Jill followed Crash up to the second floor of the apartment building, she debated the wisdom of that decision. *Oh, come on.* Staying away from relationships was one thing, but she didn't want to become a hermit in the process. Since the diagnosis, she'd been so busy rearranging her life that she hadn't made new friends other than Lauren. She liked Crash's kind, easygoing nature and her sense of humor. Why wouldn't she want to have her in her life, at least as a friend?

It's not like I'll throw her down on the nearest horizontal surface and have my way with her as soon as the door closes behind us.

Promptly, images of just that scenario flashed through her mind. Growling under her breath, she shoved them away. She could do this—just be Crash's friend. So what if she found her attractive? When she had first met Grace, she'd been attracted to her too, but over time, that had faded. While she wasn't blind to Grace's beauty, she no longer felt anything but friendship for her. All she had to do was wait until the same happened with Crash.

And ignore the way her ass looked in that pair of jeans.

She directed her gaze elsewhere as Crash unlocked the door to the third apartment on the right.

"Come on in," Crash said and led her into a studio apartment.

To the right was a tiny kitchen with dirty dishes piled up in the sink, and to the left, a couple of weights, a skipping rope, and a towel lay on a yoga mat.

With a hint of a blush on her cheeks, Crash picked up the towel. "Sorry. I wasn't expecting visitors."

"You should have seen my house before I hired a housekeeper."

Crash let out a low whistle. "You've got a housekeeper? Wow. Acting must pay better than I thought."

"I wish. Susana, my housekeeper, only comes in for an hour or two every day, and she's very affordable. She'd work for free if I let her. She kind of adopted me."

"That's good." Crash walked into the kitchenette and asked over her shoulder, "So, lots of milk, no sugar, right?"

"Right."

While Crash made coffee, Jill stepped farther into the studio apartment to look at the framed photos on the bookshelf. They showed Crash with an older couple that was probably her parents and five men that had to be her brothers. Leaned against another frame was a strip of photos taken in a booth at an arcade or an amusement park. Crash, one of her brothers, and two kids that were probably her nieces and nephews had all squeezed into the booth and were making silly faces at each other. In each picture, everyone was smiling broadly, their arms around each other. What a difference to the stiff, staged Christmas photos on her own bookshelf. Jill sighed and turned away from the photos.

This is nice, Crash thought as she popped another cookie into her mouth and chewed contentedly. She hadn't had a close female friend since Sabrina, her mentor, had betrayed her by sleeping with Kyleigh.

Granted, thinking of Jill as just a friend wasn't easy, especially not with the way Jill kept licking cookie crumbs and chocolate off her hands.

The chirping of her cell phone announced a new text message, finally making Crash look away from Jill. She put down her coffee mug and reached for her phone on the coffee table. When she pulled her hand back, her arm brushed Jill's side.

Warmth flowed through the rest of her body. She settled back on her part of the couch and glanced at her phone.

It was a message from TJ. *Want to come over and watch the game with me and the boys?*

What game? God, she was really out of the loop. She hadn't spent much time with her best friend since shooting had started. *Sorry,* she typed back. *I've got company.*

Oooh. I knew it! That's why I haven't seen you in ages! TJ's reply was followed by a string of smiley faces, hearts, and virtual kisses.

She rolled her eyes. TJ could be such a girl sometimes.

"If something has come up, I can go," Jill said next to her.

"Not necessary," Crash said quickly. She wasn't ready to give up Jill's company yet. "Just a message from a friend who invited me to watch the game." She dashed off a reply to TJ—*Not that kind of company. Talk to you later*—and then put the phone away.

"Are you sure you don't want to go?"

"Very sure." Crash gave a rueful smile. "To tell you the truth, I'm not even sure what game he's talking about."

"Baseball. The Dodgers. Hello?" Jill waved her hand up and down in front of Crash's face. "What kind of lesbian are you?"

"One who's busy having coffee with you." She took the cookie bowl from Jill, trying to ignore the tingling that went through her at the brush of their hands.

Jill peeked into the depths of her coffee mug, then over at Crash. "Can I ask you about the stunt you did today?"

Instantly, her stomachache was back. While she had talked with TJ about the mechanics of the failed fire stunt many times, she had never spoken about the emotions involved. But after Jill had driven her home and been there for her, she couldn't just shut her out, so she nodded reluctantly.

"You didn't hurt yourself when you were thrown through that wall, did you?" Jill asked.

Crash shook her head. "The wall wasn't the problem. It's the fire I didn't like." That, of course, was the understatement of the century.

"Yeah. I heard some of the other stunt performers say that fire stunts are some of the most dangerous gags around."

"That's true. If you work with fire, there's no trick involved, no illusion of danger. The fire and the danger are real."

Jill swirled the coffee in her mug as if it were wine and studied it, deep in thought.

Did she sense that there was more to Crash's dislike of fire stunts?

"Have you ever gotten hurt doing a stunt?" Jill finally asked.

Crash rubbed her neck, only realizing what she was doing when she touched the burn scar. Quickly, she snatched her hand away. "I don't like talking about stunts that went wrong. If I allow my thoughts to linger on the dangers of my job for too long, I won't be able to do what I do for a living anymore. Once I've analyzed the situation and found out what the problem was, I need to move on."

"So you did get hurt," Jill said.

Boy, she was like a terrier with a bone, not letting it go. "Nothing major. I've been lucky so far."

"Why do I get the feeling that your definition of 'nothing major' differs from mine?"

"I mostly just got bruises and cuts, really. Some were deep enough to require stitches, but I haven't had any broken bones or injuries that put me in the hospital for long."

Jill turned on the couch so she was facing Crash more fully. "*Mostly* just cuts and bruises? You did get hurt in a stunt involving fire, didn't you?"

Crash hugged her knees to her chest and put her chin on top. "Yes," she whispered.

Jill slid closer and touched Crash's leg.

It was just a fleeting touch, which didn't last for more than a moment, but it warmed Crash's entire body.

"You don't need to talk about it if you don't want to. I shouldn't have asked."

"It's okay," Crash said. She clutched her shins more tightly. One of her hands crept up and touched the scar on her neck.

Instead of pressuring her into telling her more, Jill just watched her.

"The year before last, I had a string of bad luck. First, I hurt my leg during a motorcycle stunt and was out of work for months. When my leg finally healed, I took the first job that was offered to me, even though it was a low-budget action movie with a stunt coordinator that didn't have the best reputation." She lifted her head and rubbed her knees with both hands. "I should have known better, but I was eager to work again, so I said yes. They didn't have the budget to do more than a take or two for most stunt scenes, and practice was kept to a minimum too. Everything went okay the first few days, but then…"

Jill slid onto the edge of the couch, her eyes wide. "What happened?"

"I was scheduled to do a full-body burn. The director had very specific ideas how he wanted the scene to look. He wanted the shot done during sunset. The crew setting up for the stunt ran a little behind, and we were quickly losing the light. We were in a hurry, and that's never good when you're doing a stunt."

Jill nodded. "Yeah. I realized you and Ben and the rest of the stunt crew always put a lot of time into preparing each stunt."

"I wish they'd done that on the set of *Point of Impact* too." Crash sighed. "They lathered the fire gel onto my skin and clothing, but the problem is that it only protects you while it's wet, and it dries within five minutes, so that upped the time pressure. The wind picked up just as they were about to set me on fire." Her jaw muscles were hard as stone as she ground her teeth. "We should have put it off, but we didn't."

Jill hardly seemed to breathe as Crash continued.

"The fire was supposed to be mainly on my front, where most of the fire gel went, but with the wind it crept upward immediately and snaked around to the back of my neck." She pulled down the neck of her T-shirt in the back, giving Jill a glimpse of the raised, uneven scar, which had started to itch as soon as she'd started talking about the damn fire stunt. "By the time they put me out, I had this little souvenir." She tried to sound casual, but the expression on Jill's face revealed that she saw through her quite easily.

"God, Crash." She slid over on the couch. For a moment, she looked as if she was about to touch the scar on Crash's neck, but then she put her hand on Crash's shoulder instead and rubbed gently. "No wonder having to do a fire stunt made you throw up."

Crash groaned. "Don't remind me. That wasn't one of my finest moments. If Ben had seen that…"

"What if he had?" Jill asked, sounding a bit angry. "I bet they all had moments like that. It doesn't make you a bad stunt performer. It just makes you human."

A smile crept onto Crash's face. Jill Corrigan, the woman who went out of her way to never let anyone see her vulnerable, was passionately defending her moment of weakness. It warmed Crash's heart, chasing away the memories that made her blood run cold.

"What?" Jill asked.

"Nothing," Crash said, but her smile broadened.

Jill stopped stroking Crash's arm.

Crash instantly missed the touch, comforting and exciting all at the same time.

"Nothing?" Jill playfully narrowed her eyes at her. "You're grinning like a fool over nothing?"

"Yep. That's my answer, and I'm sticking to it."

Raising up on one knee, Jill grabbed a pillow from the couch. "Oh yeah?"

"I wouldn't do that if I were you. I've got a fourth-dan black belt in Taekwondo, which means I know a lot of moves and techniques to disarm you."

A challenging glint entered Jill's eyes. "Such as?"

"Such as…this." Ducking the pillow aimed at her head, Crash started tickling her.

Laughing and shrieking, Jill tried to escape the tickling hands.

Crash stalked after her like a lioness and quickly disarmed her.

Jill squirmed and tickled back. Her palm brushed Crash's breast, nearly turning the tickling match into something else.

Breathing hard, hands on each other's bodies and faces just inches apart, they both stopped and pulled apart.

God, Crash had never wanted to kiss someone so badly. The desire to feel Jill's lips against hers was almost a physical ache. She wanted to throw caution to the wind and pull Jill into her arms. Only the knowledge of what it might do to their brand-new friendship stopped her. *Don't. She doesn't want to get involved, and neither should you.*

Jill pushed away and slid to her side of the couch.

"I'm sorry," Crash said. "I shouldn't have—"

Jill lifted her hands, then shoved them beneath her thighs as if she had trouble controlling herself too. "It's okay. I just… I hate being tickled."

"I won't do it again," Crash promised, knowing they weren't just talking about tickling.

For a moment, Crash thought Jill would get up and leave, but finally, Jill asked, "Have you ever considered giving up your job and doing something else for a living?"

Careful not to let their bodies come into contact again, Crash answered, "Never."

"Not even after that fire stunt?" Jill asked.

"Not even then." Crash smiled crookedly. "I guess growing up with five brothers made me determined to never give up, even if it might be crazy at times. What about you?"

Jill shook her head. "I grew up with just one brother, so I might have some sanity left."

"No, I mean... Did you ever consider giving up acting and doing something else for a living?"

"Never," Jill said.

"Not even when you had to work nights at a diner so you could go to cattle calls during the day—assuming that's what you had to do."

"Oh, yeah. I did. But no, not even then." Jill tilted her head and smiled at Crash. "Maybe I'm a little crazy after all."

"I think all actresses are a bit crazy. I mean, you have to be just a little off your rocker to make it in this town."

"Oh, just actresses? While stuntwomen are perfectly sane and normal, of course."

Crash gave a dignified nod. "Of course."

Jill reached over and pinched her, but Crash didn't retaliate, too conscious of the sensations that had coursed through her during their tickle match. No sense in torturing herself.

"I admit it's hard sometimes," Jill said after a minute or two, her voice pitched so low that Crash had to strain to hear her.

Crash slid a bit closer so she could catch her words. "What do you mean?"

"The cattle calls," Jill said. "They're called that for a reason. Hundreds of actors being herded in, just waiting for the casting directors to slaughter them."

Crash nodded. "I've been in a few of them."

"Really? I didn't know stuntwomen had to audition too. Or did you try out acting?"

"God, no. I prefer to make the actresses look good instead of working in front of the camera."

"Why the cattle calls, then?" Jill asked.

"The casting directors are looking for stunt people who closely match the looks of the leading actresses. Sometimes, they take just one look at you and dismiss you without even glancing at your resume. It's demeaning."

Standing in the middle of a sterile room, being paraded around in front of the blank-faced casting directors and producers who were looking her over, just to dismiss her for the size of her breasts or her hair color... Even for someone like Crash, who had never suffered from lack of self-confidence, it had been a crushing experience at times. The thought of anyone treating Jill with anything less than respect and admiration made her clench her fists until her nails dug into her palms.

"Yeah," Jill said. "It's the same for actresses. But you know what I hate even more? When the casting director smiles at me, and I can tell he and the producers really loved me for the role I'm reading for."

Crash cocked her head. "I thought that was good."

"It would be if one of them didn't start to whisper to the others, which makes them stop smiling and start regarding me with that mix of pity, curiosity, and discomfort on their faces. And the casting director who loved me a second ago suddenly tells me I'm not right for the role after all."

"Why would...?" Then it hit her. "You mean they don't hire you because you have MS?"

Jill nodded.

"They can't do that! It's against the law!" Rage bubbled up, heating Crash's chest and cheeks.

A tired smile tugged on Jill's lips. "They don't come right out and say it's because of the MS, of course. They just say I'm not the right type for the role. Not the healthy type, they mean." She shrugged. "Part of me can understand it, you know? Movies are expensive. No one wants to take the risk of having one of the leads or an actress playing an important supporting character drop out mid-filming."

"But that's just not fair!" Crash sputtered, her words nearly jumbling together. "You work harder than any other actress I know. You never ask for a break, even when you look like you're about to fall over. You would even do your own stunts if they let you."

"I'm glad they don't," Jill said after a moment's hesitation. She nibbled her bottom lip as if the admission had cost her a lot.

"Because otherwise, you wouldn't have met me?" Crash asked with a grin, trying to get some levity back into the conversation and make Jill smile.

It worked. Jill grinned and playfully rolled her eyes at Crash. "Yeah, because I would have missed out on the company of your charming self. But seriously, some of the stuff you do... I couldn't do that, even if Ben and Floyd let me."

"You think the other actresses like Nikki and Shawn can?" Crash shook her head. "That's what we stuntwomen are for."

"I'm not talking about the dangerous stunts. I'm talking about scenes in which Lucy is supposed to stumble over a bedpan or run up a flight of stairs. I can't do that anymore, at least not if the director wants a dozen takes."

She looked so sad and discouraged that Crash wanted to take her into her arms and comfort her, but she had a feeling Jill wouldn't like it. She'd mistake it for pity.

Helplessly, Crash searched for the right words to make things better but then realized that anything she said would be just empty platitudes. "You know what?" she finally said. "Having MS really sucks."

Jill blinked three times in rapid succession. Then she burst out laughing.

The sound of her laughter made Crash smile and chased away the sadness that had settled over her. "But," Crash said, nudging Jill's shoulder to get her attention, "you're still you. You're still a great actress and a wonderful woman, and nothing, not even the MS, can change that."

In the sudden silence, Jill's sharp inhale sounded overly loud.

Just as Crash was about to apologize for her sappy words, Jill reached out and gently touched Crash's face with her fingertips. She moved closer, as if to kiss her.

Crash's heartbeat picked up in anticipation. *Oh yes, please.*

But then, instead of kissing her, Jill wrapped both arms around her and pulled her close. "Thank you," she whispered against Crash's ear. She clutched her almost painfully. "I think I really needed to hear that."

"I really meant it," Crash whispered. Her chest felt tight, not just from the embrace, but from the emotions lodged there.

"I know. That's why it means so much." Jill took a deep breath, let go, and got up as if suddenly overwhelmed by their closeness. "It's getting late, and I still need to run some errands. Will you be okay on your own?"

Crash watched her retreat to the door but knew better than to follow her. "Yeah, of course." She put a hand on her belly, which had settled down—if you didn't count the flutters caused by Jill's closeness.

"Good," Jill said. "Do you want me to pick you up tomorrow morning since your car is still in the studio lot?"

Crash knew she could have gotten her friend TJ to drive her, since he was working on a nearby movie set, but she was looking forward to spending more time with Jill. "That would be great. Thanks."

"Would seven be okay?"

"Sure."

Jill opened the door and turned back around. "Thanks for...um, the coffee."

"It was the least I could do after you rescued me and drove me home."

They nodded at each other from across the room. Then the door closed behind Jill with a quiet click.

Crash sank down onto the couch until she lay flat on her back. *Jeez. What was that?* She rubbed her face with both hands. If she continued like that, she'd get burned for sure—and it probably wouldn't be during a fire stunt.

CHAPTER 8

JILL KEPT AN EYE ON Crash the next day. She seemed to be back to normal, joking around with her colleagues, unaffected by the heat and the shooting schedule.

Well, that makes one of us.

In today's scenes, Lucy Sharpe, the doctor she played, had to hurry through the burning city, chased by an inferno of fire and smoke.

Floyd and Ben wanted things to look as realistic as possible, so they opted for actual fires whenever they could, computer-generating only the burning of entire buildings and historic landmarks.

She breathed a sigh of relief when Floyd declared the last scene of the day a wrap. A thrumming sensation shot up and down her left leg. It felt as if she had her cell phone on vibrate shoved deeply into her pocket. She ignored the buzzing feeling, grateful that her leg had otherwise held up okay and she hadn't needed the foot brace today.

Lauren jogged up to her just as she was about to enter the wardrobe trailer. She was carrying a bag from Jill's favorite Chinese restaurant.

"Hey there, screenwriter lady. I see you remembered our dinner date." Jill eyed the bulging bag. "Is Grace joining us, or are you just really hungry?"

"Uh, neither. I think I went a bit overboard when I ordered because I felt guilty," Lauren said with a sheepish expression.

Jill narrowed her eyes at her. "You didn't change the script and have poor Lucy die some horrible death in the end, did you?"

Lauren laughed. "No, nothing like that. I promise not to kill Lucy off. But this has to do with script changes. Floyd wants me to rewrite some of tomorrow's dialogue, so I'll have to give you a rain check on dinner."

Jill tsked and shook her head. "What is it with women and rain checks lately?" It was out before she could think about it.

Of course, Lauren immediately picked up on it. "Women?" she repeated with a grin. "Are you saying the great Jill Corrigan asked someone out and was rejected or at least put off to another day?"

"No! I mean...no. It wasn't like that. Actually, I was the one handing out the rain check, but it was just for a conversation with a friend."

"That friend wouldn't, by any chance, have the most gorgeous blue eyes on the planet?"

A tell-tale blush swept up Jill's neck. She stared at Lauren, caught off guard. She hadn't known that Lauren had met Crash. And since when did her happily partnered friend comment on the gorgeous eyes of other women? Then it dawned on her. Lauren wasn't talking about Crash; she was talking about Grace, of course. "Uh, no. Grace said she'd invite me over for your world-famous hot dogs after we return from San Francisco."

Lauren laughed. "Oh, yeah, they're haute cuisine."

"Anything I don't have to cook myself sounds great," Jill said.

That made Lauren sober. "I'm sorry I don't have time to have dinner with you. I'll invite you to my favorite Chinese place in Chinatown when we fly to San Francisco on Monday. But for now..." She handed over the takeout bag. "Pig out on the shrimp wontons, cream cheese rangoons, orange beef, sweet-and-sour spare ribs, and moo shu vegetables."

When Lauren said good-bye and hurried off, Jill stared down at the ton of food. No way could she eat all of that on her own. *Should I...?* She glanced over at the stunt trailer, where she knew Crash was checking the equipment she would use in next week's scenes. It startled her a little how well she knew Crash's habits already. After their emotionally intense conversation—not to mention their little tickle fest—yesterday, should she really get even closer by inviting her to dinner?

She snorted at herself. It was lukewarm Chinese takeout in her trailer, not an invitation to a romantic little restaurant. They had agreed to be friends, so having dinner together wasn't a big deal.

Decision made, she entered the wardrobe trailer to finally get rid of her costume before heading over to the stunt trailer.

Crash walked down the two rows of metal shelves on either side of the thirty-foot stunt trailer, past fall pads, wire rigs, air ratchets, and a mini trampoline.

When she passed the fire stunt equipment, the sight of the heat-resistant hood and a one-gallon bucket of fire gel made her shiver. *Don't think about it. One barfing episode was more than enough.*

There would be enough time to worry about the big fire stunt in the weeks to come. For now, she would focus on the gags she'd have to do in San Francisco. At the end of the trailer, she found the jerk vest she would wear for one of the stunts and ran her fingertips over each strap and pick point, making sure the nylon wasn't frayed.

From the open door of the trailer, the tantalizing scent of sweet-and-sour sauce and stir-fried vegetables drifted over, making her stomach growl.

"Oh, come on, Rick. That's just cruel," she said without turning around. "What do I need to do to get you to share with your poor, starved colleague?"

"Hmm, I'll have to think of something." The voice behind her definitely didn't belong to Rick, their stunt rigger.

Crash let go of the jerk vest and whirled around.

Jill was standing on the top step of the stunt trailer. She had already changed out of her costume and was wearing a pair of low-rise jeans and a green T-shirt that said "my other T-shirt has a really funny slogan." Crash allowed her gaze to linger on the text for a moment, just because she found it funny, not because she was ogling Jill's attractive curves.

Yeah, right. Who do you think you're fooling? She forced her gaze to Jill's face.

Her stage makeup had been removed, revealing the cute freckles dusting Jill's nose. A grin made her green eyes sparkle.

Whenever Crash saw her like that, it was hard for her to believe that Jill had a chronic illness. She mentally chastised herself. *Oh, because all chronically ill people are required to look like they're at death's door, right?*

Jill held up a large bag with the logo of a Chinese restaurant. "Have you had dinner yet? I know you normally try to eat healthy, but…can I tempt you?"

"Oh, yeah. You can tempt me any time," Crash said with a playful leer.

Jill took a fortune cookie from the bag and threw it at her.

With her quick reflexes, Crash was able to catch it before it hit her in the nose. Grinning, she unwrapped it, put the two pieces into her mouth, and crunched happily. She shoved the wrapper along with the tiny slip of paper into the pocket of her jeans to toss it later.

"Aren't you going to read your fortune?" Jill asked.

"Nope. Not the day before a stunt." She shrugged. The tips of her ears burned with embarrassment. "Stunt people are a superstitious bunch."

Jill's face showed no judgment. "I think most people who risk their lives on a regular basis are. I once knew a race-car driver who wouldn't race without wearing a green article of clothing."

They headed over to Jill's trailer. Sitting side by side on the couch, they passed the containers of food back and forth until even the last noodle and the last shrimp were gone.

After the intense conversation yesterday, it was nice to just spend some time together and regale each other with funny anecdotes about things that had happened on movie sets.

"Oh, God." Jill dropped against the back of the couch. "I'll have to sleep here. I'm so full I can't move."

Crash folded her hands over her pleasantly full belly and sprawled out her legs. "Thanks for dinner. It was great."

Jill nodded and closed her eyes. She looked as if she was going into post-meal hibernation.

At least it gave Crash ample opportunity to study her without being caught. She took in Jill's shiny red hair. Even her fine eyebrows and her lashes were a deep auburn. Except for the smattering of freckles across her slightly upturned nose, her skin was clear. It looked so soft and smooth that Crash's fingers were itching to touch it. As Jill relaxed, her full lips parted. Crash swallowed as her gaze lingered on that lush mouth. It took her several seconds to realize that those lips were moving and Jill was talking to her. "Uh, excuse me?"

"I asked if you want the second fortune cookie." Jill opened her eyes. Her pupils widened.

Only then did Crash realize that she'd moved closer to Jill while she'd studied her features. Now their faces were mere inches apart.

"Uh, you have a little…" Her heart beating faster, Crash reached out and picked a tiny bit of ash out of Jill's hair.

"Oh. Thanks. The production crew had ash raining down on me all day, and it seems some of it—"

Crash stopped her rambling by touching her lips to Jill's.

Jill froze. Her hands came up and clutched Crash's shoulders.

Crash paused too, only now fully comprehending what she'd done. She knew she should really pull back and apologize, but with the warmth of Jill's lips against hers, reason didn't stand a chance.

For several seconds, Crash wasn't sure whether Jill would push her away or draw her closer.

Jill didn't look too sure of it either. She pulled back just a fraction of an inch. "Please, Crash," she whispered against Crash's lips.

Her warm breath against her skin made Crash shudder. "Please…what? What are you asking for?" she whispered back and looked into Jill's eyes. Did Jill want her to stop—or to kiss her again?

Passion swirled in the green irises. "Hell if I know," Jill muttered, pulled her close, and kissed her.

Crash's hands went to Jill's face and cradled it gently. She slid her tongue over Jill's bottom lip, teasing, asking, then demanding.

Jill surged against her and willingly opened her mouth.

At the first touch of their tongues, Crash's eyes fluttered shut. Her groan mingled with Jill's drawn-out moan, the sound making Crash tingle all over.

Jill clutched Crash's shoulders almost desperately before moving her fingers up, into Crash's hair, to pull her even closer. She kissed Crash as if she wanted to rip her clothes off, throw her down on the couch, and worship every inch of her body right then and there.

Their tongues slid against each other, stroking, seeking.

Heat engulfed Crash. She trailed her hands down, letting them roam up and down Jill's back. Closer. She wanted her closer. God, this woman was driving her crazy.

Jill's fingers tightened in her hair. Then, with a gasp, she wrenched her lips away.

Surprised, Crash nearly collided with her and caught herself with one hand against the back of the couch. Breathing heavily, she stared at Jill, who was licking her lips.

Jill looked just as dazed as Crash felt. "I…I need to cool down."

"Yeah," Crash croaked huskily. She fanned herself with both hands. "Me too. Jesus, that was hot."

A hint of a smile dashed across Jill's face and then disappeared. "No, I mean I really need to cool down. My legs are tingling, and it has nothing to do with your kissing skills. I need to turn up the AC."

Not really what Crash wanted to hear after a kiss like that, but maybe they could share another kiss once Jill's body temperature had gone down a bit. "Let me—"

Jill lifted her hand. "I've got it." She pushed up from the couch and crossed the trailer. The first two steps looked timid, as if her legs were shaky.

Crash hoped that at least some of it was from their kisses. Her gaze tracked Jill as she moved to the control panel next to the door and turned the air-conditioning to full blast. Her whole body vibrated with the need to pull Jill back into her arms and kiss her again.

Are you crazy? You agreed to be friends. The non-lesbian kind. That's all she wants and all you can give. But that didn't stop her from hoping Jill would lock the trailer door and proceed to kiss her silly again.

When Jill returned, she didn't sit next to her. She stopped just out of reach and looked down at Crash. "I'm sorry. I shouldn't have done that."

Those weren't the words that Crash had longed to hear. Truth be told, she didn't know what she wanted to hear. What kind of future could there be for them? She cleared her throat. "No. I'm the one who should apologize. I kissed you first."

"Yeah, but I kissed you back, even though I knew better," Jill said, her voice rough. "I'm sorry. I never meant to lead you on. It won't happen again."

Jill clearly meant it as a promise, but to Crash, it sounded more like a threat. She stood and took a step toward Jill. "I don't know." She took a deep breath. "Maybe we should talk about it. Obviously, there's something between us." There, she'd said it.

"There is no *us,* Crash. Just let it go, okay? I like spending time with you as a friend, and I don't want this stupid kiss to ruin that."

"Stupid kiss?" The words stung.

Jill sighed. "You're a damn good kisser, and I admit I enjoyed it. But it was still stupid."

"Why?"

"Oh, come on, Crash. Don't make this harder on me than it has to be. You know why. I told you I don't do relationships."

"Who's talking about a relationship? We could…I don't know…maybe go out on a date or something?" Even to her own ears, it sounded like a question, not a suggestion. She couldn't say what exactly it was she wanted; she just knew it involved more than friendship.

"And then?"

Crash kneaded the tense muscles in her neck. "I don't know. But—"

"No, Crash. It has no future. Let's just forget this ever happened."

If only it were that easy. Crash didn't think she'd ever forget the feeling of Jill's lips against hers.

"We won't have many scenes to film together in San Francisco," Jill said. "Let's take that time to get some distance, and then we'll be able to be just friends again when we're back."

From your lips to God's ear. "If that's what you want."

"That's what I want," Jill said, but somehow, there was no passionate conviction behind the words.

"All right." Not knowing what else to do, Crash got up and walked to the door. She hesitated, not wanting to leave, but what else was there to say? "I guess I'll see you at the airport, then."

Jill nodded, her lips compressed to a line. "See you."

Slowly, Crash opened the door. A part of her waited for Jill to call her back, but, of course, it didn't happen. The door closing between them sounded very final.

CHAPTER 9

FOR ONCE, JILL WAS GLAD that their cast consisted of mostly B-list actors. It made traveling to a location shoot so much easier. A year ago, things would have been very different. Back then, paparazzi had followed her wherever she went, trying to get a snapshot of Grace Durand's supposed lover and shouting a barrage of intrusive questions.

Once Jill had revealed that she and Grace hadn't been caught sneaking into her trailer for a quickie, but that Grace had merely helped her up the stairs, the tabloid sharks had lost interest.

A secret lesbian affair was great gossip rag fodder; one friend helping another apparently wasn't.

Now, as she entered the terminal at LAX with Floyd, Shawn, Nikki, and their stunt doubles, the paparazzi only snapped a picture or two and then left them alone. The technical crew had driven up to San Francisco the day before, transporting the equipment, so their group didn't draw much attention.

When they reached the gate and settled down to wait for boarding to begin, Jill immediately took her battered script out of her laptop bag and started studying her lines—or at least pretending to look at them. Pins-and-needles sensations had kept her up for most of the night, so she was too tired to make conversation with her colleagues. Most of all, she was trying to avoid talking to one colleague in particular.

Every now and then, she peeked up from the script and over to Crash, who sat across from her to the left, her legs sprawled out comfortably in front of her. Sunglasses hid her dazzling blue eyes, so Jill couldn't see where she was looking. She quickly directed her attention back to her script. But she couldn't focus today. She glanced toward the large terminal window. The sun had burned away the June Gloom, and now the tarmac shimmered with heat.

She watched the planes land and take off for a while and then went back to the script. Instead of the lines she was supposed to memorize, the only thing going through her mind were the words she and Crash had said to each other right after the kiss.

The kiss. God. What the hell had she been thinking? Okay, admittedly, there hadn't been much thinking going on as other parts of her body had taken over. Up until now, staying away from women hadn't been a problem at all. She'd spent the last two years adjusting to the MS and trying to save her career after the double outing. Romance had been the last thing on her mind.

And that isn't allowed to change, she firmly told herself. She and Crash didn't have a future, so she had to stay away from her.

But Crash's words kept echoing through her mind: *Who's talking about a relationship? We could...I don't know...maybe go out on a date or something.*

A date... Could that be an option? Just dating, without a commitment? She imagined having dinner with Crash—this time not just sharing Chinese takeout but spending the evening at a nice restaurant with low music in the background and a candle on the table. She could almost feel Crash's hand resting on hers, stroking her fingers.

With a shake of her head, she chased the image away. As nice as a date with Crash would be, it wouldn't be long before Crash would want something more meaningful. She'd want to share more of her life than just romantic dinners every now and then. But sharing Jill's life meant living with MS—and she didn't want that for Crash.

"You okay?" Lauren asked next to her.

Jill turned toward her. "Uh, yeah. Why wouldn't I be?"

"Because you have been staring at the same page of the script for the last half hour. I hope there's nothing wrong with it." Fine lines of worry carved themselves into Lauren's forehead.

"Oh, no. No, the scene is perfectly fine. I love how Lucy is not taking shit from the male doctors."

Lauren grinned. "I thought you'd like that." She sobered. "So, if it's not the script, what is it, then?"

"Nothing. I just—"

The crackling loudspeakers interrupted her. "Attention, passengers," the gate attendant said. "Flight 2760 to San Francisco is now boarding at gate 5. We're now inviting our first-class passengers and passengers who need assistance to board."

Glad for the interruption, Jill stood, grabbed her carry-on, and got into the queue at the boarding gate.

Lauren followed her. "Don't think you're getting rid of me that easily. What's going on?" She leaned closer and lowered her voice. "Is it the MS? Are you having trouble with your eyes or something?"

No, with my heart. Or at least my damn libido. "My eyes are just fine. I'm tired and a little nervous; that's all."

"Ah." Lauren nodded as if she'd had a sudden realization. "Right. Grace said you hate flying."

Jill didn't bother to correct her. It was true, after all, even though it wasn't the reason why she'd been distracted.

"So, what are you doing with Tramp while you're gone?" Lauren asked as they were walking down the Jetway.

"Susana is taking care of him. She's probably going to spoil him rotten."

They boarded the plane and took their seats beside each other in the first-class section.

But before Jill could get comfortable next to Lauren, Floyd, who sat behind them, leaned over the back of her seat. "Would you mind switching seats with me, Jill? I need to talk to Lauren about the Lotta's Fountain scene."

"Sure." Jill gathered her script and her laptop bag and squeezed past Floyd in the aisle. About to slide into the seat he had vacated, she paused when she caught a glimpse of her new neighbor.

Crash stared back, looking just as startled as Jill felt. She had shoved her sunglasses up to rest on her head, so her deer-in-headlights look was quite obvious.

So much for staying away from her for the week.

"Uh, are you okay with sitting with me?" Crash asked.

"Of course," Jill said, using her acting skills to appear at ease. "Why wouldn't it be okay? I'm used to Lauren abandoning me for another seatmate."

Lauren squawked her protest from the seat in front of them and turned around. "Hey, you offered to switch seats with me the one and only time I was on a plane with you."

"Yeah, because I didn't want to stand in the way of true love."

"Please. There was nothing going on between Grace and me back then," Lauren said. "I thought she was the very straight star of hetero romances."

Other passengers started to board, so they fell silent.

Jill bent to stash her laptop bag under the seat in front of her. She sensed Crash's gaze on her, so intense that it felt almost like a touch. After ignoring it as long as she could, she finally straightened and turned to her.

"Grace, the very straight star of hetero romances," Crash repeated, her voice so low that no one but Jill could hear. "She's not talking about...?"

"Grace Durand? Yes, she is. Grace is my best friend and Lauren's girlfriend. Didn't you read any of the gossip rags last year?"

Crash shook her head. "I try to stay away from all press about female stars. If the actress I'm risking my life for is a real bitch, I'd rather not know."

That made sense. Jill tilted her head in approval.

"So Grace Durand is gay?" Crash let out a low whistle. "Wow. I had no idea."

"Neither did she," Jill said with a grin.

"Apparently not, or she wouldn't have given a press conference claiming she was only a straight friend helping you out," Crash mumbled.

Jill turned her head in her direction. "I thought you stayed away from gossip rags?"

Was that a hint of red entering Crash's tan cheeks? "Uh, yeah, I just...I came across an article about your coming out."

"Came across?" Jill repeated with a disbelieving look.

"Yeah. Completely by coincidence."

Coincidence. Right. Jill bit back a grin.

"Stop grinning." Crash nudged her. "Okay, so I Googled you."

Maybe Jill should have disliked it, but she actually found herself flattered. At least she wasn't the only one failing miserably at pretending not to be interested.

A flight attendant stopped in the aisle next to them and offered them a pre-flight drink. Many of the people around them had ordered wine, beer, or scotch, but since her diagnosis, Jill had become wary of the effects alcohol had on her. Unlike her youth, when she had been able to stay up all night, partying and drinking, now a beer or two would get her drunk and make her feel like hell the next day.

"Just a Diet Coke, please," she told the flight attendant.

Crash ordered water. As the flight attendant handed them their beverages and moved past them down the aisle, she studied Jill over the rim of her glass. "That press conference you gave last year..."

"What about it?"

"It wasn't something you'd planned well in advance, was it?"

"No. The press forced my hand. I wasn't in a hurry to tell anyone about the MS."

Crash wiped a bit of water from her bottom lip and nodded thoughtfully. "Yet you stepped in front of the press and told them anyway. You did it for Ms. Durand, didn't you?"

Jill shrugged. "The gossip rags kept reporting that Grace and I had something going on, just because they'd seen her help me to my trailer. I couldn't allow my MS to hurt her career."

"So you sacrificed yourself, just the way you're sacrificing your own happiness so you won't burden a potential partner down the road," Crash commented.

Jill reached out and trailed a bead of condensation down the side of her Coke before looking back at Crash. "What else could I do?"

"I don't know. It was a damn brave thing to do, but then Ms. Durand turned out to be gay after all, so you basically risked your career for nothing. Doesn't that make you angry?"

Jill thought about it for a moment. It was a valid question. Amazing that no one had ever asked her about it before. "No, not really," she finally answered.

"Not really?" Crash drawled, her Texas accent becoming more pronounced.

"In the end, she probably did me a favor by forcing me to reveal it to the public. Trying to hide my symptoms was getting pretty exhausting."

"I can imagine. Then why did you do it? Hide that you have MS, I mean."

Jill shrugged. "I didn't even tell my family or most of my friends until nine months after the diagnosis, so the public certainly didn't deserve to know either."

Crash's eyes widened. "Wow. I can't imagine keeping something like that from my family. Didn't you need…or want their support during a time like that?"

"No," Jill said immediately. It hadn't even occurred to her to ask anyone for help or comfort. Her family had never been a source of either. "I was fine on my own. There wasn't much they could have done anyway."

Instead of accepting that answer, as her parents had done when she'd finally told them, Crash continued to look at her.

Jill struggled not to avert her gaze. She felt as if she'd given Crash some access into her heart and mind last week, and now that door was still ajar, enabling Crash to see much too deep.

"They could have been there for you," Crash finally said. "Held your hand in the waiting room or something."

Jill tried to imagine her mother holding her hand but couldn't. The two times in her life when she'd asked her parents for help, they'd been too busy struggling with their own emotions, adding to her stress instead of relieving some of it. "They live in Ohio."

"So? I know for a fact that there are planes in Ohio too." Crash gestured at the plane they were in, which was slowly pulling away from the terminal.

Jill's throat went dry. She fumbled for her seat belt, making sure it was buckled. "Yeah," she said, trying to focus on the conversation and not on the moving plane. "But I didn't want them there. I couldn't deal with them on top of everything else."

Crash opened her mouth, but then she closed it again. She squinted over at Jill. "Are you okay?"

Their plane taxied down the runway, quickly picking up speed.

Jill nodded, staring straight ahead, not to the small window, where the ground was flying by.

"Are you sure? You're a bit pale."

Jill couldn't answer. Her stomach lurched when the plane lifted off the tarmac. She swallowed hard and grabbed the armrests with both hands.

"Here," Crash said gently. "Maybe this will help."

Expecting some medication to settle her stomach, Jill glanced over.

Crash was holding out her hand.

Jill hesitated, wanting to tough it out, but then, as the plane climbed at a steep angle that took her breath away, she latched on to Crash's hand. Her fingers were warm and strong, not damp and trembling like Jill's. After that kiss three days ago, the touch should have felt awkward, but it didn't. It felt safe.

"I'm not afraid of flying," she told Crash but didn't let go of her hand.

The corners of Crash's mouth twitched. "Of course not."

"No, really. I'm not. It's just the takeoffs and the landings that I don't like."

Finally, the plane was safely off the ground and no longer rising so steeply. The knots of tension in Jill's stomach eased, and she exhaled slowly. "Okay. You can let go now."

But Crash didn't seem in a hurry to withdraw her hand. "It's fine. I don't mind."

Truthfully, Jill didn't either. Quite the opposite. She tightened her grip for a moment, soaking up the warmth of Crash's skin, then forced herself to let go. Her hand felt strangely cold and empty now. She curled her fingers into a fist. "What about you?" she asked to distract herself and looked past Crash to the grid of tiny buildings below them.

"Me?"

"Yeah. I guess as a stuntwoman, you're not afraid of any of this." She waved her hand in a vague gesture that could just as well mean this thing between them rather than flying.

Crash looked at her as if wondering which option they were talking about. "You saw me behind the wardrobe trailer on Thursday," she said, her voice pitched so low that no one else on the plane could hear. "What do you think?"

In the past, Jill had always assumed all stunt people were adrenaline junkies and fearless daredevils not scared of anything. But while Crash was courageous and confident in most situations, the vulnerability she had revealed after the explosion stunt had touched Jill deeply.

Before Jill could answer, Crash shook her head and went on. "We have a saying: there are fearless stuntmen, and there are old stuntmen, but there are no fearless old stuntmen. You can't be a scaredy-cat, of course, but a certain amount of fear is actually healthy. I know I wouldn't want to work with a stunt performer who is too cocky and reckless."

Fear is actually healthy, Jill mentally repeated. She sighed. *Too bad it can't heal MS.* She turned a little in her seat and studied Crash. "Have you ever...backed out of doing a stunt?"

Crash immediately shook her head. "I've suggested ways to adjust a stunt to make it safer, but no, I never backed out. I'm not the backing-out type."

The answer hung in the air between them for a moment. That was part of why Jill couldn't get involved with her. Crash would stay with her out of a sense of duty and obligation, even if it meant ruining her own life.

They sat in silence and watched the world disappear beneath them until the plane leveled off and the fasten-seat-belt light went out.

Floyd rose from his seat, stepped into the aisle, and gave Jill a questioning look. "Want to switch back?"

Jill hesitated. She turned her head and looked at Crash.

Their gazes connected, making it even harder to tear herself away.

Her mind skipped ahead to the landing once they reached San Francisco. Would Crash hold her hand again? She longed to shake her head and tell Floyd that she'd stay where she was, but, finally, reason won out. As much as she wanted to, she couldn't keep clinging to Crash—literally and figuratively. "Sure," she said and got up.

After one last glance back at Crash, she slipped past Floyd and into the leather seat next to Lauren. She felt Crash's presence in the row behind her yet refused to turn around and peek at her. Out of the corner of her eye, she saw Lauren watching her, but she purposefully didn't react.

"Are you okay?" Lauren finally asked.

"Of course. Why wouldn't I be?"

Lauren pointed down. "Because you keep rubbing your hand."

When Jill followed her gaze, she realized she'd indeed been rubbing her hand. Not the left one, which sometimes got tingly, but the right one. The one Crash had held. She snatched her left hand away and clutched the armrest. "It's nothing."

The cool breeze from the bay picked up, making Jill shiver in her damp dress. *I'll never, ever complain about the heat in LA again.* After shooting in the City by the Bay for three days, she finally understood why Mark Twain had supposedly said that the coldest winter he'd ever seen was the summer he'd spent in San Francisco.

Well, the sun had been shining earlier today, but they hadn't been able to film this scene then, because apparently rain didn't show well on film when the light came from overhead. Now with the gray clouds above and the cold wind blowing, Floyd had declared it perfect weather. But then again, he wasn't the one who needed to shoot take after take in the pouring movie rain.

Floyd looked up from the monitor showing the video feed from camera one. Lips pursed, he shook his head. "Let's go again, this time with a bit more intensity. You're shouting at the sky, angry at nature's poor timing. Take it from 'Now of all times it rains,' please."

Production assistants herded the extras back into position. They were portraying San Franciscans made homeless by the earthquake and fires.

Jill moved to her mark, careful not to slip in the puddles surrounding her. The rest of the set, where the cameras and equipment had been set up, was completely dry.

"Roll sound," the assistant director shouted.

"Speed," the sound mixer answered.

"Roll camera!"

"Rolling," the first assistant camera operator called.

"Marker!"

The second assistant camera operator stepped in front of the camera with a clapperboard and called out the scene and take number. He smacked the top slat down with a loud crack and ducked out of the frame.

"Action," Floyd called.

Big, fat raindrops began to fall down from the rain tower, which was basically a twenty-foot pipe mounted on a stand and hooked up to a tank truck via a hose.

Jill shivered as the fake rain hit her. Couldn't they have at least heated up the water a little before pouring it down on her? Then she forgot about her complaints as she sank into her role and became Dr. Lucy Sharpe.

Clutching her black doctor's bag, she stopped in the middle of the street and lifted her face to the sky. Water dripped down her chin. "Now of all times it rains?" She let out a disbelieving laugh, bare of any humor, and shook her fist as if threatening the weather gods. "We could have used the darn rain three days ago, not now when the fires are out already and most of the city lies in ruins!"

A cry of pain came from one of the nearby tents.

Lucy shook the rain out of her eyes, jumped over a foot-long fissure in the street, and rushed toward the tent. She ducked inside just as Floyd called, "Cut!"

Please, please, please. Jill clutched her ice-cold hands together and paused inside of the tent as she waited to hear if the take was finally a wrap.

"We need to go again," Floyd called, making her groan. "One of the extras is wearing sneakers, and it shows up in the shot. Where the hell is wardrobe?"

Jill inflated her cheeks and blew out a breath of frustration. "Oh, Jesus." She felt like kicking something or someone—preferably that extra with the sneakers.

"Here."

The familiar voice made Jill look up and into Crash's blue eyes. She hadn't realized that someone else was in the tent with her.

Crash held out a blanket and a hot water bottle.

"Thanks." Jill took the hot water bottle and tugged on the blanket, but instead of letting go, Crash wrapped it around her and rubbed her shoulders and arms through the thick material.

Jill knew she should protest and pull away from this intimate gesture, but it felt too good. She shivered, and it wasn't just from the cold. She clutched the hot water bottle with both hands so she wouldn't do something stupid—such as wrapping her arms around Crash and burying herself against Crash's heat. "What are you doing here? I thought you and the other stunt people had gone back to the hotel?"

"The others did, but I thought I'd stick around for a bit. After the scenes I shot this morning, I just couldn't resist seeing someone else be miserable for a change."

Despite her words, Crash didn't seem gleeful, but Jill didn't comment on it. "Oh, yeah, then take a good long look."

Crash gave her a compassionate smile. "Maybe you could have that extra fall into the fissure or die some other horrible death in the next scene."

Laughter bubbled up despite Jill's misery. When Crash settled the blanket more tightly around her shoulders, her arm brushed Jill's side, making her shiver again. She covered it by shaking herself. "Ugh. That milk is making me all sticky."

"Milk?"

Jill nodded. "Apparently, rain doesn't show up well on film, so they add a bit of milk to the water before pouring it down on me."

"Well," Crash said, giving her a crooked grin, "isn't bathing in milk supposed to do wonders for the skin? I heard it worked for Cleopatra. Not that you need any help in the looks department, mind you."

Jill burst out laughing and forgot her bedraggled state for a moment. She suppressed the urge to touch Crash's forearm and pressed the hot water bottle to her chest instead.

The sounds of the crew setting up for yet another take drifted in.

The assistant director stuck his head into the tent. He looked from Jill to Crash and back, visibly surprised to see them in this semi-embrace, with Crash still rubbing the blanket over Jill's back. "Uh, ready to go again?"

Holding on to the hot water bottle for another moment, trying to soak up every last bit of heat—and, truth be told, support from Crash—Jill nodded. She handed the hot water bottle back to Crash and gave her a nod. "Thank you."

"You're welcome," Crash said softly.

After one last glance back at her, Jill tugged her drenched costume back into some semblance of order, squared her shoulders, and marched back to her mark beneath the water tower.

Crash crossed her hotel room toward the window and glanced at the street below. Darkness had fallen outside. One of the drivers had delivered Crash and other crew back to the hotel almost an hour ago, but Jill, Shawn, Nikki, and the crew that had been shooting their first-unit scenes today still hadn't returned.

Where the hell are they? It couldn't take that long to film the last shot of the day, could it?

The more time went by without them returning, the more worried Crash became. Had Jill suffered a relapse, so they had to take her to a hospital?

Bullshit. According to her research, heat could make MS symptoms flare, but she hadn't heard of wind and rain having the same effect. Still, she couldn't help worrying.

Voices outside in the hallway attracted her attention. She hurried to the door and put her eye to the peephole.

A bald man passed by. He wasn't part of the cast or the crew, only another hotel guest.

Just as Crash was about to turn away from the door, her cell phone rang. She jerked and nearly slammed her eye into the spyhole.

Oh, yeah, that's all I need. Having to explain to Ben or the people in makeup how I managed to get a shiner when I wasn't doing a stunt. She walked over to the nightstand where she had left her cell phone. The display said, "Mom." She swiped her finger across the small screen. "Hi, Mom."

"How is my favorite daughter doing today?"

"Your only daughter is just fine, thanks." The old joke between them soothed her a little. With the phone pressed to her ear, Crash walked back to the door to take another peek through the spyhole.

The hotel corridor beyond was empty.

"So, tell me about the crazy things you did today," her mother said.

"Not much to tell," Crash answered.

Her mother snorted. "Like I believe that even for a second! Remember how you fell off that tree, broke your arm, and didn't want to tell me?"

"Mom!" Crash groaned. "That was ages ago. There really isn't anything to tell today. I have a gag scheduled for tomorrow morning, but the most dangerous thing I did all day was heat up water for a hot water bottle."

Her mother made a sympathetic noise. "Cramps?"

"Huh?" Another glance through the peephole. Still nothing. "Oh, no. The hot water bottle wasn't for me."

"Oooh! Have you been holding out on me, Kristine?"

"Holding out on you?"

"Have you met a girl?" her mother clarified.

An image of Jill flashed through Crash's mind—the way she had stood under the rain tower earlier, her face raised to the sky, the drenched dress clinging to her curves. "Not a girl," she said without thought. "She's a woman."

"So you did meet someone? What's her name? She isn't another stuntwoman, is she? Did you meet her in San Francisco? When will we get to meet her?"

"Whoa! Slow down, Mom! It's not like that."

"That's what you said when I caught you in bed with that Jennifer."

Another groan escaped Crash. "Her name was Jessica. And thanks so much for reminding me of all the highlights of my youth."

"It wasn't that bad," her mother said.

No, actually, it hadn't been. Though she would have chosen another way to come out to her parents, they had taken it in stride.

"So what's the story with…?" Her mother paused expectantly.

"Jill," Crash supplied after a moment's hesitation, knowing her mother would get it out of her sooner or later anyway. "Jill Corrigan."

For several seconds, only silence filtered through the line. Then her mother let out a shriek.

"Shit, Mom!" Crash pulled the cell phone away from her ear and then carefully moved it back. "Believe it or not, stunt people need intact hearing."

"Jill Corrigan? The Jill Corrigan?" Her mother's voice was still higher than normal, sounding like an excited teenager.

"The one and only."

"Oh, I loved her in *Coffee to Go*. She's just so funny. I stopped watching when they wrote her out of the show."

Great. Her mother was a fan. Now she would never hear the end of it.

"You have to bring her home and introduce us!"

Crash thumped her forehead against the door several times. "I told you. It's not like that. We're just friends."

Her mother let out a disbelieving huff. "Don't tell me she's not your type."

"She is, but… It's…complicated." She didn't want to mention Jill's MS, not sure if her mother knew.

Steps came from the hallway.

Crash lifted her head away from the door and checked the peephole again.

Even through the fish-eye lens that distorted her features, there was no mistaking the person that slowly walked by.

Jill!

Someone had lent her a coat, but she was still wearing her wet costume underneath. Why the hell hadn't she gotten out of that thing on the set? Had Jill been too proud to let anyone help her with the buttons?

"I need to go, Mom," Crash said into the phone. She didn't wait for an answer but hung up and threw the cell phone on the bed. With her hand on the door handle, she hesitated for a second and glanced down at herself. She was wearing just a pair of boxer shorts and a thin tank top beneath the bathrobe the hotel had provided. Shrugging, she opened the door anyway, stepped out, and pulled it closed behind her.

Too late, she realized that she hadn't pocketed her key card before leaving her room. There would be time to worry about it later. For now, she wanted to focus on Jill, who had stopped in front of her room farther down the hall.

She was fumbling the key card out of her purse. Her hands were shaking so badly that she couldn't get the card into the slot. "Come on. Open, dammit." She kicked the door.

"Hey there, Rambo. You might want to leave breaking down doors to us stunt people." Crash stepped up behind her and took the key card from her.

"What are you doing?" Jill protested.

"Opening the door for you."

"Thanks, but I can manage."

Normally, Crash tried to be respectful of her wishes, but not this time. Jill's hands were ice-cold beneath hers. She covered them with her own for several moments, hoping to warm them, before she swiped the card through the card reader.

When the door clicked open, Crash grasped her elbow and led her inside the hotel room.

Jill had just enough time to notice that the maid had been in before Crash guided her past the bed and toward the bathroom. Jill dug in her heels. "What are you doing?"

"You're shaking like a leaf. You need to warm up, and the fastest way to do that is to take a hot shower."

"I will," Jill said. "But you don't need to stay and supervise." The thought of Crash watching her undress sent goose bumps of a different kind down her body.

Crash gave her a crooked smile. "Well, I would go back to my room, but there's a problem with that. I pulled the door closed without taking my key card with me. Would you mind giving me asylum in your humble abode?"

She and Crash sleeping in the same room, with only one bed and Crash wearing a bathrobe, with probably just her underwear beneath? Jill wildly shook her head. *No, no, no, no.* She had admirable restraint, but she was not a saint.

"But I could help you get out of those wet clothes," Crash offered, managing to look completely innocent.

"Oh, I just bet you could." Jill gave her a light swat to the shoulder. "No, thanks. I suggest you go down to the reception desk and request a replacement key card for your room."

"Dressed like this?" Crash looked down at her state of dress…or rather undress. The V of her bathrobe had slid apart a little, giving Jill a glimpse of the thin, white tank top beneath. If she wasn't mistaken, Crash wasn't wearing a bra.

Jill had to swallow before she could get her mouth to work. "Then call down and have them bring up a new card. Feel free to use the phone." She escaped into the bathroom, closed the door behind her, and leaned against the wall. Her hands were still shaking, but she wasn't sure if it was from the cold. Truth be told, she didn't feel all that cold anymore. Even as tired and miserable as she was, the sight of Crash's bathrobe-clad body heated her from the inside out.

Crash's voice filtered through the door. For a moment, Jill thought she was talking to her, but then she realized Crash was probably on the phone, calling the reception desk to have a key card brought up.

She turned on the water in the shower and hesitated for several seconds, debating whether to set the temperature to hot or cold. Her libido could use the cool-off, but her body craved heat. Finally, she decided on water that was warm but not hot enough to cause her symptoms to flare. After struggling with the tiny buttons on her dress, she stepped beneath the spray. Amazing how heavenly the water flowing over her body felt after she'd been miserable in the fake rain all day.

She took her time, washing all remnants of the sticky milk from her hair, and tried not to think of the woman on the other side of the door while she ran her hands over her body to clean it.

Surely Crash was gone anyway. If she wasn't mistaken, there'd been a knock on the door several minutes ago—probably someone from the hotel had brought up a replacement key card.

When she stepped out of the shower and dried off, she realized that she'd forgotten to take clean, dry clothes into the bathroom with her. Crash did something to her brain that made clothing seem optional.

She eyed the wet costume lying in a puddle on the bathroom floor. No way was she getting back into that thing. Barefoot, with just a towel wrapped around herself, she stepped closer to the door and pressed her ear against it.

Nothing. Everything was quiet on the other side.

Crash had probably gone back to her own room by now.

She opened the bathroom door an inch and peered out.

The part of the room where she'd left Crash standing was empty.

Instead of relief, the emotion that swept through Jill felt closer to regret. *Come on. It's better this way, you know that.* But it was getting harder and harder to make herself believe it. Sighing, she opened the door more fully and stepped through.

Two steps into the room, she stopped abruptly.

Crash hadn't left. She was sitting in the armchair in the corner. The tan skin of her legs, bare up to mid-thigh where the robe had slid up, gleamed in the soft light of the bedside lamp.

Both of them froze.

"Jesus." Crash breathed out the word, her voice filled with surprise and awe. Her gaze slid over Jill's nearly naked body, making every inch of it tingle in a decidedly non-MS kind of way, before she respectfully looked away and studied the pattern of the carpet as if it were a fascinating piece of art.

"Sorry. I thought you'd left," Jill mumbled and clutched the towel against her chest.

"No, I wanted to make sure you're okay before I go. You don't need to apologize," Crash said, still politely looking at the floor. Almost beneath her breath, she added, "Hell, no. No apology needed at all."

The admiration in Crash's husky voice sent heat through her body, but she pretended not to have heard. She dashed across the room to her suitcase, where all of her clothes were because she hadn't yet had time to unpack. Getting the lock to open proved to be difficult since her fingers were trembling again. This time, the shaking definitely had nothing to do with being cold and everything to do with the heated expression in Crash's eyes when she looked at her.

"You're still trembling." Worry was obvious in Crash's voice. The armchair creaked as she stood and stepped up behind Jill.

No, no, no, don't come any closer! The resolution to send Crash away warred with the need to have her near and feel her against her own body. Sudden anger gripped her. Damn Crash for putting her into this situation. Before meeting her, she'd always known that staying away from women was the right thing to do. But now... Why couldn't Crash leave and lounge around in just a bathrobe in her own damn room?

"Are you still cold?" Crash asked.

Jill abandoned her fruitless attempts of opening the suitcase and whirled around. "No, damn you, I'm not cold at all!" She had turned so fast that she lost her balance.

Crash caught her around the waist.

The touch of her hands was barely perceptible through the thick cotton of the towel, but it still sent a shiver through Jill.

Once Jill had found her balance, Crash slowly let go but stayed close as if to make sure Jill was really okay. "Careful," Crash whispered. Her blue eyes looked nearly silver in the low light of the lamp. They were so close that the damp warmth of her breath brushed across Jill's lips.

She let out a groan. "We're not doing this again." She licked her suddenly dry lips.

Crash's eyes tracked the movement with an expression that seemed almost hungry. "Why not?"

The look in her eyes made Jill long to pull her even closer and capture her mouth with hers. Making good use of her last two still-functioning brain cells, she answered, "Because I'm not in the market for a relationship. I told you that before."

"Who said I am?" Crash gave back. "I've barely gotten over having my heart trampled on by my last girlfriend, and I'm not eager for a repeat."

Jill stared at her. "Are you saying…? Are you talking about a one-night stand?"

Crash shrugged. "If that's all you're offering, I can live with it." She pulled Jill closer, bridging the remaining space between them until their bodies pressed against each other. "I want to kiss you."

God, Jill wanted that too, but she wasn't sure it was a good idea. "Crash, I…"

But Crash didn't wait for whatever Jill would have said. Her lips covered Jill's.

The kiss instantly deepened, melting Jill's resolve. She wove her fingers through Crash's hair and kissed her back.

Then Crash moved away a bit, creating half an inch of space between their lips. A shiver ran through Jill at the sudden loss of contact.

"Kiss you all over," Crash added, her faint Texas accent becoming more prominent in her husky voice. She lowered her head and kissed the spot between Jill's collarbones, right above the edge of the towel.

Groaning, Jill tilted her head back to give her more access. If this simple touch of Crash's lips to her skin made her body react like that, she might not survive if she let Crash continue.

Crash nibbled and kissed up the side of Jill's neck, creating goose bumps along her way.

"Stop!" Jill pressed one hand against Crash's terrycloth-clad shoulder to push her away, but somehow her hand lingered.

Crash froze, her lips still pressed to Jill's skin. Slowly, she lifted her head with a look on her face as if Jill had slapped her.

"I mean…wait," Jill said quickly. "If we're going to do this, we need to establish some ground rules first."

"Rules?" Crash repeated. One of the corners of her mouth twitched as if it couldn't decide whether to lift into an amused grin or turn down into an expression of dismay.

Those full, tempting lips… Jill tore her gaze away so she could think. "Rules," she said again. "This will be just a one-time thing. Once we're back in LA, we'll go back to being just friends and never mention it again. No declarations of love. No commitment. No promises of a happily-ever-after. No expectations beyond this one night. No flowers, no dates, no endearments. Just something physical. Some safe fun, nothing else." She looked Crash in the eyes. "Can you do that?"

Crash nodded.

"Say it. I need to hear it."

"No declarations of love. No commitment. No happily-ever-afters," Crash repeated. "Just sex." Her lips quirked into a devilish grin. "Hot, steamy, mind-blowing sex."

A wave of desire shot through Jill. The wild, passionate look in Crash's eyes jolted something inside of her, but still she held back. She needed to be sure, even if it might ruin the spontaneity of the moment, so she opened her mouth to tick off more rules.

"You talk too much." Crash tightened her grip on Jill's waist, pulled her closer, and interrupted her words with a demanding kiss.

Moaning, Jill sank against her. Liquid heat seemed to pump through her veins and settled low in her belly. For a moment, she was afraid that she'd become overheated and her symptoms would flare in the middle of things. Then Crash's tongue slid against hers and she stopped worrying. Stopped thinking. She tangled her fingers in Crash's hair and angled her head to deepen the kiss.

With each stroke of their tongues against each other, with each touch of Crash's hands along her bare upper back and shoulders, the heat inside her flared higher until Jill wrenched her mouth away.

Crash stared at her, her pupils so large that only thin rings of blue remained of her irises. "What is it?" she rasped, her voice rough with passion. "Oh, please, tell me you didn't just invent another rule that forbids kissing."

The near panic in her eyes made Jill chuckle. "No, don't worry. This isn't *Pretty Woman*. Kissing is okay. Very okay. I just wanted to move this to the bed."

"Oh yeah. Good idea." Crash walked her backward, not letting go of her for even a second, and eased her down on the bed before following her, covering her body with her own.

Crash immediately kissed her again—a slow, thorough kiss that nearly drove Jill crazy. Only when Crash dipped her head and her mouth grazed the skin above her sternum did Jill notice that Crash had somehow managed to remove her towel without her being aware of it.

For a second, being completely naked while Crash still wore her bathrobe made her feel too vulnerable, as if not just her body but her soul had been laid bare to Crash's gaze.

Nonsense, she firmly told herself. *This is just a night of fun between consenting adults.* Crash wanted to explore her body, not find out her deepest fears and secrets.

From the hungry look in Crash's eyes, Jill had expected the sex to be fast and wild, but Crash didn't seem to be in any hurry.

She leaned up on one elbow and studied Jill's body with such intense focus that Jill began to squirm beneath her.

Was she Crash's type, or did Crash usually prefer women who were taller or smaller or had—? She interrupted her thoughts with a mental shake of her head. It didn't matter. This was a one-time hook-up, not a match for life. Still, she couldn't help wondering if Crash liked her body. While Jill still worked out several times a week, she had to be more careful not to exhaust herself too much or risk a temporary flare-up of her symptoms, so she wasn't as athletic-looking anymore as she had been two years ago.

Crash either didn't notice or didn't care. Nothing but admiration and passion gleamed in her eyes as she studied Jill's body.

Her worries eased, Jill just lay back and let Crash look at her.

Finally, Crash trailed kisses down Jill's chest but never ventured closer to her nipples, which were begging for attention. She flicked out her tongue as if trying to taste the freckles on Jill's chest. Her body moved slowly against Jill's, creating deliberate friction. Leisurely, as if she had all the time in the world, her fingertips followed the path of her mouth down Jill's body.

Jill's belly tightened in anticipation of where Crash's hand might end up, but instead, Crash drew lazy circles around one breast. Jill groaned. These maddeningly unhurried touches were driving her crazy. She pushed against Crash's shoulders and rolled them over until she was the one lying on top.

Their legs tangled, and one of Crash's thighs slid between hers, pressing against her.

Jill gasped and eased away. It had been too long since she'd been with a woman. If she wasn't careful, this would be over too soon. This could be the very last time she ever had sex with someone, so she was resolved to make the most out of it. For now, she would focus on Crash instead of the pleasure pulsing through her own body.

She toyed with the sash of Crash's robe, but instead of untying it, she just slid her hand into the opening of the robe. She lightly cupped one breast through the thin tank top. It wasn't too small or too large. *Perfect. Just perfect.* She moved her thumb back and forth over one nipple, which instantly hardened.

Crash bit her lip but didn't make a sound.

Jill grinned. She loved nothing better than a bit of a challenge. Keeping her gaze on Crash's face to watch her reactions, she pushed the robe from her shoulders and arms and helped Crash struggle out of the tank top without taking the time to open the sash. Immediately drawn back to Crash's body, she grazed her teeth down her torso.

Crash's chest heaved beneath her, and she clutched Jill's ass with both hands, pressing her closer, but still made no sound.

Grinning against Crash's skin, Jill moved farther down. She nipped at the soft underside of one breast, then circled it with her tongue before closing her mouth over Crash's nipple and sucking gently.

A long, throaty moan escaped Crash, making Jill smile in triumph. "That's good," Crash said, her voice hoarse. "More than…Jesus!"

Jill swirled her tongue around the hardened tip. After she had thoroughly loved the breast, she moved back a little.

"One more rule," Crash said, sounding breathless. "No stopping."

"I'm not stopping." The bathrobe, which was still tied at Crash's waist, needed to go. She wanted to see and touch all of Crash. Jill undid the knot and parted the robe slowly, like unwrapping a present. "Sit up for a moment," she said. When Crash did, she pulled the robe free and then hooked her fingers into the waistband of Crash's boxer shorts. She slid them down and dropped Crash's clothes next to her towel on the floor. Lying on her side next to Crash, she looked down at her.

Crash's body was a work of art. Her tanned skin had a golden glow in the low light of the lamp on the bedside table. Her face, more handsome than beautiful, was flushed with pleasure. Jill took in her lean muscles and taut stomach. *So stunning.* Her mouth went dry. Despite her earlier promise not to stop, she hesitated. Did she really have the right to get involved with her, even for just a one-night stand? Crash was so full of life and vitality with the body of a goddess, while she...

Crash interrupted her thoughts when she linked both of her hands in the small of Jill's back and pulled her down against her body. "Another rule," she whispered against Jill's lips. "No thinking."

When Crash kissed her again, Jill had no problem following that newest rule. For now, the MS and her unpredictable future didn't matter, only the here and now. She started exploring every inch of Crash's body with her hands and mouth. While her fingers traced the sides of her breasts, she touched her tongue to the spot where Crash's pulse pounded in her neck.

Her own heart hammered as if in response, beating a wild rhythm against her ribs. She hummed when she tasted the slightly salty skin.

A deep groan vibrated through Crash's chest.

Jill nibbled her way down the line of Crash's throat then slid lower to toy with her nipple.

Crash's strong thighs parted so she could press her body more fully against Jill's.

The hot wetness against her belly made Jill groan. God, she wanted to taste her so badly, but it seemed too intimate for what they were doing. So she circled Crash's nipple with her tongue instead before drawing it fully into her mouth. It hardened against her tongue as she sucked gently.

"Again!" Crash groaned, her voice raw with need. "Do that again."

Jill switched to the other breast and repeated her sensuous actions.

Crash cradled the back of Jill's head with both hands and pressed her closer to her breast. Her hips thrust against Jill, seeking friction. She tried to roll them over and take the lead, but Jill stopped her by pressing a hand against her chest, fingers splayed wide.

"No. Let me." She knew Crash was stronger and could reverse their positions easily if she really wanted, but apparently, Crash was willing to give her control. Being able to guide her pleasure was a powerful turn-on.

Crash dropped her arms back to the bed and grasped two handfuls of the sheet.

Jill slid a little to the side so she could have better access to Crash's body. She trailed her right hand down Crash's chest, this time not detouring to her breasts. Her fingertips traced the bands of muscles in Crash's abdomen and then teased the sensitive spot where her hips met her legs before caressing the incredibly soft skin on the inside of her thighs.

As she trailed her fingers higher, Crash's breath hitched. Groaning, she lifted her head to watch Jill's fingertips dip into her damp curls and then, with another groan, let her head fall back against the pillow.

The sounds and feel of her made Jill nearly dizzy with desire. Unable to wait any longer, she slid one finger between Crash's folds, stroked across her clit, and then slowly pressed into her.

"Jill...so... Oh, yes!"

Jill held still for a moment, marveling at the wetness and heat, then she slowly began to move.

A guttural groan tore from Crash's throat. "Faster."

At the need in Crash's voice, Jill moved her finger faster against the straining of Crash's muscles.

Crash's hips kept in rhythm with her hand. They moved together so effortlessly as if they had done it a hundred times before.

The tendons in Crash's neck stood out in sharp relief. Her breath came in ragged gasps.

Jill wished for this moment to last forever, but she didn't want to torture Crash.

When she added a second finger, Crash's back bowed. Her thrusts against Jill's hand became more urgent. The wild look of abandon on her face made Jill's belly twist with desire. Then Crash's entire body tensed. With a shout, she collapsed back onto the bed.

Once the contractions stopped, Jill withdrew her fingers and watched as Crash's eyes blinked open. Their gazes met.

A slow, satisfied smile spread over Crash's face. "Is there a rule against complimenting your technique?" she asked breathlessly.

Jill grinned back, glad that Crash was keeping this light and fun. "Nope. That's not only allowed; it's highly recommended."

"Then consider yourself complimented." A shuddery breath escaped her, and she shook her head as if having to clear it. "God, you're good. Let's see if I can keep up." Instead of rolling them over so that she was on top, she patted her muscular thighs. "Straddle me."

A jolt of desire went straight to Jill's core. Hoping her left leg would hold up, she straddled Crash's lap and slowly lowered herself. When her wet flesh touched Crash's smooth thighs, all thoughts of the MS vanished. She had to fight the urge to rub herself against Crash's gorgeous body like a cat in heat. If she did, this would be over too fast. "Touch me."

Crash rasped her teeth over her own bottom lip as if having to restrain herself. She looked up at Jill with smoldering eyes. "Don't worry. I will."

Jill loved the way she looked at her. It made her feel sexy. Alive. Healthy. God, she had missed this.

With Jill straddling her lap, Crash sat up. Her impressive abdominal muscles flexed against Jill, making her moan. Crash's skin, damp and glistening with sweat, felt like silk against her own.

Crash ducked her head and took one nipple into her mouth while rolling the other between her thumb and forefinger. Her other hand moved around Jill to massage one of her ass cheeks and pull her closer against her belly.

Groaning, Jill rocked against her. "Touch me," she said again, no longer sure whether she was giving orders or begging—and no longer sure if she cared. She grasped the hand that was caressing her breast and brought it down. "Touch me here."

"Like this?" Crash rubbed one fingertip over Jill's clit in light circles, then slipped lower to tease her entrance with soft strokes while her other hand was still kneading Jill's ass.

Jesus. Jill sucked in a sharp breath. Those hands were magic. The muscles in her belly and thighs were already starting to quiver. "Inside. Now." She clasped Crash's wrist and guided her down.

Their groans mingled as Crash slid inside with two fingers. Her other hand came to rest on the small of her back, guiding her, as Jill began to rock against her.

Crash's hot mouth was on her neck.

Through the haze of lust, Jill somehow had the presence of mind to gasp out, "No marks. Don't leave any... God, yes!"

Crash had shifted her palm a little so that she could now stroke Jill's clit with her thumb without interrupting the rhythm of her other fingers.

The movements of Jill's hips became erratic. *So close. So...* She leaned down and kissed Crash hard until she had to break the kiss to gasp for breath.

Crash flexed her fingers inside of her, at the same time raking her teeth over the sensitive area below Jill's ear.

"Oh! Crash!" She arched against her one last time, then orgasm hit and she collapsed against her with a shout.

Crash held Jill close and guided her down, onto her side. She stayed with her, stilling her fingers but not removing them.

Dazed and unable to move, Jill allowed her head to rest against Crash's shoulder. This wasn't cuddling, she told herself. She would move away as soon as she regained use of her limbs. "You should consider yourself complimented too," she said when her breathing finally slowed. Her voice was hoarse and her throat dry. "Was I shouting?"

"Let's just say I hope the people in the neighboring rooms don't belong to our crew," Crash said with a daredevilish grin.

Jill blushed, but she didn't look away from Crash's heated gaze. "Yeah, let's hope so, because we've only just gotten started." Her body felt sated and exhausted, but she couldn't get enough, especially knowing that this would be the only night they had.

"Oh, is that so?" Crash drawled. Without waiting for Jill's reply, she started moving her fingers again. It was as if she had learned to read Jill's body perfectly already; she immediately hit the right spot.

Her head falling back, Jill groaned.

"Too much?" Crash asked, stilling her fingers.

"No. God, no. Perfect."

Crash started moving again and, within moments, sent her spiraling a second time.

Crash collapsed onto the damp sheets and stared at the ceiling, nearly cross-eyed with pleasure. *Jesus.* Maybe she would miss out if she gave up on one-night stands. *Hmm, but then again, maybe not.* Because if this were a relationship and not a one-night stand, she wouldn't have hesitated to wrap her arms around Jill and cradle her against her body while they enjoyed the afterglow. She turned onto her side and regarded Jill.

Cuddling hadn't been mentioned in Jill's collection of rules one way or another, but Crash didn't want this incredible experience to end on an unpleasant note by touching Jill in a way that wouldn't be welcome.

They lay facing each other, sharing the same pillow but not touching.

Jill's normally creamy-pale skin was flushed and her breathing was still a little uneven.

During their lovemaking—*sex,* she mentally corrected herself—she hadn't thought of Jill's illness. Well, truth be told, there hadn't been much thinking going on at all. But now she worried that Jill would have a price to pay for exerting herself like that.

Crash cleared her throat. "Jill?"

"Hmm?" Jill's eyelids had drooped to half-mast, but now she forced them open and glanced over at her.

"Are you all right?"

"Never been better," Jill said. As if to prove it, she reached for Crash again.

"Oh, God." Crash grabbed her wrist and stilled her hand against her lower abdomen. "I never thought I'd say this, but you're wearing me out."

"I have a lot to make up for. Two years is a long time." Jill smiled and her tone was light as if it were just a funny quip, but there was something in her eyes that looked strangely like grief.

Crash studied her. "Two years… Is that how long you've known about the MS?"

"That's when the first symptoms started, but it took a while until the doctors came up with the diagnosis."

"And you haven't been with anyone since?" Crash couldn't help asking.

"Nope," Jill said. Her tone was still casual, but Crash sensed the emotions lurking beneath.

"I'm glad you didn't keep denying yourself this." Crash gestured at their naked bodies.

"Me too," Jill whispered. But instead of wrapping her arms around Crash and kissing her, she pulled her hand out from under Crash's and moved to her side of the bed. Something in her face closed off.

Crash stared over at her; then her gaze flicked to the door. "Do you want me to go?"

This whole situation had heartbreak written all over it. Maybe she should leave before she got even more involved than she already was. There were a dozen good reasons why she should get up, gather her clothes, and leave, yet part of her still hoped that Jill would want her to stay.

"No," Jill said and then added, "I mean, it's the middle of the night. We wouldn't want any of our colleagues to see you sneak out of my room."

"Right." Crash peeked over at her. Was that really the only reason Jill wanted her to stay? The way Jill looked at her said something else.

Jill turned around, away from her, interrupting their eye contact. "The bed is big enough for us both," she said over her shoulder. "Let's just go to sleep."

Crash turned off the light but lay there without closing her eyes, staring at the contours of Jill's naked back in the near darkness. Her body was still humming with pleasure, but the rest of her was much less satisfied.

What would happen now? Would this really stay a one-time thing? She couldn't imagine never touching Jill again. But what were the alternatives?

The darkness didn't hold any answers.

She listened to Jill's breathing as it evened out into the soft rhythm of sleep. It took a long time before Crash nodded off too.

CHAPTER 10

A FAMILIAR JABBING PAIN IN her toes woke Jill from an unusually sound sleep. She stayed still and listened. No distant hum of city traffic filtered into the room, so it was probably early. Without opening her eyes or sitting up, she took stock of her body, as she did every morning. Waves of tingling shot up and down her left leg. She gritted her teeth against the feeling as if ants were crawling all over her calf. The rest of her body felt heavy, but there was no other pain, no scary new symptom.

Something else was new, though. Her right leg and arm were draped over a warm body and her head rested on a chest that lifted and fell in the soft pattern of sleep.

Crash. Memories of last night shot through her mind in vivid images. God, no wonder she felt exhausted. She hadn't known she still possessed the energy to have sex for hours on end. Being with Crash had been like a drug, making her crave more.

Not just more sex, but more of everything. She wanted to snuggle closer, trying to shut out the world for a little longer and let Crash's calm breathing lull her back to sleep. As long as she hadn't gotten up, the day hadn't officially started, so she hadn't broken their just-one-night agreement.

She allowed herself to soak up the feeling of Crash's naked body against hers for another minute, then called herself to order.

Enough. You have to face reality sooner or later, so cut out the rosy afterglow.

The pressure in her bladder told her that staying in bed was not an option anyway. If she didn't want to wake Crash with a wetness of a different kind, she had to get up—now.

She took a deep breath, as always a little tense before first getting up in the morning. How she missed those carefree days of the past when she had just opened her eyes and jumped out of bed without being afraid to discover that she had gone blind or couldn't move.

So far, it hadn't happened, but that didn't stop that nagging fear from always lurking in the back of her mind. Another deep breath and she lifted her arm and withdrew her leg from around Crash.

So far, so good.

Her limbs seemed relatively okay. Now on to her eyesight. She opened her eyes. The gray light of dawn filtered through the curtains of the hotel room. Her gaze traced Crash's chiseled features, which were relaxed in sleep and looked even more appealing in the shadowy half-light. Her hair was disheveled from the way Jill had run her fingers through it and clutched Crash's head last night. A black lock of hair had tumbled onto her brow, and Jill had to fight the urge to push back that smooth strand and press a kiss to the sensual curve of Crash's mouth.

Annoyed with herself, she directed her gaze elsewhere. The glowing red numbers of the alarm clock told her it was nearly five. Okay, so her eyesight worked too. With that encouraging inventory of her body done, she quietly slipped out of bed.

Her legs felt weak, as if she'd run a marathon. Her body would definitely hate her later today, when she had to shoot that dancing scene in the ballroom of San Francisco's only intact Victorian building. *Yeah, but it sure as hell didn't hate me last night.*

Her bladder reminded her that there was no time to indulge in pleasant memories, so she grabbed a change of clothes and rushed toward the bathroom as fast as her wobbly legs would carry her.

At the door, she turned back around and watched Crash, who lay fast asleep, only half covered by the rumpled sheets. Her gaze traced the curve of the one breast that was visible and then over one strong shoulder and up to Crash's face, which looked completely peaceful.

For a moment, she let herself wonder whether Crash would think back to last night every now and then too. She resolutely told herself it didn't matter and entered the bathroom.

Once she had taken care of business, she stepped into the shower and thoroughly spread soap over her body, forcing herself to wash off all traces of Crash.

When she dried off and got dressed, her gaze fell on the box of syringes that she had placed on the marble counter next to the soaps and little shampoo bottles with the hotel's logo. The daily injections were supposed to reduce the frequency and severity of her relapses. Good thing she hadn't put her medication in the fridge, as she did at home. While the prefilled syringes could be kept at room temperature for up to a month, the manufacturer recommended refrigerating them. Usually, she took one out the evening before so it could warm up a little, but last night, she definitely would have forgotten. She liked to get her injection over with first thing in the morning so she didn't have to worry about it for the rest of the day, but she couldn't do that if it wasn't the right temperature.

She glanced at the bathroom door. Everything was quiet on the other side, but she still went to the door and locked it before returning to the sink. This was a ritual that she needed to perform in privacy. She laid out one of the syringes, a cotton pad, and an alcohol wipe. The gel pads she normally used to warm up the injection site beforehand and then cool it afterward were in the other room, but she didn't want to risk waking Crash by getting them.

She'd lost track of time as she often did when shooting on location, so she had to think a moment to remember that it was Tuesday. Right thigh day. Much better than Saturday and Sunday, when she had to inject herself into the back of her arms, which were hard to reach, especially since she had no hand free to pinch the skin before putting the needle in.

After pulling her jeans down and sitting on the closed toilet, she swiped the alcohol pad over her skin and removed the syringe from its blister pack while she waited for it to dry. She removed the needle cap and carefully shook a drop of the medication from the tip of the needle, knowing it would irritate the skin if it came into direct contact with it. Without hesitation, she pinched a bit of skin between thumb and index finger of her left hand and was just about to insert the needle into her thigh when a knock came at the door.

Jesus F. Christ! She barely stopped herself from flinching and stabbing herself with the needle.

"Jill?" Crash called through the door. "Are you in there?"

"Uh, yeah. Do you need the bathroom?" Jill asked, trying to sound normal, as if Crash hadn't startled her.

"No, I can wait. It's just that you've been in there for a while, so I wanted to make sure you're okay."

Crash's concern felt good, but at the same time, it reminded her that she wasn't healthy; she was someone whose well-being couldn't be taken for granted. "I'm fine," she called through the door. "I'm just…getting dressed."

She bit her lip as soon as she'd said it. *Great.* Now she was acting like a junkie who locked herself into a bathroom to shoot herself up with heroin and then lied about what she'd been doing.

"Okay," Crash answered.

Then everything was silent. Was she waiting for Jill to say something? That was exactly why Jill didn't do one-night stands. Mornings after were just too awkward.

Pressing her lips together, she again pinched up a bit of skin and inserted the needle into the side of her leg. The sting made her wince, but she ignored it and pushed the plunger all the way down. It burned more than usual. She sucked in a sharp breath as she pulled the needle out, released the skin, and pressed the cotton ball to her thigh. *Damn.* She'd injected the medication too fast. Now she'd end up with an itching red lump on her thigh. That hadn't happened since she'd gotten used to injecting herself.

"Jill?" Crash called. Her voice sounded so close as if she was leaning against the door. "Are you really okay?"

Jill bit her lip to hold back a gruff reply. "Just peachy."

"Are...we okay?" Crash asked more quietly.

"Of course." Jill stood, pulled up her pants, and dropped the empty syringe into her disposal container. "It was fun, and now that we got it out of our systems, we can move on."

Crash was quiet for a moment before saying, "I guess so. What happens in San Francisco stays in San Francisco, right?"

"Right." Even though she was finished injecting herself, Jill didn't leave the bathroom. She wasn't ready to face Crash.

Another moment of silence. "I'll head over to my own room now. I have a stunt later that I need to prepare for."

"Okay."

Her receding footsteps indicated that Crash was moving away from the bathroom door.

"Crash?" Jill called.

The footsteps stopped. "Yeah?"

Jill opened her mouth, about to tell Crash to be careful when performing her stunt but then held herself back. She and Crash were colleagues, not loving partners who worried about each other's well-being. "See you later."

"See you," Crash answered. A few seconds later, the door clicked shut behind her.

Crash shivered in the heavy, damp fog of the San Francisco morning. Chimes drew her attention up to the ferry building's clock tower. Eight o'clock and they still weren't shooting. The crew bustled around her like an army of busy ants, setting up cameras and other equipment, while the PAs tried to keep a horde of curious onlookers behind the cordons and Ben instructed their new stunt performers.

Instead of flying their entire stunt department to San Francisco, Ben had hired local stunt people for everyone but Shawn, Nikki, and Jill. In addition to doubling for their actresses, Crash and her two colleagues also stepped in as extras whose characters were involved in action-packed scenes.

Today, one of those scenes was on the shooting schedule. Thank God for small favors. At least it meant Crash wouldn't have to work with Jill today, giving them both some time to get over the awkwardness.

She should have known better. Her mentor had warned her never to sleep with a colleague or anyone else she had to work with. Maybe she should have listened to Sabrina, but she just hadn't been able to resist. And why should she? Many of her colleagues indulged in one-night stands whenever they could. It was part of their live-life-to-the-hilt-because-you-could-die-tomorrow attitude. Even Sabrina, the bitch, hadn't followed her own advice when she'd slept with Crash's girlfriend, their assistant location manager.

She shook off thoughts of Jill and the past and focused on work. Their director wanted the greater realism of shooting at the few historic buildings that had survived the earthquake and fires, so they were filming at the ferry building with its arched arcades.

Crash glanced up at the nearly one-hundred-twenty-year-old clock tower again. What the heck was taking the crew so long? They had permission to film for only two hours.

That should have been plenty of time for the one scene they needed to film, but it seemed to take forever to get everything set up the way Ben wanted it—mainly because they still needed to establish a rapport with their new colleagues, not because Crash was distracted or tired. At least that was what she told herself. Considering she'd slept for just two hours, she actually felt pretty good.

Ben did another walk-through with Crash and the San Franciscan stuntwoman, Sarah, and had them run through each of the fight beats in slow motion, almost as if they were dancing.

Dancing? Crash mentally shook her head at herself. *You're kind of poetic this morning.*

"Okay," Ben finally said. "Here we go. On marks."

Two dozen extras took their places, surrounding Crash and Sarah. When Ben called, "Action," they started shoving and jostling, nearly pushing Crash over the edge and into the harbor.

"There it is!" someone shouted.

Crash, Sarah, and the extras all paused and stared out toward the ocean. There was nothing to see, but later, a computer-generated ferry would be added, approaching the dock, where hundreds of people waited.

The jostling and shoving started again as panicked San Franciscans fought each other for a place on the ferry, desperate to get away from their burning city.

An elbow hit Crash a little too hard, making her grunt. She raised her umbrella and threatened to swing it down on Sarah's head.

As they had practiced before, Sarah threw a gloved fist at her.

Crash waited, timing it just right. As Sarah's fist crossed the bridge of her nose, she jerked her head back and pretended to be hit hard. She stumbled back and landed in the water with a loud splash.

Shit, that's cold. She flailed her arms, pretending to panic as her water-logged dress and petticoats dragged her down.

"Cut!" Ben called from above.

The crew immediately rushed to help Crash climb out.

Ben was massaging his chin—never a good sign, as Crash had learned in the past three weeks.

"We didn't nail it?" She'd thought the fight sequence had gone just fine.

"Yes, you did, but it all looked a bit too great."

Crash realized her wig had nearly been swept from her head so she tugged it back into position. "Too great?"

"Yeah. Sarah punched you like a boxing champion, not like a refined lady from 1906. We need to tone it down a little to make it believable."

Why hadn't he thought of that before making her jump into the water? Crash suppressed a sigh. "Okay. I'll get changed into a dry costume and then let's go again." She walked over to the wardrobe trailer they had set up nearby.

Sagging racks of dresses, blouses, trousers, chemises, and coats stretched along two walls. Shoes and boots of all sizes were lined up on a shelf, while hats filled the opposite wall.

The costume assistant was busy helping another actress into her corset—and not just any actress.

Even from behind, Crash recognized her immediately. She'd spent the night worshipping that body after all.

She paused in the doorway, riveted by the sight of creamy skin and gleaming, coppery hair piled up onto her head.

The costume assistant threw her an annoyed look. "Come in or stay out. Either way, close the door."

Quickly, Crash entered and closed the door behind her.

Jill glanced over her shoulder. A hint of red crept up her neck. "Oh. Hi."

"Hi." Crash stood there, her wig with the hat attached in her hands. *Say something.* "Uh, I'm wet." As soon as the words were out, she wanted to slap herself. God, one night with Jill had reduced her to a bumbling idiot who wasn't capable of opening her mouth without double entendres coming out. She pulled the wet bodice away from her chest. "Uh, I mean, I had to shoot a scene that made me end up in the harbor, and now I need a dry costume."

"Why don't you strip down, and I'll be with you in a second," the costume assistant said without looking away from where she was lacing up Jill's corset.

Crash couldn't look away either. If she had thought that the newness would wear off after exploring every inch of that body several times and they could go back to just being friends, she had deluded herself.

Come on. Be a professional. She forced herself to turn away, stripped off her wet dress, and put it on a hanger. The petticoats and the corset followed. Even the chemise had gotten wet, so she took that off too.

"You need to face away from me for this to work," the costume assistant told Jill.

A smirk curved Crash's lips. So Jill had watched her undress. Good to know that she wasn't quite out of Jill's system either.

When Jill was dressed, the costume assistant turned toward Crash and took in the wet dress. "Oh. The duplicate is still with Connie for some last-minute repairs. Let me get it." She squeezed past Crash, and the trailer door fell closed behind her.

Crash swallowed as she unexpectedly found herself alone with Jill.

They stared at each other and then glanced away at the same time.

Now what? She peeked over at Jill. God, she looked great in that dress. With her hair piled up on her head, leaving her neck bare, she appeared somehow vulnerable—or maybe it was the look in her eyes. "Are you okay?" Crash asked softly.

"Would you please stop asking me that?" Jill grumbled and then gentled her tone. "I know you mean well, but all it does is remind me that people...you...see me as an MS patient."

"I don't...I... That wasn't my intention. I just...care about your well-being." She stepped around a mannequin so she could see Jill's face better. "Is that so wrong?"

"No. Yes." She looked at Crash and then quickly averted her gaze as if wanting to avoid staring at her bare breasts. "Crash, we really can't..." Jill tugged on a strand of her hair, nearly making the entire creation come tumbling down. She quickly snatched her hand away and curled it into a fist.

"Why don't we talk about this after work?" Crash said. "We could meet back at the hotel at seven and then take a cable car up to Fisherman's Wharf and..."

A shake of Jill's head made her trail off. "I can't. I'm having dinner in Chinatown with Lauren tonight."

"Then how about—"

The trailer door opened, and the costume assistant entered with the replacement dress. "Here it is." When Crash didn't acknowledge her return and kept looking at Jill, she glanced back and forth between them. "Is everything okay?"

"Yes," they said in unison.

"We were just talking about an agreement we have," Jill added with a glance at Crash.

No commitment. No promises of a happily-ever-after. No expectations beyond the one night. Crash gave her a stiff nod. *Message received.* Even though it felt wrong to walk away, it was what they had agreed on, and she knew it was for the best. She was an adrenaline-loving stuntwoman, traveling around the globe to get the most exciting gags. A commitment to someone who might become bound to a wheelchair didn't fit her lifestyle.

Right. She took the chemise the costume assistant handed her and slipped it over her head.

Even without being able to see, she felt the moment Jill squeezed past her in the narrow space within the trailer.

"Crash?" Jill said from right in front of the door.

"Yes?" Crash struggled to pull the chemise down so she could see her. She held her breath as she waited for what Jill would say.

Jill hesitated. One hand already on the doorknob, she shuffled her feet. "I... Good luck with your scene," she said, opened the door, and walked down the three steps without looking back.

Crash imagined that she could hear the dress rustling long after the door had closed behind her.

CHAPTER 11

CRASH HEADED STRAIGHT FROM THE airport to the playground. That was what she and her friend TJ called his backyard, where he had set up airbags, trampolines, and other equipment for stunt performers who wanted to practice.

He didn't ask why she was so eager to train flips until her legs were so tired she couldn't land safely anymore and then went all out in a sparring session.

Crash hoped that by the time she got home, she'd be so tired that she'd just fall into bed and sleep for the rest of the weekend. On Monday, things would be back to normal. Just business as usual. They would hang out in Jill's trailer between scenes and share a fruit platter in the craft services tent, nothing more.

Two weeks ago, that would have been a pleasant thought, but now it left her feeling dissatisfied.

TJ finally dropped his gloved hands. Sweat darkened his gray muscle shirt. "Who is she?"

Crash looked up from trying to untie her boxing gloves with her teeth. "Who?"

"The woman you're thinking about."

"What makes you think I'm thinking about a woman?"

He snorted. "Because that was the second time in the last half hour that I nearly broke your nose because you can't focus for shit."

"I just got a lot of work stuff on my mind," Crash said.

"Right. Does that work stuff have a name?"

Crash glared at him.

"I hear the girls…"

Another glare from Crash.

"Uh, the women in San Francisco are hot," he said.

"I didn't notice." It was true. The only woman she'd looked at lately was Jill.

"Man." He shook his head at her. "For a stuntwoman, your life is really boring."

Crash finally managed to strip off her gloves and threw them at him. "You have no idea."

He took off his own gloves. "Yeah, but only because you refuse to give me any dirt."

She put him in a headlock and rapped her knuckles against his head. "Oh, you want dirt? I'm happy to oblige." She tried to drag him down to the ground so she could rub a handful of grass and earth into his face.

He grabbed her, and they both went down, tussling for the upper hand. It was like interacting with her brothers.

Men were just too easy. All you needed to do to divert their attention was to offer beer or to challenge them to a fight. Life would be so much less complicated if she were straight. But then again, she thought with a grin, it would be a lot more boring too.

Finally, TJ with his heavier weight and superior strength managed to pin her to the ground. "So? Want to tell me about this mystery woman now?"

Damn. So much for men being easily distracted. She knew he wouldn't let her up until she gave him something. "I had a one-night stand in San Francisco," she said as casually as possible.

"Cool." He let go of her.

She sat up and shrugged. "I guess."

"Wow." He laughed. "With that kind of enthusiasm, she must have been bad."

"No!" She flicked a handful of dirt at him. "No, it's not about that."

TJ brushed earth of his sweat-stained muscle shirt. "What is it, then? If you had a great time in bed, why are you in such a shitty mood?"

Crash pushed up off the ground. "I'm not in a shitty mood. I just... I've got a lot on my mind."

"Ooh, I get it now. You wanted more, and she shot you down."

"That's not it. Not really."

"So you don't want more?"

Crash flopped down on the large trampoline in the middle of the backyard. Still bouncing, she stared up into the sky. One of the clouds was shaped like Jill's car. Crash waited until she had stopped moving and took a deep breath. "I do."

The two words rattled around in her brain, leaving her breathless. It was the truth; she realized. A one-night stand wasn't enough. But the words sounded too much like marriage vows, and that was just crazy. She wasn't ready for that kind of responsibility, was she?

TJ landed next to her, bounding on his belly, and gave her an expectant look.

"I want more, but I don't know what to do about it—or even if I should."

Groaning, he rolled onto his back, and they lay side by side, looking up at the sky. "Man, women are complicated."

"Tell me about it," she muttered.

"I'm the last person on earth you should ask for relationship advice," TJ finally said. "But if you ask me, you should just stop thinking about it so much. Just get the girl and worry about the rest later."

"Woman," Crash said and climbed off the trampoline. Maybe she should take TJ's advice. The next time she saw Jill, she'd sit her down and convince her to give her a chance.

Just a date, with all the other rules still firmly in place. For now. She could handle that.

But first she needed a beer—or two. She headed toward the house and called over her shoulder, "Last one in pays for the pizza."

This was getting ridiculous. Jill had avoided her since their one-night stand in San Francisco, even going so far as to eat the hot, sit-down meals the catering service offered instead of heading over to the craft services tent at lunch time. It was almost as if she sensed Crash's resolution to ask her out on a date and wanted to avoid the conversation.

For two days, Crash struggled with her emotions in silence. She was angry and hurt at the cold-shoulder treatment, and she missed their easy banter. For a while, she was tempted to just give up. Maybe it wasn't meant to be. But she knew that was her fear talking. If she walked away now, she could blame it all on Jill, not on her own insecurities about getting involved with a chronically ill woman.

Jill wasn't as unaffected as she pretended to be either. Usually, she joked around with Shawn and Nikki in between takes, but now she withdrew into herself when the cameras weren't rolling, putting on her MP3 player so no one would disturb her.

On day three after their return to the LA studio, Crash finally had enough. She gathered her courage, got two bowls of fruit salad and two of the wraps Jill liked, and headed over to Jill's trailer.

Loaded down with food, she used her foot to knock on the door and called, "Jill? Are you there? Can we talk? Look, I even come bearing food."

But when the door finally opened, it wasn't Jill who stood in front of her.

Crash nearly dropped her offerings when she came face-to-face with Grace Durand. Even though she tried to stay away from Hollywood gossip, there was no mistaking the woman's long, golden hair, luscious curves, and eyes as blue as a tropical ocean. She had seen several actresses without their stage makeup and had been less than impressed, but Grace seemed even more attractive off screen. *Holy shit.*

She had known Jill was friends with Grace Durand, of course, but she hadn't expected to find her here, visiting her friend like a mere mortal.

Grace smiled as if she was used to that kind of reaction. "Jill? It seems someone else had the same idea as we did."

Jill appeared in the doorway next to Grace, a container of Chinese takeout in one hand and chopsticks in the other. Her hair looked as if a bird had tried to nest in it—probably from the ladies' hat and the Gibson-girl-style additions she had worn on set. She was barefoot, and a splash of what looked like sweet-and-sour sauce graced her cheek.

Her appearance was so different from her almost larger-than-life friend that Crash looked back and forth between them. Then she decided that she liked Jill's down-to-earth style better.

"Hi," Jill said quietly.

"Hi." They looked at each other, neither of them moving.

Jill eyed the food in Crash's hands. "Oh, wow, what's this? Let's-fatten-up-Jill day?"

Grace poked her in the ribs. "Hardly. We're all just trying to take care of a friend." She studied Crash with a curious expression. "Right?"

"Right," Crash said.

"Is that Crash?" Lauren called from inside of the trailer and then stepped up behind her girlfriend. "Hi. Why don't you come in? There's enough food for you too, especially since you brought your own."

Crash's gaze went from her to Jill. Somehow, she didn't give off the impression that she wanted Crash to come in and mingle with her friends. For a moment, she considered accepting Lauren's invitation anyway, but then she mentally shook her head. By now, she knew Jill well enough to realize that she wouldn't react too well to being backed into a corner. With her friends right there, they wouldn't be able to talk about what was going on between them anyway. "No, thanks. I have to get back to the stunt trailer. I just wanted to bring over some food before the burly grip guys descend on the crafty tent."

Grace gestured at the food Crash had brought. "Your grips eat fruit salad and wraps? The ones on my sets are always more the junk food types."

Damn. She's got you there, genius. Crash shrugged as casually as she could and offered a small grin. "Well, you never know. It's better to be careful than to go hungry."

"True," Grace finally said. Her face didn't give away whether she suspected that the food was just a convenient excuse to come over and see Jill.

Crash looked back and forth between Grace and Jill, not sure what to do with her food since Jill had her hands full already.

"Here." Grace relieved Crash of Jill's half of lunch.

Crash resisted the urge to shuffle her feet on the trailer's top step. She gave Grace a quick nod. "Nice to meet you. Will I see you later, Jill?"

"Um, yes. Thank you," Jill said quietly. "For the food, I mean." She looked as if she wanted to say more, but with a glance at her friend who hovered next to her, she kept silent and just white-knuckled her chopsticks.

"You're welcome." Crash tore herself away from Jill's green eyes, jogged down the three steps, and escaped to the stunt trailer, not sure if she should be relieved or disappointed that their conversation had been delayed.

Jill sank onto the couch next to Lauren and pretended to need all her attention to grab the small pieces of pineapple with her chopsticks.

Grace settled on the floor in front of the couch and casually leaned her head against Lauren's knee. "Wow. Who was that?"

Jill nudged her with her bare toes. "Stop salivating."

A delighted smile lit up Grace's ocean-blue eyes. "Oooh, you're interested in her!"

"Nonsense," Jill said firmly. "You know I'm not looking to get involved with anyone."

"Then why the jealousy?" Grace asked.

"I'm not jealous." Jill's thoughts raced, trying to come up with an explanation for what she was feeling. It was *not* jealousy. It couldn't be jealousy. "I...I'm just not used to you looking at other women like that. In all the years I've known you, I never had the slightest inkling that you are anything but straight. Heck, you were married to a man!"

Grace shook her head so emphatically that her blonde hair flew back and forth. "I was married, yes, but I wasn't happy."

Lauren put down her chopsticks and squeezed Grace's shoulder.

Grace instantly tilted her head and pressed her cheek on top of Lauren's hand. "After meeting Lauren, I have a new appreciation of women," she added.

"God," Jill said. "Sometimes watching you guys..."

"Makes you long for a relationship of your own?" Grace finished her sentence.

"Makes me want to barf," Jill said with a grin.

Lauren and Grace bombarded her with fortune cookies, which Jill caught and ate without checking what was written on the tiny pieces of paper. *What? Now you're superstitious too?*

"Back to the topic at hand," Grace said. "You have no reason to be jealous."

"I told you I'm not jealous." Jill wasn't jealous of the way Crash had looked at her friend either. She was used to men—and some women—looking at Grace that way. It didn't bother her. *Okay, not much.* "Because there's nothing going on between Crash and me."

"Crash?" Grace repeated.

"It's a nickname. She's one of the stunt performers," Lauren said. "Actually, she's doubling for Jill."

A knowing grin formed on Grace's lips. "Oh, so you work together very closely."

"There's nothing going on," Jill said. *Don't blush. Don't blush.*

Grace laughed and patted Jill's leg. "Give it up. I'm an actress too, remember? I can see right through you."

"There's nothing to see," Jill insisted.

Lauren and Grace traded glances. "Right."

Jill bowed her head over the box of sweet-and-sour chicken and shoveled some of it into her mouth, hoping to end the conversation.

But Grace seemed to have lost interest in her own food and was watching her instead.

Jill wanted to hurl her takeout box across the trailer and shout at them to leave her alone. Staying away from Crash was hard enough, but if her friends now started to push her toward her...

"Jill..." Grace put her hand on Jill's leg—the left one, so she felt the touch only as if through several layers of thick winter clothing. "What's going on? Talk to me. Please."

She shoved her chopsticks into the box, nearly piercing the bottom. "I slept with her." It was out before she could hold it back.

Silence filled the trailer for a moment.

A grin crept over Grace's face. "I knew it!" She straightened on her knees and threw her arms around Jill. "I'm so happy for you."

Jill struggled out of the embrace. "Would you hold off on printing the wedding invitations? It was a one-time thing, nothing more."

"Does she know that?" Grace asked softly.

"Of course," Jill said, a little hurt that Grace would think she'd lead Crash on. "I made that clear. Very clear."

"Hey." Grace rubbed Jill's arm. "I'm just asking because...I never had a one-night stand bring me food."

Jill snorted. "You never had a one-night stand, period."

Grace tilted her head in acknowledgment. "You've got me there. But that's beside the point. I don't know Crash, but she seemed very nice, and I just thought—"

"She is nice," Jill said. "I really like her. But as much as I'd like to, nothing is going to come out of it." She paused and bit her lip as she mentally listened to the echo of her words. *As much as I'd like to... Goddammit, Grace! Why couldn't you leave me alone with my denial?*

"Why not? You could—"

"Stop it, Grace!" She realized she was nearly shouting and lowered her voice. "This isn't up for debate. Let's just change the topic, okay?"

Grace opened her mouth, then, after a quick glance to Lauren, closed it and nodded.

Jill took several deep breaths and tried to calm her racing heart and the chaos of emotions inside of her. She took a grape from the bowl of fruit salad, then remembered that Crash had brought it for her and put it back. "So," she said after a moment of silence, "have you decided on your next project?"

Grace stole a piece of melon from the fruit salad. "Not yet. There are three scripts that I really like. Maybe you could take a look at them when you come over for Lauren's famous hot dogs on Saturday."

Jill blinked. "I'm coming over for hot dogs on Saturday? I wasn't aware we had decided on a day yet."

Grace gave her the charming smile that had won her the hearts of millions of viewers. "That's because I just decided a second ago."

Shrugging, Jill popped a piece of by-now cold chicken into her mouth and chewed. "Who am I to argue? I love Lauren's hot dogs. Besides, I could never resist a woman who offers food."

"I noticed," Grace said, looking at the fruit salad and the wrap Crash had brought.

"Grace..." Jill threatened her with the chopsticks.

Her friend lifted both hands. "Okay, okay. I'll shut up."

They continued eating in silence.

Crash was sitting on the stairs of the stunt trailer with her laptop on her knees, eating her wrap and watching the pre-visualization of the fire stunt she'd have to do shortly before filming ended, when Lauren found her.

"Crash? Do you have a minute?"

She paused the 3-D animation, closed the laptop, and looked up at Lauren expectantly. "Sure."

Lauren swept a strand of her chin-length, brown hair behind her ear, hesitated, and then perched on the step next to Crash. "Grace and I were wondering if you'd like to come over for dinner on Saturday."

"Uh..." Crash clutched the laptop with one hand. "Come over for dinner?"

"Yeah, you know, the meal that is usually served sometime in the evening," Lauren said with a smile.

Crash resisted the urge to roll her eyes. *Writers.* They all thought they were hilariously funny. "You're inviting me to dinner?"

"Sure, why not?"

"I don't know. It's just that Grace...Ms. Durand..."

"She's a normal, flesh-and-blood woman like you and me. Despite what the gossip rags might say, she doesn't spend her time off-set shopping in luxury boutiques or having dinner at restaurants where even the bread sticks cost more than most people make in a month."

"I didn't think so," Crash said. She didn't know Grace, but she had a feeling that Jill wouldn't be such close friends with her if she were one of the shallow, money-grubbing stars that were so common in Hollywood. "But why me?"

Lauren shrugged. "You're friends with Jill, so I figure you can be trusted not to lure the paparazzi to Grace's home."

Friends with Jill… That wasn't all she wanted to be, even though she didn't yet know exactly what role she wanted to have in Jill's life.

"Besides, there aren't too many other lesbians working on the set of *Shaken to the Core*, so we thought it might be nice to get to know each other a little," Lauren added.

Crash no longer hesitated. As far as she knew, Grace and Lauren were Jill's closest friends. Maybe she could use the get-together to ask them for help on how to break through Jill's reserve. "That sounds great. Do you want me to bring anything?"

"If you want beer, you can bring a six-pack, since we don't keep any at the cottage. It's totally casual, just hot dogs with a couple of friends."

Did that mean she wouldn't be the only guest? Would they invite Jill too? That possibility only made her more determined. At least then Jill would have to stop avoiding her, and they might be able to talk. "Beer it is, then. So when and where?"

"How about I pick you up at home Saturday around six?" Lauren said. "The drive up to Grace's home can be a bit nerve-racking if you're not used to navigating the steep road."

Crash chuckled. "I'm a stunt driver. I think I can manage."

"I'm not saying you can't, but you don't have to."

Who was she to argue with their screenwriter? "Okay. Saturday at six. I'll send my address to your studio e-mail."

"Great. I'm looking forward to it." Lauren stood, waved, and walked away.

Crash watched her cross the studio lot. With her tall, sturdy body, Lauren didn't look like someone who spent most of her day behind her desk.

Wow. She'd have dinner with Lauren and her superstar girlfriend. That thought wasn't what was making her heart pound, though; it was the idea of possibly having dinner with Jill and asking her for more than a one-night stand.

Blowing out a breath, she opened the laptop and pressed play on the pre-vis. An animated figure was set on fire and then ran across the screen, flames all over her body.

Crash and burn. She hoped it wasn't a preview of what was to come on Saturday.

CHAPTER 12

THE TANTALIZING SCENT OF HOT dogs wafted over from the patio when Grace led Jill into the cottage.

Tramp stuck his nose in the air and let out a woof.

Jill's stomach answered with a hearty growl.

Grace laughed. "Glad to hear that your dog and your stomach approve."

"Nothing against your hot dogs, but Tramp isn't picky when it comes to food." Jill put the cheesecake she'd brought into the refrigerator and followed Grace to the patio, where she watched her turn the hot dogs. She shook her head with a grin. "I never thought I'd see this."

Grace threw her a questioning glance. "See what?"

"You preparing hot dogs. Isn't junk food one of the seven deadly sins in your mother's book?"

"It's my mother's book, not mine," Grace said with a stubborn tilt of her chin. "If she prefers not to eat hot dogs, that's fine with me, but the world won't end because I have one every once in a while." Her lips curled into a smile. "Or two."

Jill had never thought she'd hear that either. For a lot of years, Grace hadn't questioned her mother's advice when it came to her career, and that included what she could and couldn't eat. She walked over and gave her friend a hug. "Lauren is definitely good for you. By the way, where is Wonder Woman? I thought she's responsible for cooking the hot dogs?"

"Change of plans. She'll be back in a minute." Grace put down the grilling tongs and headed inside, to the tiny kitchen.

Jill whistled for Tramp to follow her inside.

He hesitated, apparently reluctant to leave his place in front of the grill but then trotted after her.

"That wasn't what I asked," Jill said.

For several moments, Grace continued to prepare the bowls of condiments as if she hadn't heard her. Finally, she turned, leaned against the counter, and examined her fingernails. "She's picking up our other guest."

"Other guest?" Jill echoed. As far as she knew, Grace never invited anyone but Lauren and her over. The cottage up in the Santa Monica Mountains was her hideaway from the world and the paparazzi. "Who is it?"

"You'll see," Grace said, bit into a pickle, and chewed noisily.

"Why do I have this feeling you have something evil planned?"

"Because you've worked in Hollywood for too long and became paranoid," Grace answered. She pressed bowls of relish and onions into Jill's hands. "Here. Take this outside while I get the ketchup and the mustard."

Jill took the bowls and whistled for Tramp to follow her back to the patio. "Come on, boy. If that other guest is someone I don't like, you can bite him or her."

Grace laughed. "Right. The only way Tramp would ever hurt anyone is by licking them to death."

"Hey, he can be pretty scary. Remember how you and Lauren climbed the wall surrounding my house and clung to the ivy, afraid that Tramp would get to you?" The memory of that evening made her chuckle, even though her symptoms had flared that day.

Grace groaned. "Don't remind me. I ruined my best pair of shoes. Since I made that kind of sacrifice for you, you can cope with an additional guest joining us for one night. Now get those condiments outside before I eat all the pickles."

"All right, all right, slave driver. Tramp, come on."

Tramp didn't have to be told twice. He followed Jill outside to where the hot dogs were.

Ugh. Crash grabbed hold of the passenger seat. Lauren hadn't been kidding. The dirt path was bumpy, steep, and winding.

Lauren navigated it without problems, as if she had done it a thousand times before.

Just when it looked as if the dirt path would end in the middle of nowhere, the car climbed up an incline, and a lone home lay in front of them.

Instead of the luxury villa Crash had expected, it was a small, one-story house set among a grove of trees that protected it from view.

"Not what you expected?" Lauren asked with a grin.

"Uh…"

Lauren laughed. "Come on. You can admit it. I sure as hell expected something else too when Grace took me to her cottage for the first time."

When they got out, Crash noticed that there were two cars in the driveway. One was a SUV and the other Jill's Beetle convertible.

Her steps faltered. So Jill really was here, as she had half hoped, half feared. Suddenly, she was no longer sure this had been such a good idea.

Lauren opened the door, turned toward her, and gave her a questioning look. "Is everything okay? The drive up didn't make you seasick, did it?"

"No. I'm fine. I just… Does Jill know you invited me to dinner?"

"I assume Grace told her by now."

Which meant she hadn't known. Not a good situation. Didn't they know Jill hated being taken by surprise, leaving her vulnerable? "Lauren, I'm really not sure this is a good idea."

"What? Having hot dogs with a bunch of movie people? Nonsense. Like I keep telling Grace, having junk food every once in a while won't kill you."

Crash had a feeling Lauren knew she wasn't talking about the hot dogs, but she couldn't bust Lauren's innocent act without explaining what was going on between Jill and her. Even if she'd been willing to violate their privacy, she wasn't sure she could explain. No, that was for Jill and her to figure out first.

Damn. She should have driven herself. Now she was stuck here until Lauren decided it was time to leave. Reluctantly, she followed Lauren into the cottage.

If she had expected expensive designer furniture, she would have been wrong again. A rocking chair that looked as if it had seen better days was tucked into one corner of the room. A pockmarked oak coffee table and a worn leather couch faced a wood-burning fireplace. There was no bed anywhere, but a ladder led up to a loft. A glass door offered a view of a patio surrounded by trees and bushes.

This is nice. Crash hadn't known something like this existed just half an hour outside of LA.

Grace turned away from the fridge in the kitchenette that took up one wall of the cottage, a bottle of ketchup in her hand. "Good timing. The hot dogs should be just about ready. Welcome."

"Thanks for having me." Crash held out the six-pack of beer Lauren had requested, then the six-pack of nonalcoholic beer she'd brought, just in case. According to her research, most people with MS didn't do so well with alcohol. While her hostesses tried to make room in the refrigerator, Crash craned her neck. Where was Jill?

Barking came from behind the closed sliding glass door.

"Oh. You have a dog."

Lauren shook her head. "No. It's Jill's."

Jill has a dog? There was still so much she didn't know about her. She hoped Jill would give her a chance to get to know much more than just her body. "Is it…a therapy dog?"

Grace shook her head. "No. I think Jill just wanted some company."

That sounded like Jill. She had decided to live her life alone, without a human companion, so she had gotten a dog instead.

Grace pressed a bowl of shredded cheese into Crash's hands. "Why don't you take this outside and go say hello? We'll be out in a second."

Not one to delay the inevitable, Crash marched to the glass door and peeked out.

At first, she saw neither Jill nor a dog. Then she spied a mid-sized bundle of curly, golden hair sniffing one of the old oak trees surrounding the property. If she wasn't mistaken, it was a labradoodle, a mix between a Labrador and a poodle. She had to grin at Jill's choice of pet.

Then she realized that someone was lying in the hammock tied between two oaks.

Jill.

Her eyes were closed, and she looked as relaxed as Crash had ever seen her.

Well, she looked pretty relaxed after… Thoughts of their night in San Francisco made her smile. *Focus!* She slid back the glass door and stepped outside onto the stone patio.

The air smelled of sagebrush and hot dogs. The city noise was absent; only the chirping of crickets and bird song drifted over.

The dog cocked its head and then whirled around and rushed over. Its fluffy tail was wagging, so Crash wasn't worried.

"Tramp!" Jill called sharply. "Come here!"

The labradoodle stopped abruptly. After a longing glance toward Crash, he turned and ran to Jill's side.

Jill put one foot on the ground. She struggled for a moment to make it safely out of the hammock.

All of Crash's instincts urged her to hurry over and help her, but she held herself back, knowing Jill wouldn't want to be rescued like a turtle lying helplessly on its back.

Finally, Jill made it to her feet. "Sorry about that. He's not—" She turned toward the house and only then got a glimpse of Crash.

They stood staring at each other.

Crash clutched the bowl of shredded cheese. "I'm sorry. I thought they told you they invited me."

"No. It seems they forgot. Apparently, I'm not the only one with an occasional lapse in memory," Jill muttered.

"Sorry. They invited me and I—"

"I get it," Jill said. "Any lesbian between eighteen and eighty would give her right arm to have dinner with Grace Durand, so how could you say no?"

Crash looked her in the eyes. She wanted her to know how much she meant what she was about to say, "I'm not here because of Grace. I was kinda hoping you'd be here."

Jill tightly folded her arms across her chest, as if warding off the impact of Crash's words. "I'm here," she said but didn't sound happy about it.

In the silence between them, the dog's whining sounded overly loud.

Well, at least someone was eager to greet her. "Do you…want me to leave?" Not that she could, even if she wanted, since she didn't have her car. But this was about so much more than just staying for hot dogs.

"No," Jill said. "We're both adults. Just because we don't want a relationship doesn't mean we can't share a meal every now and then. I mean, we've had lunch together on the set a dozen times, so there's nothing to it, right?"

Was it really that easy for her? Or was she trying to convince herself as much as Crash? "Right," Crash said with some hesitation.

The glass door, which Crash had closed behind her, slid open. Their hostesses joined them on the patio and put a basket of buns on the table.

Jill walked over and gripped Grace's elbow. "Let me help you get the drinks."

"It's all right," Grace said. "You sit and relax. Lauren can help me."

"No. I'll help. Lauren can stay out here, get the hot dogs off the grill, and entertain your surprise guest." Jill nearly dragged her back inside.

Tramp tried to follow, but he wasn't fast enough. The door slid closed before his nose, so he instead took the opportunity to greet Crash.

While petting him with one hand, Crash peered into the cottage. God, she would pay good money to hear what was spoken inside.

"What the hell are you doing?" Jill asked as soon as the glass door clicked shut.

Slowly, Grace turned around and gave her a doe-eyed look of innocence. "Doing?"

But Jill had been in two movies with Grace, so she knew when her friend was acting. "You know exactly what I mean."

"I'm just having dinner with friends."

"Friends? Since when is Crash your friend? You don't even know her!"

"That's how you get to know people and make new friends—by inviting them to dinner."

"Cut the bullshit, Grace!" Jill realized she was shouting and snapped her mouth shut. She peeked toward the patio, hoping Crash hadn't heard her, and lowered her voice. "You really expect me to believe you invited her and me over at the same time, without any ulterior motives?"

Grace threw her hands up. "Okay. I admit it. I had an ulterior motive. I want you to be happy. Is that so wrong?"

Jill's anger deflated like a pierced balloon. She stepped up to Grace and touched her arm. "No. I appreciate it. If circumstances were different…" She trailed off. It was better not to let herself think about it. "I'm not in a position where I can look for happiness in a relationship, so please cut out the matchmaking."

"Why not?" Grace asked with a hint of defiance.

"You know why. Don't make me say it." A headache formed behind her temples, so she reached up to massage them.

"You really want to stay alone for the rest of your life, just because you have MS?"

Jill's anger sparked alive again. "Just?" she echoed. "I'd think that's reason enough!"

"That's not what I meant. I just…I really think you should reconsider and give yourself a chance to see where this is going."

"I already know where this is going! Haven't you seen what MS can do to people?"

Grace regarded her with a serious expression. "Do you honestly think Crash would lose interest in you if you had a relapse? Like you said, I don't really know her, but I didn't get the impression that she's so fickle."

"It has nothing to do with being fickle," Jill said, instantly feeling the need to defend Crash. "It's only human. How desirable do you think she would still find me if she had to change the sheets because I had an accident during sex?"

"Maybe you should ask her that, not me," Grace said quietly.

Jill shook her head. "I don't need to have that discussion with her. I've already made my decision. Look at her." She gestured toward the sliding door.

On the other side of the glass, Crash was throwing a tennis ball for Tramp. The muscles of her arm rippled beneath her short-sleeved blouse, and the breeze outside tousled her short hair.

As if sensing her attention, Crash looked over, and their gazes met.

Jill turned away. "Do you really think a woman like her should have to live with MS? What if it were you? Would you want Lauren to live like that?"

Grace stared at the tiled floor of the kitchenette. "No," she whispered. "I wouldn't want that for her. But—"

Jill cut her off with a wave of her hand. "No buts. Crash and I agreed that it would be just a one-night stand. We're both not interested in more. Please respect my wishes and just leave it at that."

A sigh ruffled the golden-blonde strand of hair that had fallen onto Grace's forehead. "All right. If that's what you want…"

"That's what I want." Jill squared her shoulders and forced a slight smile onto her face. "Well, that and a beer, but since you don't keep alcohol in the house and I couldn't have one anyway, I'll settle for you skipping the matchmaking."

"Well, actually…" Grace opened the refrigerator and took out several bottles of beer. She pressed one into Jill's hands. "Here. It's nonalcoholic. The woman who's not interested in you brought it—and I don't think it's because she knows I don't drink."

"Grace," Jill said in a warning tone.

"Okay, okay. I'm shutting up now."

Jill pressed the cool bottle to her forehead and closed her eyes for a moment before following her back to the patio. "Thanks."

"Oh, God, no." Jill quickly pulled her plate away when Grace wanted to put another piece of cheesecake on it. "I'm about to explode as it is."

She leaned back in her chair, sipped her second nonalcoholic beer, and watched the sun set over the canyon. Grace's hideaway up in the mountains was almost ridiculously romantic, and Crash's closeness didn't help.

With all of them squeezed around the small patio table, Crash's leg brushed hers whenever one of them moved. Every time it happened, the tingle shooting through her entire body became harder to ignore—and so did the fact of how well Crash fit in with her friends.

"How about you, Crash?" Grace slid the leftover piece of cheesecake toward Crash. "You do stunts for a living. That must burn calories like crazy. You can take a second piece of cake."

"No, thanks." Crash covered her plate with her hands so Grace couldn't deposit the piece of cheesecake on it. "If I want to get into Jill's drawers and dresses on Monday, I really shouldn't."

Lauren burst out laughing.

Jill nearly spat a mouthful of beer across the table. Heat crept up her neck. She threw a crumpled-up napkin at Lauren. "Jeez, Lauren. She didn't mean it like that. All she meant is that she needs to be able to wear the same costumes that I do."

Crash shook her head at Lauren. A faint hint of red suffused her cheeks too. "What is it with you writers and your dirty minds?"

"Me?" Lauren touched her own chest.

"Yeah, you," Crash and Jill said in unison.

Grace deposited the last piece of cheesecake on Lauren's plate. "Here, eat. You're the only one who works behind the camera, so you can afford the extra calories."

One of Lauren's eyebrows arched up over the rim of her glasses. "Are you saying it doesn't matter how I look?"

"Oh, it matters," Grace said, her voice gone husky.

"They're still in that can't-keep-their-hands-off-each-other phase," Jill stage-whispered to Crash. She was glad for her friends, really, but at the same time, she couldn't help envying them for what they had.

Lauren threw the crumpled-up napkin back at Jill before digging into the piece of cheesecake.

"I know how they feel," Crash whispered, her voice pitched so low that only Jill could hear.

The heat in her gaze made Jill's cheeks flame, and Crash's breath bathing her ear caused a full-body tingle, but she ignored that, too, and sent Crash a warning gaze. They had agreed to go back to being just friends, and there was no renegotiating on that.

"So," Grace said, "how did things go in San Francisco? You've been back for a week already, but neither of you told me much so far."

In an attempt not to peek in Crash's direction, Jill looked down and pretended to check if Tramp was still sleeping beneath the table. She realized the dog had moved a little so that his head now rested on Crash's shoe. *Figures. Not even my dog can resist her.*

"Not much to tell," Jill said as matter-of-factly as she could. "Just business as usual." It was a message to Crash, but she didn't turn her head to look at her and see if it had been understood.

"Oh, yeah," Crash said. "We had to make the most of our time there, so we were shooting from sunup to sundown."

Make the most of our time there... Was it just her imagination, or was there a seductive timbre in Crash's voice? She shivered as she remembered how they'd made the most of their time in her hotel room. In the past, she had always enjoyed a healthy sex life, but then the MS had messed with her self-esteem and her libido. She'd assumed that part of her life was over for good, but with Crash, a lack of libido had definitely not been a problem. She mentally shook her head at herself. *Just because you could keep up with her for a few hours doesn't mean you could always make her happy in and out of bed.*

Lauren looked up from her cake and glanced over at Crash. "I heard you had to repeat that crowd shot down at the ferry building five times."

"Six, actually." Crash groaned. "That's the thing when you work with extras. They're not trained actors or stunt people, so one of them kept messing up. I was soaking wet for most of the day."

God! Jill white-knuckled her fork. *Stop with the double entendres already!*

"Wardrobe ended up having to dry-blow my costume because they ran out of dry ones," Crash added.

"Oh, yeah, extras... Tell me about it. I think some directors would rather work with trained chimpanzees than with extras." Grace gestured over at Jill.

"Remember when we were shooting *Ava's Heart* and the prop department kept having to replace things?"

Jill needed a moment to get her mind out of the gutter and back to the topic at hand. "It turned out that one of the extras was stealing our props to take home as souvenirs," she explained and allowed herself to look over at Crash, who was listening with rapt attention, her intense gaze resting on Jill. "We only caught him when he tried to steal the scarecrow."

"What?" Laughing, Crash shook her head. "Who would steal a scarecrow?"

"Extras," they all said at the same time and shared a laugh.

Jill couldn't look away from Crash. She liked the way she laughed—and the way she looked while the sunset dipped her strong features in bronze. *Oh, cut out the romantic bullshit!*

She was dangerously emotional tonight, so it was better to leave before she did something stupid. She gestured at the horizon, where only a glowing band of orange remained. The canyon below was already dipped in shadows and growing darker by the minute so that she couldn't make out the stands of chaparral and sage anymore. "I think I'd better head out now, guys. I don't want to drive down the dirt path in the dark."

Lauren swallowed the last bite of cheesecake and traded long glances with Grace. "Um, would you mind driving Crash home, Jill? That would save me the trip to the city and back."

"You'll stay the night?" Grace beamed at her. "I thought you wanted to head back to your apartment to get some writing done tomorrow morning?"

Lauren grinned. "I changed my mind. If that's okay with you."

"Okay? That would be great!" Grace sent Jill a pleading gaze. "Do you mind? It would be wonderful to have a little extra time with Lauren."

Now they both looked at Jill expectantly.

Oh, very subtle, guys. But there was no way out. Even if Crash could get a cabbie to get her up here, Grace wouldn't want a stranger coming to the cottage. She unclenched her teeth and said, "I don't mind. Come on, Crash."

They got up and went inside, followed by Grace and Lauren. Tramp woke and bustled after them, excited at the sound of Jill's jingling car keys, because he knew that meant they were about to go for a ride.

Jill hugged first Lauren, then Grace. "You're putting me in an impossible situation," she whispered into Grace's ear. "If you keep this up, I'll call your mother and tell her what you had for dinner."

"Hey, I had nothing to do with this," Grace whispered back. "It was Lauren's idea."

"I didn't see you objecting."

"Of course not. With one or both of us shooting on location half of the time, we don't get to spend enough time with each other."

Jill sighed. At least one of them wouldn't have to spend the night alone.

Crash slid into the passenger seat of the Beetle, while Jill got Tramp secured in the backseat with some kind of dog harness and then climbed behind the wheel.

When she turned the key in the ignition, an upbeat pop song blasted through the car's speakers. "Sorry," Jill said and turned down the volume.

Crash could imagine her singing along to the songs on the radio on the drive up, the top of the convertible down and the wind in her hair. The mental image made her smile.

"What?" Jill asked.

Still smiling, Crash said, "Nothing."

"Do you want the top up or down?" Jill asked.

Temperatures had dropped after sunset, but with that earlier image of Jill driving carefree, Crash just couldn't resist. "Down, if you don't mind."

Jill pressed a button, which made the Beetle's soft-top fold back into the rear of the car. Then she guided the car down the narrow dirt path.

Crash watched the confident way Jill gripped the steering wheel. She remembered how those hands had mapped her body with the same confidence. "Nice."

"Thanks. Having a convertible is the one Hollywood-style luxury I allow myself, even if it's not exactly a sports car."

"I wasn't talking about the car. I meant your driving."

"Oh. Thanks. Well, I spend a lot of time at the cottage, so I know every bend and every stone in the dirt path."

It was the perfect opening to find out more about Jill and her friendship with Grace. Admittedly, Crash was curious. She wanted to ask if Jill and Grace had ever been a couple or slept together, but this might be her only opportunity to talk to Jill alone, away from the set, so she didn't want to waste it talking about Grace.

Okay. Buck up. It's now or never. She searched for the right words that wouldn't make Jill clam up immediately. Should she come right out and ask for a date? But that hadn't gone down so well before. Maybe she should ask her to see a movie with her, spend some time together, just as friends, and then…

Before she could decide on the best strategy, Jill glanced over and said, "I'm sorry my friends put us in an awkward situation by trying to set us up. They weren't exactly subtle about it, were they?"

"No need to apologize," Crash said. She opened her mouth to add more, but Jill was faster, as if she sensed what Crash had been about to say and didn't want to give her the chance to voice her thoughts.

"You know how it is. Whenever a woman is newly in love, she's suddenly on a mission to help all of her friends find their soul mates too."

Crash gave a noncommittal hum.

"Your friends aren't like that?" Jill asked.

"God, no. Most of my friends are stuntmen. Not exactly the settling-down types. I wasn't for the last two years either. After my last girlfriend cheated on me, I had enough of relationships for a while."

Jill reached out with her right hand as if she wanted to put it on Crash's leg but then pulled it back at the last moment. "I'm sorry that happened to you. She didn't deserve you."

"Yeah. But now…" Crash took a deep breath and held it for a moment. "I think I'm ready for something new. It doesn't need to be a white-picket-fence kind of commitment, but I want more than a one-night stand. And I want it with you."

A pained-sounding groan escaped Jill. "Crash…"

"Please, hear me out," Crash said, afraid of what Jill would say if she let her speak. "Maybe your friends are right. We could be good together. I think you can feel it too. Maybe we should give dating a shot." Her heart in her throat, she glanced over at Jill.

"We said that it would be just a purely physical one-time thing, with no expectations beyond that one night," Jill said. She kept her face expressionless, but her voice vibrated with emotion, revealing that there was a lot going on inside of her.

"You were the one who said that," Crash stated quietly.

"And you agreed to it."

Crash sighed. "Yeah. I did. But now I have a hard time…" She trailed off, not wanting to make things any harder on them both by voicing her feelings, which Jill might not even return.

Jill whispered something, but her voice was so low that Crash couldn't understand her.

Had that been a "me too," or was that just wishful thinking? "What did you say?"

"Nothing."

They reached a less curvy part of the road, and Jill drove faster, making the wind whip around them. Conveniently, it also made conversation impossible if they didn't want to shout at each other. In the backseat, Tramp stuck his nose outside, obviously enjoying the way the wind ruffled his thick fur.

Crash leaned against the passenger's side door and turned a little in the passenger seat so she could watch her. "Jill…"

Jill kept her gaze on the road, pretending she hadn't heard her over the wind.

The very last traces of sunset reflected off Jill's copper hair, making it glow as it trailed on the wind. The dim lights from the dashboard illuminated her features.

Crash wanted so much to reach out and brush a wind-whipped strand of hair out of her face, but she knew it wouldn't be welcome, so she shoved her hands beneath her thighs.

Jill slowed the car a little and, keeping her gaze on the road, leaned toward Crash.

Crash's heartbeat sped up. *What is she…?*

Their shoulders brushed as Jill opened the glove box and rummaged through it.

Warmth flowed through Crash's body, chasing off the slight chill from the night air.

Finally, Jill found what she was looking for—a hair band, apparently—and retreated back to her side of the car, leaving Crash's shoulder feeling cold. Jill tried to pull her hair back into a ponytail with one hand and grunted in frustration when she couldn't manage.

"Let me," Crash said.

"I can manage."

"I know you can, but you don't have to." Not waiting for a reply, Crash reached over and took the hair band from her. She really just meant to help Jill tie her hair back, but when her fingers sifted through the smooth strands and brushed the soft skin of her neck, all thoughts of hair bands went right out the window.

Crash lifted Jill's hair with one hand, but instead of gathering it into a ponytail, she traced the curve of her nape with her slightly callused fingertips.

The touch sent a shiver through Jill's body, all the way down to the tip of her toes. But more than that, the tender gesture made her heart clench. She nearly swerved into the left lane. "Jesus, Crash, stop it before we have an accident."

"Sorry," Crash said, but when Jill glanced over at her, Crash didn't look as if she regretted a thing. She used both of her hands to wrap the hair band twice around a slightly messy ponytail.

"Thanks," Jill said.

Crash gave a nod, and they spent the rest of the drive to Los Feliz in silence.

Jill double-parked and turned off the engine.

They sat in the quiet car for a minute. Crash seemed reluctant to get out. Truth be told, Jill didn't want to let her go either, but what was there left to say? She couldn't give her what she wanted.

Tramp stuck his nose through the gap between the seats, probably wondering what they were doing.

Yeah. What are you doing? Send her away once and for all. You already delayed it much longer than is good for either of you.

But Jill didn't. She just sat and looked at Crash.

"Do you want to come up for a cup of coffee?" Crash finally asked.

Oh, no. Coming inside with Crash was a bad idea. "I never drink coffee this late in the day, or it'll keep me up all night."

"I have tea too," Crash said with an inviting smile. "We could sit down and talk about it. About...us."

Jill firmly shook her head. "I told you there is no us. No amount of talk will change that I have MS. That's just a fact that we both have to accept."

"I do, but why does it have to mean that you and I can't even go out on a date?"

For a moment, Jill couldn't think of a reason. *Yeah, why? Why can't we just date?* a voice in her head whispered. She silenced it immediately. "Dating in a business like ours is difficult enough, but dating someone with MS... I can't even predict how I'll feel tomorrow morning, let alone next week or next month. That makes planning a date more than difficult."

Crash grinned. "No problem. Difficult is my middle name."

"You don't have a middle name."

Now completely serious, Crash looked at her. "Don't you think I'd be willing to adjust if you don't feel up to going out? So what if we watch a movie at home instead of going to a movie theater?"

"That's just it. You shouldn't have to adjust because of me. That's what people in a relationship do, and that's out of the question for me."

"I don't mind adj—"

"But I do. If you give and I take all the time, we would never be equal."

Crash quirked an eyebrow at her, either unable or unwilling to understand. "Staying home to watch a movie would make us unequal?"

"Maybe not at first. But what if we go on more dates?"

Crash grinned. "That's the idea. I hope you wouldn't run away screaming after the first one."

"So we would date...and sleep together?" Jill shook her head. "Do you know how easy it would be to slip into a relationship?" *Much too easy with Crash.*

"We'll cross that bridge when we come to it," Crash said. "For now, I'm proposing a date, not marriage."

It was tempting, so tempting. "You can afford to live your life like that, but I can't. I can't just ignore what might happen down the road. What if at one point the MS affects my libido? Are you willing to give up sex? What if I have a relapse while you are auditioning for a job? Would you just walk away from a once-in-a-lifetime career opportunity?"

Crash swallowed. She looked toward her apartment complex as if she wished herself there.

Jill clenched her teeth. *See?* That was exactly why she had to clear this up once and for all. She didn't want Crash to have to look for a way out in the future.

But instead of getting out, Crash turned back toward her. "I don't pretend to have all the answers either. But why can't we try to figure them out together?"

"Because it's not what I want," Jill said, making her voice firm. Maybe if she said it out loud often enough, she'd believe it herself. "I have my answers already."

Crash ran both hands through her wind-blown hair. "I don't think telling you again how stubborn you are would do any good, would it?"

A tiny smile darted across Jill's face. "No."

Crash nodded a few times, as if to herself, and then reached for the door handle. "Thanks for the ride. Guess I'll see you on Monday, then."

"Yes. See you Monday."

Her hand still on the door, Crash looked back over her shoulder. Her searching gaze rested on Jill's face for several seconds before she opened the door and climbed out. "Good night."

"Good night."

After another moment of hesitation, Crash shut the door and turned toward the house.

Sudden panic rose in Jill as she watched her walk away. She couldn't date Crash or start a relationship with her, but she didn't want to let her go either. Not like this. "Wait," Jill called before she could talk herself out of it.

With a hopeful grin, Crash whirled, jogged back, and jumped into the passenger seat of the convertible without opening the door, making Tramp bark and strain against his harness. "You called?"

"Showoff," Jill muttered but couldn't suppress a smile.

"Did you call me back just to insult me?" Crash asked, a hint of humor lacing her voice. But there was also something else—hope.

A hope that Jill couldn't fulfill, but neither did she want to let her go. "No, of course not. I...I just wanted... I wanted..." Oh, to hell with it. One thing she wanted was clear and uncomplicated, so she focused on that. She leaned across the middle console, grabbed a handful of Crash's shirt, and pulled her closer. Then her lips were on Crash's. She kissed her hard and hungry, letting the kiss say what she couldn't and allowing herself to get lost in the rush of sensations. One of her hands stroked up Crash's arm and came to rest on her shoulder, encountering firm muscles.

Crash moaned and clasped the back of Jill's head to bring her even closer. Her fingers set off a full-body tingle as they slid into her hair and pulled out the hair band.

God. Good thing she was already sitting down. Amazing what Crash could do to her with a simple kiss.

Finally, when their positions became too uncomfortable, they broke the kiss.

"Does that mean…?" Crash whispered. She trailed her fingers down the side of Jill's neck, but when they reached the edge of Jill's shirt, she didn't slide them farther down. She paused to wait for Jill's reply.

Jill shook her head. "I had to give up a lot since I've been diagnosed. But I realized that sex isn't something I want to give up."

"You don't have to." Crash's eyes smoldered with heat. One corner of her mouth quirked up into a grin. "I'm volunteering." She bent her head to kiss Jill again.

Quickly, Jill stopped her with one hand pressed to Crash's shoulder. If she was going to do this, she had to make one thing very clear. "But sex is all you'd volunteer for. The it's-a-one-time-thing rule is the only one I'm willing to break."

"So you still don't want a commitment. No declarations of love. No promises of a happily-ever-after. No flowers, no dates, no endearments." Crash rubbed that sexy dimple in her chin as if thinking about the offer, but Jill wasn't sure what was going on in her head.

"Exactly. All I can offer you is something physical."

"And friendship," Crash supplied.

"That too. But if you're the love-at-first-orgasm type, I'd rather not…"

"Then I'd already be head over heels," Crash said. "Because you made me come pretty hard that night."

"Three times," Jill couldn't help adding. Jeez, when had she reverted back to an adolescent who boasted about her sexual prowess?

"Showoff," Crash said, just as Jill had earlier.

They grinned at each other, and some of the tension receded.

"Listen," Jill said after a while. "I think we work really well together—on set and in the bedroom. But that's all it can ever be. This…arrangement will last only as long as we're shooting together. Once we wrap up the movie, I want us to be able to just walk away with no heartbreak. If you can't do that…"

Crash's smile looked a little forced, but she kept her tone light as she said, "Hey, I'm a stuntwoman. We learn to roll with the punches. If a strictly physical thing is all you can give me, I can live with it."

Jill bit her lip. She didn't want to flatter herself by asking Crash if she was sure. Instead, she kissed her again.

When the kiss ended, they were both breathless.

"I know you don't drink coffee in the evening, but how about we find some other ways to keep you up all night?" Crash asked, her voice husky.

Jill nodded and blindly pressed the button that would put up the car's soft-top, setting off another round of barking from Tramp.

They had to drive around the block twice before they spotted a parking space on the street, and then they walked back, giving Tramp the chance to sniff and water a few trees.

Jill's excitement grew with every step, along with her nervousness. *Calm down. You already slept with her once. No big deal. Just stop thinking and analyzing it to death.*

Crash reached for her hand as if sensing Jill's conflicting feelings. She indicated their entwined fingers with a nod of her head. "Is this okay? I mean…"

"It's fine." Jill squeezed Crash's hand and let herself be pulled inside and up the stairs.

Crash unlocked the door to her studio apartment. "Come on in." She kicked the door closed behind them with her heel and took a moment to set a bowl of water on the floor for Tramp.

With the dog distracted, she pressed Jill against the countertop in the kitchenette and kissed her.

The pressure of Crash's breasts against her own nearly made Jill sink onto the kitchen tiles. "Mmh, I… God… I like your method of keeping me up much better than caffeine," she gasped out between teasing nips and kisses. She slid her hands down Crash's muscular back and to her trim hips. Oh, she felt so good.

Crash kissed a hot path up Jill's neck and nipped at her earlobe while she moved her backward across the room. Her warm breath bathed Jill's ear, making shivers of excitement rush through her, as Crash whispered into her ear, "Good thing I didn't bother closing my sofa bed back up into a couch this morning."

Just as Crash pulled the shirt over Jill's head and guided her down onto the sofa bed, a cold muzzle, dripping with water, touched Jill's bare skin. She let out a startled shriek. "Tramp! Cut it out! This isn't playtime, dammit—at least not for you."

Tramp barked at her in reply, his tail wagging wildly.

Crash collapsed onto the sofa bed next to her and let out a frustrated groan. After a second she started laughing.

Well, at least she was being a good sport about it. Jill sent her a grateful look.

Tramp tried to jump on the bed with them.

"Oh, no, you don't. Tramp, off!" Jill pulled him back by his collar. "Is there anywhere we can make him more comfortable? Somewhere away from the bed."

"How about the kitchen?" Crash suggested.

They got up and led an excited Tramp, who was jumping and yipping, apparently thinking playtime would continue, over to the kitchen area. A high breakfast counter with two bar stools separated the kitchen from the main room. Crash took a blanket out of her closet, and Jill got him settled in the kitchen, blocking him in with two of the bar stools. She stayed with him for a few minutes, calming him down with soothing scratches to his ears, then got up. "Stay," she said firmly and pointed to his improvised dog bed. "Quiet."

Tramp whined when they washed their hands at the sink and then walked away, leaving him behind.

"No, Tramp. Quiet," Jill repeated.

He fell silent. A deep sigh drifted over as he settled down.

Jill and Crash looked at each other and exhaled at the same time.

Crash reached for her and pulled her back to the sofa bed. "Finally. The kid's in bed," she said with a grin. "Now, where were we?"

Slipping her hands beneath Crash's T-shirt and sliding it up, Jill murmured, "I believe," she bent and pressed a kiss to Crash's flat belly, "we were right here."

Then they both stopped talking as they sank back onto the sofa bed.

CHAPTER 13

CRASH WOKE AT SIX, AS she usually did. Unlike most days, she wasn't eager to get up and go for a run. The warm body behind her felt too good. Jill's front fit against her back as if they were two parts of one piece, molded for each other.

Now you've gone crazy. You agreed to keep it just physical, remember?

Carefully, she turned and watched Jill sleep. She reached out and pushed back a strand of copper hair before it could tickle Jill's nose.

Jill slept on, undisturbed.

God, she looks exhausted. No wonder. She hadn't kept Jill up all night, but she'd come close. They'd both been just as insatiable as the first time, back in San Francisco, and it had been just as good.

At least physically. She sensed that they'd both held something back. She tried to tell herself it didn't matter. It had been the norm for the past two years, when she'd stuck to one-night stands and short flings. So what if she had one more?

But Jill was not just another woman in a string of meaningless conquests. Yes, Crash had once again agreed to Jill's rules, but that didn't stop her from hoping that she'd win Jill over to the idea of dating. Just dating, not a lifetime commitment. Crash wasn't ready for that either, but a date she could handle.

Maybe Jill just needed a little time to come to the same conclusion.

What if time won't change a thing? she wondered.

Well, she would survive. It wasn't as if she was hopelessly in love with Jill, right?

Right. Resolutely, she forced herself to roll away from Jill's warmth and out of bed.

As soon as she started to move away, Jill let out an irritated groan. Her hands slid over the sheet as if looking for Crash.

Aww. How cute. She's missing me already. Crash grinned down at her, then called herself an idiot, and forced herself to walk away from the bed and the sleeping woman. Maybe a run would help her clear her head.

A cool touch to the inside of her wrist woke Jill. "Oh God, no," she mumbled, still half asleep. "Not again. I really can't, or I won't be able to walk on Monday."

Her spirit was more than willing, but her body was simply exhausted and sore in ways that weren't entirely unpleasant.

When Crash didn't answer, Jill opened one eye. Bright sunlight streamed in through the balcony doors, and she blinked a few times before realizing it hadn't been Crash that had woken her.

Instead of looking into Crash's passion-clouded blue eyes, she stared into a pair of brown ones.

Tramp nosed her bare forearm again.

Oh no. The poor guy was probably close to exploding. Thank God she'd at least fed him before heading over to Grace's cottage last night.

A quick glance over her shoulder confirmed that the spot next to her was empty. She tried not to be hurt that Crash had just gotten out of bed while she'd been asleep.

This is what you wanted, remember? Just a physical thing. No pillow talk on the morning after required.

She fisted the pillow beneath her head, which smelled of Crash and made her want to burrow deeper. With a grunt of frustration, she shoved it away.

Just when she was about to try out how steady her legs were, the door to what Jill assumed was the bathroom opened and Crash stepped out, fully dressed.

For a moment, Jill felt very naked in comparison. Well, she *was* naked, since she had fallen asleep after making love last night. She wrestled the impulse to pull the sheet higher up her body. *Don't be ridiculous. She saw every inch of you already. Several times.*

But the way Crash gazed down at her made her feel as if she saw so much more than just her body.

In a tank top and a pair of cut-off sweatpants, Crash walked over to the bed. Her hair was damp and pushed back from her face, revealing her strong features.

Jill felt an almost painful tug in her belly.

"Good morning," Crash said with a smile and settled onto the sofa bed next to Jill, close but not quite touching.

Her closeness instantly made Jill's body react, tired as it was. She struggled against the urge to touch the damp strands clinging to Crash's neck. *You can't possibly want more. Get out of bed. Now.*

But she didn't move. "Good morning. Wow. I must have been really out of it. I didn't hear you get up."

"Yeah. You were. Seems we really tired you out," Crash said with a small grin. "You can sleep a little longer if you want. It's Sunday, after all."

Jill shook her head energetically, not sure whom she wanted to convince—Crash or herself. "Tramp needs to go outside."

"I doubt it. I took him with me when I went for my run." Crash pointed to the yoga mat, where Tramp now lay, looking as if Jill wasn't the only one Crash had powered out. "I hope that was okay."

"You went for a run?" Jill echoed. How on earth could Crash go for a run after a night like the last one, when Jill wasn't even sure she could walk? She reached over and ran her hands along Crash's limbs.

Crash chuckled but held still and let Jill examine her. "What are you doing?"

"Looking for your hidden cyborg technology. You can't be human." Instead of artificial joints or super-human muscles, her fingers encountered warm skin beneath the tank top. "Hmm. Maybe I should stay in bed a little longer after all."

Crash pulled the tank top up over her head and rolled on top of her. "Maybe you should."

For once, it wasn't the little electric shocks zapping through her feet that woke Jill; it was a soft movement beneath her head. She opened her eyes and blinked into the bright late-morning light. It took her a moment to realize she'd fallen back asleep.

She settled back with her head again resting on Crash's chest, which was lifting and falling in a steady rhythm. Their legs were tangled, and one of her arms was wrapped around Crash's middle. Both of Crash's arms were holding her close, her fingers splayed across Jill's back as if trying to achieve maximum contact. Her warmth and scent surrounded Jill, creating a bubble of comfort.

For a few moments, Jill imagined waking up in Crash's arms every morning for the rest of her life.

Impossible. She mentally shook her head at herself. But for the first time there was another voice piping up in her mind. *Why shouldn't it be possible?*

She hadn't had a relapse in about a year, and her last MRI hadn't shown any new lesions. Sure, her symptoms flared every now and then, but so far, they were just minor annoyances, nothing major that put her into the hospital or into a wheelchair. She did have a few limitations, but for the most part, she could live her life the way she wanted. Maybe she was one of the lucky ones and her MS would turn out a very mild, stable form. Could she have a relationship of some kind after all, maybe just date casually, as Crash had suggested? Was it possible to keep the MS and a relationship separate, so she wouldn't end up a burden to her partner?

She tightened her hold on Crash, afraid to let herself hope. But as much as she tried to shut them out, Crash's words kept echoing through her head. *You're still you. You're still a great actress and a wonderful woman, and nothing, not even the MS, can change that.* Somehow, those words had cracked open a door that Jill had thought closed forever.

"Hmm, good morning…again." Crash's voice rumbled through her. She trailed her hand over Jill's hip.

Almost without her conscious will, Jill snuggled closer, allowing herself to enjoy the caress.

But instead of sliding her hand down to cup Jill's ass, Crash paused. A tiny wrinkle formed between her brows. She gently circled a tender spot on the back of Jill's hip with the tip of her index finger. "What's this?"

Jill craned her neck to see what she meant. When she realized that Crash was pointing at one of last week's injection sites, where a red spot the size of a quarter had formed, she stiffened. So much for being able to have a relationship without MS. "It's nothing." She slipped out of bed and reached for her clothes, which had ended up on the floor last night.

Crash sat up and watched her with a frown. "Did I say or do—?"

"No. I just have to get going. Tramp needs his breakfast." *And I need the toilet and my damn injection.* Crash's question had been a reminder that she couldn't just spend a lazy Sunday morning in bed with a lover the way most other people could. She put on her panties and her jeans, covering the red spot on her hip, and then wrestled with the closure of her bra. *Shit.* Her fine motor skills weren't the best this morning.

Crash got up and tried to take over the task. "Let me. I'm not just good at taking bras off, you know?" She winked at her.

But Jill didn't want help dressing. She sidestepped Crash's hands, stuffed the bra into the pocket of her jeans, and slipped her T-shirt over her head.

Crash dropped her hands, letting them dangle at her sides. Her gaze tracked Jill as she searched all over the room for her shoes, but she didn't try to approach her again.

Jill bit the inside of her cheek. She hated this sudden tension, but it was a good reminder of why she couldn't allow herself to get in too deep. Finally, she found her shoes beneath the coffee table and slipped them on.

Crash put on a T-shirt and a pair of sweatpants and followed her to the door, where they lingered. "Jill…"

"Shhh. Don't say anything." That was the beauty of a purely physical fling after all—no need to explain herself or to talk about her MS. Jill softly pressed her fingertips to Crash's mouth, then, unable to resist, replaced them with her lips.

Moaning, Crash wrapped both arms around her and pulled her close. Their bodies touched all along their lengths, breast to breast and thigh to thigh.

It took several minutes before Jill could force herself to back away. "See you tomorrow."

"See you," Crash said, leaning against the door as if her knees had gone weak.

With a slight smile, Jill pointed. "You're blocking the door."

"Oh. Sorry." Crash straightened and took a step to the side.

Jill clipped on Tramp's leash and headed out without allowing herself to look back.

CHAPTER 14

JILL DIDN'T SEE MUCH OF Crash the next week, mostly because Floyd had her do reaction shots—close-ups showing her character's emotional reactions to the horrible injuries caused by the earthquake and fires.

No stuntwomen were required for those scenes. Crash's absence from the set gave Jill some much-needed distance, but sometimes, when she had a quiet moment, she also admitted to herself that she missed running lines with Crash or just hanging out with her in the trailer.

When they broke for lunch on Friday, Jill had almost given up hope of seeing her before the weekend. But when she headed for the craft services tent, she heard familiar footsteps from behind.

Her heartbeat picked up. She turned and came face-to-face with Crash.

Instead of a period costume, she wore a pair of faded jeans that fit her like a second skin and made Jill's gaze linger on her athletic legs.

"Hi," they said at the same time, then fell silent.

Crash bobbed up and down on the balls of her feet and pointed at the tent. "Are you heading to lunch?"

Jill nodded, glad that Crash had broken the silence. "Yeah. I'm going to pig out for once. Floyd didn't like that burn-victim scene when he reviewed yesterday's dailies, so he had us do another dozen takes. I need chocolate, or I won't survive this afternoon's reaction shots."

"Ouch. Sounds like an emergency." Crash gave her a commiserating look and held open the flap of the craft services tent for her. Her hand came to rest on the small of Jill's back as she followed her in.

The little gesture felt good. No harm in letting herself enjoy it as long as they both knew it didn't mean they were a couple. Jill smiled and looked back over her shoulder. "Want me to grab a Snickers for you too?"

"No, thanks. I have to do a glass stunt later today, and I don't want to get the sugar jitters. Just some salad for me."

Glass stunt? Jill wondered what that involved. Nothing dangerous, she hoped. Instead of voicing her concern, she forced a grin onto her face. "Can I have your chocolate bar, then?"

"If they don't get to it first." Crash pointed to the front of the tent.

Jill turned and groaned.

It looked as if the entire grip department had descended on the craft services tent. At least a dozen broad-shouldered men were digging into the food as if they hadn't eaten in days.

"Damn. That's against Maggie's rules," Jill muttered.

"Maggie's rules?" Crash gave a slight smile, but it didn't reach her eyes. "Are they anything like your rules of no commitment?"

"No, not exactly. Well, maybe one. When I got my first role in a movie seven years ago, one of the more seasoned actresses took me under her wing. She told me that there are five cardinal rules of survival on every set."

"Ooh, I gotta hear this. So, what are they?"

Distractedly, Jill watched as the grips started decimating the pile of chocolate bars on the table. She hoped there would be at least one left by the time she reached the front of the line. "Well, we just broke rule number one. Always get to the craft services table before the guys from the grip department do."

The grip department wasn't only one of the largest on set, but the grips also worked up quite an appetite by hauling heavy equipment and sandbags all day.

"Good rule," Crash said. "What are the others?"

"Always show up on set at least ten minutes before call time."

"Check. You're always on time. What else?"

"Always turn off your cell phone on set."

"Check." Crash ticked it off on her fingers. "And?"

"Never try to guess your wrap time, or you'll jinx it."

Crash laughed. "Ha! So you're superstitious too! I take it that's also a check?"

Jill shrugged. "Whenever I thought we were going to wrap early, we ended up having to stay late because something went wrong, so I learned to respect Maggie's rule number four."

"Makes sense. So, what's rule number five?" Crash asked.

Finally looking away from the quickly disappearing chocolate, Jill glanced at Crash for a second before lowering her gaze to her fake-dust-covered boots. She wished she'd never mentioned Maggie's rules. "Uh, I think I'll go and try to charm the grips into giving me one of the chocolate bars."

"Not so fast." Crash gently held on to her arm. "You can't leave me without sharing the wisdom of rule number five. Don't force me to tickle it out of you."

The memory of their last tickle match sent shivers up and down Jill's body. She had to clear her throat twice before she could speak. "You wouldn't dare. Not here."

"Oh, you think so? There's not much a stuntwoman wouldn't dare to do," Crash said, a challenging gleam in her eyes.

They had agreed on just a physical thing, so why was it so hard to tell her about rule number five? Jill sighed and said, "Never hook up with anyone on set until the very last week of the shoot."

In the sudden silence between them, the shuffling of Jill's feet appeared to be overly loud.

Crash coughed. "Well, um…" She lowered her voice. "I guess three out of five ain't so bad, right?"

"I guess so." Jill knew she should leave it at that, but instead she found herself reaching out to touch Crash's arm. "Just for the record: I don't regret breaking rule number five."

"No?" Crash's ice-blue eyes searched hers.

"No." It was the truth. When she was with Crash, passion swept away everything else, including worries about her health. For once, her body was a source of pleasure instead of frustration. *But that's not all you like about being with her, is it?* She ignored the thought and held Crash's gaze until the intensity of their eye contact became too much. Glancing away, she added, "But I wish I hadn't ignored rule number one."

Behind them, more grips entered the tent.

"Oh-oh." Crash widened her eyes comically. "Chocolate is now on the list of endangered food items."

"Damn. Now I wish I had a secret stash in my trailer, like any other actress on set."

"You really want that chocolate badly, don't you?"

Wanting things she couldn't have… That seemed to be the norm for her lately. She nodded.

"Okay. Hold this." Crash pressed her water bottle into Jill's hands and sauntered over to the grips at the front of the line, her stride confident, as if she owned not just the craft services tent but the entire set.

Jill watched her from behind. Never had a pair of faded jeans looked so sexy, and knowing that Crash was jumping into the fray to rescue some chocolate for her made her even more attractive.

Jill couldn't hear what she said to the men, but she watched Crash's body language. Crash wasn't exactly flirting, but suddenly every smile, every subtle movement held a magnetism that was hard to resist. She leaned against the table in a pose of relaxed casualness while she gestured at the remaining chocolate bars. Her sensual lips quirked into a smile as she said something that made the key grip laugh.

God, those lips… Suddenly, the need to kiss those lips surpassed the need for chocolate.

Crash returned, triumphantly holding a Snickers bar aloft.

Instead of reaching for the chocolate bar, Jill grabbed Crash's arm and dragged her from the tent.

"Um, aren't you hungry anymore?" Crash asked.

"Oh yeah. I am."

Something in her tone made Crash follow her to the trailer without asking any other question.

As soon as the door closed behind them, Jill pressed Crash against it and kissed her. All she'd wanted was a kiss, but as soon as she touched her, she had to have all of Crash, so she slid her hand down Crash's flat belly and unbuttoned the sexy jeans.

The chocolate bar would have to wait.

They lay on the couch in Jill's trailer, in a tangle of limbs and half-on, half-off clothing. One of Crash's legs kept slipping off the sofa, but she was loath to move. The way Jill trailed her fingertips all over her back and shoulders felt too good, now soothing rather than arousing. She admitted to herself that she'd missed this—missed Jill.

"God," Jill breathed against the overheated skin of her neck, making her shiver. "Why are you still single?"

Crash chuckled. "Thanks. I'll take that as a compliment."

"It is, but seriously, why hasn't some woman snatched you up by now?"

"There were a few, but let's just say that I've got hurt more often in my relationships than in my line of work." Crash had never talked about it much, not even with TJ or her other friends, but now she surprised herself by continuing. "The first girlfriend I had after moving to LA just couldn't deal with the dangers of my job, never knowing if I would come home hurt…or not at all."

Jill trailed her fingers up and gently skirted the edges of the burn mark with the tip of her pinky. "I can understand that."

"Yeah, me too. But it still hurt like hell when she broke up with me. My next girlfriend was just the opposite. Kyleigh really liked the thrill of being around stunt people."

"That's good, right?" Jill still examined the red, uneven burn scar as if trying to memorize its shape.

It didn't hurt, but it felt very intimate. Crash realized that none of the women she'd been with in the last two years since acquiring the scar had ever touched it. "That's what I thought, but she liked it a little too much. I caught her in bed with my mentor."

Jill's touch paused, then she protectively covered the scar with her hand. "I'm sorry that happened to you. If there's one thing I could never understand, it's why people cheat on their significant other instead of getting out of the relationship if they're no longer happy."

"Don't ask me. I never understood it either." Crash knew she was partly to blame for some of her relationships failing, but she had never cheated on any of her girlfriends.

"So..." Jill paused.

She had never before hesitated to ask about whatever she wanted to know, so now her hesitation made Crash lift her head. "What?"

"I was just wondering... You're not interested in anyone right now, are you?"

Crash almost snorted. She eyed their half-naked, entwined bodies. *Uh...hello?*

Before she could point out the obvious, Jill continued, "I mean...this," she gestured at them, "is okay as long as we're both single, but if there's anyone you could have a future with..." She paused again. Her chest heaved under a deep breath as if she had to force herself to get the words out. "I know it'll only last until filming ends, but if you meet someone else before that, I don't want to stand in the way."

Crash looked into her eyes.

Shadows darkened the green irises. Jill worried her bottom lip with her teeth and directed her gaze away from Crash's.

Gently, Crash reached out and tipped Jill's chin up so they made eye contact again. "There's no one else." Lying here with Jill, she couldn't imagine that there would ever come a time when another woman would capture her attention the way Jill did. *God, you're in much too deep. Like she just said, filming will wrap in six weeks and that'll be the end of your arrangement.*

Jill took her palm off the burn mark and clutched Crash to her with both hands for a moment before letting go and sitting up. "One thing's for sure," she said as she put her drawers and petticoats back on. Her voice vibrated with emotion. "You'll make some woman very happy one day, in and out of the bedroom."

Instead of getting up too, Crash remained lying on the couch and stared up at the trailer's ceiling. The problem with that prediction was that she didn't want some woman. The more time she spent with Jill, the more the realization became clear in her mind: Jill was the one she wanted.

The problem was that Jill was a package deal. She came only with a chronic illness that neither of them seemed to know how to handle.

Now fully dressed, Jill perched on the edge of the couch, put one hand on Crash's hip, and looked down at her with an expression of concern. "What is it?"

Crash sighed, knowing she would only drive Jill away if she voiced her thoughts. "Just thinking about the stunt I'll have to do later."

"There's no fire involved is it?" Jill's brow furrowed.

"No." Crash swung her legs off the couch. "No fire involved." But as she was fast coming to realize, fire wasn't the only thing with the potential to hurt.

Since Crash still had some time until she would be needed at the second-unit set, she accompanied Jill over to where the crew had set up the conglomerations of tents that served as Dr. Lucy Sharpe's hospital.

Makeup immediately rushed over, pressed Jill into one of the canvas chairs, and reapplied her worn-off lipstick, making Crash bite back a grin.

She let her gaze trail over Jill's body to make sure no other traces of their violation of rule number five could be detected. The high-necked, white blouse looked pristine, and somehow, they had managed not to wrinkle her skirt too much, but one of the laces on her white, pointy-toed ankle boots had come undone.

Crash knew how hard it was to bend over with the corset Jill was wearing. Plus she had noticed that laces, zippers, and buttons were often daunting for Jill, either because her hands had gone numb or because the MS was messing with her fine motor skills.

It sure didn't feel like she's lacking coordination earlier. She shook off the thought. When the makeup woman finished her work and stepped back, Crash knelt in front of Jill.

"Um, what are you doing?" Jill asked from above her.

Crash smiled up at her. "Don't worry. I'm not proposing or anything." She tied the laces for her, taking care to pull the loops tight so they wouldn't come undone again.

Jill tried to pull her foot back, but Crash nudged her knee.

"Hold still. There. All done." Her fingers lingered on Jill's ankle. She couldn't resist touching her, even in this small way.

When she looked up, still in her kneeling position, there was a frown on Jill's face instead of the smile she had expected.

Jill pulled her foot out of Crash's hands. "Don't do that."

"Do what? Tie your laces?" Crash stared up at her, taken aback by the sudden coldness in Jill's voice.

"Act like you're my caregiver," Jill whispered sharply.

"I'm not. I just saw that your shoelace was undone and—"

"Then just tell me next time. I learned how to tie my shoelaces when I was three, so I'm perfectly capable of tying them myself."

"I never said you weren't."

"But you acted that way."

Crash gripped the hair at her temples with both hands. It was better than doing what she really wanted to do: grab Jill's shoulders and shake some sense into that stubborn woman. "I just tied your laces for you. I really don't understand what the big deal is, but fine. Have it your way." She got up from her kneeling position and turned to walk away, but Jill's grip on her wrist made her turn back around.

"The big deal is that we had an agreement, and you're coming awfully close to breaking it. You're not my caregiver or my girlfriend. That hasn't changed."

The harsh words made Crash flinch. "So, what am I?" she couldn't help asking, unable to keep the hurt from her voice. "Your dirty little secret?"

Jill blanched beneath her fresh layer of film makeup. She looked around the set, which was getting busier as the cast and crew returned from lunch. "You honestly think there's anyone on set who doesn't know why you're spending so much time in my trailer?" Jill asked, her voice softening a bit. "It's not about that."

Crash consciously tried to relax her hands, which had curled into fists at her sides. "What's it about, then?"

"I just told you. It's about you breaking the rules."

"I broke the rules by tying your laces?" Crash gave an incredulous shake of her head. She wasn't sure if she should laugh in disbelief or start shouting at Jill. How could Jill make love…sleep with her one minute and then not even allow her to tie her laces the next? "That's bullshit, Jill."

They stared at each other. Jill opened her mouth to say something when one of the PAs jogged up to them. "Mr. Brower is looking for you over at the stunt trailer," he said to Crash. "He wants you to pad up now."

Crash was starting to think of production assistants as the bane of her existence. Their timing really sucked. But maybe she should be glad about the interruption this time. She didn't want to lash out at Jill, but neither did she want to put up with the hot-and-cold treatment. "I have to go," she said to Jill, shook off Jill's grip on her wrist, and walked away without waiting for a reply.

Crash listened to Ben, their stunt coordinator, while they did one last walk-through of the glass stunt, but half her attention was still on the conversation she'd just had with Jill—if you could even call it a conversation.

Jill's words kept echoing through her mind. *You're not my caregiver or my girlfriend.*

It all came down to that. She couldn't be one without the other, so Jill wouldn't let her be either. How the hell could she get her to accept normal, considerate acts without freaking out or believing that every little sign of Crash's caring had to do with her damn MS?

"Crash?" Ben waved a hand up and down in front of her face. "You with us?"

"Uh, yeah." She bent and pretended to examine the dinner table she was supposed to smash into. It appeared solid, but she knew it was made of soft balsa wood, which would splinter easily under her weight. Next, she ran her fingertips over the wine glasses and the decanter on the table. They, too, looked like the real deal, even though they were candy glass, which would shatter into tiny fragments without hurting her.

At least that was the plan.

"Do you want to do a trial run with the glasses?" Ben asked. "We have a couple of extras, but the tables are too expensive to test."

Crash shook her head. She wanted to get this over and done with and then go home to lick her emotional wounds. No use in hanging around the set to have dinner with Jill tonight. "It should be fine. We did three practice runs of the scuffle yesterday. The timing isn't complicated, just one well-aimed push and—bam!"

"Great." Ben turned to the crew. "We're doing this from two angles—the homeowner's wife," he pointed to Crash, "and the looter." He gestured toward the other stuntman. "Two takes from each should do it."

While the crew got ready, Crash tried to get into the mental space that allowed single-minded focus, forgetting all about Jill and their fight.

"Ready?" Ben asked.

She exchanged glances with her colleague and nodded.

"Quiet on the set! We're shooting."

Camera and sound started rolling, and then Ben called, "Action!"

Crash let out a piercing scream as the stuntman, playing an armed looter, advanced on her.

"Cut!" Ben called before her colleague could push her into the table. He shook his head at Crash. "Scared, remember? You're scared for your life."

"Uh, yeah, I know," Crash said, irritated with the interruption.

"But that wasn't what you portrayed. That scream sounded angry and frustrated, like you were about to grab the decanter and hit him over the head."

Shit. Maybe she hadn't been as successful at forgetting about Jill as she had thought. "Sorry. I've got it now." *Scared, scared, scared,* she mentally chanted while she waited for the cameras to start rolling again, but her frustration with Jill threatened to break through. *Come on. Method Acting 101. You can do it.*

She tried to think of a situation in which she'd been scared. An image of her being set on fire immediately came to mind.

This time, she had no problems sounding panicked when Ben shouted, "Action!"

The stuntman advanced on her and roughly pushed her out of the way, making her fly backward and smash into the table.

The balsa furniture collapsed into a pile of wood debris. The candy glass shattered beneath her back as she landed on the floor, little fragments flying everywhere, so Crash kept her eyes shut for safety reasons until Ben called, "Cut. Nice job."

Grinning, Crash got to her feet and shook tiny pieces of candy glass from her costume.

Someone from the makeup department came over and used a brush to remove the littlest fragments from her clothes and skin.

The crew immediately got to work, clearing the set of wood and glass and setting up a new table.

"Oh, shit." His forehead set into more furrows than a basset hound's, Ben strode over to her. "You're bleeding. Are you okay?"

With her adrenaline still pumping, nothing hurt. Crash scanned her body and realized that a piece of candy glass was embedded into the side of her hand. She had probably broken her fall with that hand and landed on the glass fragments.

The set medic, who stood by during every stunt, rushed over.

"I'm fine," she said. Truth be told, she would have said that even if the cut had been worse. As a stunt person, you didn't want to appear weak, especially if you were a woman trying to make it in the good old boys' club. She prided herself on never crying, never complaining, and—most importantly—never holding up production. Little cuts like this one were nothing out of the ordinary when doing a glass gag.

Ben shook his head. "A bleeding wound isn't fine in my book." He stepped aside so the medic could take a look.

Crash suppressed a flinch when the medic pulled a glass shard out of her hand with a pair of tweezers. He pressed a piece of gauze against the cut to stop the bleeding and then placed two transparent butterfly bandages on it that wouldn't show up on film. "That should take care of it for now, but I'm not sure the Steri-Strips are enough. As soon as you finish here, you should go to the ER and get a couple of stitches."

Wonderful. Crash suppressed a curse. *Great ending to a great day.* She sighed.

Ben looked over the medic's shoulder with a concerned expression. "Want me to call Jill so she can take you to the ER?"

She gave him a surprised look.

"I mean… You're…uh, friends, right?" Ben said.

So Jill had been right. Most people on set probably suspected that there was something going on between them. Well, Crash didn't care, at least not for herself. Stunt performers had a reputation as bold daredevils, so people assumed her to be the love-them-and-leave-them type anyway. But she didn't want him to think Jill was acting unprofessional by starting an affair with her stunt double. "We became friends when she let me hang out in her air-conditioned trailer."

Ben waved her explanation away. "Air-conditioned trailer, huh? Whatever. I think they already wrapped for the day on the first-unit set, so I'm sure she could take you. Want me to call her?" He gestured at a PA with a walkie-talkie around her neck.

"Nah." Jill had made it clear that she didn't want mutual care and support. "Let's do take two. If it still looks like I'm going to need stitches after we shoot the last take, I'll drive myself."

"Do you think you'll be able to work tomorrow?" he asked with a skeptical glance at her hand.

Crash peeked at her hand and experimentally curled her fingers. Despite the butterfly bandage, blood oozed from the cut. *Damn.* "Sure. If I can wear gloves, they'll even hide the stitches if I get any."

Ben shook his head. "You can't. I need you for a scene in which the soldiers force people to help remove debris from the streets. It's a bare-handed shot." He tapped his chin with his index finger.

"Can we switch around the order of scenes on the call sheet? Maybe do this one a little later? I'm a fast healer." She didn't want to give up any of the stunt scenes if she could help it. From the very first day on set, she'd taken on as many gags as Ben allowed her to do, even several in which she wasn't doubling Jill. If she played her cards right, this movie could be her ticket to more steady work and doing stunts for more well-known actresses. Then her career would be back to where it was before the motorcycle accident and that damn fire stunt.

Ben dashed her hopes when he shook his head. "No. Floyd doesn't like shooting around such inconsequential scenes. I'll get one of the other stuntwomen to do it. Take the day off tomorrow and get some rest."

"But I'll still get to do the other stunts, right?"

"Yeah, of course. Luck isn't on your side, but I like your work."

Crash pressed her lips together and gave him a tense nod. "Okay. Let's do the final takes so I can get this taken care of."

For once, they had wrapped early, but instead of enjoying her afternoon off, Jill was moping around the house, wandering from room to room without settling anywhere for long.

Tramp followed her and let out a whine as if sensing her restlessness.

She reached down to scratch behind his ears. "It's okay, boy." Truth be told, nothing was okay. She was still angry—at Crash, but mainly at herself.

Why the hell couldn't she stay away from Crash and avoid all that drama?

She flopped down onto the couch and buried her face in her palms. *You know why.* Despite what she kept telling Crash—and herself—this went way beyond something just physical. She felt herself drawn to Crash, not just in a sexual way. But every time she had almost convinced herself that it was okay to explore what was happening between them, even if just a little, something happened that reminded her why that wasn't a good idea.

The shoelace incident proved that Crash would never see her as an equal partner, especially as the MS progressed, which it most likely would at some point.

An image flashed through Jill's mind—Crash down on one knee, tying her laces for her as if Jill were a helpless child. The memory made her hands clench into fists. She knew Crash had meant well and that she'd hurt her by pushing her away. The memory of the hurt in Crash's eyes and the frustration obvious on her face played on auto-repeat through her mind, but she'd been just as helpless to take it away as she was against her MS.

She couldn't let Crash help her every step of the way. Not if she wanted to be Crash's equal, someone Crash didn't need to take care of. She wouldn't be able to stand it if Crash started treating her the way her parents did. For them, all she seemed to be anymore was a patient, someone with MS.

She jumped up and paced about the living room but didn't find answers to the questions running through her mind. "Maybe I should end it."

The thought stabbed her with the sharpness of a knife.

Tramp let out a low whine. It didn't sound as if he agreed.

"Oh, yeah, sure. Take her side, traitor." She scratched him behind one ear again, sank back onto the couch, and pulled her laptop over to check her e-mail.

No message from Crash. Jill's shoulders slumped. She realized how much she had come to look forward to the funny pictures and short messages Crash sometimes sent her.

Now just a new e-mail from her mother sat in her in-box. She clicked on it and scanned it. A long groan escaped her when she saw that it was another link to a website that held information about the latest miracle drug her mother had researched online.

Her mother just didn't get it. Or maybe she didn't want to get it. There was no cure for MS. But her mother kept e-mailing her newspaper clippings or website links about the latest health fad that promised to help MS patients. It was probably her way of dealing with the powerlessness and making herself feel as if she was doing something to help, but to Jill, it was just another painful reminder of her illness.

She left the e-mail in her in-box to answer it later, closed the laptop, and slid down into a lying position. She pressed a sofa pillow onto her face and groaned into it.

Tramp jumped up onto the couch. Normally, he wasn't allowed on the sofa, but now she just didn't have the energy to order him down. His warm body pressed against her legs was comforting.

The pillow still over her face, she had nearly drifted off to an exhausted sleep when the ringing of her cell phone pierced the silence.

With another groan, she lifted the pillow away from her face and debated with herself whether to pick up. She half hoped, half feared that it might be Crash, but the ringtone—ABBA's "Money, Money, Money"—indicated that it was someone from the studio. "Yes?"

"Ms. Corrigan? This is Nancy Abbott."

Their second AD. Jill sat up.

"I just e-mailed you a copy of the new call sheet for tomorrow," Nancy said. "We had to move back your call time a little. The stuntwoman can't make it before nine, so how about you be in makeup by seven thirty?"

The stuntwoman? Jill's hazy brain had trouble catching up. "Crash? Uh, I mean, Ms. Patterson?"

"No," Nancy said. "Her replacement."

Jill jumped up from the couch so fast that the room started spinning around her. She clutched the back of the couch with one hand, holding on desperately. Had Crash quit her job just because she didn't want to work with her anymore? She couldn't believe Crash would do something like that. "She...she quit?"

"What? Oh, no. It's just for tomorrow. She'll be back the day after. Ben just thought it might be better not to let her handle the debris scene with her hand."

Jill tightened her grip on the couch. Why was Nancy suddenly talking in riddles? "With her hand?" she repeated. "What's wrong with her hand?" An image of Crash's hands—strong and tan and gentle—flashed through her mind. She shook it off so she could focus on the conversation.

"Oh. I thought you knew."

"Knew what?" Jill's impatience grew, and she had to force herself not to shout at the second assistant director. "What's going on?"

"Uh, there was an accident on the second-unit set this afternoon, and—"

"What?" Her legs gave out, dropping Jill back onto the couch.

Tramp immediately put his muzzle onto her knee and looked up at her with his soulful brown eyes. A low whine rose up his chest.

Jill put her hand on his head to silence him. "What happened?" she asked, raising her voice so she could hear herself over the thumping of her heart. "How bad is it?"

"It's not that bad, really. Just a cut from the glass, as far as I know."

Her vivid imagination showed her images of jagged glass shards tearing through Crash's wrist and an artery spurting blood. Queasiness hit her. She mentally gave herself a good shake and took a steadying breath. *Calm down, will you? If it were that bad, she wouldn't be back on set the day after tomorrow.*

"Ms. Corrigan? You still there?"

Jill took a steadying breath. "I'm here. I'll take a look at the new call sheet."

"Good. Thanks. Let me know if you need a driver to pick you up."

Nancy always asked, and Jill's answer was always the same. "No. I'll drive myself."

"Okay. Good night, then."

"Good night." Jill dropped the cell phone onto the couch. "She'll be fine," she whispered into the room. Crash had probably sustained worse injuries in her line of work.

But as much as she wanted, Jill couldn't turn off her worries. She wouldn't be able to relax until she'd seen Crash for herself.

Decision made, she jumped up, grabbed her car keys, and rushed to the door as fast as she could.

Tramp bounded after her.

Within a minute, they were on their way to Los Feliz.

Crash had just returned from her visit to the ER when the doorbell rang. Expecting either her friend TJ or some studio clerk sent over to fill out an accident report, she headed to the intercom. "Yes?"

For a moment, all she heard was static. Then someone—a woman—cleared her throat. "Um, Crash?"

"Jill? What are you doing here?" Crash stared at the intercom as if that would reveal the answer.

"I... The second AD called because of tomorrow's call time."

"And?" Crash asked, not bothering to sound friendly. After the day she'd had, her emotions were just too raw.

Another moment of silence. "Can I come up? I think we should talk."

Crash ran her unhurt hand through her hair. She was tempted to send her away, but if Jill was finally ready to act like an adult, she didn't want to be the childish one. Without answering, she pressed the buzzer and automatically looked around her studio apartment while she waited for Jill to make it up to the second floor.

A dumbbell lay on the kitchen counter, and her sneakers and socks formed a path from the door to the couch. She moved to pick them up but then stopped.

She hadn't invited Jill over, so her surprise guest would just have to deal with the mess. But she couldn't resist moving to the door and peeking through the peephole, watching Jill approach. The sight of Jill in a spaghetti-strap top nearly made her smile. She gritted her teeth and tried to hold on to her anger as she swung the door open.

Tramp rushed up to her, wagging not just his tail but his entire rear end. He jumped around Crash excitedly and tried to lick her hands.

"Tramp! No!" Jill pulled him back before he could get to Crash's injured hand. She stood in the doorway and stared at the gauze pad that the doctor had taped over the stitched-up cut. A bit of iodine-stained skin peeked out from beneath the dressing. "Is it bad?"

The concern in her voice made it hard to stay annoyed with her—as did the jean shorts she was wearing. "Nah," Crash said. "Just three stitches."

"Stitches are bad in my books."

Crash shrugged. "I've had worse."

They stood facing each other across the doorjamb.

Jill shuffled her feet. "Can I come in? I won't stay long. I just want to…" She lowered her gaze and stared at her feet, which admittedly looked pretty cute in a pair of strappy sandals.

Crash steeled her resolve to stay angry. "You want to do what? Hand out another lecture about me breaking the rules?"

"No, I…" Jill's gaze veered up, then back down. "I just wanted to make sure you're okay."

"I'm fine." Against her will, her tone softened a bit. Jill's concern for her felt good. She sighed. "Come on in."

As if understanding the invitation, Tramp bustled past them into the apartment. He started sniffing and exploring the room as if he hadn't been there before.

When they settled on opposite ends of the sofa, Tramp trotted over, proudly presenting the sock he held in his mouth. He shook it and then offered Jill one end for a game of tug.

"Tramp, no! Drop it!" Jill pointed to the floor.

Clamping his canines down on the sock, Tramp tilted his head and gave her a pitiful look.

"Drop it!" Jill stabbed her finger in the direction of the floor more energetically.

Tramp dropped his bounty and retreated.

Crash bent and picked up the soggy, ripped article of clothing, pinching it between thumb and index finger of her uninjured hand. "You owe me a new pair of socks."

Jill took a deep breath and finally lifted her gaze to meet Crash's. "I also owe you an apology."

Crash sucked in a breath. She hadn't expected that. But then again, Jill rarely did what people expected of her.

"One second." Jill jumped up to rescue the second sock and Crash's sneakers from Tramp before returning to the couch. She shifted as if she couldn't find a comfortable spot and clutched the sneakers as if they were a lifeline. Finally, she peeked over at Crash. "I...I overreacted earlier. I mean, I stand behind what I said, but I shouldn't have been such a bitch about it. I should have found another way to let you know I don't want to be coddled."

"Coddled?" Crash echoed. "I tied your shoelaces for you because you were wearing a corset. That's hardly coddling."

"It is when you're fighting for your independence every day," Jill said quietly but firmly. "Has Nancy ever asked you if you want someone to pick you up and bring you to the set?"

"Uh, no, but that's just a common courtesy to actresses."

"Not if she offers because she thinks you shouldn't be allowed to drive yourself," Jill said. "Have you ever been forbidden from doing even the simplest stunts because everyone is afraid that you might trip and hurt yourself?"

"No. Jill—"

"Have your colleagues ever vacated their chairs for you as soon as you enter a room, as if you're eighty years old and can't be on your feet for even a minute?"

Crash held up her hands. "Okay, I get it."

"Do you?" Jill's gaze drilled into her.

Crash started to nod but then paused. "I don't know if anyone who doesn't have a chronic illness can understand completely, but I'm really trying. I didn't tie your laces for you because I was coddling you or thought you couldn't do it yourself. I'd like to think I would have done it even if you were perfectly healthy."

Jill clamped her teeth around her bottom lip, a deep sadness darkening her eyes to a murky olive color instead of the vivid green Crash was used to. "I guess we'll never know."

Sudden anger bubbled up in Crash. "Would it be so bad if I tied your laces because your hands are giving you trouble? I wouldn't think anything of it if you tied my shoelaces because I can't do it with my stitched-up hand. How is me helping you any different from you coming over to make sure I didn't hurt my hand too badly?"

"I... I don't know. It just is."

"Now there's a mature response," Crash muttered.

Jill's jaw muscles bunched. "Your hand will heal, Crash. The MS won't—ever. If anything, it will only get worse. That's the difference."

"But if the MS is here to stay, doesn't that make it all the more important to simply accept a helping hand from your friends every now and then so you can conserve your energy for more important things than tying shoelaces?" Crash asked but didn't wait for an answer before continuing, "Don't you think Lauren or Grace would have tied the shoelace for you too if they'd been there? Would you have told them off too?"

Jill opened her mouth but then hesitated. She slumped against the back of the couch and rubbed her eyes, suddenly looking exhausted.

The remainder of Crash's anger evaporated like water in the California sun. She wanted so much to wrap one arm around Jill and let her rest against her shoulder, but she knew it would most likely spark another fight.

"Probably," Jill finally said. She nibbled on her lip and then added, "But I admit that I might not have reacted quite so strongly."

That admission hurt. Jill was sleeping with her but didn't even trust her on the same level that she would a friend. She hesitated, not sure if it was a good idea to say what was on her mind or if Jill would throw those words back into her face. Finally, she decided to voice her feelings anyway. "You know," she said softly, "it might be against your rules, but I care for you." The words hung between them. God, that sounded almost like a declaration of love, and that wasn't what she meant, was it? "I mean, we agreed to be friends, right?"

"Yeah. We did. We are." Jill reached over, laid her hand on Crash's, and squeezed.

Pain flared through Crash's hand. Suppressing a curse, she pulled it back.

"Oh God. I'm so sorry. I didn't mean to… Shit."

Cradling her hand, Crash took a deep breath as the pain faded away. "Phew. It's okay. It only hurt for a second. All good now."

"Really?" Jill searched her face.

"Yeah. I'm sure I'll survive."

"No, I mean…are we good?"

Crash had rarely heard her sound so insecure. She looked into Jill's eyes and nodded. "We're good."

"Can we agree that you won't try to tie my laces again?"

Crash sighed. "Honestly, I'm not sure I can promise never to lend you a helping hand again." Seeing Jill struggle and waste her energy on simple things like opening buttons was just too hard. "That doesn't mean I think you're helpless. I know you can do it, but when I'm there, I might as well do it for you."

"You won't always be there," Jill said quietly. She held up her hand before Crash could think of something to say to that. "I know you think I'm overreacting, and maybe you're right, but this is important to me."

Crash suppressed a sigh and regarded Jill with a shake of her head. "No commitment. No declarations of love. No tying shoelaces. That list of rules is slowly becoming a weighty tome."

Jill looked away and fiddled with the laces of the sneakers she still held. "I'm sorry. If this is getting too complicated for you—"

"It's okay." Things were getting complicated. But what were the alternatives? Walking away for good? Crash wasn't ready to do that. "I'll try to respect your wishes in this."

"Thank you." Jill lifted her hand as if to touch Crash again but then seemed to change her mind. "I should go. I'm not the one who can laze around at home tomorrow after all." She winked at Crash with a levity that seemed a little forced and then powered herself up from the couch as if it took all her strength to do so.

Despite the promise she had just made, Crash struggled not to grip Jill's elbow to steady her. "Are you okay?"

"Yes. I'm not the one who got hurt today."

Was she talking about Crash's hand or about their fight? Crash wasn't sure. She followed Jill and Tramp to the door, where they stood facing each other for several seconds.

"Take care," Jill finally said and reached for the doorknob.

"You too." Crash gave Tramp a parting pat to the back, then the two stepped outside. Slowly, Crash moved to close the door.

"Crash?" Jill called through the crack in the door.

"Yeah?"

"I do too."

Before Crash could figure out what she meant, Jill's footsteps retreated.

Crash swung the door open and stuck her head out. "What do you mean?" she called after Jill.

At the end of the corridor, Jill paused and turned back around. She hesitated, jiggling Tramp's leash. "I care for you too."

Stunned, Crash stared at her. A wild wave of hope rushed through her, and she made one step forward, toward Jill.

"I mean, we're not robots," Jill added quickly, stopping Crash midstep. "It's perfectly normal to become a little attached to the person you're sleeping with, especially if you're friends, isn't it?"

Ouch. The words were true, but still...ouch. Crash had hoped for a little more. "Yeah," she murmured.

Jill gave her a smile, but the expression in her eyes was sad. She lifted her hand in a wave and disappeared around the corner.

Crash stared after her. After a while, she stepped back inside, closed the door, and leaned against it. "Perfectly normal." She sighed, rubbed her chest with her good hand, and went to throw away the chewed-on sock.

CHAPTER 15

Jill breathed a sigh of relief as she entered her air-conditioned trailer. The heat outside had been almost unbearable for the last hour, but she'd gritted her teeth and finished her reaction shots.

She plopped down onto the couch and waited until the air had cooled down enough to lower her body temperature. Within just a few minutes, the fog lifted off her brain and the numbness in her legs all but vanished.

Only then did she even attempt to open the buttons on her costume. Once she'd taken a quick shower and changed into her own clothes, she mentally calculated the distance from one air-conditioned refuge to the next. Production office. Car. Home.

That should work. She nodded with satisfaction and headed out.

Fran was manning the production office when Jill stepped inside. "Hi, Jill. Are you here for your call sheet?"

Jill nodded.

Seconds later, Fran's printer spat out several sheets of paper. "Are you on your way out, or are you heading back to the set?"

"I'm finished for today."

"Too bad," Fran said. "I thought you could take their call sheets back to Nikki and Shawn."

Jill shook her head. "They aren't shooting. They headed over to that empty storage building where the stuntmen train to run through a couple of action sequences with the guys from the stunt department." The guys and Crash, to be more exact.

Crash... Thinking about her instantly made Jill want to see her. Just to check to make sure Crash wasn't hurting her hand by overdoing it in training. *Yeah, right.* Her lies to herself were no longer working.

After a moment's hesitation, Jill waved her fingers at Fran. "You know what? Hand them over. I'll drop them off on my way to the car."

Fran gave her a dubious look. "On your way to the car? That building isn't anywhere near the parking lot."

She was right. It was stupid. The storage building was all the way at the other end of the studio lot, and it wasn't air-conditioned. Not a place where she should want to be. But even knowing she was probably making a fool of herself, she couldn't resist. The urge to see Crash was just too strong. "I don't mind."

Call sheets in hand, she made her way to the storage building and pulled open the door. *Just drop off the call sheets, wave hi to Crash, and get out,* she firmly told herself.

To her relief, it wasn't as hot or stuffy as she had expected. The training stunt performers were sweating like crazy, though. Jill's gaze immediately found Crash.

She was wearing baggy cargo shorts and a sweat-dampened tank top that clung to her breasts and her athletic torso. Sweat gleamed on her muscular arms, and her dark hair stuck to her neck in wild waves. She expertly swung something that looked like a long stick, smashing it against one held by a stuntman. Both sticks were moving almost too fast for Jill to follow.

She paused in the doorway. Dry-mouthed, she watched the play of Crash's lithe muscles, the wild grin on her face, and the joy in her eyes as Crash fought, testing her strength and her agility against those of her training partner.

Watching Crash train was a guilty pleasure, but at the same time, it acted as a reminder of why it was a good idea not to let herself get any closer. Crash was strong and healthy—and she wasn't.

That didn't stop her from watching and wanting, though. Despite her resolution not to stay for longer than a minute or two, she couldn't tear her gaze away.

"Hey, Jill!"

It took a second for her name to register. Reluctantly, she looked away from Crash.

Nikki waved at her from where she was sitting against the wall with Shawn, out of the way. She indicated for Jill to join them.

Still watching the stunt fight, Jill walked over and settled down between them. "I thought they were supposed to be training you?"

"We already finished," Shawn said. "Now they're just blowing off some steam."

Jill could think of more pleasant ways to do that, but she bit her lips and just nodded.

"God," Nikki whispered, watching the two stunt people with rapt attention. "Do you see those muscles?"

"Yeah." Jill's gaze was glued to Crash and the way swinging that stick made the muscles in her arms flex.

Shawn laughed. "I don't think you two are talking about the same muscles." She nudged Jill. "Girl, you're a goner."

"What? No, I... I'm not. I... We..."

Shawn wrapped one arm around her. "Hey, it's okay. If I were gay, I'd definitely make a play for her too."

Jill opened her mouth for another denial but then snapped it shut. She wasn't kidding anyone, not Shawn and not herself, so she directed her gaze back to Crash and watched her in silence.

Finally, Crash planted one end of the stick on the floor and flung herself up into the air. Her feet hit the stuntman's chest, catapulting him back.

He went down but jumped back up to the applause and cheering of the two actresses.

Wow. Jill clapped her hands too, dropping the call sheets in the process.

Crash, who was casually leaning on her stick, looked over. The wild, triumphant glow in her eyes softened as she walked over to Jill, focusing just on her.

Jill got up, relieved when her limbs cooperated and didn't leave her stranded on the floor. "Hi," she said as she stood eye to eye with Crash. She found herself a little tongue-tied. They'd been shooting mostly on different sets all week, so she had barely seen Crash since apologizing after their fight last Friday.

"Hi."

Jill reached out, but with their colleagues' watching, she touched Crash's weapon rather than her arm. "That's a dangerous stick."

"Staff," Crash said with a smile.

Waving her hand in a *whatever* gesture, Jill asked, "Are you okay to fight like this?"

Crash flexed her fingers to show off the functionality of her stitched-up hand. "Good as new." She leaned on the stick…staff again. "So, what brings you here?"

Jill bent and picked up the call sheets she'd dropped. "Just bringing over the call sheets for Nikki and Shawn."

"Now they have you working as a PA too?" Crash asked, arching her brows.

"No, I…" *Volunteered.* She bit her lip so she wouldn't say it, not wanting to reveal how eager she'd been to see Crash. "It was on my way out."

"And here I thought you'd missed me," Crash said. She flashed one of her grins, but there was more than teasing behind it.

"Nah. I just wanted to see you put Nikki and Shawn through their paces, but it seems they already finished their training session," Jill said as lightly as possible and pointed over to her colleagues, who were now talking to the stuntman.

Crash laid the staff across her shoulders and hooked her arms over it. "Yeah, you know actresses…fragile egos, fragile bodies." She echoed Jill's playful tone. "Not much you can do with them."

"Hey!" Jill tried to swat her on the shoulder, but Crash neatly sidestepped. Leaning closer, Jill lowered her voice and said, "There was a lot you could do with this actress's fragile body, if I remember correctly."

Crash's eyes lit up, burning into Jill like a laser. Her breathing, which had calmed while they talked, hitched and then picked up. "Present company excluded, of course," she said huskily.

"Of course," Jill murmured.

They stood without talking, just looking into each other's eyes, until Shawn and Nikki joined them.

Jill handed over the call sheets.

"Thanks," Shawn said without looking at the sheet of paper. She gazed at Crash instead and smiled at her. "Thanks again for showing me that flip."

The way she looked at Crash made Jill remember what Shawn had said earlier, about making a play for Crash if she were gay. *Too bad for both of them that she isn't.* She kicked at the edge of a gymnastics mat. Shawn wasn't handicapped by an illness. She could do flips with Crash all she wanted, and she wasn't even aware of how lucky she was.

"Will you have to do a flip in tomorrow's scene?" Jill asked. "I thought it was just a jump."

"It is, but it was fun trying some of the other stuff," Shawn said. Then the younger actress's enthusiasm dimmed. "Too bad you can't try any of it."

Yeah. Thanks for the reminder. Jill bit back the remark and just shrugged, not wanting to admit how much her colleague's insensitive comment hurt.

"Who says she can't?" Crash turned to face Jill as if they were alone. "Do you want to try a stunt?"

Jill hesitated. On the one hand, she would have loved to do even a simple stunt, to prove to herself and the world that she could do it. But, on the other hand, if she got hurt, she would hold up production for weeks or even months. Could she really risk it just for her ego's sake?

"Trust me," Crash said, her voice low. "You won't get hurt."

"Okay. What do you want me to do?"

Crash turned, put down her staff, and rummaged through some of the equipment set along the wall.

It took considerable effort on her part to not watch the way the cargo shorts stretched over Crash's ass, but Jill wasn't an actress for nothing. She managed to appear entirely engrossed into the small talk with her colleagues.

Soon, Crash returned and handed Jill a bottle. "This is your chance to hit me over the head."

Jill stared down at what looked like a wine bottle. "You want me to hit you... with this?"

"It's just candy glass," Crash said.

"Candy glass?" Jill repeated. "So the worst thing that can happen is that you get a sugar rush if you accidentally lick it?"

Crash laughed. "No. Stunt glass used to be made of sugar, but nowadays it's made of a special kind of plastic. We still call it candy glass, though. It crumbles into tiny pieces, not into long shards like the real thing would. You can still get hurt, but it's much more unlikely, unless you land directly on the shards, like I did when we filmed that intruder scene."

Jill tapped her nails against the fake glass. Okay, clearly not real glass, but still... "Didn't you have enough of glass stunts?"

"You know what they say... If you get thrown off the horse, you have to get back up on it as soon as possible. So..." Crash pointed at her head.

Hesitating, Jill hefted the bottle in her hand. This would have been a lot easier on Friday, when she'd been angry with Crash. But now...

"Let her be the person who gets the bottle smashed over her head," Crash's colleague said.

Now Crash was the one who hesitated. "I'm not sure that's a good idea."

"I thought it's safe."

"It is, but..."

"What?" Jill asked, narrowing her eyes. "You think I can't do it?"

Nikki laughed and nudged Crash. "Oh, now you did it. Telling Jill she can't do something is like handing a match and a can of gasoline to a pyromaniac."

A chuckle escaped Crash, and she gave Nikki a rueful nod.

"Come on, guys. I'm not that bad."

"Right," Nikki and Crash said in unison.

"I'm not." Not backing down from a challenge was a good thing, wasn't it? Jill looked at Crash. "So?"

Finally, Crash held her hand out, and Jill laid the bottle into it.

"Do you want me to pretend to attack you?" Jill asked.

"No. If I hit you while you're moving, it gets harder to calculate the best angle. Let's do this one nice and easy." Crash eyed Jill's head as if looking for the best spot to hit. She turned the neck of the bottle in her long fingers over and over.

Was it really as safe as Crash said? Why was she hesitating for so long?

"Ready?" Crash finally asked.

Jill nodded.

"Okay. Turn away from me a bit. It's best if I do this from behind, where your head is protected by your hair."

Crash had probably done this a thousand times, and Jill trusted her skills, so she turned around without hesitation.

Behind her, Crash took an audible breath.

The bottle came down on the back of Jill's head and shattered with a sound that resembled that of breaking glass. Jill let out a pained groan and collapsed onto the gymnastics mat. Tiny fragments rained down around her.

Crash instantly crouched down next to her. "Jill! Oh God! Are you hurt?"

Jill sat up and laughed. "No. I just thought I'd give the stunt a little acting flair." Being hit by the candy glass bottle hadn't hurt—at least not more than a light slap to the head.

"Wow. That looked cool," Shawn said.

"It looked scary," Crash grumbled. "The way you collapsed..."

"I'm fine." Jill reached up to remove some little pieces of the fake glass from her hair.

"No!" Crash grabbed her hands and gently pulled them back down. "Don't do that. The fragments can still cut you." As if to prove it, she pointed at her healing wound that no longer had a dressing over it. She guided Jill to bend over and carefully ran her fingers through Jill's hair.

Shivers ran through her, from her scalp to her toes, her body instantly reacting to Crash's touch. *Jeez. Now I have a Pavlovian response to her.*

"You okay?" Crash asked.

"I'm fine." With the last pieces of glass removed, Jill got to her feet and looked over at her colleagues. "Ta-da. There. I finally got to do a stunt."

"Now you get to make a wish," the stuntman said.

"A wish?"

"Yeah." Crash nodded. "It's a tradition in the stunt business. When you get a bottle broken over your head for the first time, you get to make a wish."

Jill gave her a teasing slap to the shoulder. "Oh, so that's why you wanted me to smash the bottle over your head—so you could make a wish."

"Nope. I had my first bottle smashed over my head a long time ago," Crash said.

What was it that Crash had wished for back then? It saddened Jill that she couldn't even guess what it might have been and that she would never know these intimate little details about her—and that no one would ever know things like that about her in return. These were things to share between life partners, not friends with benefits.

"So, what did you wish for?" Shawn asked.

Jill wagged a finger at her. "It won't come true if I tell you." This time, she was glad she could hide behind the old superstition.

"Spoilsport," Shawn said but smiled. She, Nikki, and Crash's colleague said good-bye and walked out of the building together.

Jill hung back for a moment and watched Crash pack up her equipment.

"So," Crash said when she turned and shouldered her duffel bag, "have you made a wish?"

"Not yet."

"You should."

Making wishes on a superstition was a stupid thing children did. The logical part of her brain knew that. But she couldn't help it. A dozen different options shot through Jill's mind. They all came back to one. If her MS magically disappeared, she could have the life she wanted without having to struggle for it every day. She would no longer be limited in the roles she could play. She could look into the future without being afraid of what it might bring. And she could allow herself to be with Crash—really be with her, without holding anything back.

She peered at Crash and then mentally shook her head. That kind of wishful thinking didn't work, and she'd never been one to indulge in it. But she could still enjoy Crash's company in the here and now, so she finally nodded. "Yes, I did."

"Good," Crash said. "I hope it comes true."

They walked to the door together.

"I want you to have dinner with me—my treat—as an apology for me being such a bitch on Friday," Jill said before she could change her mind.

The door, which Crash had just opened, fell closed before her nose as she let go of it. She tilted her head and regarded Jill with wide eyes. "Are you...asking me out?"

"No! No, like I said, it would be an apology dinner, just two friends sharing good food, not a date."

"Would it really be so bad if it were?" Crash asked quietly.

It would be wonderful. The thought came unbidden. "No. Any woman would be lucky to date you."

"I'm not asking out any woman. I'm asking you out."

"*I* asked *you* out," Jill reminded. She bit her lip at the Freudian slip. "I mean, I asked you to have dinner with me so I can apologize."

Crash couldn't quite hide her grin. She pushed the door open with her shoulder and then held it so Jill could pass through too. "You really don't have to apologize again. Once is enough for me."

"Does that mean you're not accepting my invitation to dinner? That's the wish I made, so you should be required to fulfill it, seeing as you're the one who took my bottle virginity."

Crash's step faltered. Then she burst out laughing. She turned toward Jill, her blue eyes dancing with mirth. "Bottle virginity?"

"Yes," Jill said, trying to keep a straight face. "It's in the dictionary. Look it up."

"Oh, I will. And if it's not in there, you'll owe me dessert too."

The seductive timbre of her voice sparked a memory of their naked skin sliding against each other. Jill shivered despite the warm temperatures. "No problem. I can provide that too."

"Then we've got a date."

This time, Jill decided not to fight over that one word. She would just pretend that it was only a figure of speech, not what Crash—what both of them—really wanted. "So, when would be good for you?"

Crash tugged on her tank top, which still clung to her chest. "How about Saturday? The way I look and smell right now, not even a hot-dog stand will sell me anything. Do you want me to pick you up at, let's say, eight?"

"Saturday at eight sounds good, but parking can be really bad around the restaurant I have in mind. Why don't we meet at my place and then walk over?"

"Sure. Where do you want to go?"

"There's a great Persian place in Glendale, not too far from where I live. Do you like Persian food?"

Crash thought for a moment. "I don't think I ever had it."

A grin spread over Jill's face. "Oh, so you're going to lose your Persian food virginity to me."

"Let me guess. That's in the dictionary too?"

"But of course."

They walked to their cars together, and Jill gave Crash her address. After a quick wave, she climbed into her car, turned the key in the ignition, and put the air-conditioning on high. She sat there, letting the cool air blast her face, and shook her head at herself. "What the hell are you doing?"

"I can't talk right now, Mom," Crash said. She tried to balance her cell phone between her ear and her shoulder while she perched on the sofa bed and tied her laces. "I'm on my way out the door."

"Are you going out with someone?" her mother asked predictably.

God, why couldn't her mom be like the mothers of so many other lesbians—ignoring her daughter's love life, in deep denial about her sexual orientation? "No, Mom. Just going out for a bite to eat with a friend." She bit back the *unfortunately* on the tip of her tongue.

"What are you wearing?" her mother asked.

"I told you it's not a date, so it doesn't matter what I'm wearing," Crash said. Under no circumstances would she admit that she had dug out her best pair of slacks and the sleeveless white blouse that usually made women's gazes linger on her arms.

A moment of silence filtered through the line; then her mother cleared her throat. "You aren't having dinner with Jill Corrigan, are you?"

What was that tone supposed to mean? "I thought you were a fan of Jill's?"

"I am."

"Then why do you sound so disapproving now?"

"I don't disapprove of your friendship if it's really just that, but…" Her mother sighed. "I'm a fan of her acting, but I didn't know much about her personal life. After you told me you're…friends with her, I looked her up on Wikipedia."

Both were silent for several moments.

Laces tied, Crash dropped her foot back to the floor and stared down at it. "You know about the MS." She made it a statement, not a question.

"Yes. I'm sorry I nudged you to date her. Now I understand why you won't."

Crash's stomach churned. She flopped down onto the sofa bed and rubbed her eyes with her free hand. "It's not like you think. It's…complicated."

"You don't need to feel guilty," her mother said. "You'd be a fool not to consider the long-term consequences of getting involved with her. Do you remember Brett, that quarterback your father coached when you were little?"

Images of the big, burly teenager carrying her around on his shoulders flashed through Crash's mind. She couldn't have been more than six at the time, but she still remembered him. "Yeah. What about him?"

"He'd been offered a full-ride scholarship by several major colleges, but right before he finished high school, he was diagnosed with MS. He had to kiss his scholarship good-bye. By the time he graduated from college, he was in a wheelchair. Now he can't even tie his own shoes."

Tie his own shoes… An image of her kneeling to tie Jill's shoelaces shot through Crash's mind. Would that be Jill's future as well? And if it was, would someone be there to tie her laces for her? She wanted to push the thought away, as she had done for weeks, but this time, she didn't allow herself to do that but instead asked herself the question that had been on her mind all along: Could she be the one to be there for Jill? If push came to shove, did she really have what it took to be a long-term caregiver?

"Kristine? Are you still there?" her mother asked when she didn't say anything.

"Uh, yeah. Mom, that was twenty years ago. There was no medication whatsoever to help delay the progression of MS back then. Now there are twelve, and there's a lot of research being done. In five or maybe ten or fifteen years, there could be a cure."

"Let's hope so," her mother said. "But until then, I don't want you to live your life waiting for a 'could be.' It might be selfish, but I'm your mother, and I don't want that for you."

Crash ducked into the bathroom to comb her hair and spray a bit of perfume on her neck and wrists. "I don't want that either, but…"

"Then why did you just put on perfume, which you rarely ever do?"

Wha...? Crash glanced at the bathroom mirror as if expecting to see a hidden camera. "How did you...?"

Her mother chuckled, but it sounded a bit sad. "I know you."

Yeah. She did. And that was why she would find out sooner or later anyway. Crash took a deep breath. "We said it would be just a dinner between friends, but if Jill were open to it, I'd want it to be a date."

Her mother gasped. "No. Kristine. That's not a good idea. I'm sure Jill is a lovely woman, but getting involved with someone who has MS and could end up in a wheelchair... How would that fit into your life?"

"*She* would fit into my life. Besides, I said date, not get married, Mom."

"Like I said, I know you. And I know you're loyal to a fault. Once you're in, you're in. You wouldn't break up with her even if you have to spoon-feed her and change her diapers."

Crash squeezed her eyes shut against the mental image of Jill bedridden or wheelchair-bound.

"You'd have to give up everything that has been important in your life so far—traveling, going out, sports," her mother said into the silence. "You've always been so active, even as a child. If you get involved with her and her illness progresses, you'll be tied to the house along with her."

"I know," Crash croaked out. "Don't you think I did a lot of research and soul-searching about that?"

"Soul-searching... That sounds like you're considering more than just a date."

Crash sank against the doorjamb. "I don't know, Mom. I'm not sure of much these days. Maybe I'll end up regretting it, but I think I'm going to regret it more if I pushed Jill away just because I'm afraid." A sigh escaped her. "She's doing enough of that for the both of us."

"So she doesn't want to date you?"

"At least that's what she says." Crash glanced at her wristwatch. *Shit.* If she didn't hurry, she'd be late. Not a good way to start their dinner that might or might not be a date. She hurried out of the bathroom and grabbed her car keys and the dark gray blazer with the Chinese collar on the way to the door. "Mom, I really have to go now. Say hi to Dad and the boys for me, if you talk to them. And don't worry so much about me, okay?"

Her mother snorted. "I'm your mother. It's my job to worry."

Crash didn't know what to say to that. "I'll call you next week. Good night." After pressing the end-call button, she stood there for a second, letting the entire conversation play back in her mind. She shook herself out of her morose mood.

For now, she would focus on having a nice evening—and maybe a night full of passion—with Jill. She would worry about the rest tomorrow.

It was one minute past eight, and Crash still hadn't arrived. Not that Jill was watching the clock or anything. She peered through the blinds, even knowing that the ivy-covered brick wall surrounding her house would block her view.

"Your date isn't going to stand you up, is she?"

The sudden voice behind her made Jill clutch her chest and whirl around. She'd forgotten that Susana was still there, cleaning the house in preparation of the Fourth of July, even though Jill had told her it wasn't necessary since she wouldn't have anyone over. She had a feeling that her curious housekeeper had stayed longer so she would still be there when Crash arrived, not because of dusty cabinets.

"Would you stop it? I told you Crash is just a friend."

"Crash." Susana smacked her lips as if tasting the word. She wrinkled her nose. "What kind of name is that?"

Jill shrugged. In the beginning, she had found it strange too, but now she no longer thought about it. "She's a stuntwoman."

"Ooh! She's an adventurous one, sí?" Susana grinned at her.

Jill just shook her head. It still amazed her a little how casual her housekeeper was about her sexual orientation, even though she'd come to the US as a child and grown up in a Catholic family. If only her own parents could be more like that.

"Crash's adventurous nature is none of my business—or yours," Jill said, playfully wagging her finger at Susana. "We aren't dating."

"Oh, so that must be why you're wearing such nice clothes...and why you put on perfume."

Jill peered down at the jade-colored blouse and the brand-new jeans that hugged her figure nicely. "There's nothing wrong with smelling good and looking nice while having dinner with a friend, is there?"

"No. Nothing wrong with that," Susana said. "Nothing wrong with going out on a date either."

"Do we really need to have this discussion again? It's bad enough that Crash is constantly trying to get me to reconsider."

"Oh, she does?" Susana smiled broadly. "I like her already."

Me too. And that was the problem.

The gate buzzer sounded.

Tramp jumped up from his bed and started barking.

"Tramp, hush!" Jill hurried past Susana to the intercom next to the door. "Yes?"

"Hi, it's me—Crash."

Jill's heart beat faster as she buzzed her in.

A minute later, a knock sounded on the door.

Tramp was still barking and blocking the door in his excitement to greet the visitor first. He danced around in the hall, sniffing and then wagging his tail as if he knew exactly who was on the other side of the door.

Jill pushed him back with one hand, straightened the collar of her blouse with the other, and swung the door open.

Suddenly, she was glad for Tramp's eager greeting, because it gave her a moment to collect herself and to force some fluid back into her parched mouth so she could speak. "Uh, hi," was the culmination of her efforts as her gaze roved over Crash's bare arms and the sporty blazer she had casually tossed over one shoulder.

"Hi." Crash bent to greet Tramp and then straightened.

Was there a handbook for this kind of situation? If there was, Jill wanted a copy. How did you greet a friend with benefits? As much as she wanted to kiss Crash, it seemed too intimate without the context of sex, especially with Susana watching. A handshake was too clinical. Their simple "hi" was a bit lame.

Crash solved her problem by stepping closer and giving her a short hug.

The scent of her perfume—clean and fresh with a spicy edge—made Jill weak in the knees. She melted against Crash's body until their heat mingled.

Very aware of Susana lingering somewhere behind her, she forced herself to back away after a few seconds.

"You look great." Crash let her gaze rove over Jill's blouse and jeans.

"So do you." Good thing they were going to a restaurant, not to a lesbian bar, because Jill had no intention of spending the evening chasing off all the women salivating over Crash. Not that she had a right to chase them off, she reminded herself. She cleared her throat and tore her gaze away from Crash's arms, left bare by her sleeveless white blouse.

"Nice house," Crash said, peering past Jill into the living room. "Yours?"

"Yes. Well, mine and the bank's. My grandparents left me some money, and I'm still paying off the rest. Shall we?"

"Aren't you going to ask her in for a tour?" Susana asked from behind her.

Grudgingly, Jill stepped back to let Crash enter. She hadn't wanted her to get too familiar with her home—or with Susana. It felt too much like introducing a date to her family. "Crash, this is Susana Rosales, my housekeeper and friend…and Tramp's grandmother," she added, earning her a swat to the shoulder. "Susana, this is Crash…Kristine Patterson, my…friend."

"Pleased to meet you." Crash flashed one of her charming smiles as she shook Susana's hand.

Susana returned the smile and the handshake.

"Come on. I'll give you the nickel tour." Jill tugged on her arm, drawing Crash with her before Susana could interrogate her.

Tramp followed them as they went from the kitchen to the office and from there to the living room.

Crash looked around with obvious interest, and Jill wondered what she made of the butter-soft leather couch, the long bookcase, and the exercise bike set up along one wall so Jill could watch TV while she exercised.

Crash wandered to the single French door that led to the backyard and peered out. "What's that?"

Reluctantly, Jill joined her and saw that Crash was pointing at the tire jump, the short tunnel, and the modest A-frame in her backyard. "Oh, those are just a few obstacles that I set up for Tramp. We're taking agility classes once a week. Nothing too ambitious, but it's fun and it helps me stay fit." When someone had voiced doubts that she'd be able to run alongside Tramp to guide him, it had only made her more determined to try. And when her left leg was acting up, Susana's son ran him through the course for her.

"Wow," Crash said. "That's impressive."

Jill grinned. "What? I think she thought we're just beautiful blonde airheads, Tramp." She caressed the dog's golden fur.

"You're not a blonde," Crash said, grinning back.

"No, but I played one on TV."

Crash laughed.

The sound of her laughter poured over Jill like sunshine and made her smile reflexively. If only things could always be like this.

They continued the tour.

"And what's up there?" Crash asked, pointing to the stairs.

"Just the master bedroom, my bathroom, and a guest room," Jill said but didn't take her upstairs. Fatigue had weighed her down all day, and she didn't want to exhaust herself before the evening started by climbing the stairs. She'd rather conserve her energy for later tonight. The thought made heat pool low in her belly. "We should go. I booked a table for eight."

"Have a nice evening," Susana said with a broad grin and held on to Tramp so they could leave the house without him following.

They walked the five blocks to the restaurant side by side, glancing at each other out of the corner of their eyes.

God, Crash looked good. Jill's gaze trailed down her bare arm to her hand. She wanted so much to reach over and entwine their fingers, but she had been the one who insisted it wasn't a date, so she couldn't very well...

Before she finished the thought, Crash's hand slid into hers.

Startled, Jill looked over at her.

"Is this okay?" Crash asked. "I know you said you didn't... It just feels so natural."

Yes, it did. Jill curled her fingers around Crash's. "It's okay." No harm in allowing herself to dream a little, right?

They continued their way without saying anything else about it.

"Sorry I was a bit late," Crash said before the silence could grow awkward. "My mother called just as I was about to leave, and she wanted to know all the details about where I was going. You know how mothers can be."

"Not really. When my mother calls me, it's either to brag about my brother's latest success in his job as an insurance agent or to give me health advice."

"Is she a doctor?"

Jill snorted. "No. She's a housewife. She just makes it her mission to read up on any new health fad that could help MS patients."

"That's good, right? I mean, she's trying to be there for you."

"That's not the best way to do that. Most of these so-called miracle cures are just wasting my valuable time."

"Have you told her that?" Crash asked softly.

Jill nodded. "More than once. But every time I do, she claims that I'm just stubborn and in denial."

"Which you, of course, aren't." The corners of Crash's mouth twitched as if she was trying not to grin.

"No. Yeah, okay, maybe I can be a little stubborn at times, but I'm not in denial." At least she didn't think so. She was injecting herself and taking vitamin D pills every day; there was always a fold-up cane and a foot brace in the trunk of her car, just in case, and she avoided getting involved with anyone. She was facing her MS with her eyes wide open, wasn't she?

The warmth of Crash's hand holding hers told her that she might not be as successful avoiding emotional involvement as she wanted to think.

But Crash's fingers entwined with her own felt too good to let go. "So, what did you tell your mother?" she asked to distract herself.

"That it's complicated," Crash said and left it at that.

"I assume she knows you're gay?"

Crash smiled. "I think she knew when I kept asking for more private lessons because I had a crush on Delia, my math tutor. Normally, she couldn't keep me inside long enough to even open the math book."

"How old were you?" Jill asked.

"Nine or ten. Delia broke my little heart when she started dating one of my brothers." Crash clutched her chest in a theatrical gesture.

Jill chuckled. "That bitch."

"I got over it. Now we laugh about it every time we talk about it."

"You're still in contact with your math tutor?" Jill asked. She hadn't kept in touch with anyone from back home when she had moved to LA. Somehow, she felt she'd outgrown her old friends and no longer had things in common with them.

Crash nodded and smiled. "I'd better. She's now my sister-in-law."

Wow. Her family gatherings must be interesting. Their conversation made the walk to the restaurant pass by quickly, but Jill was glad when they approached the red brick building. Her legs felt like lead, and she had to look where she was stepping because her feet were numb, not giving her any sensory feedback.

She ignored it, not wanting the MS to intrude on their evening. "Here we are," she said and pointed over to the restaurant's entrance, which was flanked by two palm trees.

She stopped and looked back and forth between the door and the restaurant's courtyard. The sun was about to set, and the lights wrapped around the tall trees in the courtyard were twinkling invitingly.

She should steer them inside, where air-conditioning would help keep her body temperature down and where the setting wasn't as romantic.

But she wanted Crash to experience the best of what her favorite restaurant had to offer. For just this evening, she wanted to let herself imagine what it would be like to really be on a date with Crash. "Want to sit outside?"

"Sure, that sounds nice."

They stepped onto the large outdoor patio, where two rows of tables were set up beneath striped awnings.

The hostess approached immediately. "Hi, Jill. Table for two?"

"Hi, Laleh. Yes, please." Jill could feel Crash's surprise as she looked from Jill to their hostess.

Laleh seated them at a small table in a quiet corner, away from the busiest section of the patio. She handed them the menus, lit a candle in a glass globe in the middle of the table, and asked for their drink order. Before she walked away, she winked at Jill.

Obviously, she had seen them walking hand in hand.

"It seems you've been here before," Crash said.

Jill shrugged. "What can I say? The food is great."

Crash studied the wall next to their table, which was decorated with a mural of a beautiful seascape. Finally, she turned her attention to the menu. "Anything you can recommend?"

"Everything is good, but the portions are gigantic," Jill said and nodded toward the plates that were being served at the table next to theirs. "Want to share something?"

Crash didn't hesitate. "Sure. Why don't you pick since you've been here before?"

Hmm. A woman who wasn't afraid to hand over control. Jill liked that. Again, she couldn't help noticing how compatible they seemed to be. It was a bittersweet realization.

When Laleh returned to bring Crash's Armenian light beer and to refill Jill's water, Jill ordered the chicken soltani for them to share.

"Excellent choice," Laleh said with a nod of acknowledgment. "You're a woman of great taste."

"You say that every time, no matter what I order."

Laleh grinned. "That's because everything on the menu is an excellent choice. I'll be right back with the lavash."

Crash watched her leave before turning back toward Jill. "Is she just super friendly, or did the two of you use to date?"

Was it just her imagination, or did Crash seem a little jealous? "I told you I don't date."

"Maybe not right now, but you didn't always have MS."

The intrusion of her multiple sclerosis into the evening made Jill flinch. Couldn't she have even one evening alone with Crash? "No, we never dated. Perhaps Laleh just likes me because I tip well," she answered, trying to keep her tone light.

Laleh returned with a stack of thin, soft lavash bread, plates of fresh herbs, and bowls of different dips that came before every meal. "Don't listen to her," she said to Crash. "I like her because she gets me tickets to movie premieres."

Crash looked back and forth between them.

"We've been friends ever since I bought the house a couple of years ago," Jill finally explained as Laleh walked away. "Her family owns the restaurant, and since I'm not much of a cook, I spend a lot of time here."

She showed Crash how to sprinkle basil and mint on the lavash, roll it up, and dip it alternately in the eggplant dip, the hummus, and the yogurt-and-cucumber dip. She enjoyed being the instructor instead of the student for once. It was a nice change of pace from their interactions on the set, where Crash was the one teaching her how to move when they filmed the lead-ins for the stunts. This was what a relationship was supposed to be like—them taking turns helping each other, not her always being on the receiving end.

"Ooh, this is good," Crash said between two bites. "Tell them to forget about the main dish."

Jill laughed. "Oh, you say that now. Wait until you taste the charbroiled chicken."

"I usually don't eat like this." Crash gestured at the linen-topped table, which was already covered with plates and bowls.

"I noticed." On the set, Crash ate even less than Jill did—usually just a salad for lunch, and if they started shooting early in the morning, she came in with a smoothie while other actresses were sipping their coffee. "Stuntwomen are probably under the same pressure to stay thin as actresses, right?"

"Worse, actually," Crash said and, as if to contradict or rebel against what she was saying, reached for another piece of bread.

"Worse?" Jill paused with a piece of eggplant-dipped bread hovering in front of her lips. "Why's that? I would have thought that stuntwomen needed to be athletic, not rail-thin."

Crash reached out for one of the bowls, hesitated, and then seemed to decide against putting onions on her bread. "They need to be both. For some stunts, you have to put on hip, butt, and thigh pads, so you appear bigger than the actress you're doubling for. You can imagine that most actresses wouldn't be pleased if their stunt doubles make them look fat on camera."

"Well, this actress is very pleased with the way her stunt double looks," Jill commented.

They shared a grin across the table, the magnetism between them in full force.

Jill could only hope that she'd have the energy to end the night the way she wanted it to end—in Crash's arms. "Trying to be thinner than most actresses in Hollywood is just crazy," she added.

"Tell me about it. I don't like it, but that's the way it is. Which is why you need to take this bread away from me."

Jill, of course, didn't. She enjoyed seeing Crash lick bits of dip off her fingers too much. "Stuntwomen are much more physically active than actresses, so you must burn off a lot more calories."

"True," Crash said and took another piece of bread. Finally, she pushed her plate back and leaned her dimpled chin on her hand. The candle cast a soft glow over her features. "But let's not talk about me all night. Tell me about yourself."

Jill hesitated. The soft music, the romantic lights, the getting-to-know-each-other conversation... This really was a date, wasn't it? Was she ready to have that happen?

"I told you my math-tutor story," Crash said when Jill remained silent. "Tell me how you realized you're a lesbian."

Okay, that was a harmless enough story. "I don't really remember it, but when I was five, I apparently told my parents that I wanted to be an actress and marry Sandra Bullock when I grew up."

"Cute," Crash said with a wide grin.

Jill gave an impish smirk. "Me or Sandra Bullock?"

"Well, Sandra Bullock looks great for a woman her age, but I was talking about you," Crash said.

Laleh returned with their food in record time. Skewers of chicken breast kabob and ground chicken stretched from one end of the plate to the other. Both skewers lay on a huge pile of safran-tinted basmati rice and came with grilled tomatoes and peppers.

Jill spooned half of it onto the empty plate Laleh had brought for Crash. Her mouth watered, and she quickly got started on her own dinner. The chicken was tender and moist and charbroiled to perfection, just the way it always was. She hummed with satisfaction.

Crash tried a bit of the meat and let out a moan that made Jill's body heat as memories of what she'd done to make Crash sound like that in the past washed over her.

Crash's voice pulled her from her erotic haze.

"...that declaration?"

"Uh, excuse me? I was a little distracted for a moment."

Crash grinned as if she knew exactly what had distracted her. "I asked what your parents said to the declaration that you wanted to marry Sandra Bullock."

"They just laughed. No one took it seriously. I came out to them before I moved to LA."

"I bet they didn't laugh then," Crash said.

"No, they didn't. They didn't say much either. Well, except for James. My brother had plenty to say." Jill couldn't keep the hint of bitterness from her voice.

Crash lowered her fork and glanced over at her. "Is that the religious one who always quotes from the Bible before dinner?"

Wow. Jill was impressed that Crash actually remembered that. "Yes, that's him. I only have one brother."

"What about your parents? How did they react?"

"That's just it. They didn't," Jill said. "There were no tears, no shouting, no attempts to convince me it was just a phase. Nothing. They choose to ignore it for the most part. That's what they always do whenever I do something they don't approve of." The cold-shoulder treatment hurt, but she was used to it.

Crash slowly shook her head. "I can't even imagine what that must be like. In my family, nothing is ever ignored. Everyone is in each other's business all the time, especially my mother."

"So if she knew about..." Jill bit back the *us* on the tip of her tongue and instead said, "...that we're sleeping together, she'd be on the next plane to LA with her shotgun, demanding that I make an honest woman out of you?"

Crash laughed. "Not exactly, but she would demand that I bring you home to meet the family somewhere around the second date."

Even if she knew about the MS? Jill couldn't believe that. "Well, maybe there is something to be said for my family's don't-ask-don't-tell policy."

During the rest of dinner, conversation flowed smoothly. Jill didn't want the evening to end, but exhaustion hit her long before they finished their meal. She struggled to suppress a yawn. It was more than merely being tired. She had never been able to explain MS-related fatigue to a person who didn't suffer from it. It felt as if she'd been awake for twenty-four hours, and sometimes, that feeling hit her out of the blue, occasionally even in the morning after a good night's sleep.

She declined dessert when Laleh asked, and to her relief, Crash didn't want anything either, so Jill asked for the check.

When they eventually got up and started to make their way across the patio, Jill stumbled—maybe over an uneven patch of floor, maybe over her own numb feet. Only Crash's fast reflexes and her secure grasp around Jill's waist prevented her from landing face-first in someone's dinner.

"You okay?" Crash asked right next to her ear. She still didn't let go, even after Jill had regained her footing.

Jill slowly exhaled. "I'm fine. Thank you."

Hesitatingly, Crash relinquished her hold.

Laleh rushed over. "Jill! Are you all right?" She patted Jill down, brushing her hand over Jill's clothes as if she had actually taken a header into someone's food and needed to be cleaned up.

The people at the tables surrounding them looked over.

All the attention made Jill's cheeks heat with embarrassment. She ignored the glances and gently brushed off Laleh's helping hands. "I'm fine," she said again. "I just didn't pay attention to where I was going. Guess the great chicken soltani put me into a food coma."

Laleh laughed. "It's been known to happen."

Crash didn't laugh. She stuck close to Jill as they made their way out of the restaurant and down the street.

"Stop it," Jill said.

"Stop what?"

"Hovering and looking at me."

Crash smiled. "Maybe I like looking at you."

Even though her near fall made Jill a bit grouchy, she couldn't hold on to her bad mood.

Crash shortened her steps and took her hand again, and Jill welcomed it—only because she liked the feeling, not because she needed the support.

When they reached Crash's car, which was parked along the wall surrounding Jill's house, they kept walking as if by silent agreement. At the gate, they paused and faced each other.

"So," Crash said.

"So," Jill repeated.

A soft smile curved Crash's lips. "I believe someone promised me dessert. Can I come in?"

Jill hesitated. She wanted to ask her in; she really wanted to, but she just wasn't sure if she had enough energy for sex tonight. Did she have the right to ask Crash to just hold her, without anything else happening?

Before she could decide, Crash bent her head and started nibbling on Jill's neck.

All of Jill's bones seemed to liquefy in an instant. A wave of desire washed away her exhaustion. She clutched Crash's back with both hands, enjoying the feeling of slender muscles beneath her fingers as Crash's lips wandered up to her earlobe.

"Code," Crash breathed into her ear.

"Huh?" Jill's brain had trouble processing thoughts. It was too busy with the sensations coursing through her body. Never before had a woman reduced her to three-letter words so easily.

Crash let her hands run up and down Jill's sides. "We need the security code to get inside and into the house."

"Yeah." It took Jill a moment to remember that she was the one who had the code. She kicked herself into gear and entered the four digits into the panel next to the gate.

They tumbled inside, up the driveway, and into the house, arms around each other, mouths fused.

Jill slid her hands beneath Crash's blazer, pushed it back, and let it drop to the side table, eager to get to some bare skin. Her fingertips explored the gentle curve of Crash's biceps, then up to strong shoulders. Still moving them through the hall, she struggled with the top button on Crash's blouse.

Tramp came running, nearly making them trip over him. He sniffed to see if they had brought him anything, then trotted off when it turned out they hadn't.

Jill tugged her toward the stairs leading to the master bedroom. Halfway up the stairs, her left foot started dragging, instantly cooling her libido as she struggled not to fall or to draw Crash's attention toward her leg.

Crash looped one arm around her, either to bring her closer or to steady her; Jill wasn't sure. "You should move your bedroom downstairs," Crash said in a light tone.

Jill pulled free of her gentle grip. Grace and Lauren had suggested the same, and other friends such as Amanda and Michelle had commented on it too, but Jill didn't want to take that step before it became absolutely necessary. Reorganizing her home would have felt like an admission that the MS was the mistress ruling her life. "That's not necessary. I can manage."

"Yeah. But maybe I can't wait. If your bedroom were downstairs, I could already…"

At the tone of Crash's voice, a shiver went through Jill. "You could already do what?"

On the top step, Crash wrapped both arms around her and kissed her with a passion that made Jill's legs feel even weaker than they already did after navigating the stairs. "I could tell you," Crash whispered against her lips. "Or I could show you." She looked at Jill, her eyes burning with desire. "Your choice."

Instead of a verbal answer, Jill took her by the hand and pulled her into the bedroom.

Crash guided Jill backward toward the bed, taking a moment to look around Jill's bedroom—light cream walls, a wooden dresser with deep red drawers, and syringes on the bedside table—before the back of Jill's knees hit the mattress.

She ran her hands over Jill's hips. That curve felt so good, as if it had been made just for her touch. The urge to feel Jill naked beneath her gripped her, and she struggled not to rip Jill's blouse open.

Slow, slow, she urged herself. Even though Jill had extended their "just one time" arrangement, she feared that Jill might pull the plug any day and decide that they were getting too close and needed to end things. So Crash was determined to enjoy this night, because it might be their last one together.

She held her breath as she reached for the top button on Jill's blouse, not sure if Jill would allow her to undress her after the shoelace incident.

But in this context, Jill seemed fine with it. Her face was flushed, and her lids heavy with desire. She kicked off her shoes and struggled with her belt while Crash slid the blouse down her creamy-pale arms. At Jill's wrists, the blouse caught, for a moment shackling her arms to her sides.

Crash pulled the blouse off Jill's hands and let it drop to the floor. Her own top and Jill's jeans and bra followed. Impatient to feel Jill against her, she guided her onto the bed and immediately covered her body with her own. Jill's heat filtered through the fabric of Crash's slacks. She leaned over Jill, balancing on her elbows to keep most of her weight off her, and kissed a path down Jill's neck.

By now, she was familiar with Jill's body and knew where to touch her to make her sigh and moan and whisper Crash's name in that breathless, husky tone that made Crash's head spin with the excitement of it all.

She placed a string of open-mouthed kisses down Jill's chest and licked the underside of one breast.

Jill's hands came up, and her fingers tangled in Crash's hair, trying to guide her to her breast.

Crash playfully resisted. She nibbled the outer curve of one breast and took her time caressing Jill's sides and the arch of each rib before moving on and kissing a slow trail down her belly.

A red mark, like the one she'd found on Jill's hip, graced her belly. This time, she knew better than to ask about it. A bit of research online had revealed that it was probably a skin irritation on one of the alternating injection sites.

She kissed Jill's skin all around the mark and paused with her lips hovering just above the lacy edge of Jill's panties. That close, she imagined she could already smell Jill's musky scent. With her fingers on the elastic, she hesitated.

The previous times they had slept together, they had both avoided oral sex. But now it was becoming harder and harder to resist the urge to taste Jill.

Jill didn't stop her as Crash pulled the panties down a bit, but neither did she encourage her by guiding her hands or her head or by lifting her hips off the bed so Crash could strip off the last article of clothing.

Crash looked up to gauge her reaction.

Jill's eyes were closed—not in pleasure, but in deep sleep.

No. She didn't...? Crash squinted and took another look to make sure she wasn't imagining things. Sure enough—Jill had fallen asleep. Her bare chest lifted and fell in the regular pattern of sleep.

Sighing, Crash rolled off her and lay next to the sleeping woman, staring up at the ceiling. She could honestly say that something like this had never happened to her before. Huffing out a frustrated sigh, she let her hand trail down beneath her own legs and squeezed softly. God, she was so turned on. She could feel the heat and the wetness even through the fabric of her slacks. For a moment, she was tempted to slide her hand down her pants and take care of herself, but with Jill peacefully sleeping next to her, it felt too weird.

She pulled her hand away and shook her head at the situation. A wry grin turned into a quiet chuckle. When she had read about the effects MS could have on Jill's energy level and her libido, she had wondered how she would deal with a situation like this. Well, now she had a chance to find out.

She turned onto her side and watched Jill sleep.

In repose, the witty, always strong woman looked very young and vulnerable.

Crash wanted to wrap her arms around her and protect Jill, but she knew it was impossible. Jill would never allow it anyway; she insisted on being her own protector.

She eyed her shoes and her blouse, which formed a trail from the door to the bed. Should she get up, dress, and leave? But she didn't know the security code that would lock the door and secure the home behind her, and she didn't want to leave Jill defenseless. Knowing Tramp, he would greet any burglar with friendly licks.

Truth be told, she didn't want to leave. Moving carefully so she wouldn't wake Jill, she stripped off her slacks and her bra and dropped them on the pile of clothes next to the bed. After one last glance at Jill, who still slept soundly next to her, she turned off the light, moved closer until she felt the heat of Jill's skin against hers, and closed her eyes.

Despite the uncomfortable pressure between her legs, Jill's soft breathing quickly lulled her to sleep.

CHAPTER 16

An uncomfortable sensation in her left leg woke Jill. That wasn't anything unusual. But when she shifted, trying to ease the discomfort, she discovered that it wasn't the MS that created the strange sensation this time.

She opened her eyes. Sunlight was streaming in through her bedroom window. Another woman's bare leg lay across her equally naked one, pinning her thigh to the bed.

Wait a minute! How had she gotten into bed, much less naked with another woman?

Even without looking, she knew who it was. By now, she was familiar with the toned body that was pressed up against hers. *Crash.* As soon as she thought the name, the fog of sleep cleared and she remembered. *We got home from the restaurant and went upstairs, and she undressed me and started kissing my chest and then...*

Nothing. She couldn't remember what had come after that.

Oh no. She pressed her forearm over her eyes, covering half of her burning face. *Don't tell me I fell asleep on her!*

She took stock of her body, then slid her hand down Crash's, who mumbled something unintelligible and pressed closer but didn't wake. Jill discovered that they were both still wearing their panties. The rest of their clothing was strewn around the bed. *Shit.* She had indeed fallen asleep in the middle of things.

And that's why you have no business being with her. You don't even have the energy for a sexual fling anymore. Damn fatigue. Tears burned in her eyes.

Then Crash flung her arm over her too, now trapping her completely.

Yet she's still here, even though I left her with the lesbian equivalent of blue balls. Her body was warm against Jill's, the hard muscles softened by smooth skin. Jill had missed waking up in her arms. For a moment, she allowed herself to imagine again what it would be like to always wake up like this, to share her life with Crash.

But last night had been proof that it wouldn't be fair to Crash. It was enough to have her own life destroyed by the MS; she wouldn't allow it to rule Crash's too.

Jill was just about to slip out from under Crash without waking her when the gate buzzer sounded and Tramp started to bark downstairs. She froze.

Crash's relaxed body took on the tension of wakefulness. Her right arm flexed around Jill. Her eyes blinked open, and she looked at Jill from just inches away. A smile formed on her face, so tender and intimate that Jill was torn between sinking back into her arms and fleeing downstairs. "Good morning."

"Morning. The bell rang. Someone's outside the gate." Jill pointed in the direction of the front door. "I need to get up."

"Oh. Sure." Crash took her arm away and rolled to the other side of the bed.

Jill instantly missed their body contact.

The buzzer sounded again.

"Yeah, yeah. Hold your horses. I'm coming." Her days of jumping out of bed were over. Jill rose slowly until she was sure that both legs felt steady. When everything seemed to be in working order, she reached for a robe and made her way down the stairs. She pressed the button for the intercom so she could talk to the person outside of her gate, while using her free hand to rub Tramp's ears. "Yes?"

"Finally," a male voice said. "What took you so long?"

Jill's jaw gaped open. "James?"

"The one and only," he answered.

"What are you doing here?" Her brother had visited her only once since she'd moved into the house, and they hadn't talked at all in the last year since she'd told him she had MS and he had declared it God's punishment for her being gay.

"It wasn't my idea. I was in LA for a conference this week, and Mom insisted I stop by and make sure you're doing okay before I fly back."

"I'm fine," Jill said. Why was it that she had to say that so often nowadays?

"So you aren't going to let me in?" James asked.

Jill sighed. No doubt he'd report back to their parents if she didn't. He'd always been a little tattletale, even as a child. Whenever Jill had been up to any kind of mischief, he'd run straight to their parents and had given her away. No wonder perfect James was their favorite. Gritting her teeth, she pressed the button that would open the gate.

When she opened the door for him, Tramp rushed outside, and this time, Jill didn't hold him back. Let James be scared for a moment before he realized Tramp was just a cuddly teddy bear, eager to be petted. Not that James would ever pet an animal when he was dressed in his pinstriped suit, as he was now.

He stepped around Tramp and into the house and let his disapproving gaze wander over her bathrobe-clad body. "You're not even dressed? It's after nine already."

"So what? Is there a law that forbids bathrobes after nine?" Jill asked, folding her arms over the terrycloth robe.

He shook his head at her. "Of course not. But do you really have to live up to all of the stereotypes about Hollywood starlets?"

"What stereotypes are that, pray tell?"

"Staying up late, partying and doing God knows what, and then sleeping all day."

"How would you know that's what I've been doing?" Jill asked, not even trying to hide her bitterness. "You haven't been part of my life for a long time."

He slowly straightened his tie. "I don't need to be part of your life to know the obvious. There's an SUV parked right outside your property, you're still in bed after nine, and I can hear someone moving around upstairs."

"That's none of your business." Jill's muscles tensed until she thought they would start to cramp.

"The heck it's not! You're still my sister!" He slammed his hand against the wall next to her head, but Jill tried her best not to flinch.

Tramp started to growl, which Jill had never heard him do.

"What am I supposed to tell Mom when she asks about you?" James asked with a challenging stance. "That I found you in bed with another woman? I thought you gave that up when you found out about the MS? You know, I always thought it was a good thing that you got the illness. It stopped you from acting on your attraction to women."

Jill had heard him say similar things before, so it shouldn't have been a surprise. His words still hit her like a punch to the gut. How could he, her own brother, say something so hateful? Anger and sadness warred with each other, surpassed only by disbelief.

Before she could think of an answer, Crash was suddenly next to her, dressed in the sleeveless blouse and the pair of slacks from last night. For once, her blue eyes appeared cold, narrowed to slivers of ice. "I think it's time for you to go."

"Who are you?" James asked, squaring off against her.

"Someone who won't allow you to talk to Jill that way," Crash said. Her voice was controlled, but it vibrated with tension, and her hands were curled to fists at her sides. She stabbed her finger toward the door. "Go. Now!"

His face turned red with anger. For a moment, he looked as if he wanted to get into a fight with her, but then his survival instinct kicked in.

The normally easygoing Crash radiated danger, making even Jill's jackass of a brother think twice about getting into her face.

Jill almost wished he were less of a coward. She was pretty sure that Crash could have kicked his butt from here all the way back to Ohio without even breaking a sweat. A part of her would have loved nothing better than to see that.

James turned toward Jill. "Will you really allow your...your...girlfriend," he spat out the word, "to treat your own brother like that?"

A grim smile stretched across Jill's face. "Yes," she said, not bothering to correct him about who Crash was to her. "You don't deserve any other treatment.

Mom sent you to make sure I'm okay. Not to criticize the way I live my life or to make hurtful comments. If that's all you can do, then we have nothing to say to each other."

He regarded her for a moment and then shook his head. "I will never be able to understand how two siblings can be so different."

"That might be the only thing we will ever agree on," Jill said and opened the door for him. "Good-bye, James. And don't come back until you can accept me for who I am, not who you want me to be."

After glancing back and forth between her and Crash, James finally turned and stepped outside.

Jill didn't wait for his parting words, knowing she wouldn't like them. She closed the door in his face before he could open his mouth.

Crash stared at the door and then at Jill. "What the hell was that?"

"My brother."

"I gathered that. But what he said about you and the MS..." Crash shook her head, her puzzlement and shock obvious. "My mother would wash out their mouths with soap if my brothers ever dared to say such a thing to me."

Jill sighed. "I wish I could say he's not usually like that, but sadly, he is. We have never been overly close, and telling him I'm gay didn't exactly bring us any closer. He told me he could accept my being gay as long as I don't act on it."

"How generous of him," Crash said, hurling an angry glare toward the door.

Jill took several steadying breaths and tried to calm the raw emotions coursing through her. It wasn't just the anger toward James; she was embarrassed that Crash had to witness her brother's behavior. Jill had never wanted or needed a knight in shining armor to fight her battles for her, but a part of her had to admit that it felt good to have Crash kick out her brother and become so upset on her behalf. Her parents had never defended her like that when James started with his homophobic rants.

The funny thing was that nothing had even happened between her and Crash last night, no matter what James thought. Heat suffused her cheeks as she was reminded of her falling asleep in the middle of things. "I'm sorry."

"You don't have to apologize. It's not your fault that your brother is a homophobic asshole."

"I'm not just talking about my brother," Jill said. She would rather forget about it, but she forced herself to continue. "I'm talking about last night too."

Crash waved her away. "No need to apologize for that either. Last night was great."

Her kindness only sparked Jill's anger. "Yeah, up until I fell asleep in the middle of making...in the middle of sex. I bet that never happened to you before."

"So I'm expanding my horizons," Crash said with a shrug and a grin. "Nothing wrong with that. It's not the end of the world."

"Let's cut the bullshit, Crash." She had never allowed herself any cop-outs and excuses, and she wouldn't start now. "Being left to take care of your own needs while I snored next to you in bed and then having to face my homophobic brother the next morning is not what you signed up for."

"Like I told you before, as a stuntwoman, I have learned to roll with the punches."

Jill shook her head. "You shouldn't have to. Adjusting is what people in a relationship have to do. Not someone who's having a sexual fling."

Crash clamped her teeth onto her bottom lip as if holding back what she really wanted to say. "God, Jill. You hold yourself to damn high standards. Doesn't it get exhausting?"

You have no idea. Jill rubbed her forehead.

"Listen," Crash said when Jill didn't answer. "Things like that happen, especially if you work long hours and have to deal with fatigue. It's not a big deal."

"Maybe it is to me," Jill whispered, talking more to herself than to Crash.

"So, what do you want to do?" Crash asked. "End things just because you can't stand having me see you weak, even for a moment?"

The words shocked Jill into silence for a moment. "No. I... It's not about..." She drilled her fingernails into her palms. Dammit. Crash was right. She'd always hated for anyone to see her weak, but with Crash it was even worse—maybe because what Crash thought of her mattered more than anyone else's opinion. "No," she finally got out. "No. I never said I wanted to end it now. I just... I want you to know that it wasn't you. I still find you desirable. It's just... It was a long week, and I was pretty tired."

"It's okay," Crash said softly. "Really. You don't have to explain yourself."

Her easy acceptance felt good, especially since it was the opposite of what she got from her family, but at the same time, Jill hated that it was necessary.

Crash nudged her. "If it makes you feel better, you could give me another rain check." She gave Jill one of her sexy grins.

She couldn't help returning it with a smile of her own. "You want me to make you out a rain check on sex?" She mimicked writing a note. "Good for one orgasm?"

Crash laughed, and a bit of the carefree mood that Jill always enjoyed in Crash's presence returned. "At least one," she said, the seductive timbre of her voice making Jill shiver in the best of ways. "But how about we start with breakfast?"

Breakfast sounded good. It seemed she needed all the energy she could get. "All right. Since I couldn't keep my promise of dessert last night, the least I could do is make you pancakes."

"You said you weren't much of a cook. Do you know how to make pancakes?" Crash asked.

Jill smirked. "You're about to find out."

Jill tried to forget her stupid brother, the MS, and every other negative thing in her life while she cracked the eggs. There would be time to deal with all the emotions brewing inside of her later. For now, she just wanted to have a relaxing Sunday morning, like any normal person.

She hadn't bothered getting dressed, and the front of her bathrobe slid apart while she stirred the pancake batter.

Crash sat with both elbows leaned on the breakfast bar, her head in her hands. Her gaze followed Jill around the room as if she were watching her accomplish some fascinating feat and didn't want to miss even a second.

Those glances were a balm for Jill's bruised ego. She soaked up Crash's admiration and grinned to herself as she poured a bit of the batter into the hot frying pan. Maybe they could go back to bed after breakfast, and Crash could cash in that rain check.

They bantered back and forth while they ate, stealing bites of food from each other's plates. It reminded Jill of having breakfast with a lover—someone she loved and was in a relationship with—and she allowed herself to indulge in the illusion for a few minutes.

Then, just as she swiped the last piece of pancake through the puddle of maple syrup on her plate, she remembered that she had yet to inject herself. With everything that had been going on that morning she had completely forgotten, something that had never happened before.

For a moment, she was tempted to skip the injection just this once. Was it so wrong to want to feel like a normal person for one morning, someone who didn't have to start her day by sticking herself with a needle? The painful injections didn't even help with her everyday symptoms; they were meant to delay the next relapse.

She wanted to stay in the kitchen, do the dishes with Crash, and playfully flick sudsy water on each other. But finally reason won out. If she started skipping injections, the "just this once" would quickly become a habit. *The way it did with Crash.* She couldn't allow that. Suppressing a sigh, she returned to the reality of her life and got to her feet. "Would you excuse me for a minute? I'd like to get dressed."

Crash looked disappointed—maybe because she had entertained fantasies of going back to bed with Jill too—but she adjusted quickly. "Sure. I'll get started on the dishes."

Without another word, Jill walked toward the stairs.

"Jill?" Crash's voice reached her just as she'd set her foot onto the bottom stair.

She turned back toward the kitchen, expecting Crash to ask where she kept the dish towels or something like that. "Yes?"

"Are you okay?"

God, when had Crash gotten so good at reading her moods? Jill forced an upbeat tone to her voice as she answered, "I'm great. Be right back." The climb up the stairs, away from Crash, felt endless, this time not because of exhaustion, but because she knew what awaited her upstairs.

She hated arm days with a passion. The needle needed to be inserted into the back of one arm, which was hard to reach without help. It was also impossible to pinch a bit of skin since she needed her only available hand for handling the syringe. Over the course of the last almost two years, she had developed a routine. She prepared the injection, slid out of her bathrobe, and swabbed the back of her arm with an alcohol pad before straddling the chair she kept in her bedroom for just this purpose. Now came her little trick. She used the back of the chair to push the skin of her arm to the side so she could reach it better.

The angle didn't make it easy. It took her three tries before the needle finally pierced her skin, making her wince. Slowly, she pushed the plunger.

By the time Crash had cleared away the dishes and washed the frying pan, Jill was still upstairs. Crash stepped into the hall and listened, but everything was quiet in the bedroom.

Tramp bustled over. She scratched behind his ears and sent him a questioning look. "You wouldn't have any idea what's up with your mom, would you?"

Jill had appeared cheerful and relaxed during breakfast, but Crash sensed that a lot had been going on beneath the surface. Had she finally managed to get through to Jill and make her realize it wasn't necessary to hold her at arm's length? Or was Jill still thinking about the confrontation with her brother or her embarrassment about having fallen asleep?

Whatever it was, Crash didn't want to wait to find out. Tramp followed her as she climbed the stairs.

The bedroom door was ajar, and Crash peeked inside.

The first thing she saw was Jill's naked back. Crash's mouth went dry, and she marveled at how just seeing a bit of bare skin and that sexy flare of Jill's hips could have that effect on her.

Then she realized Jill wasn't sitting on that chair to put her socks on or something like that. She had her left arm up on the back of the chair and was using her right hand to insert a needle into her skin.

Crash stood frozen, any amorous thoughts gone. Instead, other emotions rushed through her, just as strong as that wave of desire—compassion, shock, even anger. How unfair that Jill had to go through this every day, probably for the rest of her life. Crash had known that Jill wasn't as healthy as she looked; she had witnessed symptoms such as stumbling, fighting with buttons, and being exhausted, but seeing her inject herself drove Jill's sickness home like nothing else before. In her line of work, Crash saw a lot of injuries, some of them horrific sights such as fractures with bones sticking through the skin, but nothing had ever shaken her the way seeing the needle pierce Jill's skin had.

Speechless and knowing that nothing she said or did could help Jill, she was just about to turn away and tiptoe back downstairs, when Tramp pushed past her and nudged the door open completely. He let out a low whine.

"What are you doing up here, boy? You're supposed to—" Jill turned. Her gaze met Crash's. Instantly, she jerked the needle out of her arm and dropped it to the dresser. Her cheeks flushed, but Crash couldn't tell if it stemmed from embarrassment or anger or a mix of both.

They stared at each other for several seconds, neither of them saying a word.

Then Jill reached for the abandoned bathrobe and slipped it on as if feeling exposed. Her movements were abrupt and jerky. "Could you give me a minute?" Her tone was rough and distant, so unlike the laughing, joking woman who had eaten pancakes with Crash just a few minutes ago.

"Uh, of course." Crash whirled around and quickly retreated. She paced the kitchen while she waited for Jill to come downstairs. Every second seemed to stretch and last an eternity. Would it be better if she just left, sparing Jill the need to face her? *Don't you mean sparing yourself the need to face her?*

In the end, she decided to stay where she was. It was how she handled tough situations at work—facing her fears instead of running away.

When Jill finally entered the kitchen, the bathrobe was nowhere to be seen. She was instead wearing a pair of jeans and a thin sweatshirt. Its long sleeves covered her arms, hiding any injection marks she might have.

"I'm sorry," Crash said immediately. "I didn't mean to intrude on your privacy. I know you don't—"

Jill lifted one hand. "It's okay." She sounded shaken, so her words weren't convincing. "Maybe it's for the best. I think we both needed the reminder."

She didn't elaborate; she didn't need to. Crash knew exactly what she meant: the reminder of why it wasn't a good idea to get involved with Jill. But as much of a shock as it had been to see Jill inject herself, it only made Crash more determined to be there for her.

Silence spread through the kitchen, interrupted only by the overly loud dripping of the tap.

Jill walked over, turned it off, and then leaned against the sink, keeping the breakfast bar between them as if she needed it as a barrier.

Crash took a step toward her. "Jill…"

"Please don't say anything. It is what it is."

"Which is…?" Crash wasn't even sure if Jill was talking about the MS or about them. "Talk to me, Jill. Please."

Jill white-knuckled the edge of the breakfast bar. "I can't."

"Please."

"You don't understand how it feels to…" She looked away.

Crash leaned against the breakfast bar from the other side and covered Jill's hand with her own. "I want to. I really want to understand you."

For a moment, Jill looked as if she wanted to spill out everything that bothered or hurt her, but then she once again held herself back. "Maybe it would be for the best if you left."

To hell with the rules. She wouldn't leave Jill. Not like this. "Why do you keep pushing me away?"

"It's for your own good."

A bit of anger sparked alive in Crash. "For my own good? Don't I get a say in deciding what is or isn't good for me?"

Jill wildly shook her head. "You're not thinking straight."

Crash gave her a half-smile. "Thinking straight is overrated."

"Dammit, Crash, that's not funny. We're talking about your future! Why would you want to live with a disease that isn't yours?"

"I don't want to, but—"

"Then don't. You've got a choice. I don't."

"Well, apparently, I don't have a choice either because you won't give me one," Crash muttered.

They stared at each other across the breakfast bar. The air seemed to crackle with emotions.

Crash waited for Jill to say something, to give in, just a little, but she just stood there, now both fists curled around the edge of the breakfast bar.

When Crash's frustration reached a boiling point, she threw her hands up. "I might as well talk to a brick wall. I'm going." Digging in her pocket for the car keys, she whirled and marched to the door. Despite her anger, she hoped with all her might that Jill would stop her before she reached it.

But everything behind her remained silent.

The door thudded closed between them.

Outside, Crash stopped and leaned against the door for a moment. Her body was so tense that the shaking of her muscles made the wood vibrate. With a grunt, she pushed away from the door and jogged to her car.

When the door closed behind Crash, Jill ran after her, into the hall. With her hand on the door knob, she paused. Everything in her urged her to call Crash back. *Yeah, but what then?*

She could pull Crash back inside and take her upstairs to have makeup sex. They could go on another date—and this time even openly call it that. They might even whisper words of love and be happy together, at least for a while. But what if she had a relapse? What if her MS turned into a more aggressive form?

Would Crash walk away, as she had done now? She didn't want to think so, but she wasn't sure. Not that she could blame Crash. If she stayed, at least initially, that might be even worse. Crash would ignore her own needs to be there for her until she was as close to an emotional meltdown as Jill felt right now. Eventually, she would start resenting Jill for everything she was missing out on. That would slowly but surely strangle the life out of their relationship and smother the affection, desire, and maybe even love that Crash felt for her.

No, it was better not to let it come to that. It hurt enough as it was, so she didn't even want to image how much it would hurt a few years down the road, when she'd opened up to Crash completely. Slowly, she turned away from the door.

Her gaze fell onto Crash's blazer, which she had eagerly stripped off her and thrown onto the side table the night before. When she picked it up, Crash's perfume clung to the article of clothing. Groaning, Jill buried her face in the blazer's collar and breathed in Crash's scent.

She sank to the floor, her back against the door. With her arms wrapped around her legs, she sat there and pressed her face against her knees in a desperate attempt to hold back tears.

The ringing of the phone made her jerk.

Crash! Her heart started thumping against her ribs. She wanted to talk to her so badly, but what would she say? Trembling, she reached for the phone on the side table.

It wasn't Crash.

Of course not. After the way they had left it, she might not call her ever again. The thought hurt.

The phone rang again. An image of her mother flashed across the display.

Sighing, she accepted the call.

"Your brother just called me."

Jill rubbed her stinging eyes. She couldn't deal with this today.

"He was very upset."

"*He* was upset?" Jill echoed.

"James said there was some woman in your house who kicked him out. What's going on for heaven's sake? You don't do things like that to your own brother."

Jill tightened her grip on the phone until the edges dug into her fingers. Her mother hadn't even asked her how she was doing or listened to her side of the story before making accusations. "You do, if he says the kind of hateful things he did. Mom, he—"

"Who was that woman?" her mother asked.

The answer was more complex than her mother realized. For a moment, Jill considered scandalizing her by saying something like, *The woman I'm having a torrid affair with,* but then she just said, "A friend."

"In my time and age, friends didn't get involved in family affairs," her mother said.

"Yes, Mom, they did. At least the real friends. James didn't even ask how I'm doing. The moment I opened the door, he started criticizing and making stupid assumptions. He even said the MS is a good thing because it stops me from acting on my attraction toward women."

Her mother was quiet for a moment, then she said, "I'm sure he didn't mean it like that."

"Like hell he didn't! He meant every word. He'd rather have a sister with MS than a sister who's a lesbian."

"Let's not fight about it, honey."

Jill huffed into the phone. That's what her mother always said when she ran out of arguments. "Fine. I have to go anyway. I've got agility training in an hour." Agility was on Thursdays, not Sundays, but her mother didn't know that. She barely knew a thing about Jill's life.

As fast as possible, Jill ended the call. She let out a groan and barely held herself back from throwing the phone against the wall. Instead, she stared down at it.

Should she call Grace? God, she really needed someone to talk to, and she knew Grace would listen without judgment.

But she would try to talk Jill into giving a relationship with Crash a chance. Same thing with Amanda, her ex-girlfriend-turned-friend. Since she had moved in with Michelle, she saw the world through rose-tinted glasses.

Jill didn't need that kind of unrealistic encouragement. It was hard enough to stop herself from dreaming of things that could never be.

There was no one she could talk to. She was alone, and that was how it would always be. In the past, that had never bothered her. Being on her own, without someone who loved her, had never been that hard before. She almost—just almost—regretted ever meeting Crash. For the first time in a long time—maybe ever—she longed to spend her life with someone.

Not someone, she admitted to herself. *Crash.*

Tramp bustled over and pressed his cold nose to her neck, whining as if he sensed that she was having some kind of breakdown.

"I'm okay, boy," she croaked out.

He licked her hand, sniffed the blazer she was still clutching, and then let out a woof, probably recognizing Crash's scent.

Jill's throat tightened. She wrapped both arms around Tramp and buried her face against his curly fur.

CHAPTER 17

CRASH HIT THE PUNCHING BAG so hard that the chains suspending it from the ceiling of TJ's training shed rattled. She felt the shock all the way up to her shoulder, but she kept punching.

Grunts and curses tore from her throat. "Damn stubborn, frustrating woman!" The battered red leather of the bag groaned under a particularly hard hit.

The jabs and punches kept coming faster, and the force behind them increased until her gloved hands started to hurt. Her muscles protested, and her punches lost their finesse. Still she didn't stop. There was too much frustration bottled up in her.

"Okay, you can stop now," a voice said from behind her. "It's dead."

Crash whirled around, fists raised.

The heavy punching bag smacked her in the back, nearly making her tumble into TJ's arms.

She caught herself, stopped the swinging bag, and took several heaving breaths before she could speak. "Sorry for making such a ruckus. I would have done this at home, but you know I don't have a punching bag in my apartment."

"It's okay. You know you're welcome here any time." He came over, untied the gloves for her, and pulled them off. "Any particular reason why you're over here on a Sunday morning, beating the shit out of my punching bag?"

Crash sighed. "A woman, what else?"

"Still the same one?"

"Yeah. I haven't even thought about other women since I met her. Jill." Even saying the name made a mix of longing, sadness, and frustration tumble through her.

TJ straddled the weight-training bench and looked over at her. "Sounds pretty serious."

Crash nodded. Her feelings for Jill had stopped being casual sometime ago. "Yeah, it is. Otherwise, I wouldn't put up with all that shit."

"What shit? Don't tell me this is going to end up being another disaster like the one with Kyleigh?"

She barely stopped herself from bristling at him, her defensive instincts on full force. "Jill isn't anything like Kyleigh. She doesn't want to get involved with one woman, much less two."

A frown dug a furrow between TJ's brows. "She's not straight, is she?"

Crash had to laugh. "No, trust me. She isn't."

"If she's gay and just not interested, then why all that...?" He waved at the punching bag. "If she doesn't appreciate what you have to offer, just walk away. There are a lot of beautiful women in this town."

If the situation were reversed, Crash would have said the same. But she knew there was more behind Jill's refusal to even date than a disinterest in her. She sensed that it was also more than just stubbornness and pride that made Jill keep her at arm's length. "It's not that she doesn't want to get involved. I think she does. She's just... I think she's scared."

"Scared? Why would she be—?"

"She has MS."

The weight TJ had just picked up clanked to the floor. "Jesus, Crash! That's the sickness where your muscles waste away and you end up in a wheelchair, isn't it?"

"No. You're thinking of MD—muscular dystrophy. MS affects the nerves, but yeah, some of the people suffering from MS end up in a wheelchair."

TJ stared at her and opened his mouth to say something, but Crash stopped him by holding up a hand, palm out.

"I know, I know. I'm crazy for even thinking about getting involved with her, yada, yada. My mother already made that clear, so save your breath." Crash lashed out with her foot, hitting the bag so hard that it shook.

TJ was still staring at her. After a while, he asked, "What are you going to do about it?"

"There's not a damn thing I can do about the MS," Crash grumbled.

"Not about that. I mean...are you sure you want to take on that kind of responsibility?"

Crash caught the swinging bag and held on to it with both hands. She looked TJ in the eyes. "I think I'm ready."

"You think?" he echoed. "You'd better be damn sure about it. Remember Jimmy?"

Of course Crash remembered. Their colleague had broken his neck during a wire stunt and was now paralyzed from the chest down. His fiancée had been supportive during his recovery, and they had even gone through with the wedding but then had divorced after less than a year. It had devastated Jimmy.

TJ was right. She needed to be sure before she tried again to convince Jill. "I've been racking my brain over this for weeks, but I still don't know how I can be sure before I'm actually in the situation."

She sank next to TJ onto the weight-training bench, and they sat there mulling it over for some time.

"Therapy?" TJ finally suggested.

Crash shook her head. "I don't think talking to someone who has no idea about MS would help." But his suggestion sparked another idea. Her fingers were smarting a little as she pulled her phone out of her pocket, brought up the small browser window, and typed, *MS caregiver support group.*

"What are you doing?" TJ asked.

"Making sure I'm sure," she mumbled while scrolling down the list of search results. When she found what she'd been looking for, she pocketed the phone, jumped up, and gave the punching bag one final tap with her bare fist. "See you later."

On Friday, Jill didn't have any scenes on the shooting schedule, so she stayed home and lingered in bed until eleven. She wasn't sleeping, but she didn't seem to have the energy to get up today. For once, her fatigue wasn't to blame.

The constant mental replay of last Sunday sucked the energy out of her. She couldn't forget the hurt and frustration in Crash's eyes before she'd walked out, and her words kept echoing through her mind.

I don't have a choice either because you won't give me one.

Had that been wrong? Could she offer a choice, maybe some kind of don't-ask-don't-tell relationship in which neither asked about or mentioned the MS? But multiple sclerosis had an ugly way of making itself obvious. It wouldn't work, at least not for long. She couldn't have a relationship without the MS, and she couldn't be a true partner for Crash with it.

She rolled over in bed, onto her back, put the pillow over her face, and screamed her frustration into the feathers.

That didn't work either. All it did was make Tramp come running to see if that noise meant she was finally ready to get out of bed.

"Okay, okay. I'm getting up." She wriggled the toes on her left foot, making sure it would hold up, then crawled out of bed.

Thoughts of Crash followed her into the bathroom and then downstairs. Her house was full of memories. Here, on the top step, Crash had kissed her with such passion that Jill had felt like one of the swooning ladies in a historical drama. In the hall, Crash had squared off with James, defending Jill. And in the kitchen, they had sat sharing pancakes and easy banter.

In the five days since, nothing had been easy. They had barely talked. She tried to tell herself it was better that way. Things between them would end after the wrap party anyway, so what if it ended four weeks earlier?

She let out an unladylike snort. Even an actress in a cheap B movie could have portrayed indifference more convincingly. "Let's hope you can do better when you're in front of a camera, Jill Corrigan."

Okay, time for a distraction. All that moping around was disgusting. Watching TV was out; she wasn't in the mood and any action scenes would only remind her of Crash, so she marched to the hall closet and took out the cleaning supplies. Maybe cleaning the house would help declutter her mind too.

She had just gotten started when the front door opened. Susana stood in the doorway, her hands on her hips. "What do you think you're doing?"

Jill froze, a duster in one hand. "Um, isn't it obvious? I'm dusting."

Susana tsked and bustled over. "You're paying me to do that. Besides, I just dusted yesterday. Give me that thing."

Jill held on. "What else am I supposed to do?"

"What other people are doing on their day off—relax, have fun, enjoy life."

Sighing, Jill let go of the duster.

"Here." Susana pressed Tramp's leash into her hand. "Take him for a walk so I can hide the cleaning supplies while you're gone."

They both chuckled.

When Jill returned an hour later, she headed straight for the kitchen, filled Tramp's bowl with fresh water, wrenched open the door of the fridge, and noisily rummaged through its contents. She needed chocolate. Lots of it.

Susana looked up from scrubbing the sink. "The walk didn't help?"

Jill smashed the fridge closed and ripped open the wrapper of a chocolate bar. With her mouth full of chocolate, she mumbled, "A little."

"Is this about Kristine?"

"About Crash? Why would you think that?" Jill bit off another big piece of chocolate.

"Because you have been moping around ever since she took you on that date last Saturday," Susana said. "Did something happen while you were out with her?"

"It wasn't a date," Jill said. "And I'm not moping."

Susana folded her arms over her apron, gave her a look, and muttered something in Spanish.

Had she just been called a stubborn mule?

"Do you want to talk about it?" Susana asked, her expression softening.

That motherly tone was nearly Jill's undoing. Her nose started to burn as if she was about to cry. Quickly, she shook her head.

Susana walked over and pulled her into a hug.

"The chocolate is melting," Jill protested but still sank willingly into the warm embrace.

Susana held her for a few seconds, then pulled back and took the chocolate bar out of her hand.

"Hey! My chocolate!"

"You can't eat it. We'll need it to decorate the cake."

Jill frowned. "What cake?"

"The cake we're going to make. Come on. Baking helps with everything, even lovesickness." She opened a drawer, took out another apron, slid it over Jill's neck, and tied it in the back for her.

Tears burned in Jill's eyes. *Jeez. Stop it.* "Thank you," she whispered.

"No thanks necessary," Susana said. "I'll make you do all the work. Now shoo! Get the eggs!"

"Aye, aye, ma'am."

Crash shut off the engine and sat there in silence for a moment, staring at the house across the street. Being here felt strange and inappropriate, as if she was fulfilling a morbid curiosity. Last Thursday evening, she had sat in her car, hesitating for a long time too. She hadn't been sure if she had a right to participate in the caregiver support group meeting since she wasn't a caregiver.

But the people there had been very welcoming, especially Sally, the leader of the group. She had even invited Crash into her home so she could meet her husband and see for herself how they managed their everyday lives.

Before Crash could gather her courage and head over, the front door of the house opened and Sally stepped onto the veranda. She waved at Crash, whose cheeks started to burn.

Quickly, she climbed out of the SUV and willed her blush to disappear while she crossed the street. *Oh, the things we do for love.*

The thought made her pause. *Love?*

But she had no time to obsess over it, because she'd reached Sally now. "Hi. I was just..." She gestured back to the SUV.

Sally smiled, the crow's feet around her eyes deepening. "It's okay. I imagine it must feel a little weird to be here."

"Isn't it weird for you?" Crash couldn't help asking.

"A little," Sally said with the same honesty that had impressed Crash at the support group meeting on Thursday. "But I really don't mind. And it's good for George to feel he can help other people." She led Crash to the door. "Ready?"

Not really, but Crash nodded anyway and followed Sally inside.

The house was completely wheelchair-accessible, with wide doors and no thresholds or carpets. A chair lift provided transport to the upper floor. In the past,

Crash might not have noticed these little details, but now she was paying attention, hoping to learn as much as she could.

Sally led her into a spacious living room, where a thin man, whom she guessed to be in his mid-fifties, sat in a recliner. Crash eyed a nearby wheelchair. Did Sally transfer him back and forth all on her own?

"Look who I found outside," Sally said to him. "George, this is Kristine Patterson. Kristine, this is my husband, George."

She stuck out her hand. "Thanks so much for having me. Please call me Crash."

He smiled up at her but didn't reach out. "Um, I'm not much for handshakes these days. Not that I don't want to, but..." He nodded down at his hands, which rested limply on his lap.

"Oh. I'm sorry." Crash quickly pulled back her hand and shoved it into her pocket. Maybe this visit hadn't been such a good idea after all.

Sally pressed her down onto the couch. "Sit and tell us how you got a nickname like Crash."

Grateful for the innocuous topic of conversation, Crash told them.

"Wow! You're a stuntwoman!" George's eyes twinkled with excitement. "I was into motocross racing when I was younger, but nowadays, I confine my racing to this." He nodded over to the wheelchair.

Crash didn't know what to say to that. She couldn't tell if he was bitter about no longer being able to race.

"It's for the best," Sally said. "You get into enough trouble with the wheelchair as it is."

"Hey, you were the one who steered me into the flower bed and ruined Mrs. Baker's beloved zinnias!"

"Me? I'm just the engine in our little operation; you're the navigator, Mister."

Crash looked from one to the other as if watching a tennis match, observing their banter and the loving look in their eyes as they teased each other.

This, she thought. *This is what I want.* For her and Jill to make the best of what life threw at them—together. Watching them made her hopeful that it was possible. Now the only question was: Would it be possible for Jill and her too?

Only when Sally looked at her expectantly did Crash realize that they had stopped their bantering and she had missed a question directed at her.

"Uh, excuse me?"

"I asked how you take your coffee," Sally said.

"Please don't go to any trouble on my account."

"It's no trouble at all. We have one of these fully automatic coffee machines that have more electronics than a spaceship."

"Then I'd love to have a cup," Crash said. "Plain old black, please."

Sally nodded and walked away, leaving her alone with George.

Swallowing, she turned to him.

He gave her a smile as if sensing her nervousness. "So," he began, "Sally says you're thinking about becoming involved with someone who has MS."

"You're not going to tell me to think twice about it, are you?"

He gave a rueful smile. "Didn't do me any good with Sally, and since you're here, it probably won't do me any good with you either."

"So Sally never hesitated?" Crash asked.

"Oh, yeah, I did," Sally called from the kitchen. "Have I told you our last name?"

What did that have to do with anything? "Uh, no, you didn't." In the support group, only first names had been given.

George rolled his eyes. "My last name's Dork. There are worse. I went to school with someone whose name was Loser."

Becoming Mrs. Dork... Crash grinned. Was his last name really all that had made Sally hesitate to marry him?

Sally came back into the living room with a tray of mugs. "We had the longest engagement in history before I finally agreed to marry him."

George snorted. "Agreed to marry me? You were the one who proposed." He glanced at Crash. "Four times."

Sally balanced a plastic cup with a lid on George's chest, tucked his hands around it to hold it in place, and then put a straw through a little hole in the lid. "There you go. Careful, it's still hot."

"Thank you," George said.

She kissed his cheek before settling down at the end of the couch closest to him.

Crash watched them. They both seemed so at peace with their routine. Would she do as well as a caregiver? And would Jill ever become so comfortable accepting help if she became this disabled? Finally, she asked, "So she was the one who proposed to you?"

"I had to," Sally said. "Aptly named Mr. Dork here kept wanting to do the honorable thing by not tying me to him."

That sounded very familiar. "What did it take to finally convince him?"

"Time," Sally said.

At the same time, George said, "A baseball bat."

"He's a bit old-fashioned, you know?" Sally reached over and patted her husband's arm. "He felt as if he, as the man in the relationship, should be able to take care of me, and if he couldn't, he wasn't worthy of being my husband."

George pressed his lips together, and for the first time, the light in his eyes dimmed. "I couldn't even carry you over the threshold. I felt like a terrible excuse for a husband." He lowered his voice and added, "Still do, sometimes."

So it wasn't all roses and sunshine for them either.

"You're the best husband I could wish for," Sally said.

They looked into each other's eyes, seeming to forget about Crash for a moment, before George said, "Maybe your boyfriend is struggling with the same."

"Um, actually..." Crash cleared her throat. "The person I'm interested in is a woman. Her name is..." She hesitated. While she didn't want to lie to them, violating Jill's privacy felt wrong. "Lucy."

Sally smiled knowingly. "I thought you might be gay, but I didn't want to stereotype. Don't worry. We're fine with it. Two of the few friends who still stand by us are lesbians."

"So your girlfriend's issues are probably different from mine," George said.

Crash shook her head. "No, I think she's struggling with some of the same things. She hates feeling dependent and unequal. Getting her to accept any help is like pulling teeth. She isn't used to relying on anyone. Her parents and her brother are too busy judging her for being gay, for being an actress...and maybe even for having MS."

"I'll never understand people." Sally sighed and got up. "Let me get us some cookies."

They were silent for a moment after she disappeared into the kitchen.

"She's a great woman," Crash said quietly.

George's eyes held a mix of love, pride, and sadness. "Yes, she is." He bent his head to take a sip of his coffee, but the straw escaped him.

It was hard to observe him chase around the straw with his mouth. The thought of watching Jill be as helpless made her stomach hurt. Should she offer her help? She didn't want to take away the little bit of independence that he still had, so she remained where she was.

Finally, he managed to grasp the straw with his lips and took a healthy sip. "Damn. That's hot," he gasped out and started coughing. Coffee drenched his mustache and dribbled down his chin.

Crash jumped up. She looked around helplessly and then took one of the paper napkins from the coffee table. Hesitantly, not wanting to hurt him, she dabbed his chin, preventing the coffee from dripping down onto his shirt.

"Thanks," he said, his voice a little rough, either from coughing or from embarrassment.

Sally rushed back into the room. "Is everything all right?"

"Everything's fine," George said with an innocent expression.

Crash sat back down, hiding the wet paper napkin behind her back.

George grinned at her, and she smiled back, like two co-conspirators.

"You two aren't fooling anyone," Sally said. "I told you that coffee was hot."

She had probably developed some kind of sixth sense when it came to her husband, always aware of how he was doing. Crash wondered if she would have the same kind of strength.

They sat, talked about Jill and life with MS, and ate the cookies, with Sally feeding him in between taking bites of her own cookie.

Crash had worked with some of the most heroic stunt people in the business over the years, but she couldn't remember when she'd last been so impressed by two people she'd just met.

Finally, when the last cookie was gone and George seemed to get tired, Sally walked her to the door. "So?" she asked. "What did you think? I hope we could help you."

Crash nodded. "I think so. I'm not sure I could handle it as well as you do, but I'm ready to try my best."

Sally patted her arm. "I didn't get there overnight. You should have seen me in the beginning. Besides, it doesn't just matter how ready you are."

"What do you mean?"

"Lucy has to be too," Sally said. "She has to be ready to accept your love and your help."

A sigh escaped Crash. Jill had a long way to go—if she'd ever get there.

"Why don't you bring her along the next time you visit us?" Sally suggested.

Crash tried to imagine Jill having coffee with George and Sally but couldn't. "I don't think she's ready for that either." Seeing George being fed by his wife would only remind Jill of her own uncertain future, and Crash wasn't sure if that would help or make Jill even more determined to avoid tying another person to her.

"Don't give up on her," Sally said.

"I won't." Crash gave her a short hug. "Thank you. If you ever need some time away and don't have anyone who could keep an eye on George, let me know."

"You're a keeper. Lucy would be stupid to let you get away."

Crash smiled and said good-bye. As she jogged to her SUV, she hoped that Jill would realize that too.

Crash sat on the steps of the stunt trailer, her laptop balanced on her thighs. She was watching the pre-visualization of the big fire stunt, which was now just three weeks away. The thought was making her palms clammy, so she wiped them on her knees, never taking her gaze off the screen, even though she already knew every second of the video by heart. Recently, Jill and what was happening between them had helped push aside her worries about the fire stunt, but now that she and Jill weren't talking, her ruminations about it had come back in full force.

She watched the screen as if her life depended on it. *And it might.* In a fire stunt, every move had to be timed just right. There was no room for error.

Only one thing could direct her attention away from the video: every time footsteps approached, she looked up, hoping it might be Jill.

It never was.

Crash had been giving her space since that morning eight days ago, when she'd walked out of Jill's house. Truth be told, Crash also needed some space. She was sick of always being the one to make the first step after Jill had pushed her away. This time, she'd wait for Jill to come to her.

But with every hour that went by, her resolution wavered a bit more. What if Jill wouldn't come? Was she making a total fool of herself by attending the caregiver support group and visiting with Sally and George, preparing for a future with Jill that might never happen?

Footsteps interrupted her thoughts.

When she looked up, her hopes were dashed once again. It was Lauren, not Jill.

"Hey," Lauren said and sat next to her on the top step.

"Hi." Quickly, Crash closed her media player, not wanting Lauren to question her about why she was watching the fire stunt. Too late, she realized that the browser window that was open behind it was one of the MS websites she had bookmarked.

Lauren glanced at the screen before Crash could close the laptop. "You're reading up on MS?"

Crash nodded but didn't provide any explanation.

"Are you just curious or...?" Lauren trailed off and studied her.

"No." Crash squared her shoulders. Talking about it with Lauren, one of Jill's best friends, made her commitment more real. "I'm serious about Jill, and I want to be there for her—if she'd let me."

"I hope she will," Lauren said and gave her a pat to the arm. "Grace and I really hate Jill being alone."

"Me too," Crash said quietly.

"Are you planning on doing that?" Lauren pointed at the screen.

Crash scanned the website to see what she meant. At the top of the page was an ad for the MS walkathon, a charity event raising money for MS research.

"Uh, I hadn't thought about it."

Lauren nudged her. "You know what? Let's all do it—the entire crew and cast. It would be great publicity for the movie, and we could show our support for Jill. We could be Team Jill." She trailed her hands over her chest as if she could already see the name printed on her T-shirt.

It was easy to imagine what Jill would think about that. Whenever possible, Jill hid her symptoms from her colleagues, not wanting to be thought of as the actress with MS. She would probably be less than enthusiastic about the entire cast and crew showing up to walk for her. To her, it would mean accepting help—and accepting her role as an MS patient. "I don't know, Lauren. Jill might not like that."

"Nonsense," Lauren said. "Jill is always up for contributing to a good cause. Last year, she participated in a celebrity waitress dinner benefitting unemployed actors and their families."

"Yeah, but there she was the one raising money for other people and didn't belong to the group being helped."

Lauren rubbed her chin. "You know what? Let's just do it anyway. If Jill wants to join us, great. And if not, it's still a really good cause."

It was, no doubt about that, so Crash nodded reluctantly.

"Good. Then let's go over and ask her." Lauren stood, walked down the three steps, and turned back. "Aren't you coming?"

"Uh, I need to...finish up here." She gestured vaguely at her laptop. After hardly talking to her for eight days, she'd rather not be the one ambushing Jill with the walkathon.

When Lauren nodded and walked away, she opened the media player again. But now, not even the pre-visualization of the fire stunt could hold her attention. She would have paid good money to be a fly on the wall during that conversation.

CHAPTER 18

Jɪʟʟ ᴡᴀs ᴀʙᴏᴜᴛ ᴛᴏ ɢᴇᴛ into her car after a long day of shooting when someone called her name from across the parking lot.

Crash? Her heartbeat sped up. Aside from the interactions their jobs made necessary, they hadn't talked for eight days. Jill missed her, and that was a completely new experience. She had never missed anyone before. But she didn't know how to bridge the distance between them without agreeing to date Crash. Slowly, not ready to face her but unable to resist, she turned.

It wasn't Crash.

"Hi," Lauren said. "Are you okay? You just looked at me like you didn't know whether to hug me or kick me."

"No. I'm always happy to see you, screenwriter lady." Jill forced a cheerful smile. "What's up?"

"There's something I wanted to ask you."

"No, thanks. I don't think I'm up for a threesome with you and Grace today."

Lauren snorted. "You wish. No, I have a proposal of a different kind. A local MS group is organizing a walkathon at the Rose Bowl in Pasadena this Sunday. I was thinking we could all walk together—the entire cast and crew of *Shaken to the Core.* What do you think?"

An MS walkathon and Lauren wanted all of her colleagues to participate? Everything in her screamed, *No.* She struggled to compose her features. "I don't know about this, Lauren. Shooting keeps me pretty busy."

"We're all busy. But the walkathon is on the weekend. So?" Lauren looked at her expectantly.

"If you don't mind, I'd rather pass."

"But it's for a good cause. All money raised goes to MS patients who can't afford their medication and into promising research projects trying to find a cure for MS."

Jill leaned against her car and pressed both hands against the sun-warmed metal. "I know that's important..."

"But? I thought you were always happy to support nonprofit organizations?"

"I am," Jill said. "You know that. I was a waitress at that celebrity dinner last year, remember?"

"I know. I was there."

Jill snorted. "Like you had eyes for anyone but Grace in that cute waitress apron."

"I was just keeping an eye on her to make sure she was fine waitressing with her broken arm."

"Her arm? And here I thought you kept your eyes on a pair of completely different body parts."

Lauren cleared her throat. "Back to the topic at hand. We were talking about the MS walkathon."

If not even talking about Grace could distract Lauren, Jill knew she was a woman on a mission. "Why are you so hell-bent on getting me to participate?"

"Well, for one thing, it's great publicity. I'm sure I can get several well-known actresses to participate, including a certain Grace Durand, so it would be good for your image."

"That might be, but you're no longer my publicist."

"But Marlene is, and I know she would say the same," Lauren countered.

Jill jingled her car keys. If only she could escape into her car. "I just... I like to keep my job and my private life separate."

"No one can understand that better than I. In my previous job, that was essential. But some of these people...Nikki, Shawn, Crash, and me...we aren't just your colleagues. We're your friends."

That made it even worse for Jill. If she agreed to walk with them, she would become the face of MS to them. She would lose the fight she fought every day—to establish herself as a good actress, a reliable colleague, and a loyal friend—and become a person suffering from MS. It would give the MS a status in her life that she didn't want it to have. But she didn't want to talk about that with Lauren, so she said, "You weren't very successful in keeping your job and your private life separate, seeing as you got involved with one of your clients."

"Since you're trying to change the topic again, I take it that's really a no on participating in the walkathon?" Lauren asked. "Crash said you might not want to do it. Guess she was right."

Crash? Lauren had talked to Crash about the walkathon? Had Crash agreed to participate? "Did she think I wouldn't be able to complete the walkathon?" As soon as she'd said it, she knew that wasn't it. Crash knew her better than that. She had to realize why Jill wouldn't want to participate.

"No, she never said that. Besides, you could use a scooter, if that's what has you so worried. There was a picture on the website that showed some of last year's participants using one."

A scooter? No. If she did this, she'd cross the finish line on her own two feet. Finishing wasn't her problem; showing up was.

"Will you at least think about it?" Lauren asked. "There are less than four weeks of shooting left, so this might be the last chance for all of us to do something together. It would be great."

Jill sent her a doubtful gaze.

"Come on. Say yes. Or I'll..."

"Yeah?" Jill drawled and then paused when it instantly reminded her of Crash and the way she sounded when she teased Jill. She shook off all thoughts of Crash and continued, "Or you'll do what? You don't have any dirt on me."

"Or I'll rewrite your character's storyline."

"You wouldn't let Lucy die," Jill said, her hands on her hips.

Lauren seemed unimpressed. "Who said anything about letting her die? I'll give her a seedy sex scene with...let's say...the corrupt mayor."

Jill shuddered at the mere thought. "You wouldn't do that to your script."

"Why not? Now that I think about it, I can see the possibilities of such a scene now. A night of passion with the upright doctor could be the motivation he needs to redeem himself and—"

"I'll think about it, okay? That's all I can promise."

"All right. Just let me know, okay?"

Jill nodded and unlocked the driver's side door with unsteady fingers.

"Oh, Jill?" Lauren called before she could settle into the driver's seat.

Jill gritted her teeth so hard that she thought she'd crack a molar. "What?" she asked without turning around. She knew Lauren meant well, but this was just too much.

"If you decide to participate, I'll need to know what size you're wearing. I want to get team T-shirts made, and I need to move quickly since it's just six days until Sunday."

Team T-shirts? God. She could see it already—ugly oversized T-shirts with a *Walking for Jill* slogan. No. She didn't want that. If her colleagues insisted on participating in the MS walkathon, fine, but she didn't want to be their charity case.

"And could you ask Crash what size she wants?" Lauren continued.

So Crash was participating. Jill turned around. "Why don't you ask her yourself?"

"I have a feeling you'll see her before I do," Lauren said with a knowing smile.

"No," Jill said firmly. "I won't. You'll have to ask her yourself."

Brow furrowed, Lauren stared at her. "I thought...you and she are..."

"Friends," Jill supplied before Lauren could say something else. "Yes, we are. We're just...taking a break."

Lauren's eyebrows arched up over the rim of her glasses. "From friendship?"

Jill regarded the tips of her shoes and shrugged. "I really have to go, Lauren. I'm late picking up Tramp." She nearly dove behind the steering wheel, closed the door between them, and sped off before Lauren could say anything else.

When they wrapped the last scene on Friday, every member of the cast and crew called, "See you on Sunday" over to Jill, obviously expecting her to show up for the walkathon.

She still wasn't sure she would. In fact, she had almost convinced herself that it was okay for her not to participate. There would be thousands of people there, so what difference would one person make?

But her colleagues didn't want to walk for the thousands of other people. They wanted to walk for her.

She was touched, really, but she didn't want that kind of support. It came too close to admitting she needed to be pitied and helped.

"See you," Crash murmured as she squeezed past her in the wardrobe trailer on her way to the door.

She hadn't added an "on Sunday," as the others had. Didn't she expect Jill to come? She stared after her. "Crash?" she called just as Crash had opened the door.

Crash turned back around. Incredible how much she could say with just a look. There were so many emotions in her eyes—hope, wariness, relief, and affection.

"Will you...?" Jill licked her lips. "Will you be at the walkathon?"

"I'll be there."

The words were reassuring, maybe because she trusted Crash more than the others to see her as more than just a person with MS.

Crash stepped back inside and closed the door so that no one but the wardrobe assistant helping Jill with the costume could overhear. "How about you?"

So Crash didn't take it for granted that she'd participate. Jill wasn't sure if that made her feel better or even worse. She was starting to feel like an ungrateful coward. "I don't know."

"I think it would be important," Crash said quietly.

Jill sighed. "I know it's for a good cause and all, but—"

"Important for *you*," Crash said. She looked into Jill's eyes for a few moments; then, without additional explanations, she gave a short wave and left.

When Crash parked her SUV in one of the parking lots of the Rose Bowl in Pasadena, there had to be thousands of people getting out of their cars or gathering in groups.

Wow. So many lives touched by MS. She had jogged the three-mile loop around the Rose Bowl stadium before, but she had never seen it like this. Tents and registration tables had been set up at the end of the parking lot. Music blared from speakers, and people were laughing and shouting greetings to each other. Some of them were dressed in athletic clothes and looked like experienced runners, but Crash also saw many families with strollers, men and women with scooters, and some in wheelchairs. A few were even preparing to walk the loop with canes.

As Crash climbed out of her SUV, she recognized several members of the cast and crew, all in the orange T-shirts of team *Shaken*, as Lauren had named their team. Some of her colleagues and two people she knew from the support group meeting waved and pointed at the registration tables and the tents where people were handing out bottles of water.

Crash shook her head. She wanted to stay in the parking lot a little longer, keeping an eye on the new arrivals just in case Jill was among them.

She hoped Jill would come and be able to embrace her colleagues' support, but she was afraid that Jill couldn't bring herself to do it.

The closer it got to ten, when the walkathon was supposed to start, the more she lost hope. Still, she wanted to wait until the last possible moment to move to the registration tables, so she instead walked over to the large board at the edge of the parking lot. At the top, bold orange letters read, "Why I walk." Many people had already scribbled their answers onto the board, and Crash stepped closer to see what they had written.

A teenaged girl who'd just finished writing down her reason turned and gave Crash a smile before handing over the black marker. Before Crash could protest, she was holding the marker and the girl was gone. She stared down at the thick pen, then at the board, rubbing her chin. What was she supposed to write?

Only one thing came to mind, so she uncapped the marker and was about to write "Jill" into one corner of the board when someone stepped next to her.

"Hi."

Crash would know that voice anywhere. *Jill. She came. This is big.* Crash wanted to let out a shout of sheer joy and relief, but she was afraid to startle Jill away. With a lump in her throat, she turned toward her.

She took in the shorts and the copper hair tied back into a short ponytail, exposing the creamy skin of Jill's neck, before her gaze zeroed in on Jill's T-shirt. It was the same orange article of clothing Crash was wearing, *Team Shaken* written across the front.

Crash had never wanted to hug anyone so badly. It was as if her entire body was pulled toward Jill, vibrating with the longing to hold her, to touch her, to establish some kind of contact. But she held herself back, not knowing if Jill would allow it. "Hi," she said, her voice barely more than a whisper. "It's great to see you."

"You too," Jill said, just as quietly.

Still not able to avert her gaze for even a second, Crash pointed at the T-shirt. "You look good in that."

Jill tugged on the orange material. "It's a little too big."

"You'll grow into it," Crash said.

They were both silent for several moments, just drinking each other in.

"So," Jill finally said, her voice cracking a little, "are you going to write something down?" She pointed at the black marker in Crash's hand.

Crash looked back and forth between her and the board. Should she really do this while Jill was watching? *Do it.* Jill had proven her courage by showing up, so she could be brave too. She inhaled deeply and then let the breath escape, as she did when preparing for a stunt. She lowered the tip of the marker to the board and wrote "Jill" into the bottom right corner, forming each letter with the utmost care until Jill's name was staring back at them.

Jill looked at her name as if she had never seen it before, then turned to face Crash.

Crash forced herself to straighten and hold her head up high. Jill might not like it, but she was the reason why all of their colleagues were here on the only day off they got this week. "Your turn." She pressed the marker and its cap into Jill's hand.

Their fingers brushed, and the touch lingered for a moment longer than necessary.

"I'll do it later." Jill capped the marker and tried to hand it back.

Crash refused to take it. "Showing up was the hardest part. You can do this."

With an audible intake of breath, Jill turned toward the board. She uncapped the marker with a jerky motion. Her entire body stiffened as she faced the empty space on the board where she was supposed to write her reason for walking. The tip of the marker hovered over the board for a long time.

Her obvious struggle made Crash wince in sympathy. She barely dared to breathe while she waited for Jill to write something—or to walk away. If she did, she would be walking away from much more than just words on a board.

Finally, the marker touched the board, and after a few more seconds, Jill started writing. Her scrawl was almost illegible—either because her fine motor skills weren't the best today or because she wanted her reason to remain private.

But Crash had read Jill's comments scribbled in the margins of scripts often enough to be able to decipher the words.

Because I'm sick of being sick, Jill had written.

A lump formed in Crash's throat. She trembled with the effort it took not to pull Jill into her arms.

Jill met her gaze. Gone was the spunky facade she displayed at work. Emotions that were too complex to name seemed to flow back and forth between them.

"Ah, you came!" someone said behind them. "So you didn't want to be set up with the mayor after all."

Reluctantly, Crash turned away from Jill.

Lauren and Grace stood in front of them, both wearing the same orange T-shirts. Grace's world-famous blue eyes were hidden behind dark sunglasses and her golden-blonde hair shoved beneath a baseball cap.

While Jill greeted Grace with a hug, Crash regarded Lauren curiously. "Set up with the mayor?"

"I threatened to include a sex scene between Lucy and the mayor in the script if she didn't show up for the walkathon," Lauren said with a smug grin.

Crash looked back and forth between Lauren and Jill. Did Lauren really think a harmless threat could have changed Jill's mind? *Wow. She doesn't get it, does she?* Even Jill's friends had no clue what participating in this event meant for Jill.

Nikki, Shawn, Ben, Floyd, and several crew members joined them as they headed toward the registration tables. It took some time to get them all registered. Finally, they walked over to the starting point.

Crash fell into step next to Jill.

Jill turned her head and looked at her. They nodded at each other; then smiles crept onto their faces. "Save me a hot dog when you get to the finish line," Jill said.

"I would if I got there before you."

"Why wouldn't you?" Jill looked her up and down, causing pleasant shivers to course through Crash's entire body. "5k is nothing for you."

Shrugging, Crash said, "I figure it's called a walkathon for a reason, so I'll walk, not run."

Jill put her hands on her hips. "You're not just doing that to keep an eye on me, are you?"

"Maybe I like keeping an eye on you...both eyes, actually." Crash gave a playful leer, wanting to lighten the mood.

Jill grabbed one of the long, orange balloons from the start line and pretended it was a baseball bat as she whacked Crash left and right.

Crash ducked one swing that was aimed at her head, grinning like a fool. The static from the balloon made her hair stand up in all directions, but she didn't care. All she cared about was that she and Jill had gotten their old, easy way of interacting back.

No, she corrected herself after a moment. At first glance, it might seem like everything was the same, but beneath the surface was a new understanding between them.

When Jill finally put down her balloon weapon, Crash lightly touched her arm. "Can I walk with you?"

Jill stopped laughing and looked at her, searching her face. After a couple of seconds, she nodded. "I'd like that." Then, as if unable to stand the intimacy of the moment, she tore her gaze away and set off across the start line, following Lauren, Grace, and Floyd. "But only if you can keep up," she called over her shoulder.

"Aye, ma'am." Grinning, Crash hurried after her.

The loop around the Rose Bowl was paved and relatively flat, with only tiny inclines at some points. Two years ago, Jill would have finished the three miles already and would have been on her second hot dog by now. But running this distance was no longer possible. Not that it was required today. With the wheelchairs in the crowd surrounding them, it was slow-going and the entire loop would take them two hours.

Part of Jill wanted to charge ahead and leave them all behind, but she knew that doing this together was the point of the event. If she was honest with herself, the slow pace fit her just fine, allowing her to save her energy instead of exhausting herself trying to keep up. Besides, she was too busy looking around, observing the other participants, to watch where she was going.

Somewhere to her right, Lauren and Grace were walking hand in hand. Behind her, several of the stunt people were giving piggyback rides to tired kids. A lot of her colleagues had brought their families, so Jill was surrounded by people in orange. Even babies pushed in strollers were wearing the team T-shirts.

All of this because of me. It was a weird feeling. Overwhelming, but not entirely negative. The most overwhelming of all was the woman walking next to her. She peeked over at Crash in her orange T-shirt with the *Team Shaken* slogan.

Shaken. That was exactly how she felt around Crash, especially today.

Crash had written her name onto the board of reasons. It was solid proof that she was here just because of Jill. They all were, but with Crash, it meant more.

The young, magenta-haired woman in the motorized wheelchair directly ahead of them bumped over a crack in the pavement. The water bottle on her lap rolled off and landed on the ground. As much as the woman tried, she couldn't reach it.

Before Jill could think about it, she took a step forward, bent, and picked up the bottle. Wordlessly, she handed it back.

"Thank you." The young woman beamed at her. Apparently, the little mishap hadn't clouded her mood at all.

"You're welcome."

Just as Jill stepped back, a little girl came running, dragging a man by the hand behind her while clutching a balloon with the other. "Look, Mom! I got a balloon! Can I tie it to your wheelchair?"

Jill couldn't help staring. "She's got a kid?" she whispered. What kind of woman would have a child, knowing that she might not be able to care and provide for it as it grew older and her illness progressed, leaving her husband with the burden of taking care of her *and* the child?

"She's got three, actually," Crash said next to her, "but I think the twins are with their grandparents today."

Jill stumbled over the same crack in the pavement.

Crash caught her by the elbow, and Jill was too astonished to struggle against her gentle grip on her arm.

"You know her?"

"I know her husband," Crash said slowly, as if hesitant to admit it. "Well, not really know, but I met him when I went to a caregiver support group meeting."

Jill gaped at her. "You were…? You went to…?" She couldn't even finish the sentence.

Nodding, Crash directed her gaze to the woman in the wheelchair. "I needed to see."

Dazed, Jill continued to stare at her. What had she needed to see? How bad MS could get? What burdens the caregivers struggled with? If she could be a caregiver if push came to shove? Had she found her answers?

But as much as she longed to know, Jill couldn't ask. She wasn't ready to deal with what Crash would say. A date…yeah, maybe, just maybe, she could handle that. But Crash's visit with a caregiver support group reflected a willingness to commit to more than just a couple of dates. Before, the thought had scared her—and it still did—but now it also caused a warm feeling to spread through her chest.

Oh, no. Forget it. As much as she wanted to, she couldn't have anything long-term with Crash. She looked at the couples around her, who seemed happy with each other despite the MS. *Can I?*

For several moments, they marched on in silence.

They approached the one-mile point, where tents had been set up with refreshments. The little girl ran to get her mother some water.

"Look at them," Crash said.

Jill watched as the little girl climbed onto her mother's lap and received a hug and a kiss in return for the bottle of water. The husband laughed about something the girl said and then lovingly rubbed his wife's shoulder. They seemed like any other family. In fact, they seemed more loving and normal than her own family had ever been.

"Don't you want that?" Crash asked.

"Kids?"

"Happiness."

The sadness inside of her threatened to turn into anger. "Of course I do. I'll just have to find it elsewhere, not in a relationship."

"You haven't let the MS stop you from doing what you want in your job. You fought Floyd and Ben every step of the way when they wouldn't allow you to do the smaller stunts. Why do you let it stop you from having a relationship?"

"That's different," Jill said. Admittedly, it sounded a bit lame, even to her. She realized that she didn't have an honest answer to Crash's question.

"Does anyone need a ride to the finish line?" one of the walkathon's organizers shouted, pointing over to a couple of golf carts waiting for passengers.

Jill wanted nothing more than to escape the conversation but was determined to cross the finish line on foot, come hell or high water.

Others seemed just as determined, even though a few of them were heavily leaning on canes or stopping every few steps to rest.

As they continued walking, all the impressions from the walkathon and Crash's question kept buzzing around in her head, which felt as if it were about to explode. Everything she had accepted as an unshakable truth was now being challenged.

Crash was mercifully silent for the next two miles, granting Jill a much-needed respite.

They rounded a bend and strolled along the golf course. The sun shone, without burning down on them and making Jill's symptoms flare, and the hum of a lawn mower drifted over from the golf course—a sound that reminded her of the long, lazy summers she'd spent with her grandparents as a child. A chipmunk chattered in the trees to their right, probably complaining about all the people passing through its territory. Crash's arm brushed hers every now and then as they walked.

If not for the battle being fought inside of Jill's mind, it would have been peaceful.

Someone in the crowd ahead of them let out a triumphant yell as they rounded another bend and the finish line appeared.

A live band played Queen's "We Are the Champions." People laughed, high-fived, and hugged each other as if they had just won an Olympic gold medal.

Yesterday, Jill would have thought it silly, totally over top for a leisurely stroll. But now she had seen some of the participants struggle to finish the loop, and the wave of euphoria sweeping through the crowd seemed to be contagious.

"Yay! We made it!" Crash pumped her fist. She hadn't even broken a sweat, but she still looked proud of herself.

Or maybe proud of me, Jill thought.

Then she stopped thinking, because Crash pulled her into a jubilant hug.

She sank against Crash's body, all of her defenses instantly gone. After the injection incident two weeks ago, she had told herself to keep her distance, but that resolution melted away as she wrapped her arms around Crash and ducked her head to inhale her scent. Incredible how good Crash's body felt against hers. It wasn't just a sexual reaction. Having Crash be proud of her made her feel as if she'd just been crowned queen of America.

Pats on her back made her open her eyes, which had closed without her noticing.

The entire *Shaken* team surrounded her, celebrating as if they had just won some major sports event.

Jill's cheeks heated. She let go of Crash and stepped back to accept hugs from Grace and Lauren and some of the cast members.

When the last hug ended, everyone looked at her expectantly.

She had to say something.

Crash gave her an encouraging nod.

After taking a deep breath, Jill looked at the dozens of people surrounding her and smiled at them, albeit a little shakily. "Thank you, guys, for turning out on your only day off to walk with me. I really appreciate it." It was the truth, she realized. Walking with them had been empowering instead of making her feel weak, as she had feared.

Many shouted something back, but their voices all mingled, thankfully relieving Jill of the need to reply.

More participants crossed the finish line behind them, so they moved away to make space. Benches and tables had been set up in one of the parking lots, where food was being sold.

Crash stuck her nose in the air, reminding Jill of Tramp. "Do you smell that?"

"Smell what?"

"Hot dogs!" Crash said with an eager gleam in her eyes.

Jill laughed, her tension nearly forgotten for the moment. "It seems someone missed breakfast." Truth be told, she had skipped breakfast too. She had been too nervous to get anything down.

Hooking her arm through Jill's, Crash steered them toward one of the tables. "There's someone I want you to meet. Are you feeling up to it?"

God, would it be like this all day? How many more people with MS did Crash know? Jill wasn't sure she was ready for this. But clearly, this was important to Crash, so she nodded.

Crash stopped at a table where a middle-aged couple sat, eating hot dogs. The sturdily built woman hugged Crash as if she were a long-lost friend, and the man, who was in a wheelchair, beamed up at her. "Jill, these are Sally and George. George, Sally, this is my...friend, Jill."

Jill tried not to stare at the wheelchair-bound man. "Uh, hi. Nice to meet you." She didn't dare hold out her hand, not knowing if his arms were paralyzed too.

"Jill?" Sally's brows bunched together. "I thought her name was Lucy?"

A blush crept into Crash's cheeks, and she fingered the neck of her T-shirt. "Uh, I... It's not that I don't trust you, but I didn't want to violate Jill's privacy."

Her consideration touched Jill deeply. She reached out and squeezed Crash's arm.

"Why don't you sit with them," Crash said. "I'll get us our hot dogs."

Oh, no, no, no. Don't leave me alone with them! But her pleading look didn't help. Crash strode away, her long steps eating the ground toward the hot-dog vendor.

Jill's gaze followed her. "No mustard for me," she called after her.

"I know," Crash called back.

Jill stood there for a moment, a bit overwhelmed by the entire event going on around her.

"We don't bite," Sally said.

"Other than hot dogs," her husband added with a grin.

Jill gave herself a mental kick and sat at the table across from them.

True to his word, George wolfed down his hot dog. Sally fed him bite by bite with her right hand while holdings hers in the other.

Jill swallowed. She wanted to avert her gaze but couldn't stop watching them.

To her surprise, both of them were laughing as she fed him another bite of hot dog and his graying mustache came away covered in mustard. Sally looked around for a napkin, but she had already used the ones that had come with their hot dogs.

Jill reached out and handed her a stack of napkins from the empty table next to theirs.

Sally smiled warmly. "Thank you. I shouldn't have ignored rule number one when eating out with my dear husband." She waited a beat, and then she and George grinned at each other and said in unison, "You can never have enough napkins."

"You're a lifesaver," George said. "Well, a mustache-saver."

His sense of humor was impressive, considering the circumstances.

She looked back and forth between them. Were they always like this, or were they putting on a show for the benefit of the people nearby? Surely Sally had weak moments when she regretted ever meeting him. Taking care of a wheelchair-bound husband couldn't be as easy as Sally made it seem.

"You can ask, you know?" Sally said.

Jill blinked at her. She couldn't possibly mean...?

"Crash didn't tell us a lot about you, but I'm guessing you might have a lot of questions, and how will you get any answers if you don't ask?"

True. But she couldn't ask what she wanted to know, especially not in front of George.

"Go ahead," George said as if guessing her thoughts. "You won't hurt my feelings."

She squeezed her eyes shut and rubbed her forehead, hiding her heated face for a moment. "Is it...? I mean, do you...?" So many things were going through her mind that she couldn't articulate even one of them.

"It's okay," Sally said with a light touch to Jill's arm. "It hasn't been very long since you've been diagnosed, has it?"

On the one hand, it felt like yesterday that her doctor had tilted her world on its axis with his words, *I'm pretty sure it's MS*. On the other hand, she could barely remember life without MS. "Actually, it's been almost two years."

Sally looked surprised for a moment before shrugging. "We all deal with it in our own time."

What was that supposed to mean? She had dealt with it already, hadn't she? Squaring her chin, she stared at Sally, who only gave her a mild smile in return.

Something quivered inside of Jill. God, was Sally right? Admittedly, she felt pretty out of her depth lately. Had she just deluded herself into thinking she had coped with her condition when in reality she'd been in denial all this time?

Jill had a feeling that the answer to that question was a resounding *yes*. She hadn't come to grips with many of the aspects of MS, and that included her stance on relationships. Instead of carefully examining her options, she had closed that door once and for all.

"How long did it take you?" she finally found the courage to ask, looking from Sally to George.

A quiet sigh escaped George. He and Sally exchanged wry smiles. "It's an ongoing process," George said. "We pretty much spent the last twenty years dealing with one change after another. Having to give up my job. Going from using a cane to a walker and then a wheelchair. No longer being able to drive myself. Losing some of our friends who couldn't deal with the helplessness."

Jill's stomach bunched itself up into a massive knot. She remembered the YouTube video she had watched right after being diagnosed. That woman's boyfriend had left her because he couldn't deal with her condition. She peeked over at Crash, who waited in line at the hot-dog stand. What if she couldn't deal with it either, despite what she said? She shook off the painful thought and returned her attention to Sally. "Do you ever...?"

"Regret marrying him?" Sally finished for her.

Unable to look her in the eyes or look at George, Jill nodded.

Despite the grief that had been apparent in her eyes when her husband had listed his losses, Sally sounded strong and determined as she said, "Not even for a second." She put her hand on top of his limp one. "We met after George was diagnosed, so I entered into this relationship with my eyes wide open. Some days are harder than others and a few are hell, but just having him in my life makes it all worthwhile."

They looked at each other with a gaze so loving that it almost hurt Jill to watch.

"Ditto," George said, more to Sally than to Jill. Then he looked over at her. "Sometimes I worry about leaning on Sally too much. This," he nodded down at his paralyzed body, "is a lot to take on. I didn't want her to live like this. I still don't. But what am I to do? This stubborn woman won't leave me, so I might as well accept her love."

Could it really be that easy? Jill's world seemed to tilt beneath her. She clutched the edge of the table. Little electric shocks stabbed her left leg, a poignant reminder of her own illness, but they were nothing in comparison to the pain in her heart.

"And from what I know of your girlfriend, she's just as stubborn," George added.

"Oh, no, we're not... She's not..."

"It's okay," Sally said and touched her arm in a motherly gesture. "We already know the two of you are gay."

"That's not... We're really not... I mean, we are gay, but—"

Crash returned to the table with two bottles of water and two hot dogs. She settled down next to Jill and handed over one of each. "Did I miss anything?"

"No," Jill, George, and Sally said in unison.

Jill started eating, glad for the distraction, but while the others talked, she was still thinking about George's words.

When George tired and they prepared to leave, Sally pressed a card into Jill's hand.

Confused, Jill stared down at it. "What...?"

"It's the web address for the support group George is running," Sally said.

George was running a support group? She hadn't thought that possible.

"It's an online group, since some of us can no longer drive," George said. "The chat room we're using is compatible with my dictation software, so I can do this on my own. Why don't you drop by one evening and give it a try?"

"Self-help groups aren't my thing." She tried to hand back the card, which seemed to burn in her hand, but Sally refused to take it.

"That's what I said in the beginning, but the meetings really help," George said. "Now I'm even running my own group, and it's great to be able to give back some of the help I received."

Sighing, Jill pocketed the card. "I'll think about it."

The parking lot was almost empty, and all of their colleagues were long gone, but neither Crash nor Jill were in a hurry to leave. Crash had enjoyed spending the last few hours with Jill, playfully arguing about who got to pay for the hot dogs and talking about everything under the sun. Once they left here, she wasn't sure what to expect—would Jill shut her out again, overwhelmed with everything she had experienced today?

She watched Jill, who was nibbling her bottom lip as if she needed to digest something. Crash had a pretty good idea what it was, but she wanted to hear it from Jill and help her deal with it. "Penny for your thoughts."

"I don't think they're worth that much."

"They are worth much more than that. At least to me," Crash said, gazing into Jill's eyes.

Emotions were swirling through the green depths. For a moment, Crash thought Jill would refuse to answer or would make some kind of joke, but then Jill cleared her throat. "Sally and George." She shook her head with puzzlement. "Weren't they amazing?"

Crash nodded. "There were a lot of amazing people doing the walkathon. I know how hard it was for you to come here today."

Jill was silent for several seconds. Just when Crash thought she might not answer, she said, "It was the hardest thing I've ever done. Well, other than dissecting a frog in biology class. I still don't know how I managed not to puke."

Of course Jill would add a joke to that emotional confession. It was so typically Jill that Crash had to smile. "Well, you conquered this frog." She indicated the Rose Bowl loop.

"You've been a big part of it," Jill said. "Thank you."

"My pleasure." Crash squeezed her hand, and then neither of them let go.

They leaned against Jill's Beetle holding hands, watching other participants leave.

Anna and her husband waved as they passed them with their little girl.

"Having three kids while suffering from fatigue," Jill murmured. "I don't know how she does it. I get tired just thinking about it."

Crash studied her, taking in the shifting emotions on her expressive features. "You haven't spent much time around other people with MS, have you?"

"I didn't know that was required," Jill said, a bit tersely. Then she pressed her lips together and squeezed Crash's hand. "Sorry. I didn't mean to be so bitchy. It's just… I feel a bit…raw today."

"I know what you mean." Crash debated with herself for several seconds before deciding to go ahead and voice her thoughts. If they kept dancing around each other, they would never be able to build any kind of deeper relationship. "That's how I have felt since…well, pretty much since I met you." She held up her hand before Jill could speak. "I know we won't ride off into the sunset together anytime soon. That's all right. Just don't shut me out again, okay? I want to be part of your life beyond the bedroom, in whatever capacity you'll allow."

Instead of her features closing off, as Crash had feared, a slow smile crept onto Jill's face. "Ride off into the sunset?"

Crash shrugged. "I guess I saw too many westerns as a kid."

They both shuffled their feet and looked around the parking lot instead of at each other.

Ridiculous. Crash had never been at a loss for words around women, at least not since leaving her teenage years behind. Tensing more with every second that went by, she waited for Jill to acknowledge what she'd just said.

"I don't know what exactly I want from you…from our…from us," Jill said, staring down at the car keys in her left hand as if they were the most fascinating thing she'd ever seen. She peeked up. "Actually, that's not true. I know what I want, but I have no idea what I can have."

Crash's heart gave an excited thud. Admitting that was a huge step for Jill. She pressed her lips together, afraid that anything she said now would be too much and scare her away. Finally, when Jill kept looking at her, she said, "That's okay. We've got time to figure it out."

She hoped that was the truth. Filming would end in less than three weeks, and their initial agreement had been that their fling would end then. Would Jill, in a final, desperate attempt not to let her close, insist on it, even though so much had changed? She was determined not to let that happen, but it all depended on Jill.

When Jill just nodded in reply, Crash figured she had reached the capacity of what she could process in one day. "So," she said in a lighter tone, "what are you going to do with the rest of the afternoon? Any plans?"

"Not yet. But, well…" Jill peered up from under half-lowered lashes, heat and shyness mingling in her gaze. "I seem to remember giving you a rain check, if you're still interested."

The hint of vulnerability beneath her seductive tone touched Crash's heart. "Oh, I'm definitely interested. I mean, the walkathon was a rather leisurely affair, so I should do something to get my heart rate up."

Jill quirked a smile. "Need a sparring partner to assist you with that?"

Crash chuckled and tipped the brim of an imaginary hat. "That would be very much appreciated, ma'am."

Grinning, Jill unlocked her car. "Well, then, follow me."

"Crash?" Jill said quietly as they lay tangled together in her bed. She lifted her head off Crash's chest.

Something in her tone made Crash open her eyes and try to make out Jill's expression in the near darkness. "Hmm?" She trailed her fingers in soothing circles over Jill's shoulder blades, enjoying the smoothness of her warm skin.

"Do you think the couples we met today can still have this?" Jill gestured at their naked bodies.

"You mean sex?"

Jill nodded.

"Well, since they can't be with you, it won't be as amazing," Crash said with a grin. Then, sensing how serious this was for Jill, she sobered. "I'm not sure, Jill. I assume many of them manage some kind of sexual intimacy."

Jill was silent for a while. "Even the ones who ended up in a wheelchair?" she asked, sounding skeptical. "How's that supposed to work?"

"The handicapped partner could tell the other how to touch herself, for example." Crash rolled them around and nibbled Jill's neck, tasting the resulting goose bumps with her tongue. She trailed a string of kisses up Jill's neck and then whispered in her ear, "Wouldn't that be hot?"

A shiver went through Jill. She clutched Crash's bare back, digging in her nails in a way that made Crash groan with pleasure. "Oh yeah. At least for a change of pace. But if that was the only thing I could do…"

For a moment, Crash considered showing her how creative they could get in their lovemaking. But that wouldn't help Jill with all the doubts that were apparently going through her mind. She rolled them onto their sides and held Jill in her arms. "I hope it'll never come to that. But if it happens, we would figure it out together."

Jill leaned up on one elbow and stared down at her as if amazed that Crash had openly used the word *we*, but instead of protesting, she sighed and nestled closer.

"You've got a lot more to offer than just sex," Crash said and kissed her softly.

"Amazing sex," Jill corrected.

Crash smiled against her lips. "Even more than that."

For a moment, Jill looked as if she was tempted to show her just how amazing it could be, but then she put her head on Crash's shoulder and closed her eyes.

Crash held her until they both fell asleep.

CHAPTER 19

Jᴵʟʟ ɢʟᴀɴᴄᴇᴅ ᴀᴛ ᴛʜᴇ ᴄʟᴏᴄᴋ in the right-hand corner of her laptop's task bar. One minute to eight. She stared at the dialogue box that had been on her screen for the last five minutes. Should she log in or not? If she waited much longer, the meeting would start without her.

Sweat broke out all over her body while she paused with her fingers over the keyboard. *Come on. You can do it. It's anonymous.*

Not giving herself time to back out, she chose a username, typing the first thing that came to mind.

A message appeared at the top half of the screen.

Actress_lady has entered the room.

Jill gripped the laptop with both hands and looked around the group's meeting room. The right side of the screen listed the usernames of the other participants: LeaM, Momof3, Jennacbarton, Stacy123, Wishbone, Sucks_to_be_me, and Totally_dorky. She chuckled at what she assumed to be George's nickname.

Another message, this one in red, popped up.

Totally_dorky: Hey there, actress_lady. Glad you could join us. Like my wife said, we don't bite.

Jill froze. Sally had said that at the walkathon. So much for staying anonymous. How had George guessed who she was? Had Crash told him she was an actress?

LeaM: Welcome.

Wishbone: Hi.

She answered with a smiley, hoping they would get the message. She was here to watch, not to talk.

Totally_dorky: Does anyone have any questions or things you want to talk about tonight?

Jill waited, hoping someone else would come up with something and she wouldn't be called on.

Stacy123: My mom's on the warpath again.

Sucks_to_be_me: What crawled up her ass this time?

Stacy123: The appointment with my neurologist was on Monday, and I refused to let her come. The last time I allowed her to come in with me, she wouldn't stop crying and then she wasted all my time by explaining her crazy treatment ideas to my doctor and insisting that we try them.

Maybe she was related to Jill's mother. That sounded like something her mom would have done—if she had ever accompanied her to a doctor's appointment. The last time they had talked on the phone, her mother had gone on and on about the benefits of cod liver oil, right after she had asked Jill if she had finally talked to her brother.

Stacy123: That's more stress than I can deal with right now, so I told her to stay home. It's hard enough to remember all the things I want to talk about with my neuro without her there to create drama.

Jennacbarton: Yeah! Finally!

Momof3: Go, girl!

Wishbone added an icon displaying a pair of clapping hands to the discussion.

LeaM: You did the right thing. Your doctor's appointment is for you.

Sucks_to_be_me: Yeah. If your mother can't deal, she should make her own appointment—preferably with a therapist.

Jill chuckled. Sucks_to_be_me seemed to be quite the character. She wondered what his or her story was.

Totally_dorky: Do you have someone else who could come with you, maybe drive you and then wait in the car or the waiting room?

For several seconds, nothing moved on the screen. Then Stacy123's answer popped up.

Stacy123: I could ask my boyfriend, but he's working a lot and I don't want to impose on him all the time.

Sucks_to_be_me: Impose? Hello? He's your boyfriend, so he should be glad to be there for you.

Totally_dorky: Tone it down, Sucks. It's not an easy balance to achieve for most people. Mrs. Totally Dorky and I struggled with it for a long time. I don't want to shut her out and be a stubborn jerk, but I also don't want to give up what little independence I still possess and have her carry too much of my burden.

A new message from actress_lady appeared on the screen. Jill stared at the sentence in blue and then at her fingers, which had moved over the keyboard as if on their own accord.

Actress_lady: How do you do it? How do you achieve a balance?

Sucks_to_be_me: Ooh, so the newbie can talk.

Momof3: Shut up.

Jennacbarton: Dorky, I think Sucks needs a reminder of the group rules.

Sucks_to_be_me: Okay, okay. Sorry, actress_lady.

Jill ignored them all, waiting for George's reply. The red type finally appeared on the screen:

Totally_dorky: The same way we all are.

Which was? She hesitated and then typed her question.

Totally_dorky: You put together a network of supportive people who are there for you when you have a relapse or become disabled, so that not everything rests on the shoulders of your main caregiver.

Sucks_to_be_me: Duh. Bet she did that already.

Her fingers frozen on the keyboard, Jill shook her head. No, she hadn't. Sure, she knew Grace and Lauren would be there for her if push came to shove. Susana wouldn't hesitate to help either. But she had never made any formal arrangements or talked to them about it.

Sucks_to_be_me: Here's my advice.

Jill wasn't sure she wanted to know what he or she had to say, but she read on anyway.

Sucks_to_be_me: If you can afford it, pay someone to help you. I always found people most reliable when I had my checkbook with me.

That was the grand pearl of wisdom? "Wow," Jill mumbled at the screen. "It must *really* suck to be you." What kind of family and friends did this person have to end up with such a sarcastic attitude? Or had his or her attitude chased all the willing helpers away?

Totally_dorky: Thanks for the tip. Getting professional help is indeed a good option for some things. But, Sucks, wallowing in your bitterness really isn't. We want actress_lady to get something positive out of this meeting, not chase her away.

Jill already knew that, if nothing else, she had already learned something from this meeting: she never wanted to end up like Sucks_to_be_me. While she didn't want to give up her independence, she realized that she had to let other people in and take active steps toward dealing with her MS. How she would do that, she wasn't sure yet, but maybe tonight could be the first step.

CHAPTER 20

WHEN THE GATE BUZZER SOUNDED, Jill beat even Tramp to the door. "Yes?" she said into the intercom, even though she had a pretty good idea of who was standing on the other side of her gate.

"Hey. It's me."

No name necessary. Jill buzzed her in. Since the walkathon two weeks ago, they had spent every break on the set and almost every night together. She had never thought that she could spend so much time with one person and not get sick of her—quite the opposite.

When she opened the door, Crash greeted her with a kiss that nearly made Jill sink to the floor in a puddle of goo.

Then Crash stepped past her and set down the bag she carried to greet Tramp, who was going crazy, barking and wagging his rear end so hard that even his front shook.

"What's that?" Jill pointed at the small duffel bag.

Crash followed her gaze. "I need to be on the set very early tomorrow, so I brought a change of clothes...just in case I would end up staying over."

"Good thinking," Jill murmured, fighting down a hint of panic. Crash needed clean clothes in the morning. It wasn't as if she was asking to move in.

They settled down on the couch, cuddling and exchanging a kiss every now and then while they talked about their days. Finally, they each picked up their own work, Jill studying tomorrow's lines, while Crash watched something on her laptop.

Jill had come to love evenings like this. If only this sharing of their evenings could last beyond the wrapping of the movie next week... She still wasn't sure what the best option was—or even if there was a best option.

Sighing, she curled her legs under her on the couch and tried to focus on her script pages, but her attention kept wandering off—mostly toward the woman next to her.

Normally, Crash's presence was soothing, but today, she radiated an edginess that made the air around her seem to hum with energy. Crash sat on the couch, her laptop perched on her knees, watching the screen with rapt attention.

Jill had seen that kind of intense focus on the easygoing woman's face just when Crash was preparing for a stunt...or when they made love.

Weeks ago, she would have admonished herself for that phrasing of her thoughts, but now she could admit—at least to herself—that they were making love, even though having sex was all she was able to openly acknowledge.

She slid a bit closer on the couch to see what had captured Crash's attention so completely.

A cartoon woman in a 1906-style dress moved across the laptop screen, rushing out of a house with her eyes and her mouth wide open. Crash had the laptop's speakers off, but the woman seemed to be screaming at the top of her lungs. Flames danced along her back, quickly engulfing her entire body.

At first, Jill thought Crash was watching a cartoon or an animated movie, but when the sequence repeated over and over, she realized that it was a 3-D visualization of the fire stunt that was scheduled for tomorrow.

In less than twenty hours, it would be Crash's body, not the cartoon woman's, that was being set on fire.

She had known about the big fire stunt for weeks, of course, but she hadn't allowed herself to think about it much. There had been other things to focus on. But now Jill's throat tightened, and she struggled to breathe normally. She had to reach out for her water bottle and take a big sip before she could speak. "Crash?" She lightly touched Crash's knee.

"Hmm?" Crash answered without looking away from the laptop screen.

"Are you worried about tomorrow?"

Crash closed the laptop, put it down on the coffee table, and turned on the couch to face her. "We've planned this stunt for months, and we did about a million run-throughs. There'll be a fire marshal and several people with fire extinguishers on the set. Every crew member knows exactly what to do. Statistically, I'm taking a greater risk every time I'm taking my car out on an LA highway."

By now, Jill knew her well enough to hear what she wasn't saying. "That's good to know, but it doesn't answer my question."

Crash clutched her knees with both hands. "I..."

Jill put one hand on her arm. The muscles and tendons under her palm felt like steel, and she rubbed gently to loosen them. "This is me, Crash. You don't need to be the heroic, fearless stuntwoman here."

Crash's shoulders slumped. "I'm scared shitless. What if I freeze or my timing is off or—"

"You won't," Jill said firmly, not just to convince Crash but also to chase away the image of Crash burning from her mind. "You went over this stunt so often, you could do it in your sleep."

A sigh escaped Crash. "You're right," she mumbled but didn't sound convinced.

"Did I ever tell you that I first started acting in elementary school?" The tension in Crash's arm receded. She shook her head.

"I was a donkey in our Christmas school play."

That put a smile on Crash's face. "Aww. I bet you were cute."

"I didn't have any lines, but I was nervous as hell," Jill said. "I was about to throw up behind the stage. I was so afraid I'd bump into the manger with my cardboard costume and knock it over, baby Jesus and all. My teacher took me aside. Want to know what advice she gave me?"

"To picture the audience naked?" Crash guessed.

"That's the kind of advice you'd give a seven-year-old?" Jill lightly pinched her. "Good thing you're a stuntwoman, not a teacher. No, she told me to imagine the worst thing that could happen—"

"I don't know," Crash murmured. "I liked the idea of picturing you naked better."

Jill pinched her a little harder and continued, ignoring the interruption, "And then to think of a way that I could still come out on top of the situation. So I pictured myself picking up baby Jesus and cradling him in my...uh, hooves, keeping him warm. The audience couldn't hate me if I did that, right?"

Crash leaned forward and kissed her. "I don't see how they could," she whispered against Jill's lips.

Quickly, Jill pulled back before Crash could distract her from what she wanted to say. "So, even if you freeze or your timing is all wrong..." She looked at Crash expectantly.

"I could always drop down to the ground. That's the sign for my team to put me out. They'd have me covered in foam within seconds," Crash said as if to herself. Her hand went to her neck and covered the burn mark protectively. "This isn't the set of *Point of Impact*. I know what to do to avoid that snafu. If the wind is too strong or coming from the wrong direction, I'll tell Ben we have to wait."

"Exactly." Jill nodded with vigor. She pulled Crash's hand away from her neck and held it in both of hers. "I know fire stunts are hard for you, but I know you'll get through this like a champ. I believe in you."

"Thank you," Crash whispered, sounding a little choked.

Jill pulled Crash's legs up onto the couch and encouraged her to extend them across her lap so they could be even closer.

"I know your call time is only at eleven tomorrow and the fire gag is at eight, but...will you come watch?"

She sounded so vulnerable that Jill wanted to wrap her in her arms and never let go again. "Are you sure you want me there?" She didn't want her presence to make Crash even more nervous. And, truth be told, she wasn't sure if she could stand to see Crash be set on fire. A shiver went through her at the thought.

Crash looked her in the eyes and nodded.

"Then I'll be there."

"Hey, you okay?" From her now lying position, Crash studied Jill's face.

"Me?" Jill laughed, a sound bare of any humor. "I'm not the one who is going to be set on fire tomorrow."

"But you're the one who's trembling," Crash said.

"Must be because I'm so close to you." Jill gave her voice a seductive timbre. She didn't want to make Crash even more worried by voicing her own fears. Instead, she trailed one finger up the inside seam of Crash's jeans, all the while looking into her face to see if Crash would be receptive to a little distraction.

A groan rose up Crash's throat. Her breathing instantly quickened. "Jill..."

Jill pressed a finger to Crash's lips. "No talking."

"No talking," Crash whispered against her finger. "I can think of better things to do with my mouth." She sat up and kissed Jill forcefully, as if she wanted to imprint herself on all of her senses. One of her hands slid beneath Jill's shirt and her thumb brushed the underside of one breast, driving Jill crazy with desire. She wanted to feel Crash's touch higher or lower on her body. Preferably both.

She pressed herself against Crash and moaned. "Touch me."

"I am touching you," Crash murmured against her lips.

Only then did Jill realize that Crash's other hand had moved down and was stroking the inside of her thigh, which was left bare by her shorts. She watched Crash's fingers caress her leg, but she couldn't feel the touch at all. That part of her left leg was completely numb. It had happened before, so Jill wasn't worried, but now for the first time someone other than her doctors was touching the limb while it was numb. It was a distancing feeling, as if she were watching someone else making love. She wanted to push Crash's hand away and touch her instead, knowing that she would still get a lot of pleasure just by watching her come.

But Crash was faster. She moved her other hand down too, unbuttoned Jill's shorts, and managed to shove them and Jill's panties halfway down her legs without letting go of her. Her fingertips slid up and to a spot that wasn't numb at all.

"Oh, God." Jill gasped. "I can feel you."

Then Crash pressed closer and shifted her fingers, making Jill forget about her numb leg and about tomorrow and about anything but how incredible Crash's touch felt.

"Are you really sure you want to drive me?" Crash asked for the fifth time as Jill grabbed the car keys. "You could have slept a little longer and still made it to the studio in time to see the gag."

More sleep sounded good. Jill hadn't slept much last night, and when she had fallen asleep, nightmare images of Crash burning and screaming in panic and pain had woken her up.

"I'm driving you," she answered, just as she had the other four times. God, was she as annoying when she refused to let other people help? She hoped not.

Crash was silent on the drive to the studio. Jill knew she was running through the stunt in her mind, so she didn't try to make conversation, but she kept her hand on Crash's knee the entire way.

Tension lay in the air when they passed the guard and drove onto the studio lot. More crew members than usual were bustling about the second-unit set, double-checking fire extinguishers, blankets, and other safety equipment, while others were there to watch the stunt. Six cameras were being set up, because this was a scene they had to capture in one take.

Firefighters and medics were waiting at the edge of the set. Maybe their presence should have been soothing, but to Jill it drove home the dangerous nature of this stunt. If this gag went wrong, Crash wouldn't walk away with a few bumps and bruises.

She tried to tell herself that there was nothing to it; she had watched Crash perform other dangerous stunts since their first day on set.

But this was different, not just because this stunt scared even the normally confident Crash. When she had watched her do the first stunt involving fire, she hadn't been in love with her.

She squeezed her eyes shut as dizziness gripped her. Yet as much as she tried to, there was no denying it, at least not to herself. But then again, loving Crash had never really been the issue; allowing herself to be loved back was.

Drawing on her acting skills to keep a neutral expression, Jill walked side by side with Crash until they reached the point where the crew had set up the facade of a house that had been seriously hit by the earthquake.

Ben looked up from his conversation with two crew men Jill didn't know and waved Crash over.

"I need to go," Crash said but didn't move. Her face was expressionless, but her eyes were filled with fear.

Jill reached for both of her hands, finding them clammy. She squeezed softly. "The hardest part was showing up. You can do this."

A smile flitted across Crash's face as Jill repeated her words from the walkathon. "See you at the finish line." Her grip on Jill's hands tightened for a second, then she let go, gave her one last glance, and walked away.

Jill watched her go, her hands clutched around each other.

"Hey, Jill!"

When she turned, Lauren waved at her from behind the security barricades.

Jill headed over. "Good morning."

"Morning. Seems no one wanted to miss this." Lauren gestured at the other cast members who had shown up early to watch the big fire stunt.

"Seems so," Jill murmured.

All around her, colleagues were talking to each other, excited as if they were a bunch of kids visiting the circus.

Lauren seemed to sense her nervousness. She didn't try to make conversation while they waited.

Crash and the stunt coordinator disappeared into the stunt trailer for one last run-through. When Crash returned to the set, she wore a thin, white full-body suit that looked like long johns.

The material was fire-resistant, Jill knew.

Ben and two other men surrounded Crash. The stunt coordinator talked to her, gesturing, while the two men slathered her in a clear gel, which made the full-body suit semi-transparent and slicked it to Crash's body, revealing her athletic shape.

"Wow." One of the PAs watching from behind Jill let out a whistle.

Yeah, Crash looked sexy, but Jill was too worried to muster any amorous thoughts.

When the white undergarments were completely covered in the gel, the burn team helped Crash into a layer of black clothing and covered her with gobs of the gel again. Her hands, covered by silicone gloves, were coated in the fire-resistant gel too.

Then she struggled into her costume, an oversized dress, and Ben sprayed something onto its back. One member of the crew bent, dipped both hands into a bucket, and rubbed more of the gooey stuff over Crash's face and hair until it dripped off her nose.

Jill remembered what Crash had told her about the fire gel—it would only protect her for a few minutes, so everything would move fast now. She wanted to walk away, avoid seeing Crash being set on fire, but she stayed where she was, wanting to be there for Crash. Her heart thumped against her ribcage in a frantic rhythm.

"You okay?" Lauren asked next to her.

She felt Lauren's hand on her shoulder and nodded, her gaze still on Crash.

"Camera ready?" Ben called. "Sound ready?"

Two of the crew shouted confirmations.

"Roll sound."

"Speed," came the reply.

"Roll camera," Ben called.

"Rolling."

With every command, Jill's tension rose. She wanted to shout, "Stop," but of course she didn't. She stood rooted to the spot, every muscle in her body rigid.

Then, just seconds before she was lit on fire, Crash looked up and directly at her.

Instantly, Jill's fear disappeared, replaced with the need to be there for Crash. Everything around her seemed to disappear until just she and Crash existed. *You can do this,* she mouthed to Crash and gave her an encouraging nod, hoping Crash could see her despite the gooey stuff all over her face.

Crash shivered and tried to stand still while the burn team covered her face, hair, and hands with one last layer of the freezing cold gel. The Nomex undergarments had been soaked in the gel and then put in a cooler at forty-two degrees. The only place on her body that felt warm was the burn mark on her neck, which seemed to be on fire again.

Forget about that. It'll be different this time.

But the memories of her last full-body burn flooded her. The light flutter of anxiety that came with most stunts threatened to grow into full-fledged panic. She focused on her breathing—in, out, in, out—knowing she would get hurt or even killed if she didn't get control of her fear.

Even a look at the three safety guys, who waited, fire extinguishers at the ready, didn't help calm her, so she instead gazed at the cast and crew gathered to watch the stunt. Her mind didn't register faces, except for one.

Jill. The sight of her gave Crash confidence. Jill's last words to her echoed through her mind like a mantra. *You can do this.*

Sound and camera started to roll. Ben stepped forward and caught her gaze. "Ready?"

One last glance over at Jill, then Crash nodded. If Jill believed in her, she could handle anything. She took up position inside of the fake building and forced herself to breathe as calmly as she could. In, out, in, out. *You can do this.*

"Here we go." Ben moved around her. "Hold your breath in three, two, one—now!"

She stopped breathing, knowing that she'd singe her airways if she inhaled.

A hissing sound behind her indicated that Ben had torched the back of her dress. He rushed out of the cameras' frame.

Heat crept up her back. Not being able to see the flames licking up her dress made Crash even more nervous, but she trusted her team to keep her safe.

Seconds ticked by, each feeling like an hour. She could no longer see Jill, but she knew Jill was there, watching, trusting her not to fuck this up.

Finally, Ben raised his hand to signal that the fire had risen high enough to look spectacular on film.

Now fully engulfed in flames, she ran through the facade's doorway. Her last bit of air escaped her lungs as she let out a blood-curdling scream. The stunt script called for it, but she didn't need to act much. It was a struggle to flail her arms just the right way to show off the burning areas of her body to the cameras, but not to move in ways that would make the flames climb too high too fast.

A spot on the back of her neck felt uncomfortably hot—never a good sign. It could mean that she was about to get badly burned, but she wasn't sure if it was real or just her imagination playing tricks on her. The urge to flop down on her belly, the sign for the safety guys to put her out, was almost overwhelming. *Wait, wait. Not yet.*

She needed to give the camera operators enough material first. *You can do this!* Several seconds went by as if in slow motion. The burning sensation along her neck increased.

Her mentor's voice echoed through Crash's memory. *If anything hurts during a fire stunt, you're screwed. You need to be put out before that happens.*

Only Jill's voice in her mind kept her from dropping to the ground. Finally, the freeing hand signal and shout came. "Put her out now!"

Crash collapsed to the ground.

Jill gasped as Crash went down face-first, her entire back, including her neck and head, still engulfed in flames and her arms spread wide.

One of the safety operators threw a wet towel over Crash's head, probably to protect her from inhaling the chemicals, while three men with fire extinguishers sprayed her from head to toe.

Steam rose, and the white foam covered everything, making it hard for Jill to see. Was Crash moving? Was she okay? Jill couldn't tell.

She's okay. She has to be okay. But she needed to see for herself. Using her elbows without mercy, she shoved past several onlookers and rushed over to where stuntmen, the guys with the fire extinguishers, and the medics still surrounded Crash.

Finally, the ring of people around Crash moved back, allowing Jill a glimpse of her.

Crash was getting up, a wet blanket hanging around her shoulders so she wouldn't re-ignite. The once cream-colored dress hung around her in black tatters. The clear gel made her hair stick to her head. Gobs of the gooey stuff still clung to her face and throat. Foam from the fire extinguishers dripped off her. God, she was a mess—and the most beautiful sight Jill had ever seen.

Other people shouted congratulations, but Crash ignored them all. Her gaze zeroed in on Jill immediately, and a grin spread over her face.

Instead of stopping a few feet away, Jill approached Crash with her arms opened for a hug.

"Uh, I'm a mess and—"

Not caring, Jill threw her arms around her. With Crash's body pressed against hers, alive and healthy, she could breathe freely for the first time all morning. "You did great," she whispered into Crash's ear. "I knew you could do it."

"Thank you," Crash whispered.

The heat radiating from Crash and her tattered clothes made Jill worry about her MS symptoms flaring up, but she held on anyway. "Wow," she mumbled. "You're still pretty hot."

Crash burrowed closer.

Jill peered at her. "What? No jokes about your hotness?" That wasn't a good sign.

"Later," Crash mumbled against her shoulder. "For now, I just want to enjoy the moment." Jill felt her shake her head. "Wow. I did it. I really did it. How did it look?"

"Scary," Jill said.

"That's good," Crash said, sounding more collected now. With a glance at the people around, she lowered her voice and added, "I was close to hyperventilating for a second, but it really helped to have you here."

When they finally let go of each other, Jill flicked a gob of gel from her shoulder.

Crash's gaze swept over her. She gestured at the gel and the foam that now clung to Jill's front. "Now you're a mess too."

Jill forced a wry smile. *Truer words were never spoken.* She was more conflicted about Crash and the future than ever. After what they had shared, how could she just walk away in a week? But then again, how could she stay, knowing it would condemn this courageous woman to a life with MS?

She stepped back. "I think I'd better go and give the makeup artist some time to make me look halfway presentable."

"You're beautiful already, foam and all," Crash said. From everyone else, it would have sounded like a line, but she knew Crash meant it. After stripping off one of her silicone gloves, Crash lifted her hand and wiped a bit of foam off Jill's chin in a gesture so tender that it made Jill's heart ache. "Thanks again for being there for me."

Always, Jill wanted to say but knew she shouldn't make that promise. "You're welcome," she answered instead, gave Crash a quick hug, and hurried off to the wardrobe trailer. If only the wardrobe assistant could fix her messed-up emotions as easily as her clothing.

CHAPTER 21

Usually, Jill loved wrap parties. They were the culmination of months of hard work and one last occasion for the crew and the cast to come together to celebrate the end of filming, especially if they had managed to bring in the movie on time and on budget, as they had this time.

She was proud that she had made it through three months of filming without delaying production even once, but as she headed into the club where the wrap party for *Shaken to the Core* was being held, she didn't feel like celebrating at all.

Back in June, she and Crash had agreed that the end of shooting would also mean the end of their fling. Was that agreement still valid, even though what was happening between them had clearly surpassed being a fling weeks ago?

Maybe that agreement was more important than ever, now that she had fallen in love with Crash. Why keep torturing herself with what she couldn't have, at least not forever?

But there was that new voice in the back of her mind whispering, *Are you sure you can't have it?*

No, she wasn't. She wasn't sure of much these days. The only thing she knew was that she couldn't fathom never seeing Crash again, never touching her again, never hearing that contagious laugh again.

Music pounded through the nightclub's speakers, making the floor beneath her and the brushed aluminum bar vibrate as Jill made her way through the crowd inside. The executive producers had rented the entire club for this one night, but there were still a lot of people around Jill didn't know, probably guests of the cast, studio employees, or supporters of the movie.

She scanned the crowd for familiar faces—one familiar face in particular.

Strobe lights flashed in the rhythm of the music's beat, and a fog machine filled the club with a dense vapor, making it hard to see much more than entwined shapes writhing on the dance floor.

Was Crash part of the crowd on the dance floor? The thought of Crash dancing with someone else, the other woman rubbing her body along Crash's, made her clench her teeth.

Someone waved at her from the edge of the dance floor, but it was just Nikki, who was dancing with one of the camera operators.

Jill waved back and greeted several other colleagues but didn't join them. Finally, she spotted Lauren, Grace, and Shawn sitting at one of the tables against one wall and flopped down onto the only free chair. She leaned over and hugged Grace warmly. "Hey!" she shouted to be heard over the loud music. "I didn't know you'd be here. I thought you were still in New York, being paraded from talk show to talk show."

"I was," Grace shouted back. "I headed here straight from the airport. I wouldn't miss the wrap party of Lauren's first movie for the world."

"*First* movie?" Lauren repeated. "Who says there are going to be more? There's no guarantee anyone will take an interest in my new script."

"Oh, they will. It's too good not to attract interest."

Her friends gazed at each other in mutual adoration. "So," Grace said when she finally managed to drag her gaze away from Lauren, "how did the filming go for you? Lauren says you did great, even with all of the physical scenes the script called for."

Jill snorted. "They hardly let me do any of the physical scenes. Dr. Lucy Sharpe is at least half Crash."

As if conjured up by the mention of her name, Crash stepped up to the table. "Hi."

Jill's mouth was suddenly too dry to return the greeting.

Crash wore that sleeveless white blouse that always made Jill torn between wanting to look at it forever and wanting to take it off immediately. Tight black slacks emphasized her trim hips, and a thin leather jacket was casually slung over one strong shoulder.

Crash pulled a chair next to Jill, sat, and leaned over to kiss her hello.

The gesture made Jill's heart beat faster, not only because the touch of Crash's lips felt oh-so-good, but also because it felt so much like being part of a couple. It was scary and exciting all at the same time.

Shawn sighed and playfully nudged Jill's shoulder. "I'm starting to feel like a fifth wheel with all you newlyweds at this table."

Cheeks heating, Jill ignored the comment. Shawn had no idea what she was talking about.

"So," Grace asked after a while, "what will happen now that filming ended?"

For a moment, Jill thought she was asking about her and Crash, but then Grace added, "Do you have other work lined up already? With all the traveling I've been doing, I'm totally out of the loop and have no idea what's next for all of you."

Shawn gave an excited hop, almost spilling the drink she held in the process. "My agent just sent over the contract for my next movie. I'm not allowed yet to reveal who else is in it, but oh my God... It's a dream come true."

"Congratulations," Jill said along with everyone else. She was glad for her colleague, really. If only producers were as eager to send contracts to her agent too. None of her cast mates seemed to have problems getting roles. Grace would be in Ireland starting next Tuesday to shoot her new movie. Jill felt like the only out-of-work actress on the planet.

"What about you?" Grace asked, nodding at Crash.

"Ben got me an audition on *Engine 27*. No guarantees that they'll take me, but I'll meet with their stunt coordinator on Monday."

The legs of Jill's chair scraped across the floor as she turned to stare at Crash. "Wow. That's fantastic! Why didn't you tell me?"

Crash rubbed her neck. "It's a TV show about a bunch of firefighters, so up until last week, I wasn't sure I'd want to do it."

Jill squeezed Crash's knee under the table. "And now you are? It'll probably mean a lot of fire stunts, won't it?"

"A fair share, probably."

Jill wanted to ask if that was okay with her, but that would reveal Crash's fears to the entire table.

"It's still not my favorite kind of stunt, but I think I'm slowly getting over it," Crash said as if sensing the unspoken question.

"...you, Jill?"

Grace's voice interrupted the eye contact between them. Jill turned to look at her friend. "Uh, excuse me?"

"I asked what's next for you," Grace said. "Are you going back to TV work?"

Jill suppressed a sigh. "I wish. I don't have any offers so far, so it seems I'll be back to doing cattle calls and throwing myself to the mercy of casting directors next week."

"Well," Grace said, "if you can bear to work with me again, I could try to get you a role in my next movie."

It was how Hollywood worked, but Jill hated mooching roles off her friends. *Hey, you wanted to let other people in a little more, remember? Besides, pride won't pay your bills.* So she forced a smile and nodded. "That would be great, thanks."

Grace blinked. "Wow. That was easy. I thought I'd have to go nine rounds with you before finally getting you to accept."

With heat tinging her cheeks, Jill just shrugged.

Beneath the table, Crash reached over and squeezed her knee.

Grace started tapping her fingers on the table to the beat of a pop love song that the DJ had just put on. She looked over at Lauren, her famous ocean-blue eyes pleading. "Dance with me?"

Lauren didn't have to be asked twice.

Shawn got up too to search for a dance partner, leaving Jill and Crash alone at the table.

Jill watched her friends for a moment.

Lauren's tall frame fit against Grace's curves perfectly, and they held each other so close as if they never wanted to let go. Jill was fairly sure that they didn't even notice that there were other people surrounding them on the dance floor. With the paparazzi constantly following Grace around, the two probably didn't get the chance to dance with each other very often.

God, she missed dancing too. When the pain behind her sternum became too much, Jill had to look away.

Crash held out her hand, palm up. "How about it? Want to dance too?"

"I hung up my dancing shoes for good when I nearly did a face-plant at the wrap party of *Ava's Heart*," Jill said. She hated the thought of other people watching her dance, possibly on the lookout for any uncoordinated movements on her part.

Crash kept her hand extended. "Come on. I promise I won't let you fall."

Too late. I've already fallen. Jill sighed. She didn't know what the future would bring for her and Crash. Maybe this would be their only chance to dance together. After one last moment of hesitation, she put her hand in Crash's. Those slightly callused fingers immediately wrapped around hers, safe and warm.

"Ready?" Crash asked, looking into her eyes.

Were they still talking about the dance? Jill took a deep breath and nodded. "Lead the way."

Crash pressed her cheek to Jill's and settled her arms around her more securely, holding her close and protecting her from other dancers jostling her, disturbing her sometimes precarious balance.

If only she could always hold and protect her like this. But Jill wouldn't let her. Well, she wouldn't give up. Crash was determined that this would be the night when she'd change Jill's mind once and for all. She had to try, at the very least. Tonight was the official end of their arrangement, and she wasn't sure if Jill would insist on sticking to it—maybe even walking away from the friendship part of their friends-with-benefits affair, so Crash had nothing to lose.

When the song ended, they looked at each other and then, as if by mutual agreement, waved their good-byes to their colleagues and made their way through the crowd to the door.

A light breeze hit Crash as soon as they stepped outside. She sucked in a lungful of air and tilted her head up, trying to make out stars in the night sky, but there were none.

Instead, two security guards and a couple of paparazzi hung around. They snapped a photo or two, but then quickly lost interest when they realized they weren't big stars. The guards retreated too as if sensing that they wanted some privacy.

They stood in companionable silence, watching partygoers pass by on the busy street.

Now or never. Crash clenched her hands to fists in the pockets of her slacks. "Do you—?"

"So," Jill said, cutting off Crash's question.

It was almost as if she didn't want to let her finish, afraid of what she would ask—or maybe afraid of not having the strength to say no.

But this time, Crash wouldn't let Jill be the one who made all the decisions. "Come home with me," she said, not phrasing it as a question.

They looked at each other. Jill's green eyes, nearly black in the near darkness outside, searched Crash's face.

Crash's shoulders stiffened as her tension rose. What would she do if Jill said no? Just let her walk away, or—?

Jill nodded, nearly making Crash pitch forward in relief.

She kept peeking over at Jill as they made their way to her SUV, but Jill gave no indication of whether this would be one final good-bye or the beginning of something new for her.

The one time they had made love in Crash's studio apartment before, they had tumbled onto the sofa bed and practically ripped the clothes off each other, eager to get to bare skin, but this time, things were different.

For once, Crash's apartment was tidy—no socks or weights on the floor. Even the yoga mat had been rolled up, as if Crash had expected to bring her back here and had wanted everything to be perfect.

Crash led her by the into the apartment, closed the door, and threw her keys onto the table without looking away from Jill.

The intensity of her gaze made Jill's chest tighten with a mix of desire, joy, and fear.

Crash directed her to sit on the edge of the sofa bed and stepped into the space between her legs. Without saying anything, she wrapped her arms around Jill and pulled her close, cradling Jill's head gently against her belly. It wasn't a sexual gesture but one of comfort and love.

Jill slung her arms around Crash's hips and returned the hug—as well as the feelings it conveyed.

As long as neither of them said it out loud, she didn't have to worry.

Finally, Crash let go and moved her hands to the buttons of Jill's blouse, where she paused and tilted her head. "May I?"

Her throat too tight to speak, Jill nodded. For once, she had chosen to wear a blouse despite the buttons, wanting to look good at the wrap party. She watched as Crash's fingers slowly opened button after button without hurry, as if it were a sacred ritual that needed to be savored. Was Crash taking her time because she, too, assumed that this might be the very last night they spent together?

When the last button slid through its hole, Crash pushed the blouse back. She kissed first one bare shoulder, then the other, before kneeling. Her lips caressed Jill's collarbone, nuzzled the vulnerable spot at the base of her throat, and moved down.

Her breath warmed Jill's chest and sent shivers through her body.

When the material of the bra stopped her access to Jill's skin, Crash looked up. She slid her hands around her, a silent question in her eyes.

Again, Jill nodded.

Crash fumbled with the hooks of the bra for a moment, not at all the bold stuntwoman and seductress others thought her to be.

Jill loved her all the more for it.

Finally, Crash slid the straps down and the cups fell away. With just her fingertips, she traced the curve of one breast.

The touch was barely perceptible, but Jill felt it everywhere.

Crash kissed the slope of the other breast. Instead of continuing on to her nipple, she moved her head away and slid her hands down Jill's belly, which started to quiver in expectation. Another quick glance up, into Jill's face, then Crash opened the button and zipper of Jill's pants.

Wriggling from side to side, Jill allowed her to pull the pants down. As they slid down her thighs, a thought shot through her mind. *The foot brace!* Hastily, she covered Crash's hands with her own. "Let me…"

"It's okay," Crash said as if she knew exactly why Jill wanted to take over.

Jill gripped the pants.

For a moment, both paused and held on to them. "Please," Crash whispered.

Something inside of Jill melted. She let go.

The pants slid down, revealing the L-shaped piece of plastic that rested against the sole of her foot and the back of her calf, keeping her foot from dropping when she got exhausted.

Crash opened the Velcro straps around Jill's lower leg as if she had done it a thousand times before, her movements sure and confident. She pulled the foot brace free and set it aside. Her hands gently massaged Jill's calf muscles, making her groan in relief, then they moved upward.

Another groan tore from Jill's throat when Crash's fingertips brushed the inside of her thigh, now not a sound of relief but of arousal. She lifted up when Crash stood and pulled down Jill's panties.

Before she could lose complete control, she grabbed on to Crash's tight ass and pulled her flush against her own body. The material of Crash's slacks provided delicious pressure, distracting her from her mission to undress Crash. She moved away a fraction of an inch. Her hands went to the buttons on Crash's short-sleeved blouse, but, as usual, the damn things wouldn't cooperate and open as fast as she wanted.

"Rip them," Crash whispered.

"Oh, no. This is my favorite blouse. It shows off your arms so nicely." Did it even matter? There was a chance she wouldn't see Crash in it ever again after tonight or, if she did, would never get to undress her again. Anger and sadness clutched her at the thought. She gripped both sides of the blouse and wrenched them apart.

Buttons ricocheted everywhere.

Eyes wide, Crash stared down at her own chest, then at Jill. "I thought—"

"Changed my mind." She stopped speaking and explored Crash's flat belly with her lips and tongue and then pulled her down a little so she could reach one breast.

Crash's nipple instantly hardened as she sucked it in.

A long moan rumbled through Crash's chest. "More."

When Jill sucked a little harder, Crash gripped her shoulders with both hands as if she were the one with the balance problem. Gently, Crash urged her to crawl back onto the bed.

The satin sheets felt cool against Jill's overheated skin. Immediately, she held her arms out to Crash, missing the contact between them.

After shucking her slacks and underwear, Crash sank down and covered Jill with her own body.

Oh. So good. Jill's eyes fluttered closed at the skin-on-skin contact. She loved feeling Crash against her like this. Her world narrowed until nothing but Crash's touch existed.

Crash pressed one muscular thigh against Jill's already soaked center and, leaning up on her elbows, moved against her in a slow rhythm. Her mouth found Jill's breast and closed over one erect nipple.

The dual sensation was almost too much. She already felt herself spiraling out of control. One of her hands came up and pressed against Crash's shoulder to roll her around and take over, but Crash wouldn't budge from her spot at Jill's breast.

Crash added a gentle nibbling that made Jill let out a sharp hiss. Her hips arched up, seeking more contact. She wanted Crash to touch her—right now—but she knew it would be over too fast, so she let her continue the slow torture.

Weakly, she lifted her head to watch Crash make love to her.

The little sounds of pleasure escaping Crash as she licked and suckled were as arousing as the sensations coursing through her. The scent of their desire hung in the air.

As if sensing her gaze, Crash looked up.

For one eternal moment, neither of them moved or spoke, but an entire conversation took place.

That wasn't just passion in Crash's heated gaze. That was love.

Jill clutched her shoulders, urged her up, and kissed her deeply.

At first, their lips and tongues moved against each other achingly slow; then their bare breasts touched, making both arch into the kiss. Passion took over.

"I want you so much." Crash's warm breath caressed her lips.

Jill shuddered and pulled her hard into her parted thighs. "Then take me."

With a wild groan, Crash slid her hand down, between them.

The first touch of Crash's fingertips against her wetness made Jill gasp. She wanted to tell her to go slow so this wouldn't be over so fast, but she couldn't.

Crash circled her clit in just the right way to drive her even higher without sending her over the edge.

Jill spread her legs wider, urging her on. She wanted to make it last, but when Crash's fingers filled her, holding back was not an option. Her head spun. She arched against Crash, taking her deeper. Her clit throbbed in time with the wild beat of her heart.

Her eyes were heavy with pleasure and had nearly closed, but she forced them open. She needed to see Crash.

Their gazes connected.

The desire in Crash's irises, just thin rings of blue, made Jill's own arousal soar even higher.

"So beautiful." Crash brought her free hand up and raked her thumb across Jill's nipple, sending her senses reeling.

She rocked her hips faster against Crash and clutched her back with both hands, feeling the defined muscles contract beneath her fingers. "Yes, yes!"

Crash was panting too, her desire slick against Jill's leg.

Oh God. She was so close. So close. Jill slid her hands down and gripped Crash's behind. She felt her drive deeper into her in response. A half moan, half shout escaped her. "Crash!"

Her legs started to shake. A nonstop stream of gasps, moans, and whispers of Crash's name fell from her lips. She clenched around Crash's fingers. She pressed her mouth against Crash's shoulder as her hips bucked up once more. Orgasm hit her, making light explode behind her eyelids.

When her eyesight started working again, she became aware of Crash sliding up her body to cradle her face in her hands and kiss her tenderly.

Jill couldn't speak. Instead, she kissed her back, first languidly, then, when she regained some strength, with hunger. She drifted one hand down, between Crash's legs, moaning at the wetness she found. She rubbed her fingers over Crash's clit, gently at first, then with more insistence.

Crash thrust against her with an expression of helpless surrender. "Jill..."

"I..." *I love you.* "I'll make you come."

"Oh yeah." Crash jerked. She shivered and thrust herself against Jill's fingers. Then her body went taut, and Jill knew she was right at the edge.

That knowledge made her burn with desire, almost as if she could come again, along with Crash. Staring up into Crash's flushed face, not wanting to miss a second, she pressed a little harder.

"Oh! Jill!" Crash collapsed onto her with a choked cry.

Jill caught her and held her close, marveling at how she could feel so protective of her and at the same time so wild, as if she wanted to do this all over again. She skimmed her hands over Crash's back from her shoulders to her butt as Crash's breathing calmed.

"Jill?" Crash asked a few minutes later, quietly speaking into the darkness of the studio apartment.

Jill squeezed her eyes shut and didn't lift her head from its comfortable spot on Crash's shoulder. She knew what was coming; she had felt it in their lovemaking. Crash wanted to talk about them.

Crash turned on the light. She ran her fingers up Jill's neck and gently guided her head up to make eye contact. "Look at me, please."

Blinking against the sudden brightness, Jill looked at her.

Crash kept both arms wrapped around her, as if afraid that she'd leave if she didn't hold on. "Do you remember what you said the last time we made love here in my apartment?"

Made love, not had sex... Crash had said it. Jill's heart leapt with a mix of dread and joy, but she ignored it and nodded to the rest of her words. "That we would walk away after filming ended."

"Well, I won't. I can't."

"You have to," Jill whispered.

Crash lifted her dimpled chin in a gesture of defiance. "Says who?"

"Says the damn MS, that's who!"

"You'd just let the MS take away something else from you?" Crash shook her head. "You're a fighter, Jill. Why don't you fight for us?"

"Don't you get it?" Jill tried to pull back, but Crash held on. "I am fighting. I'm fighting for you. I don't want you to have to live with MS."

"You never asked me about why I visited the caregiver support group," Crash said after a moment of silence. "Why not?"

Because I was afraid of the answer. Jill dug her teeth into her bottom lip. "I...I guess...I just..."

"I needed to be sure," Crash said.

"Sure of what?" Jill whispered before she could stop herself.

"Sure of myself and my feelings. Sure that they are stronger than whatever the MS could throw at us. Sure that I would be able to do what Sally is doing for George, if necessary."

Something inside of Jill vibrated like one of the stunt wires holding a huge weight. "Are you?" she breathed. "Are you sure, I mean."

Crash looked her in the eyes, her blue irises glowing with determination. "Yes. I want you. A life with you. I can deal with everything else if only I have you."

A groan wrenched from Jill's chest. No one had ever said those words to her, and only now did she realize that she'd waited to hear them all her life. She wanted to rain kisses all over Crash's face and assure her she wanted the same, but as much as she longed for happiness with Crash, she wanted to protect Crash even more. "How can you be sure? We've barely known each other for three months. How can you know after such a short time?"

Crash shrugged. "My father proposed to my mother after knowing her for just two weeks. Sometimes, you just know."

Jill couldn't argue against it. Her feelings for Crash were already stronger than anything she'd ever felt for another woman. "But are you sure you'll still feel the same ten years down the road?"

"Sally still feels the same for George, so why would my feelings change?" Crash said.

"Yeah, they obviously love each other, but are you sure it's the way one spouse loves the other?" Jill voiced what she'd wondered since meeting the couple. "With Sally being the caregiver and George being the helpless one in the relationship all the time, that changes their dynamic. I'm not sure they are really partners—and that's the only way a relationship would work for me."

"You want our relationship to be a partnership, not a dependency. I get that, Jill. But being partners isn't about being able to do the same things. It's about supporting each other as much as you can in any given situation."

"That's just it." The words burst out of Jill with desperation. "How much support could I possibly give you if I ended up in a wheelchair?"

"You were the one who helped me through the fire stunt. I know you didn't want to see me being set on fire, but you stayed to show your support. Are you saying you couldn't have done that if you were in a wheelchair?"

Jill blinked, and this time, it wasn't because of the bright light. "I...I could, couldn't I?"

Crash nodded firmly. "Without you, I doubt I would have found the courage to audition for *Engine 27*. That's the kind of support I'd want from a partner."

A warm kernel of hope nestled in the center of Jill's chest. "Do you really think it could be that easy?"

"I don't know about easy," Crash said. "Sometimes it probably won't be. But I'm prepared for that."

"I'm not," Jill said, knowing she could be honest with Crash. "But..." She sucked in a breath, held it for a moment, and then slowly let it escape. "Neither am I prepared to walk away."

Crash pulled her closer, holding her so tight as if she wanted to fuse their bodies. "Then don't. Please, Jill. Give us a chance."

An enthusiastic yes trembled at the tip of Jill's tongue, but she hesitated, a thousand *buts* and *ifs* tumbling through her mind. Finally, a glance into Crash's eyes, reading the hope and the fear, was her undoing. "I'll think about it, okay?"

"Okay." Crash didn't loosen her grip on Jill. She waited a few heartbeats before tilting her head and giving her a questioning look. "So?"

Despite her tension, laughter bubbled up from Jill's chest. "Five seconds? That's all the time you're giving me to think about it?"

An impish smile spread over Crash's face. "It feels as if I already waited forever."

Jill hesitated. She still wasn't sure what was the right thing to do. But would she see things more clearly in a month or a year? She doubted it, and it wasn't fair to make Crash live her life in a holding pattern. She either had to send Crash away for good or take a leap of faith. Her last relapse had been a long time ago, and apparently, the first years were often a good indication of how the disease would progress. If that was true for her too, her chances of not ending up like George were probably pretty good. It was even possible she wouldn't have another relapse. She didn't want to look back at her life a few decades in the future and realize she'd refused herself—and worse, Crash—happiness for nothing.

"All right," Jill said on an exhale.

"All right?" Crash's voice came out in an excited squeak. "You mean...?"

Jill nodded shakily. She felt as if she were walking on a tightrope, barely keeping her balance. "Let's do this the way you suggested some time ago—go out on a date and then see where things are heading." It still felt like a risky thing to do, but she could handle it—especially with the happiness radiating from Crash. "We'll take it slow."

"Oh yeah. Slow. I can do slow."

"Yeah?" Grinning from ear to ear, Jill slid her hand down Crash's body and teased at the apex of her thighs. "Are you sure?"

Crash groaned. "Tomorrow. We'll start taking it slow tomorrow."

CHAPTER 22

When Jill woke again, the sun was shining into Crash's studio apartment and the spot on the sofa bed next to her was empty. A disappointed sigh escaped her. Now that she'd worked up the courage to allow herself to give a future with Crash a chance, she had wanted to start the day by kissing her awake.

Then she heard Crash whistle in the bathroom, and her smile returned. Even better. She would join Crash in the shower. When she slid her legs out of bed, she felt a bit shaky but told herself it was caused by thoughts of pressing herself against Crash's athletic body, trailing her soapy hands over her abs. Or maybe it was just jitters. After denying herself any kind of relationship for two years, this tentative commitment to Crash was scary—and exciting.

Calm down. You agreed to take it slow. Start with a date and then take it from—

She took one step out of bed. Her left leg gave away without warning, and she collapsed to the floor, barely avoiding hitting her head on the coffee table. She lay there, dazed, for a moment not feeling anything except for shock. Then pain shot through her elbow and her hip. She gazed down her body, trying to understand what had happened.

"Jill?" Crash called through the closed bathroom door. "Everything okay out there?"

A rush of panic hit her. "I'm fine," Jill called back. She didn't want Crash to hurry out of the bathroom and find her on the floor. Gritting her teeth, she tried to get up but quickly found that she couldn't. Her entire left side felt numb up to her waist, and her leg was completely useless.

She hadn't noticed before. For once, she had skipped her morning routine of checking her body for symptoms before getting up, her thoughts only on Crash and their relationship. *Relationship?* That familiar voice in her mind returned. *You really thought you could have a relationship? You can't even get off the damn floor!* Instead of striding into the bathroom to make love to Crash in the warm shower, she was lying naked on the cold floor, staring at the dust bunnies under the sofa bed and trying in vain to get up. How could she expect Crash to deal with this if not even she could? It had been stupid to believe that a future with Crash was possible. Her hope of having just a mild form of MS had shattered like a fragile piece of glass.

Grief and anger flooded her. She held on to the latter, using it to power herself up.

Just as she was dragging herself onto the sofa bed, the bathroom door opened and Crash stepped out. "Hey, good morning. Do you want—? Jill! What's wrong?" Crash rushed over and helped her settle more fully onto the edge of the sofa bed.

"Nothing," Jill mumbled.

"Did you fall?" Crash sank to her knees next to her and ran her hands over Jill's legs, from her ankles to her thighs.

Under different circumstances, Jill would have enjoyed the gentle touches, but now she barely even felt them on her left side. Her cheeks burned with embarrassment at having Crash see her like this. "I'm fine." She tried to pull the covers around herself, but Crash tugged it back down.

"You're bleeding," Crash said, her face gone pale. She pointed at Jill's arm.

Jill craned her neck and discovered a bleeding scrape on her elbow.

Crash jumped up, ran to the bathroom, and returned with a first-aid kit.

Jill held still while Crash pressed a clean piece of gauze against the scrape to stop the bleeding and then put a Band-Aid over it. As long as Crash was focused on her elbow, she at least wouldn't question her about why she had fallen.

Finally, Crash took her hands away and regarded her with a concerned gaze. "Are you hurt anywhere else?"

"No. I don't think so." The tender area on her right hip wasn't worth mentioning. It was probably just a bruise, and there was nothing Crash could do about it.

Crash frowned. "Did you fall out of bed?"

"Something like that," Jill mumbled.

"Jill..."

She sighed. Trying to hide it was stupid. She wouldn't even make it to the car on her own. The thought made her grit her teeth. "I can't walk," she said, keeping her voice low, almost to a whisper. "My left leg is completely out of order, and the right one," she poked it repeatedly, "doesn't feel quite normal either."

Her lips compressed to a razor-sharp line, Crash reached for the cell phone on the coffee table.

"What are you doing?" Jill asked.

"I'm calling an ambulance."

"No!" Jill reached for her arm and held on to it. "No ambulance."

"But if your leg is numb, you can't even tell if you hurt yourself."

Jill shook her head. "I would be able to tell, believe me."

"Still." Crash didn't let go of the phone. "If this is a relapse, you need—"

"We don't know if it is. Maybe I just got overheated." She forced a smile. "Last night was pretty hot." She hoped that was it, but she had a feeling this was something else. Her leg at times felt weak or numb, but she had always been able to walk, even if it was with a limp.

Crash gave her a doubtful glance. "What if it's more than a little flare-up?"

"I don't know. Guess I'll know by tomorrow." Jill marveled at how she could sound so calm. Her head was spinning. How had everything gone to hell in a hand basket so fast? Just a few hours ago, she'd been so happy and hopeful for the future, and now...

Crash plopped down on the couch next to her and wrapped her arms around Jill, who squeezed her eyes shut to stop the tears burning in them from leaking out.

She hadn't had a relapse for so long that she'd started to hope that she was one of the lucky few who, after an initial exacerbation or two, remained stable for decades, living a normal life. Now the cruel reality had slapped her in the face. Who knew how many more relapses would be coming? She wouldn't allow Crash to live through them with her.

"What do you need me to do?" Crash asked.

Jill pulled back, out of the embrace. This was her battle to fight, not Crash's. "Could you drive me home?"

A wrinkle formed between Crash's brows. "Home? You need go to the ER or be seen by a—"

"This isn't an emergency, Crash," Jill said, trying to be patient with her and not let herself be affected by Crash's sense of urgency. This was scary enough as it was. "Very few things that happen with MS are. The doctors won't even call it a relapse unless it lasts for more than twenty-four hours. If I'm not doing better by tomorrow morning, I'll call my neurologist."

Crash regarded her with a concerned gaze, clearly not liking what she heard. "And how will you get around until then if you can't walk?"

"I have a cane at home."

"Jill, you can't navigate the stairs with—"

"I'll sleep downstairs on the couch," Jill said. "I'll manage."

"You? *You* will manage?" Crash asked, hurt in her voice and her eyes. "What happened to *we*?"

There was no we; there couldn't be. She never should have given Crash—and herself—false hope. Now it hurt even more to recognize the truth that she should have stuck to all along. She didn't have the strength to tell Crash. "Let's talk about it later. I need to focus on this," she waved at her useless left leg, "right now."

"Sounds like you made up your mind already," Crash mumbled.

"Please, let it go. I can't fight this relapse—or whatever it is—and you. Please just take me home."

The muscles in Crash's strong jaw bunched. "I don't like this at all."

"Crash, please. I don't have the energy for long discussions."

Crash inhaled and exhaled, but her tense posture didn't relax. Finally, she nodded. "All right. Let's get you dressed and get you home, where you can be more comfortable."

Needing help to put on her pants and button her blouse drove home the fact that Crash might end up her caregiver if Jill didn't break things off.

As Jill powered herself up from the sofa bed, her right leg felt a bit more steady, but the left one was still as numb as a piece of wood. A new wave of anger and despair gripped her. She resolutely pushed back the rising panic. *You'll figure it out as you go. You always have, and this isn't any different.*

Crash wrapped one arm around her, steadying her.

With Crash supporting some of her weight on the left side, Jill wobbled to the door and allowed herself a quick glance over her shoulder at the unmade sofa bed she had shared with Crash, knowing she'd never be back. Her fall had made it more than clear: It had been crazy to let herself hope for a life with Crash. There was no future of any kind for them.

After a tense drive to Glendale, Crash helped Jill into the house and to the living room.

"Where's Tramp?" Crash asked, looking around for the labradoodle.

"I dropped him off with Susana before going to the wrap party yesterday," Jill said.

God, had that really just been yesterday? Crash mentally shook her head. It felt a million years ago. She'd been so happy last night, but now the door that had cracked open had slammed into her face again. With the physical exacerbation, it seemed Jill had also relapsed into her old kind of thinking.

She helped her settle on the couch and then stood there, looking down at her. Her hands felt strangely empty now that she wasn't holding on to Jill. She rubbed them on her jeans. "Do you need anything?"

"No, thanks."

A sudden idea pierced Crash's helplessness. "What about your medication? Could it alleviate your symptoms?"

Jill shook her head. "I'll inject myself later, but it's a long-term medication. It won't have any influence on acute relapses."

"Oh. Okay." Rarely before had she felt so stupid and helpless. She looked around for something else she could do. "Do you want me to pick up Tramp?"

"No, thanks. Susana will be by later and bring him with her," Jill said.

"What about your car?" It was probably still parked near the club where the wrap party had been held. "I could get it for you."

"How would you do that? You're just one person and can't drive two cars at the same time."

"I could call TJ and—"

Jill shook her head. "That's not necessary. I'm sure Susana and her husband would be happy to get it."

Crash pressed her lips together and said nothing, but she was seething inside, the anger, frustration, and hurt eating away at her. Why couldn't Jill just let her help? This damn relapse wasn't her fault, so why was she being pushed away?

But she couldn't start a fight right now; it would only deplete Jill's energy.

She looked down at her, taking in the pale face, the way Jill unconsciously cradled her left leg with both hands, and the stubborn tilt of her head. Behind that thin layer of stubbornness and strength, she could sense Jill's fear. If she pushed just a little, Jill might break down. *I can't do that to her.* Not now, when Jill needed her strength to fight the relapse.

"All right," she said. "What time do you want me to pick you up tomorrow, assuming the neurologist can squeeze you in somewhere?"

"No, Crash. You've got your audition with the *Engine 27* stunt coordinator tomorrow morning, remember?"

Crash had indeed forgotten about that. "To hell with the audition. I'll pick you up. Better yet, I'll stay and—"

"No." Jill's tone was final. More softly, she added, "Go home and rest or do whatever you need to do to prepare for the audition. One of us being in this mess is bad enough. If you lost that job because of me..." She shook her head. "I'll get Grace or Lauren to take me."

Crash hesitated. "Promise? You won't do something crazy and try to go by yourself?"

"Promise," Jill said. "Don't worry about me, okay?"

Yeah, that's easy. Just open my chest and rip my heart out. Crash made a face. "You can leave, really."

"Oh, no. I'm not leaving. What if you need the bathroom or something?"

Jill sighed. "Okay. I'll call Grace and have her come over to help me."

Crash took the phone from the coffee table and pressed it into Jill's hand. "Call her now."

"What? Don't you believe me?"

"I know you, Jill Corrigan."

Averting her gaze, Jill pressed an icon on her smartphone and lifted the phone to her ear. When she ended the call a few minutes later, she gave Crash a nod. "She's on her way. Happy now?"

"Happy? No." How could she be happy while Jill was going through a relapse—and instead of letting her help, she was calling over her best friend? That hurt more than she could say, but she didn't want to make this about herself. "I'm glad you won't be alone. I'll be going, then." She waited, hoping Jill would change her mind but knowing she wouldn't.

And she didn't. She just nodded.

"Jill..." She took one step forward, toward the couch, then stopped when Jill stiffened. "What I said yesterday about wanting a life with you... That didn't change. I still want that, and I'll be there for you every step of the way. You can call me any time, for anything. I mean it. I don't care if it's the middle of the night. Call me, okay?"

Jill nodded again, but Crash knew she wouldn't call. Something had changed inside of Jill.

Dammit. This was ridiculous. Now they were caught in the old, frustrating pattern. She didn't know if she had the strength to get through to Jill a second time. She wanted to hit something—or at least grab Jill and shake some sense into her—but of course she didn't. Her hands clenched into fists at her sides as she walked to the door, where she turned and glanced back.

"Thank you, Crash," Jill said softly. "For everything."

"Anytime. You're not in this alone, okay?" Their gazes connected, and Crash stood in the doorway for several seconds before finally tearing herself away and walking out.

The door closing behind her sounded overly loud. It felt wrong. So wrong. Crash turned around and stared at the damn door before slowly making her way to her car.

Instead of starting the engine and driving off, she sat behind the wheel and waited for Grace to arrive.

Either Grace hadn't been up at the cottage, or she'd broken every traffic law on her way to Jill's home, because forty minutes later, the gate swung open and Grace's red SUV passed through.

Crash gave a short wave and drove off, her hands clenched around the steering wheel.

CHAPTER 23

On Monday, Jill's left leg was still numb like a log. Her neurologist declared it a relapse and sent her over to the infusion center for a more aggressive treatment.

The nurse who greeted them at the door gave Grace an inviting smile. "You're welcome to accompany Ms. Corrigan inside. We allow first-timers to bring a friend, spouse, or family member."

Jill was beginning to feel like a first-grader clinging to the hand of her mother on the first day of school, and she didn't want that dependency.

"What do you think, Jill?" Grace asked. "I'd be happy to go in with you."

Jill looked up at Grace from the wheelchair that her neurologist had lent them to navigate the hall from his office to the infusion center. She opened her mouth to tell her she could leave but then hesitated. Truth be told, she didn't look forward to what would happen in the sterile-looking room. While she didn't want Crash to have to live through everything with her twenty-four/seven, letting a friend help was different. At the end of the treatment, Grace would get to go home to her own life—a life without MS. Unfortunately, Grace wasn't just her friend; she was also a famous actress.

"I don't know," Jill said. "I don't want to cause a stampede, with all of the patients dragging their IV bags across the room to get your autograph."

"Autograph?" The nurse looked from Jill to Grace. Her eyes widened, and she looked as if she were about to fall to her knees and worship Grace. "Oh my God. You're Grace Durand, aren't you?"

In moments like this, Jill was glad that she'd worn a blonde wig while she'd starred in *Coffee to Go*. Few people ever recognized her. "See?" She gave Grace a gentle push. "It's better if you go. I'll be fine."

"Are you sure?"

"I'm sure. Go."

Grace sighed and glanced at the nurse, who was still staring at her. "Can you give her something for her stubbornness too?"

The nurse grinned and finally shook off that starstruck look. "They haven't found a cure for that yet, but if they do, I'll make sure she gets a dose."

Great. The first treatment of her three-day course of corticosteroids hadn't even started, and they were already talking about her as if she weren't sitting right next to them.

"We have a waiting room," the nurse said. "It's empty right now. If you want, you can wait there. The infusion will take about two hours. We like a slower drip rate so our patients don't get a headache."

Grace nodded. "I'll be in the waiting room, then."

Jill wanted to protest and tell her she had more important things to do. Grace would fly to Ireland tomorrow to shoot on location for an entire month, and she probably hadn't packed yet. But Jill had promised herself to make better use of her support system and not waste so much energy trying to take on the world alone, so she gave in and nodded.

The nurse pointed Grace toward the waiting room and stared after her. "Wow. Grace Durand in our infusion center. Wow!"

Yeah, and she'll be in the infusion center a lot longer if you just stand there without getting me my treatment! Jill bit back the comment, not wanting to take out her bad mood on the nurse.

Finally, the nurse turned toward her and pushed Jill's wheelchair into the treatment room.

Eight lounge chairs were placed along two walls, separated by privacy curtains. Most of them were open, so Jill could make out several other patients, already hooked up to IV lines. None of them looked sick, but then again, neither did she—yet here she was, about to get one thousand milligrams of Solu-Medrol pumped into her veins. Most of the patients had brought books or their e-readers, and some were chatting with other patients across the space between their reclining chairs, catching each other up on what had happened in their lives since they had last seen each other.

Obviously, they were all veterans at this IV thing.

Jill wasn't. The two attacks she'd had so far hadn't been treated with steroids. *Well, first time for everything. Let's get this over with.* As soon as the nurse stopped in front of a free chair, Jill hobbled over to it on one leg, ignoring the curious gazes of her fellow patients, and sank into the recliner. She tried to relax as the nurse took her blood pressure and prepared the infusion.

The nurse searched for a good vein in the back of Jill's left hand.

Wanting to face the harsh realities that came with her MS, Jill forced herself not to look away as the needle went in.

"Okay, it's in." The nurse pulled back the needle, making Jill breathe a sigh of relief.

That hadn't been too bad.

The nurse taped down the catheter, hung the bag on the IV pole, connected the tube, and started the infusion. She patted Jill's arm—the one without the catheter—and gave her a motherly nod. "I'll be back in fifteen minutes to check your blood pressure again. Do you need anything else?"

Jill shook her head. When the nurse walked away, she watched the steady drip of the clear liquid and imagined what it would do to her body. What she'd heard about the side effects of corticosteroids wasn't too promising, but she'd deal with those if it meant she could walk out of here without having to rely on a wheelchair.

"First time?"

A voice from the recliner next to her made Jill look up and into the friendly face of a young girl. She barely looked old enough to have her driver's license, but there was an expression in her eyes that told Jill she'd already seen and endured more than others twice her age.

"Uh, excuse me?"

The girl smiled over at her from her reclined position. "Is this your first time for that?" She nodded toward Jill's IV pole.

Jill nodded. "First—and last, hopefully."

The teenager lifted her water bottle. "Here's to that. Carol," she pointed to a middle-aged woman across the aisle, who was trying to knit without moving her hand with the IV too much, "calls it 'PMS in a bag.'"

Jill had to chuckle. "Why's that?"

The girl just grinned. "You're about to find out."

"Hi, Mom," Crash said, trying to sound cheerful as she picked up the phone.

"What's wrong?" her mother asked immediately.

Tears sprung to Crash's eyes, and she dashed them away with her free hand. *Great. You're supposed to be a tough stuntwoman.* But she didn't feel very tough right now; she felt helpless, worried, and hurt. "It's Jill," she got out. "She relapsed."

"Oh God. I'm so sorry, Kristine. How is she doing?"

Crash snorted. "I wish I knew. I haven't seen or heard from her since yesterday. She's not even answering the phone."

"Is she in the hospital?" her mother asked.

"No. She's getting steroid treatments for three days, but she's allowed to go home after each one," Crash said. "I wouldn't even know that if Lauren—her best friend's girlfriend—didn't keep me posted. She's totally shutting me out."

"Maybe that's just how she deals with things. Your father is like that too when he's sick."

"This is MS, Mom, not the flu! She can't deal with it on her own."

"As hard as it is for you to accept, it's her choice," her mother said.

Pressure constricted Crash's chest and made her temples pound. She barely resisted the urge to hurl the phone against the wall. "But I love her, dammit!"

Only silence filtered through the line.

Shit. She hadn't meant to reveal that, knowing her mother viewed her interest in Jill with a wary eye. "Mom..."

"It's okay," her mother said. "It's not like I didn't already suspect. Normally, when you call home, all you talk about is the exciting stunts you get to do. But in the last few weeks, you couldn't stop talking about Jill."

Crash rubbed her heated face. Had she really mentioned her that often?

"Believe me, I know what it's like to be in love. It can be the most wonderful feeling in the world—but also the most awful one, if the person you love doesn't return your feelings...or if she's not doing so well." Her mother sniffled. "I don't want you to keep getting hurt whenever she has a relapse."

"I can't help it, Mom," Crash whispered. "It's not like I can just shut off my feelings."

A sigh reverberated through the phone. "No, I guess you can't."

Crash let her head rest against the back of the couch and stared at the wall. "Jill apparently doesn't have a problem shutting off her feelings. I really thought we were beyond that. After the wrap party on Saturday, she finally agreed to give a relationship with me a chance, but now she's back to not accepting my help, much less talking about any future we might have as a couple. I think she wants to end it for good."

Her mother was silent for several seconds; only the sound of her breathing could be heard. "So that's it?" she finally asked.

"What do you mean?"

"You're just going to accept her decision and give up? That's not the kind of daughter I raised."

Crash jumped up from the couch and started to pace the length of her studio apartment. "What am I supposed to do? Kidnap her and make her listen?"

"If that's what it takes."

"I thought you were against me getting involved with Jill?"

Her mother sighed. "I have nothing against Jill. She's a great actress, and I'm sure she's a wonderful woman, but I've seen what MS can do...not just to the people who have it, but to their caregivers too."

Crash dropped back onto the couch. "I know. But that wouldn't matter to me. I mean, it matters, but not as much as being with Jill."

"That's why I'm telling you to fight for her."

Sucking in a deep breath, Crash nodded to herself. Her mother was right. She was done honoring Jill's feelings and letting Jill push her away. Now it was time to get Jill to listen to what *she* wanted. "I will," she said. "Thanks, Mom."

"Anything for my favorite daughter."

The old joke made Crash smile. "I'm your only daughter."

"That doesn't matter. And, Kristine? Keep me posted."

"I will." Crash ended the call, already thinking about how she could make the most stubborn woman on earth talk to her.

Jill found out why the infusions were called "PMS in a bag" on the second day of the treatment. Good thing she wasn't driving herself. The way she felt, she would have gotten out of the car and strangled several of the drivers in the dense LA traffic on her way home.

The mood swings she experienced were worse than PMS. Earlier today, she'd felt energized, almost giddy, and had talked the poor nurses' ears off. Now, as she sweated in the backseat of a cab despite its air-conditioning and stared at the stop-and-go traffic behind a haze of car exhaust, she was so grouchy that the cabbie had stopped trying to talk to her. Her nagging hunger didn't help her mood either.

Apparently, that was another common side effect of the corticosteroids—she was so hungry that she immediately devoured every bit of food in sight, despite the awful metallic taste in her mouth.

Well, at least the steroids' more desired effects had also begun to set in. Her left foot was still dragging a bit, but she could make her way around with the help of a quad cane and no longer needed the hated wheelchair or a walker.

When the cab approached her house, she pulled the remote control for the gate from her pocket and then frowned.

An SUV was blocking the gate.

Who the hell...? Wait a minute! She knew that midnight-blue SUV! Her heart started to beat faster. *Oh no.* She didn't want Crash to see her like this—barely getting by on her granny cane with its four rubber-tipped feet, her face flushed and puffy from the steroids. But she couldn't stay in the cab forever.

"Just let me out here." She pressed the fare and a generous tip into the cabbie's hands.

He got out and opened the door for her.

It was a bit of a struggle, but she finally climbed out of the car.

As the cab pulled away, Jill tightened her grip on the four-pronged cane and hobbled toward the gate, hoping to make it past the SUV.

No such luck. The driver's side door opened, and Crash got out.

Seeing her brought a mix of emotions, pleasure and pain. She longed to sink into her arms and cry, but Jill shoved those feelings back.

Crash approached Jill slowly, almost hesitantly, and held out a bottle like a peace offering.

"What's that?" Jill heard herself ask. *No. Don't talk to her. Send her away.*

"Chocolate milk," Crash said with a hint of the grin Jill loved so much. "According to George, it helps with that metallic taste in your mouth. Lauren said they put you on corticosteroids, so I asked George about the side effects. Lauren also told me when you'd be back from the infusion center."

Great. Jill gritted her teeth.

"Don't be angry with Lauren. She and Grace are just worried about you. And so am I." The expression in Crash's eyes was so soft and tender that Jill had to look away. "So? How about that chocolate milk? I also have some lemon drops. I hear they help too."

Jill bit her lip and hobbled past her without accepting the bottle. "No, thanks. I don't have a metallic taste in my mouth."

Crash followed her. "Okay. Then I'll drink the chocolate milk while you tell me how you're doing. I called you yesterday and this morning, but you didn't pick up, so I had to resort to this." She gestured at her SUV blocking the access to the house.

Jill paused in front of the wrought-iron gate. She kept her gaze on the number pad and didn't face Crash. "Please, Crash, go home. I want to be alone right now."

"Is that really what you want?" Hurt and doubt vibrated in Crash's voice, nearly making Jill turn around and hug her.

She braced herself. "I can take care of myself."

"That's not what I asked. Look at me."

Willing herself not to look at Crash, Jill struggled to focus on the number pad. She reached out to tap the security code into the panel, but her fingers were trembling too much. *Damn.*

Gently, Crash gripped her shoulder and pulled her around, keeping one hand on Jill to steady her. With her free hand, she reached up and ran her knuckles down the side of Jill's face in a caress so tender that it made Jill ache much more than the steroids or the MS ever could.

She leaned into the contact for a second, then pulled away and desperately shook her head. "Don't you understand, Crash? I'm not a person you should get involved with. It was foolish to think otherwise, and I'm sorry if I gave you false hope."

Crash didn't move an inch. Her blue eyes were stormy like the ocean during a wind-whipped, cloudy day. "You're the one who doesn't understand. I don't care about the MS."

"But I do, dammit!" She shoved Crash back with all her strength, nearly falling in the process. At the last moment, she caught herself with one hand on the brick wall next to her and the other clutching the cane. "Go, and don't come back!"

She whirled around, not wanting to see the expression on Crash's face. It broke her heart—both their hearts, probably—but it was better to end it now, once and for all, instead of prolonging the hope and the pain. She remembered only now that she still had the remote control in her pocket. With one press of the button, the gate sprang open. Jill stumbled through. A sob rose up her chest as she reached back and pulled the gate closed, forever shutting Crash out of her life, but she choked it back. *Inside. Not here.*

She didn't dare peek through the iron bars to see if Crash had left. It would hurt too much to see her standing there—and even more if she'd left already.

Maybe it was a blessing that she needed all of her focus to make it down the uneven driveway without falling.

Something—someone—landed on the gravel next to her.

Jill whirled around and lost her balance.

Crash caught her and pulled her against her chest, steadying her.

"What the hell are you doing?" Jill shouted, caught between wanting to hit her and wanting to hug her.

"Climbing your wall. I heard Grace and Lauren did it once."

She took a tighter grip on her cane and pulled away from the tempting heat of Crash's body. "That's not funny!"

Crash shook her head, her expression sober. "I'm not trying to be. I don't remember ever being so serious about anything in my life."

Tears burned in Jill's eyes, but she refused to let them fall. "Please, Crash. You have to go. I can't do this."

"I will," Crash said. Her voice was rough. "But first, I want to cash in that rain check you owe me."

"What? What rain check?"

"Remember that day I helped you out of the stunt harness and you invited me to Greek takeout in your trailer? Okay, I invited myself, but we had a nice conversation. You asked me about my real name and how I got into stunts, and you promised that I'd get to ask you two questions in return. Well, I never got to ask that second question."

Jill squeezed her eyes shut and nodded. "I remember." Only too well, actually. She could still feel Crash's fingers on her as she'd opened the stunt harness's Velcro straps, and she could still see how warm Crash's blue eyes had been while she talked about her parents and her five brothers.

"You gave me a rain check on that second question, and now I want to cash it in."

The only thing Jill wanted was to escape into the house, but she owed Crash that much. Her throat was raw with pain, so she said just one word. "Ask."

Crash gently touched two fingers to Jill's chin and tilted her head up so they were looking into each other's eyes. Her fingers were clammy and trembled. "What are you so afraid of?"

"I'm not afraid," Jill said as if out of reflex, but even to herself, she sounded like an actress who had over-rehearsed her lines—not convincing at all. For the first time, she admitted that yes, she was afraid. Scared to death, actually.

"For once in your life, forget your pride and tell me the truth," Crash said. "I love you, dammit, and I think you love me too, so why do you keep pushing me away?"

They both froze and stared at each other.

Now the tears Jill had been trying to hold back spilled over. One ran down her cheek. She had known or at least suspected for a while that Crash loved her, but hearing her say it took her breath away. If they had met two years ago, those three little words from Crash would have made her jump into her arms and cover her face with kisses, but now they wrapped around her heart like a fist and squeezed painfully.

"I didn't mean to say it now, but I'm not taking it back," Crash said, her posture rigid and her head held up high.

"Don't do this," Jill whispered. "Don't do this to yourself. I don't want you to have to go through this too."

"Don't you see? It's already too late. I'm in this with you, heart, body, and soul. There's no such thing as keeping things just physical when you're in love."

Jill stared at her through the veil of tears.

Crash—the woman who fearlessly jumped from buildings—was trembling. Jill's throat tightened when she saw the tears glittering in Crash's eyes.

"I'm in love with you too," Jill whispered. Maybe it was cruel, but she wanted to say it just once. When Crash reached for her, she struggled backward, heavily balancing on the quad cane. "But that doesn't matter."

"It's all that matters," Crash said. "We agreed to give a relationship between us a chance, and I'm not letting you back out now."

"That was before…" Jill gestured down at her leg. "Before this damn relapse."

"The way I see it, the MS is like a fire stunt. Okay, you got burned. So what? I know it hurts and you're afraid of it happening again. But you can't let it stop you from getting back on the proverbial horse, or you'll live in fear for the rest of your life. You have to plan ahead for everything bad that could happen, but then trust your team and take the leap."

Jill dashed the sleeve of her sweatshirt over her eyes. She sank onto a nearby aluminum garden chair, no longer able to stand. "Don't you think I want to? But I can't do it. I have no right to be in a relationship."

Crash looked at her. "What about my right to be in a relationship?"

Jill squeezed her eyes shut, unable to look at the pain on Crash's face. "Crash…"

Gravel crunched, and then Crash lightly touched Jill's knee—the one on her good side.

Hesitantly, Jill opened her eyes.

"All this time, I let you be the one to make all the decisions. But if you want to be equal, you can't have all the power. You don't get to make the decisions alone. I made my decision. I know I won't be any happier without the MS if it means I'll be without you."

"That's what you think now, but how can you know that's how it'll always be?"

Crash shrugged. "I can't. The future doesn't come with any guarantees—and that's not just true for people with MS. That's where trust comes in. I have trust in us to make the best of whatever life throws at us." She tilted her head and studied Jill. "But maybe that has been your issue all along. I don't think you ever trusted anyone enough to really let yourself need that person."

Each word pierced Jill like painful little darts. She shook her head to stop them, but they kept coming.

"That's what you're so afraid of, isn't it? What if you let yourself rely on someone and then that person one day walks away?"

Abandoning her tight grip on the cane, Jill put her elbows on her thighs and covered her face with her hands. But she couldn't stop the sobs that shook her or the tears that kept falling, no matter how often she wiped her eyes.

Crash shoved the now free-standing cane out of the way, knelt on the gravel, and wrapped both arms around her. One of her hands came to rest on the back of Jill's head, cradling her protectively, while her other hand rubbed soothing circles along Jill's back. She held her close without saying a word, not telling her that everything would be fine or that she should stop crying.

Not that Jill could have stopped, even if she'd wanted. It was as if Crash's words had put a hole in her chest, and now all the bottled-up pain came spilling out, like an unstoppable flood.

Her tears soaked Crash's shirt where she had her face buried against Crash's shoulder. It was a bit humiliating, but mostly it was freeing. She clung to Crash until the storm of her emotions passed and she became aware of how uncomfortable their positions were.

Sniffing, she pulled back. "God, I hate crying. I need a tissue."

Crash searched in her jeans pocket and handed her one. She was sniffling too. Groaning, she got up from the gravel that must have hurt her knees.

Jill noisily blew her nose and wiped her eyes with the back of her hand. *Ugh.* She probably looked a sight, her face even redder and more puffy than before.

But Crash regarded her as if she had never seen anything more beautiful in her life. "Better?" she asked.

The tenderness in her voice made Jill's eyes fill with renewed tears. Annoyed, she wiped them away and nodded. "Yeah." She blew out a shaky breath and whispered, "You're right. I thought I trusted you, but...I don't think I really did. I didn't trust myself to keep you interested if my health started to deteriorate. I mean, how could you still love me if I'm a useless—"

Crash pressed a finger to her lips. "I know what word you're thinking. Don't say it. Don't even think about yourself that way. You're lovable, just the way you are, and that won't change."

"Hollywood doesn't seem to think so."

"Forget Hollywood. They're a fickle bunch. But that's not real life."

"It is, if you're an actress. Besides, my parents treat me the same way." She blew her nose again before stuffing the tissue into her pants pocket. Her eyes were still burning, and she wanted to avert her gaze, embarrassed by her unexpected breakdown, but she forced herself to look at Crash. She found no judgment in those blue eyes, so she continued. "If the same happened with you, I..." She pressed the heels of her hands to her eyes. "I couldn't stand it."

Gently, Crash pulled her hands down and looked into her eyes. "It won't. I didn't just inherit my good looks from my parents, you know? They've been together for thirty-five years, and they're still deeply in love. That's what I want with you. So?" She rocked back on her heels. "Ready?"

"To trust you? To commit to a relationship with you?" Jill swallowed. She clutched her knees with both hands and realized distractedly that she could feel that tight grip on her left side too.

"For chocolate milk," Crash said with a gentle smile and pointed at the bottle that was lying on the gravel, unharmed.

The pressure on Jill's chest eased. She laughed through renewed tears. God, that PMS in a bag was killing her. But maybe she should be grateful that the stuff had made it impossible to keep her emotions under wraps.

"Ready," she said. She sucked in a breath, held it for as long as she could, and then blurted out, "For all three."

The smile that spread over Crash's face was all the reward Jill needed for gathering her courage. Some doubts still remained, but Crash was right—she had to trust her to make her own choices instead of deciding for them both. "Thank you for...for not giving up on me," Jill said.

Crash reached out and traced the tear tracks on Jill's face with her thumb. "Never. Just don't push me away again."

"I...I won't." Jill covered Crash's hand with her own, cradling the warm palm against her cheek for several moments before letting go.

When Crash held out her hand, she took it and allowed herself to be pulled up and helped inside.

CHAPTER 24

CRASH CAREFULLY NAVIGATED BACKWARD, STRUGGLING not to lose her grip on the mattress as she and Lauren slowly made their way down the stairs with the unwieldy thing.

"How did you get her to change her mind about moving the bedroom downstairs?" Lauren asked. "I know Grace tried, but Jill was her usual stubborn self and refused to even consider it."

"I didn't," Crash said. "She made that decision all by herself."

"Well, she has been sleeping on the couch for weeks. Maybe she was just sick of it and wanted something more comfortable."

Crash nodded and bit back a grin. The couch being uncomfortable wasn't the problem, but it didn't fit two people, and Jill had gotten sick of Crash having to help her up the stairs to the bedroom. At least they had held each other while they slept, even though Jill hadn't been up for more while she recovered from her relapse.

When she reached the bottom step, a warm, familiar body squeezed past her and tried to nudge her aside. "I can take it from here," Jill said.

Crash didn't let go of the mattress. "I know you could." She turned her head so that her mouth was next to Jill's ear and whispered, "But now that we'll finally be able to share the bed again without having to climb Mt. Everest a.k.a. the stairs first, don't you think you should conserve your energy for more interesting things than lugging the mattress around?"

Jill slumped against her for a moment as if her knees had weakened at Crash's words. A noticeable shiver went through her body, then she moved away. "All right," she said grudgingly. "I'll take Tramp outside so he doesn't get in the way and then get ready for my PT session with Jennifer, the slave driver."

Crash laughed at the affectionate nickname. While they slowly carried the mattress around the corner to the former office they were converting to a bedroom, Crash watched Jill retreat, glad to see her move so easily.

After two weeks of being "brain dead" following the highly dosed steroid infusions and then three weeks of physical therapy, Jill had been able to abandon her "granny cane," as she called it. She still used a lightweight folding cane when she left the house, but that was more for added security than because she couldn't walk without.

"Wow," Lauren said, nodding toward Jill. "I never thought I'd see the day when Jill accepted help without a major battle first. Too bad Grace isn't here to see it."

"It's still hard for her, but she's trying." It was an ongoing process—for both of them. Crash struggled not to help her too often and to avoid taking over tasks that Jill could do herself, and Jill was learning not to shut her out and to accept help whenever she needed it.

A phone started to ring in the living room just as they slid the mattress onto the bed frame.

Crash patted her pockets to see if it might be hers.

"It's mine," Jill called from the living room. Then her voice drifted over as she talked to someone on the phone.

"Do you need help with anything else?" Lauren asked.

Crash shook her head. "That's okay. I know you have to pick up Grace from the airport. TJ, Amanda, and Michelle will come over tomorrow and help us bring down the bedside tables and the dresser. The rest is just some decorative touches. Jill and I can do that easily." The *Jill and I* made her grin. She loved saying that; the newness still hadn't worn off.

When Jill appeared in the doorway, Lauren gave her a hug.

"I have to go," Lauren said. "I don't want to be late and make Grace wait." The usually composed woman was nearly bouncing with excitement. Apparently, the newness hadn't worn off for her either, even after being with Grace for more than a year. With a wave at Crash, she was gone.

Jill walked over, and they stood looking at the new bedroom, their shoulders touching lightly.

"Who was that on the phone?" Crash asked after a while.

"The clinic," Jill said. "Jen's got a family emergency and none of the other PTs are free either, so they had to reschedule my PT session."

Crash turned to face her fully, a smile curling up her lips. "Ooh. So does that mean we get to spend the afternoon together—alone?" Since she had started doing stunts for *Engine 27* two weeks ago, that had rarely happened.

Jill returned the smile. Her green eyes sparkled in the sunlight streaming through the window. "Looks like it. No stunts, no PT, no doctor's appointments, no MS support group. Whatever will we do to pass the time?"

"Well, let's see…" Crash pretended to think about it. "I seem to remember a certain someone owing me a rain check."

Jill shook her head, making her red hair—now back in a cute pixie-style cut—fly. "Nope. You already cashed that in when you asked me that question, remember?"

Crash would never forget that day five weeks ago. Seeing Jill break down and cry had been hard for her too. "I'm not talking about that rain check. You gave me another one when you took a little nap at a time that…well, let's just say it wasn't quite ideal for it."

"Oh." Jill's cheeks flushed a bright pink.

"Hey. I was just teasing you." Crash trailed her fingertips over one of the rosy cheeks. "You know that, don't you? Besides, I already cashed in that particular rain check."

A challenging gleam entered Jill's gaze. "Well, maybe it was a two-for-one rain check. Too bad you were only teasing, because I'm in the mood to get better acquainted with my new bedroom." She shrugged and prepared to walk away.

"Not so fast!" Crash grabbed her by the wrist and then hesitated. *Don't treat her like she's fragile. Treat her like the desirable woman she is.* She gave Jill a little push, making her fall onto the still-bare mattress, and landed on top of her. Before they stopped bouncing on the mattress, she started covering Jill's neck with kisses, little nips, and playful licks.

A low moan escaped Jill, and she buried her fingers in Crash's short hair, pulling her closer.

God, she tasted so good. Crash wanted to kiss her all over and caress every inch of her—and then, once Jill came, do it all over again. Impatient to feel more of her skin, she sat up, straddling Jill, and dragged Jill's T-shirt up and over her head, revealing a simple white bra.

Cotton had never looked so sexy on any other woman.

Crash cupped both of Jill's breasts through the soft material and swayed a little at how good they felt in her hands. As nice as the bra was, it had to go. She bent her head to kiss Jill's upper chest and then urged her to sit up so she could unhook the closure. Once it opened, she slid the bra down Jill's shoulders, following its path with eager kisses. Her gaze trailed down Jill's half-naked body, lingered on her full breasts, and then wandered lower, to the pleasing curve of her belly. "There's so much I want to do to you right now."

"Yeah?" Jill's voice sounded breathless. "Like what?"

"Like kiss you." She did it, teasingly flicking her tongue over Jill's top lip, then the bottom one before slowly sliding it into her mouth.

Moaning, Jill dug her fingers into Crash's shoulders and returned the kiss. Finally, Jill tore her mouth away. "What else?" she rasped.

"Lick you." Crash swirled her tongue down the column of Jill's throat. "All over."

Jill shivered against her. Her voice sounded even more breathless when she asked, "Aaand?"

Crash slid off to the side and trailed her right hand down, over the sexy curve of Jill's hip, then pushed beneath the waistband of the sweatpants Jill wore. "Take you," Crash whispered into her ear.

A sense of urgency gripped her, but she forced herself to go slow. This wasn't the first time she'd been with Jill—not even the second or the third—but she sensed that this time was different, different even than that time in her studio apartment, right before the relapse. This time, neither of them was holding anything back.

Judging by Jill's moans, Crash's fingers, slightly callused from her stunt work, provided just the right amount of friction as she trailed them over the baby-soft skin of Jill's inner thigh.

A quiver went through Jill's body, and she strained upward.

Crash echoed her groan as her fingertips found Jill's panties already damp. She started stroking her through the soaked fabric.

Jill's hips undulated against her, then she stopped all movement with noticeable effort. "Hmm, kissing...licking...taking. I like that plan. But there's one problem with it," she got out.

Crash was quickly losing interest in any kind of conversation. "What's that?"

"That rain ch—God!" Jill threw her head back as Crash dipped one finger beneath the elastic leg band of her panties. She pressed her hand on top of Crash's, stopping her. "That rain check is good for me giving you an orgasm, not the other way around."

"At least one," Crash repeated what they had said on the morning Jill had given her the rain check. She ducked her head to gently nip Jill's earlobe. The feel of Jill, hot and wet against her hand, nearly drove her insane. "And I don't mind sharing."

"Good," Jill said with a roguish grin. "Then I hope you won't mind sharing the top position either." She hooked one leg around Crash and pushed against her shoulder.

With only slight hesitation, Crash let herself be rolled onto her back. The move dislodged her hand from beneath Jill's sweatpants, and Crash groaned at the loss of contact.

Jill pressed their lips together, swallowing the sound and making Crash forget everything else.

The erotic slide of Crash's tongue against her own made Jill's head spin with desire. She wrenched their mouths apart only long enough to pull Crash's T-shirt over her head, then her lips were back on Crash's.

When the kiss ended, she was panting. She traced Crash's strong jaw and then her sensuous lips with her fingertips and gazed down at her in wonder. "You might just be the best kisser I've ever encountered."

"Might?" Crash repeated with that daredevil gleam in her eyes that she sometimes got just before doing a challenging stunt. She kissed Jill again, teasing her with sensuous licks and playful nips.

"Are," Jill whispered against her lips. "You definitely are the best kisser."

With a satisfied hum, Crash started trailing kisses down Jill's neck.

Goose bumps spread all over Jill's body. She had to struggle to speak. "Well," she said and winked at Crash, "except for me, of course."

Crash laughed. "Of course." Then her lips were back on Jill's skin.

Gentle sucking just below her ear nearly made Jill's bones liquefy. She forced her protesting limbs to push back, out of reach of Crash's talented mouth. If she let Crash do whatever she wanted—what they both wanted—she had a feeling she would end up unable to move, possibly even falling asleep again. *Oh, no. Not again. Not today.*

Lying half on top of Crash, half next to her, she started to explore. Even though she had been with Crash several times before, her memory didn't live up to how amazing Crash's body really was. She trailed her fingertips over the dip below her triceps, then around to the gentle bulge of her biceps, and finally up her strong shoulders. She'd never cared much for muscles on women, but on Crash, she found them incredibly sexy.

Crash quivered beneath her touch but otherwise lay completely still and let Jill do whatever she wanted.

That in itself was a huge turn-on.

When Jill reached Crash's chest, just touching her was no longer enough, so she added her lips to the exploration. Pausing for a second, she pulled the sports bra up and over Crash's head and threw it onto the pile of clothing on the floor. Then her mouth was back on Crash's body.

She nuzzled the spot at the base of Crash's throat, inhaling her scent before sliding lower. Crash's heartbeat thrummed beneath her lips, echoing the hasty rhythm of Jill's own heart. She cupped one of Crash's breasts in her hand and kissed it in a wide circle. It was smaller than her own but so incredibly responsive. The nipple tightened before she even touched it.

Crash's hands slid up and into Jill's hair, trying to direct her.

"Patience," Jill whispered against her breast. "I'll get there."

"Not fast enough."

Jill looked up and into Crash's eyes. The blue irises were reduced to thin rings around passion-dilated pupils. "You want fast?"

"I want you," Crash answered without hesitation.

Jill tried to chase away the sudden tightness in her throat by lowering her head the rest of the way and taking Crash's nipple into her mouth. She caressed it with her flattened tongue, keeping the strokes light at first.

The fingers in her hair tightened, and Crash's free hand slid beneath the sweatpants to clutch Jill's ass.

A moan escaped Jill, vibrating against Crash's nipple. She started sucking on the hardened tip until Crash arched up. Their bodies pressed against each other, reminding Jill that there were still barriers between them—barriers she needed gone. Now.

Without letting go of Crash's nipple, she slid her hands down her sexy body, unbuckled the leather belt, and pulled it free. Next, she fought to open the button fly of Crash's jeans, but the buttons refused to budge. Never had she hated buttons as much as she did right now. She took her mouth off Crash's breast to mumble a curse.

"What's wrong?" Crash peered up at her with flushed cheeks.

"Buttons," Jill gasped out.

Crash covered Jill's hands with her own and squeezed softly. She lifted one of Jill's hands to her mouth and tenderly kissed each finger before letting go. "Take off yours, and I'll take off mine."

Jill bit her lip, for a moment annoyed that she couldn't even undress her lover, but then she shook it off. *Come on. Don't spoil it with your stupid pride.* It didn't matter who opened the damn buttons as long as they were gone—preferably within the next five seconds.

She sat up and dragged her sweatpants down her legs along with her panties, her gaze fixed on Crash's strong fingers and the buttons, which were being undone with an aching slowness. Crash's fingertips circled the last button in a teasing caress.

Jill held her breath in expectation. As soon as the button slipped free, she grabbed the legs of Crash's pants and pulled.

Crash lifted her hips off the bed, willingly letting herself be undressed.

They repeated the maneuver with Crash's boy-cut panties.

For a moment, Jill knelt above her and drank in Crash's body before the urge to touch overwhelmed her and she was back in Crash's arms.

The slide of their bodies against each other, skin on skin, sent a thrill through Jill. Their hearts beat wildly, so close that she couldn't tell which was hers and which was Crash's. Nothing had ever felt like this before. She just lay there, soaking up the feeling, until she couldn't stay still for even a second longer. Her thigh drifted between Crash's, and the wetness against her skin made her moan.

Suddenly, the one thing she wanted more than anything else was to taste that wetness. So far, she had denied herself that experience since it had seemed much too intimate for the nature of their arrangement. But now she no longer had to pretend that things between them were just physical, and she craved tasting Crash with a fierceness that surprised her.

"Crash," she murmured against her lips, her hands roaming restlessly against her warm sides. "Can I taste you?"

A tremor raced through Crash as if she could already feel it. "God, yes. I thought you didn't..."

Jill pressed her index finger to Crash's lips. "I did. I do. I just couldn't allow myself... But now I want all of you." She took her hand away and slid a little lower in bed. With her lips, her tongue, and her teeth, she made love to Crash's breasts until Crash was moaning and writhing beneath her. After pressing one last kiss to a hardened nipple, she moved downward and traced the arc of Crash's ribs with her hands and her mouth.

Goose bumps followed in the wake of her touch, and she traced them with her tongue, fascinated by how responsive Crash was to her. Every kiss to her sensitive sides made Crash arch up against her; every touch produced a moan, and every lick made her muscles quiver.

It was an incredible experience, and Jill had to squeeze her thighs together as she slid even lower. With her fingertips and her tongue, she traced the defined planes of Crash's belly.

"Jesus." Crash gasped. "I feel like I'm going to come any second."

Jill peered up at her, taking in the lovely flush that had spread all over Crash's body. "Not yet," she murmured. She softly stroked the tender skin where Crash's abdomen met her thigh.

Crash's breath hitched, so Jill did it again. And again, each time with the same result.

Then, taking mercy, she slid lower and started exploring Crash's legs.

The strong muscles vibrated beneath her touch.

Jill planted kisses just above one knee, then moved upward, licking a hot trail along one outer thigh.

Crash shifted her legs apart, silently telling her where she wanted her touch, but Jill ignored it for the moment and repeated her caresses on the other leg.

"Jill..." Crash groaned and wove her fingers through Jill's hair. "Save the teasing for later. Much later."

"I'm not teasing," Jill answered. "I'm loving you."

Crash lifted her head, and their gazes connected. Crash's eyes shone with emotion as she caressed Jill's hair, tucking a strand of it behind her ear. Then she dropped her head back to the bed and let Jill take the lead again.

Jill pressed a loving kiss to the inside of one thigh. She snuggled her cheek against the soft skin and breathed in Crash's enticing scent. Not too long ago, she had thought she would never experience this again, and now she was about to taste the woman she loved. The thought made her mouth water and her head spin.

Crash tenderly trailed her fingers through Jill's hair.

Holding on to a muscular thigh with one hand, Jill used the other to spread Crash open. Slowly, she slid her tongue against her.

Crash made a strangled sound deep in her throat and gasped out Jill's name.

The sound sent shivers down Jill's spine. Her whole body tingled with excitement. She immediately went back for more. She took her time, savoring Crash's taste—salty yet sweet at the same time—and caressing her with languid strokes of her tongue, and then, when Crash began to move beneath her more urgently, she made her touch firmer.

A shudder went through Crash. She brought her knees up and dug her heels into the mattress, pressing herself closer.

Jill reached up, caressed one sweat-dampened leg, and then guided them both to rest over her shoulders. Using her moans and gasps as guidance, Jill swiped her tongue over Crash's clit, then glided the tip lower, dipping into her, then back up.

The sounds of pleasure coming from Crash were incredibly arousing.

"Jill," Crash whispered, sounding vulnerable.

Dazed, Jill looked up until their gazes met. The expression of open need on Crash's face made heat pool low in her belly. Groaning, she curled her lips around Crash's clit and sucked gently.

Crash's hips surged up. Her hands clutched at Jill's head, her hair, the bare mattress. Urgent sounds came from her, but the only words Jill understood were her name and "don't stop."

Not that she had any intention of stopping. With Crash straining against her, she alternated between quick flicks, firm strokes, and gentle suckling. A slight tremor started against her tongue. In response, pressure grew in the pit of Jill's belly until she felt she might come right along with her. She cupped Crash's muscular ass with both hands, holding her against her.

Crash's body arched up once more. With both hands, she clutched desperately at the back of Jill's head and her hair.

Maybe the tug on her hair should have hurt, but instead, it translated into sparks of pleasure rushing down Jill's body.

Crash's strong legs tensed to either side of her face. With a shout, she fell back onto the bed.

Jill stayed with her, enjoying the musky taste of her for several more moments before sliding up the sweat-slicked, quaking body. Quickly, she wiped her mouth and trailed kisses all over Crash's flushed cheeks.

For several seconds, Crash just lay there, panting, then she clutched Jill against her body and held her close. Groggily, she lifted her head and kissed Jill, moaning into her mouth. She gazed up at her with an expression of wonder, her blue irises still just thin rings. "God, Jill. You ruined my stunt career. I may never be able to move again."

Jill chuckled, flushed with this powerful experience. "Too bad," she said, her voice husky. "Because I'm in urgent need of some touching too. But if you're out of order, I guess I'll have to…" She slid her hand down between them.

A growl rose up Crash's chest. She rolled them over with a quickness that belied her earlier words and shackled Jill's hand to the bed with one of her own. Her other hand went down and pressed between Jill's legs. "Mine!"

Jill struggled to hold back a moan. "Oh, is that so?"

"Yeah." Crash's eyes flashed as she held Jill's gaze.

Jill had always hated that look of possessiveness on her girlfriends' faces. But with Crash, it sent pleasant shivers down her body. She no longer worried about giving up too much, making herself too vulnerable. After all, she knew Crash was just as much hers. "Then what are you going to do about it?"

"This." Leaning over her, Crash bent her head and kissed her so fiercely that every cell of her body seemed to turn into liquid heat.

Still, she craved more, and Crash seemed to know it intuitively. Not interrupting the kiss, she dipped her fingers into Jill's wetness.

Jill had to wrench her mouth away to suck in a much-needed breath. Her head was starting to spin already, and she knew she wouldn't last long.

Maintaining eye contact, Crash brushed her fingers over Jill's clit.

When Jill threw her head back, Crash immediately took advantage and softly grazed her teeth down her neck. A path of heat rushed down Jill's body as Crash kissed, nipped, and licked along her neck, across her collarbone, and down her chest until her warm breath teased Jill's nipple.

Jill couldn't wait. She slid both hands into Crash's short hair and drew her down.

Crash's hot mouth settled over one nipple while she gently rolled the other between the strong fingers of her free hand.

Sensations pummeled Jill from several locations at once, almost too much for her to process. She gasped helplessly as Crash slid one finger into her, adding another source of pleasure.

Crash paused. "Is this okay?"

"You need to ask?" Jill got out between ragged pants.

A grin curled up Crash's lips. "Asking never hurt, right?"

Her ability to hold an even halfway intelligent conversation was rapidly dwindling. She clasped Crash's forearm. "Less asking. More taking. Now."

"As you wish." Then Crash's grin disappeared and an intense expression took its place as she started to move, withdrawing and then easing back inside.

Jill arched against her, feeling the pressure build. Her eyes fell closed. "God, you…" She rolled her head back and forth on the mattress. "More."

Crash pressed inside with a second finger and began stroking in just the rhythm Jill needed. "Look at me," she murmured, her breath hot against Jill's ear.

It took some effort to force her eyes open. She gazed into the swirling depth of Crash's now almost electric-blue eyes as they moved together. She ran her hands down the muscular planes of Crash's back, clutching her, wanting to feel even more of her. Close. So close already.

Crash's callused thumb rasped lightly over Jill's swollen clit. Once. Twice.

The third stroke sent Jill plummeting into a free fall. She thrust against Crash's fingers once more before she stiffened. Her eyes fell shut again. Shouting something, not sure what, she fell back.

The next thing she became aware of was Crash's arms around her, rolling them around and cradling her still quivering body.

"Jesus," she whispered against Crash's sweat-dampened shoulder. "That was…"

"Yeah." Crash kissed her forehead, her cheek, then her lips, the earlier wildness replaced by tenderness.

Jill kissed her back before collapsing once again onto Crash's body. She nuzzled the salty skin. When her thrumming heartbeat finally started to settle, she lifted her head and smiled at Crash. "If I had known it would be like this, I'd have moved my bedroom downstairs months ago."

They looked into each other's eyes and then burst out laughing.

CHAPTER 25

"Maybe this wasn't such a good idea after all," Crash said and tenderly stroked the skin of Jill's arm, causing a rush of goose bumps from the tips of her fingers to her bare shoulder. "I hope I didn't pressure you into—"

"No," Jill said quickly. "I want you to do it." It made her feel vulnerable, but she wanted to share this with Crash.

Crash leaned against Jill's body from behind and kissed the side of her neck. "I want it too, but I admit I'm a little scared. I don't want to hurt you."

Jill turned in the circle of her arms and pressed a tender kiss to Crash's lips. "You won't. Just don't put it in too deep."

The familiar daredevilish grin inched onto Crash's face.

"What?" Jill asked. What could be so humorous in this situation?

"You know, it just occurred to me that if anyone were to eavesdrop on us right now, they would think we're talking about something else. Something much more pleasant." Her voice dropped a register, to a seductive drawl that sent shivers through Jill.

She frowned for a moment before the penny dropped. "Ooh." She gazed at Crash, searching her face. "Would you be interested in trying that sometime? Toys, I mean?"

A moan rose up Crash's chest. "That's a rhetorical question, right?"

Jill grinned. "Yep." She kissed Crash again, this time with more heat. When the kiss ended, she clutched Crash more tightly and sighed. "I'll have to give you another rain check on that, though, because we have to take care of this first." She gestured at the prefilled syringe, the alcohol wipe, and the cotton ball laid out on the dresser in front of them.

"I know." Crash inhaled and exhaled audibly. "Ready?"

"No. But let's get it over with anyway." Jill moved out of Crash's arms and closer to the dresser. "God, I hate arms." Not only were they the hardest to reach of all the injection sites, they also hurt more than other places.

Crash bent and kissed the back of Jill's arm, where the needle would go soon. "I love them." She straightened, pulled her around, and looked into her eyes. "I love you."

The words brought a smile to Jill's face, despite her nervousness. "I love you too." She still marveled at her ability to say it out loud. With a deep breath, she reached for the alcohol wipe, only to have Crash's fingers cover hers.

"Let me. Please."

Other than the very first time, when a nurse had shown her how to inject herself, Jill had never let anyone do this. She didn't even use an auto-injector because doing it manually allowed her more control. It was scary to let Crash take over, but she had promised not to shut her out of this part of her life. The MS was here to stay, but so was Crash.

Without saying a word, she let go of the alcohol wipe.

Crash tore it open, stepped behind her, and gently swiped the alcohol pad over the back of Jill's arm.

Her tenderness made Jill's breath catch.

Crash moved around her and removed the syringe from its blister pack. With a focused expression, as if she were about to perform a stunt, she pulled off the needle cap.

"Remember that you need to hit—"

"Fat, not muscle. I know. I read every article and watched every YouTube video there is about your kind of injections."

Jill had to smile. How typical of Crash to approach everything like a stunt—preparing as much as she could, then facing her fears head-on. She vowed to do the same. "I'm ready."

Crash's thigh brushed Jill's as she took up position behind her. She gently pinched a fold of skin on the back of her arm. Her warm breath bathed Jill's neck as she exhaled.

It occurred to Jill how very intimate this experience was—something that could bring them closer instead of pulling them apart.

She barely winced when the needle went in. The familiar burning started as Crash pressed the plunger and the solution went into her arm.

At the count of ten, Crash slowly pulled out the needle and disposed it in an old detergent bottle Jill kept on the dresser for just that purpose. She pressed a cotton ball to the injection site and stepped around to face Jill, still applying pressure to her arm. "How was I?" The grin on her face belied the worry in her eyes.

"Wonderful," Jill said, meaning it.

"No burning?"

"Just a little." Her eyes and her heart actually burned much more than her arm—and in a more pleasant way.

Crash cupped her cheek with her free hand. "Are you really okay?"

Jill nodded. "I'm fine. This was just pretty...emotional for me."

"I know." Crash caressed her face with her fingertips.

Jill leaned even closer and brushed her lips against Crash's. "Thank you," she said, for so much more than just injecting her arm.

"You're very welcome." Crash threw the cotton ball into the trash can and wrapped both arms around Jill, her hands sliding up Jill's bare back to find the hook of her bra. "Now let's see if we can't take your mind off that residual burning..."

If you enjoyed *Just Physical*, you might want to check out the first two books in Jae's Hollywood series, *Departure from the Script* and *Damage Control*, the novel which first introduced Jill.

ABOUT JAE

Jae grew up amidst the vineyards of southern Germany. She spent her childhood with her nose buried in a book, earning her the nickname *professor*. The writing bug bit her at the age of eleven. For the last eight years, she has been writing mostly in English.

She used to work as a psychologist but gave up her day job in December 2013 to become a full-time writer and a part-time editor. As far as she's concerned, it's the best job in the world.

When she's not writing, she likes to spend her time reading, indulging her ice cream and office supply addictions, and watching way too many crime shows.

Connect with Jae online

Jae loves hearing from readers!

E-mail her at: jae@jae-fiction.com
Visit her website: jae-fiction.com
Visit her blog: jae-fiction.com/blog
Like her on Facebook: facebook.com/JaeAuthor
Follow her on Twitter: @jaefiction

OTHER BOOKS FROM YLVA PUBLISHING

www.ylva-publishing.com

DAMAGE CONTROL
Jae

ISBN: 978-3-95533-372-0
Length: 140,000 words (347 pages)

When actress Grace Durand is photographed in a compromising situation with a woman, she fears for her career.

She hires PR agent Lauren Pearce to do damage control, not knowing that she's a lesbian.

As they run the gauntlet of the paparazzi together, Lauren realizes how different Grace is from her TV persona.

Getting involved would ruin their careers, but the attraction between them is growing.

DEPARTURE FROM THE SCRIPT
Jae

ISBN: 978-3-95533-195-5
Length: 52,000 words (240 pages)

Amanda isn't looking for a relationship—and certainly not with Michelle.

She has never been attracted to a butch woman before, and Michelle personifies the term butch. Having just landed a role on a TV show, Amanda is determined to focus on her career.

But after a date that is not a date and some meddling from her grandmother, she wonders if it's not time for a departure from her dating script.

CAST ME GENTLY
Caren J. Werlinger

ISBN: 978-3-95533-391-1
Length: 100,000 words (353 pages)

Teresa and Ellie couldn't be more different. Teresa still lives at home with her Italian family, while Ellie has been on her own for years. When they meet and fall in love, their worlds clash. Ellie would love to be part of Teresa's family, but they both know that will never happen. Sooner or later, Teresa will have to choose between the two halves of her heart—Ellie or her family.

ALL THE LITTLE MOMENTS
G Benson

ISBN: 978-3-95533-341-6
Length: 132,000 words (350 pages)

Anna is focused on her career as an anaesthetist. When a tragic accident leaves her responsible for her young niece and nephew, her life changes abruptly. Completely overwhelmed, Anna barely has time to brush her teeth in the morning let alone date a woman. But then she collides with a long-legged stranger...

COMING FROM YLVA PUBLISHING IN WINTER 2015/2016

www.ylva-publishing.com

REWRITING THE ENDING
hp tune

A chance meeting in an airport lounge and a shared flight itinerary leaves Juliet and Mia connected. But how do you stay connected when you've only known each other for twenty four hours, are destined for different continents and each have a past to reconcile?

STOWE AWAY
Blythe Rippon

Brilliant, awkward Samantha Latham couldn't wait to leave rural Stowe for an illustrious career in medicine. But when an unexpected call from a hospital forces Sam to move back home to care for her ailing mother, a life of boredom and isolation seems imminent—until a charming restaurant owner named Maria inspires Sam to rethink everything she knows about Stowe, success, and above all, love.

Just Physical
© by Jae

ISBN: 978-3-95533-534-2

Also available as e-book.

Published by Ylva Publishing, legal entity of Ylva Verlag, e.Kfr.

Ylva Verlag, e.Kfr.
Owner: Astrid Ohletz
Am Kirschgarten 2
65830 Kriftel
Germany

http://www.ylva-publishing.com

First edition: December 2015

Credits
Edited by Lauren Sweet
Proofread by Joan Bassler
Cover Design by Streetlight Graphics

Made in the USA
Monee, IL
06 February 2023

27188694R00169